Fifty
Georgia
Stories

Compiled by

ANN E. LEWIS

Illustrated by

JOHN KOLLOCK

**SUSAN
HUNTER**
Publishing
Atlanta, Georgia

GEORGIA STORIES
Copyright © 1969, by GEORGIA MAGAZINE
Decatur, Georgia 30031
Second Printing, 1970
FIFTY GEORGIA STORIES
Copyright © 1977, by GEORGIA LIFE
Second Printing, 1987
SUSAN HUNTER PUBLISHING
Atlanta, Georgia
All rights reserved
Printed in the United States

ISBN 0-932419-16-X

Library of Congress Cataloging-in-Publication Data

Fifty Georgia stories.

Enl. ed. of: Georgia stories. 1969.
1. American prose literature--Georgia. 2. Short
stories, American--Georgia. 3. Georgia--Fiction.
4. Georgia--Social life and customs. I. Lewis,
Ann E., 1903-   . II. Georgia stories. III. Title.
IV. Title: 50 Georgia stories.
PS558.G4F54 1987   813'.01'089758   87-26193
ISBN 0-932419-16-X

INTRODUCTION

I AM delighted to offer the next chapter in a proud history of publishing Georgia stories. In true Southern fashion, Ann E. Lewis was introduced to me by Patsy Wiggins, the Coordinator of the Museum at Crawford Long Hospital of Emory University, who was referred to me by Margaret Perrin, one of Atlanta's most gifted and popular musicians.

Ann Lewis is a remarkable woman. She took hold of the idea of publishing stories by Georgia writers in her two magazines, GEORGIA and GEORGIA LIFE. Then she gathered those stories into book form, first in *Georgia Stories,* and then, with the addition of fifteen more, in *Fifty Georgia Stories.*

This year, 1987, marks the tenth anniversary of the publication of *Fifty Georgia Stories.* As a Georgian and as a publisher in Atlanta, I celebrate Ann's wonderful foresight and work in preserving the storytelling tradition of Georgia. I feel fortunate to bring these stories to new readers.

SUSAN M. HUNTER
Atlanta
August 5, 1987

FOREWORD

IN 1969 we published a collection of thirty-five Georgia stories selected from those published in GEORGIA Magazine during its first twelve years. The first edition was quickly sold and a second printing made.

In the meantime, six other fine stories were published in the old GEORGIA Magazine while I was its editor and since we began publication of GEORGIA LIFE, nine stories have appeared that we believe are worth preserving in a fine book.

The first edition of *Georgia Stories* contained thirty-five stories written by twenty-seven Georgia writers. In this volume we bring you fifty Georgia stories written by thirty-five writers. All stories have been illustrated by northeast Georgia's artist, John Kollock, whose book, *These Gentle Hills,* has been widely acclaimed.

Some of these stories are true, or partly true. Some are fiction all the way. Others are reminiscences. But all of them, whether fact or fiction, are Georgia stories.

iii

Though limited in locale these stories have great variety and universal appeal. Hamlin Garland—himself a regional writer of an earlier day and of the midwest—described regional literature as having "... such quality of texture and background that it could not have been written in any other place or by anyone else than a native."

The stories in this collection have been written by many natives of Georgia—school teachers, college professors, a dean of the University of Georgia, housewives, professional and amateur writers, other magazine editors, a newspaper editor and a newspaper columnist.

There is humor and pathos, legend and dialect. A few are love stories. There are nine Christmas stories and several ghost stories and six of Frances Greene's delightful Billy Nichols episodes.

All were written expressly for GEORGIA Magazine or for GEORGIA LIFE with the exception of the old plantation Christmas story, *The Cowbells,* written long ago by Mary Roxie Edwards, wife of Georgia's beloved storyteller, Harry Stillwell Edwards. It is from her book, *In Daddy Jesse's Kingdom,* distributed by the Eneas Africanus Press, Macon, and used with the permission of the author's granddaughter, Nelle Edwards Smith.

It is with pleasure that we bring you *Fifty Georgia Stories.* It is our wish that you will read them with pleasure.

ANN E. LEWIS
Publisher & Editor
GEORGIA LIFE
July 1, 1977

CONTENTS

Each in His Time

Cecil Cobb Wesley

THE DAY was as unlike other days as if it had become detached from the regular succession, having little relationship to yesterday or tomorrow. Winter had passed but spring had not yet come. It was a day of jonquils and of frost, whose damp, Atlantic wind, lifting dead leaves from the edge of farm yards, uncovered the first green shoots of hyacinths. And I knew that somewhere on a hill near the Chattahoochee, another wind was fragrant with the first arbutus.

It was a day of upheaval, forcing me from the simple routine of my simple life and sending me on a journey. It was a day of homecoming, but the large, old farm house that used to be my home wasn't home any longer, and the aging people gathered there were no longer the boys and girls of my childhood. It was a day of sadness, but it was the quiet, down-hill sadness of resignation. I had come home to bury another brother. Once there were twelve of us—now there were seven.

The funeral was over and I was standing in the front-room, greeting faces that bore some vague resemblance to other faces I had known, youthful faces of long ago. When all the people had gone but the kin, I walked through the house, opening doors and peering into rooms overflowing with memories.

Footsteps were behind me, yet no one was there. It seemed strange how memory could take the usual sounds

of farm and household and transmute them into the remembered sounds of childhood, and how voices of old
people in another room sounded like the gay voices of
half a century ago.

The rooms were just as I remembered them, yet
change had been at work. The atmosphere of children
growing, of running footsteps, had given way to an atmosphere of waiting to hear the end of a familiar tale. Although we knew the end, still we waited to hear the trite
words over and over again. Five of us wouldn't be here
any more, and the other seven walked with slow and
dragging feet through the rooms.

Someone was coming. "Why, Margaret," I said,
startled, as I turned to see my sister come bursting into
the room. Just then she reminded me of a dried arrangement. The form and shape of spring were there but the
fragrance, the color, and the life were gone. There was
a studied imitation of youth about her but in spite of it,
there was also the look of the brown leaf. She had that
same expression that I remembered from childhood—she
had something startling to tell. Margaret always startled
people, even when she brought the ordinary gossip and
news of the countryside. She would come into the front
room where the family was sitting on a Sunday afternoon:
"Guess who's going to get married? Just guess. Everybody guess. They've tried to keep it a secret, but I found
out. She has light brown hair, is nineteen years old . . ."

And again, she would run into the kitchen where
Mother and the rest of us girls were busy making peach
pickles (she having been absent when the project got
under way). She would shout: "Guess whose horse ran
away with him and pretty nearly killed him. You can't
ever guess. . . . Oh, well, he had some cuts and bruises."

And now she was hurrying toward me with that same
expression, worn now, on a face slightly puffed with fat.
And she was bursting with something to tell.

"Sadie, oh, Sadie, wait a minute. I've got something
to tell you, something so weird and crazy you won't
believe it."

I knew it.

"Have you seen that picture in the back hall?" she
asked, breathless.

"Do you mean that old picture of us children, Mother's favorite of them all?"

"That's the one," she replied.

"Why, you know I've seen it. I can't remember when I didn't see it. It has hung in the hall for at least forty years."

"Oh, I know that you have looked at it, but have you REALLY seen it? Have you ever looked at it and examined the way we are standing, the order, I mean."

"There wasn't any order, but a zigzag one. We were just standing around."

"Oh, no, we were not 'just standing.' There's an order all right and it is the most terrible thing you ever heard of. The way we are standing in that picture is the way we are—are—passing on. And guess who's next? Guess who is standing next to Millard? I am. We buried him today and I'll go next, for I'm next in that picture. I'll be next to go—"

I hurried to the hall and looked again at the picture. I felt a sudden chill that I cannot explain. It was a nervous chill as soon as I realized that Margaret was right. I never saw anything so weird and terrifying. Our family WAS dying in the same order in which we were standing in that picture.

"A coincidence," I heard a voice similar to mine saying. I tried to be calm but Margaret noticed the quiver in my voice, for I was standing next to Margaret.

"A coincidence nothing!" she snapped. "Now how could that be a coincidence? How could we be—er—passing away—just as we are standing in that picture? Now explain that to me."

We twelve children were not standing in any special order in that picture, certainly not in the chronological order in which Mother used to arrange us for our pictures. She used to be the patron saint of itinerant photographers and every one that came through the countryside headed straight for our house where he was certain to get a job. Mother always called us in from play or work and lined us up in some order. Usually Brother, the oldest and therefore the tallest, stood on the left, then stairsteps ran on down to the current baby. Again, she would place Brother in the center with the lines falling off on each end, and in one or two pictures, she arranged us in a semicircle, the five girls on one side, the seven boys on the other. But this picture lacked arrangement and I always thought, if I thought at all about it, that that was the order in which we came in from play or work.

Margaret was certainly right. There was an order in that picture, and oh, how terrible it was to see! Vincent, and not Brother, was on the left this time and Vincent was the first to die, having been killed in the first World War. Emma Lou stood next to him and she died in the flu epidemic of 1918. Ruth came next, snuggled close to Emma Lou, and she was gone now—died when her twins were born. Then came Charlie who died three years ago, and next to him stood Millard, buried today. And Margaret was next.

We stood there and didn't speak until Margaret broke the silence: "You see I'm right. We are—er—er—I hate to use that ugly word."

"Yes, I see that we are dying just as we are standing, or rather, that we have died in that order. But that doesn't mean a thing. Mother loved to have our pictures taken." I tried to be casual, even flippant. "She had one a year to keep a record of our growth. She had us stand in every sort of pose."

"You needn't be so superior about the whole thing."

"Mother had other pictures taken of us."

"But this was the last. There wasn't a picture after this. This stands as final."

"That was because Brother went away to college soon after this, Lucinda married, Vincent went to war, and we soon scattered."

"This picture," Margaret said, with a solemn look on her round face, "was the last. Five are gone and I'm next."

"Ah, you look healthy to me. But you'd better quit brooding, or you *will* be sick."

"What difference does it make whether I brood or not? The picture has already been taken."

"Margaret," I said, speaking to my little sister again, "It's only a coincidence that we just happened to be standing that day in that order and it was only a coincidence that the others died first. It doesn't mean that you will be next. I may be next. We all have to go sometime. Somebody must be next. But what could that ignorant old photographer have to do with it?"

"He isn't ignorant, but I'm sure he's very old."

"By this time he's dead himself."

"That man will never die," Margaret assured me, solemnly.

"Why, Margaret, what are you talking about? Who do you think he was?"

"I don't know who he IS and you don't know either. But I know what he looked like. I'll never forget as long as I live—which won't be long. But I can see him now. I'll never forget."

"I don't remember him and I'm older than you."

"Some people have better memories than others. I'll never forget those scary eyes. They were deep and stared at and through me and through everything. And that's not all I remember about him. I remember his long overcoat. It was a warm day but he wore this long overcoat, with the collar turned up around his ears. He would point his long, bony finger at us and say 'Stand there' and his voice was so cold and deep and scary it sounded like it was coming out of a grave somewhere. He made us stand just where he wanted us to stand, just in the order in which we are—. I remember I was afraid not to mind that queer old man and you see what's happening, Vincent, Emma Lou, Ruth, Charlie, Millard, then me."

I couldn't believe that a sister of mine was so superstitious. We were an intelligent family, I always thought. I took great pride in our accomplishments, our college degrees, our success in life. And yet here was one of us worrying herself sick because an itinerant photographer came through the countryside nearly half a century ago and cast some sort of spell over us. He was actually killing us off. I turned and walked away from Margaret and from the picture.

The following day I went home but I couldn't dismiss the thought of that picture. Sometimes it would be amusing, that is, if my mood were light and gay. Then I would laugh at Margaret's foolish fears. Again I would feel ashamed of her ignorance and superstitution. Margaret might die next, who could say? But that picture wouldn't cause it. I might go next but I wouldn't go to that picture like a heathen consulting an oracle or a fortune teller. Then, again, I would be seized with the same sort of frantic helplessness that Margaret was, especially about

the time of day when the colors were wiped out by the
gray of dusk and night was coming on. Then I would
feel the helplessness of all things at the approaching night.

"Life is a trap that catches us all," I would meditate
and the slow fear would come over me.

But, usually, when I thought of the picture it was
with a sort of curiosity and amazement that things could
work out as they had in our family and that the picture
had been right so far.

"Coincidences," I told myself just as I had told Margaret. "Nothing more than five coincidences."

I saw Margaret the following Christmas when we all
met at home again, all the remaining seven of us and our
children, and spouses, and grandchildren. Margaret was
unusually gay, and, for an aging woman, I thought a little
giddy, but then she was Margaret and I was Sadie and
we were always different. She had apparently forgotten
the picture and I didn't mention it at so happy a time.

The picture and all its weird ramifications grew dim
and dimmer in my memory so that I might never have
recalled its sinister influence over Margaret if it hadn't
been for that long-distance call.

When the operator spoke (I don't get many long
distance calls) I waited with a mingling of wonder and
dread. Then I recognized Lucinda's voice and a shudder
ran through me as I sensed what was coming:

"There's been an automobile accident and Margaret
was killed."

The Lord Giveth

Marjorie Shearer

HER VOICE was flat. Her eyes were still. "The Lord giveth," Carrie said, "and the Lord taketh away." They were the same words she had said the day they buried her little girl. There was no wonderment in the words, nor bitterness, only calm resignation.

Acceptance without question was the pattern of the people Carrie knew. And so she had schooled herself to hide her emotions, that she might seem like the others. Her eyes and her voice betrayed none of the grief she had known, none of the joy, the beauty, the longing.

But as she conformed, she wondered why it was wrong to cry, why it was wicked to feel tears crowding her eyes when the morning plucked at the strings of her being with all the freshness, the tenderness of its beauty. Crying for nothing, laughing for nothing, the others said, was wasteful. And the Lord God did not want His folk squandering their time on things that did not matter. Would the cribs hold less corn because a child—or a bird— had died? Could you wear the beauty of the morning to keep out the cold? Then you'd better think on something to eat and something to keep you warm. Slop the hogs and make the bread; bear sons to help in the field. That is woman's work, they said. That is what the Lord God intended you to do.

Carrie turned her face to the mountains and her eyes were still.

But beneath the placid face, grief had throbbed in its full turbulence. In the drab days and dark nights when she had listened for a child's voice, laughter she would not hear again, grief had claimed her for its own, had torn her courage, bruised her spirit. She knew that living with grief was living in sin, and had fought its possession of her; then in bewilderment, she had succumbed. In silence, she had cried out to the Lord God, "Why?" Wickedly, she questioned His wisdom, His goodness. Bitterness thrashed and churned within her, dashed by the relentless grief. But gradually her soul twisted until once again she could mean in her heart the words her lips spoke: "The Lord giveth and the Lord taketh away. Blessed be the name of the Lord."

During the long months of suffering and rebellion, her face remained set in the accepted mold. Her eyes held the calmness they had been taught.

But behind her careful facade, other times she had been intimate with joy. Often it sprang from some secret niche to course recklessly through her being, surging, undulating, leaving a trail of happiness glowing like sparkles over her soul. Yes, she knew joy well! And beauty.

When the first blue violets came, she was careful that no one saw her gather a few to tuck into her pocket so she could stroke the cool petals. No one saw her bury her face in the pink mist of the laurels which came later; and when the cardinal sang outside, she went right on mixing her batter, not pausing to stay her spoon unless she were alone. Then she put down her bowl and tip-toed to the window to watch him tilt his head and flirt his tail as he sang. Ah, he was a gay one! She was afraid to let her eyes dance and her lips curve in the delight of his song, but the sparkles danced inside her just the same. Once as a child, she had cried when she found a bird such as he, dead on the ground. The others jibed at her. Who but a fool would waste tears on a bird? But Carrie fondled the soft feathers, marveled at the brilliance of their color, and realized with sudden clarity the greatness of the Lord God who would take the time and use His patience to make perfect so small a creature as this crimson spark. Now that she was a woman grown, whenever she heard a cardinal sing, she remembered the feel of the downy breast, the eyes like small shiny berries. She was glad there was no one to say to the cardinal that none but a fool would sing about nothing.

And there was the way she felt about Ephraim, her husband. From the first, she had loved him with all the joy and sadness of her heart. The love was like a river flowing through her, rich and exciting, with music sweeter than the cardinal's. But she did not tell him how she felt. How could she, when he never told her?

Ephraim was a large man filled with strength. He was proud of his broad back, of the thick muscles of his shoulders. His arms were hard as the granite in the earth, and other men respected his might. He thought he need ask nothing, that he was self sufficient. But when he saw Carrie, he had to have her, and was ashamed of his weakness. He did not forgive himself for depending as he did on a small woman whose hair curling away at the nape of her neck made him forget what he was thinking. So he spoke to her no more than he had to, told her nothing of what he thought and felt. He did not tell her with words, that is, though he told her a great deal more than he imagined.

She knew, for one thing, of the longing he had. Ephraim thought it was a secret, but Carrie, watching his eyes as he looked toward the mountains, knew that more than he wanted a mule or a barn or a plow, he wanted to cross the valley and climb the steep sides. He had lived within sight of those mountains all his life, but they were always in the distance, always standing against the sky. Sometimes they were blue, and sometimes purple, sometimes gray. Ephraim's eyes were ever upon them. He would pause in his work to look toward them; he set his chair at the table so he could watch them as he ate. They changed with the seasons, with the hour of day. Ever changing, yet constant, they beckoned him with increasing power.

That was the closest he ever came to confiding in her, but there was the longing in his eyes as he looked at them, the way some men look at a woman. She knew how much Ephraim wanted to stand on the top of the tallest mountain, look out over the valley, see the ridges, the rivers, the roads, and what sort of land lay on the other side. He wanted to fill his lungs with mountain air which was said to be different from other air, so fresh and moist it had its own taste. Oh, it was a great longing he had, and Carrie understood, for she had a longing, too.

Actually, her longing was composed of many small things which were jumbled together into a great unrest. Though she had been fretted by this longing most of her life, she had never put it into words for herself, nor did she quite comprehend it. It was only that she wanted to laugh when she felt like laughing, and to weep when she felt sad. And sometimes she wanted to sing, to push the music in her heart up through her throat and out into the air.

When she was younger, she had wanted to dance. She fought especially hard against this desire, for the preacher had said many times that dancing was a sin, and the Lord God did not hold with His children flaunting their bodies about. Whoever danced on earth would later dance in hell. He promised that. But Carrie had seen the leaves throb with ecstasy, rocking on their branches. She could feel the ecstasy inside herself, tingling her blood so that she wanted to join the leaves in their gladness. She had seen water dance in the river, and flames leap and swirl. She could not believe there was anything sinful in moving to the music her soul was forever humming. She thought the Lord God Himself had put the music there, but the preacher said the devil had. She obeyed the preacher, but she did not stop wanting to dance.

Another of the things which disturbed Carrie was the way she felt about the Lord God. They said He would smite down sinners, that He would send famine and disease to punish His children, that He would order them to burn forever if they disobeyed Him. She went regularly to meeting, and heard the preacher read from the Book. She heard him read, "The wages of sin are death," and "Be sure your sin will find you out." She heard him describe the torments of hell, the cunning of the devil, and she heard him say they were all sinners. She guessed they were, if he said so. He was a man with learning, a man who could read from the Book. If they were all sinners, then they would all go to hell.

14

Carrie tried to believe what he said. She kept telling
herself that she could not read from the Book, that she
must believe the preacher. She believed the Book held
God's truth, but it was all mixed up inside her, what she
thought and what she believed. Carrie could not agree
that He who had made stars and mountains and forests
would set fire to His children for sins they could not help.
If He hated His children, He would not have put blue
violets upon their world, nor clear, sweet water. There
would be no brightly colored birds to make music; no
grapes to grow free for the taking; nor dogwoods to splash
the hills with snowy splendor in spring, and scarlet pen-
nants in the fall. Surely, the Lord God must love His
children to give them such things as these. And was it
wicked, then, for her to take time from her own work
to look at His? Or was it wicked to hurry past without
noticing?

When she went into the woods to hunt the hog which
had got loose, she paused to examine the windflowers
growing there. She looked in wonder at their fragile
beauty, feeling awe that the Lord God had cared enough
about these blossoms deep in the woods to fashion them
with such delicacy. They swayed on their slender stems,
bowing shyly. Carrie felt a bliss spread through her, a
bliss pricked with sadness. There she was again, jumbled
up, crazy. Happy and sad at the same time. She wanted
to look toward the scraps of sky showing through gnarled
gray branches, and say to the Lord God, "Thank you for
the windflowers," but even though she was alone in the
woods, she did not dare. Anybody would have said to her,
"You're a fool for wasting your time and God's with them
weeds. Better you ask Him to help you find the hog you
lost. You can eat the side meat, but you'd get poor for
certain was you to try living on windflowers!"

A great part of the longing was wanting to talk with
the Lord God who had made her.

And Ephraim, if she could only talk with him! There
wasn't much she wanted to tell him, just little things she
thought of. She wished he would look at her when he
spoke, and she wished he would say her name. He had
never called her "Carrie," never in all the years. Even in
the darkness when, after fighting with himself, he groped

for her, he did not whisper her name. He gave her no words she could treasure, only the memory of his taking her brusquely. She knew he was ashamed. Carrie was not ashamed. Perhaps it was a sin, but she could not be ashamed of loving Ephraim.

Sometimes she wondered if it were herself he wanted, or the sons. These she gave him as freely as she gave herself. Six of them, fine and strong. Big men like their father. Only Jeptha was small. But because of his size, he spoke with a louder voice than the others, and he walked with a swagger they did not need. She had no fears for Jeptha, for his back and his arms were as strong as his brothers'. He was a man, albeit a short one. They had ever been Ephraim's sons more than hers; but the little girl had been Carrie's.

She, with the twinkly eyes and the laugh like a carol, had fetched her mother colored leaves and fuzzy caterpillars, and smooth stones to feel, blossoms to smell. She had been the one who snuggled against Carrie, listened to her crooning. She was her mother's child, and Carrie did not think it unfair that Ephraim should have six, and she, one, when hers was such a one. But they buried the little girl on a winter day, and Carrie stood, dry-eyed, watching.

"The Lord giveth," she said, "and the Lord taketh away."

And now they had buried Ephraim, too. On this September forenoon when the sky was blue as his own eyes, the clouds soft and drifting lazily, the sun warm, the big pine box was lowered into its resting place. Carrie had seen to it that Ephraim was buried facing the mountains.

And she sat on the porch now, looking toward the peaks he loved. He was there among them, she knew. The sons and their wives had gone, and now she could relax. Now she could let the tears flow into her eyes. The outline of the mountains looked dim, and she brushed away the tears to see better, knowing more would come. Bright and shiny they appeared, trembled beneath the lids, then spilled over onto her cheeks, down onto the dark stuff of her dress. She did not try to stop them, for they were peaceful tears, tears of happiness.

Yes, happiness. For she knew that the longing would no more fret her. Now that Ephraim was gone, she could whisper his name with the tenderness she had in her heart for him as she had never whispered it while he lived. She could look at the mountains and know that he was there, smiling upon her, loving her. Just before he died, he had called out suddenly, sharply, from his mist: "Don't leave me, Carrie!" And then he said softly, "My little Carrie," in the same hushed tone that she had crooned to their girl-child. And though she knew her husband was dying, she was electrified with the greatest joy of her life.

She raised her eyes from the mountains and looked to the sky. "I thank you, Lord God," she said aloud, "For a-giving me Ephraim."

And when the flow of tears had diminished, she rose and went to the edge of the clearing where the purple asters bloomed. She gathered a few and mixed them with leaves from the sour-wood tree, leaves as bright as the cardinal who sang from a pine branch.

"Look, Ephraim," she said. "Look what the Lord God has give me."

Kings Are Lonely Men

Joseph H. Baird

FROM the library window of his white-pillared Colonial house on the hilltop, Parthon Rowe could see in panorama the whole town of Huntsville stretched out below him. He had stood there many mornings before going to his desk at the bank, smiling at the town like a benign father who rejoices in the virility of an adolescent son. But today he looked at it through a mist of tears.

At the foot of the graveled drive that led from the highway through the tree-studded lawn of his estate, he saw a blue convertible turn in. Flashy, he thought for the hundredth time. He fancied heavy, powerful black sedans. A trivial point, he realized, but one that underscored further the sharp differences between him and his son, Jonathan.

After the boy's mother died, he had hoped that the gap between them might be narrowed. He glanced now at the silver-framed portrait of Kathleen, taken only a few weeks before her death three years ago. The same laughing grey eyes, the same capricious curl at the end of the lips that Jonathan had. They both lacked—well, what *was* it they lacked? A sense of values, he supposed. To them the blooming of the first yellow jonquil or a funny quip from Charlie, the butler, was more reason for elation than the coming of a new million-dollar industry to Huntsville.

No, he had ceased to hope that the passing of years

would give Jonathan the dignity and sense of responsibility that he and his father before him had possessed. But, even knowing this, it was hard to believe that the boy would spurn all he had to offer, even defy him, because of a woman who was hardly more than a stranger.

Parthon Rowe left his post by the window and moved across the room to the leather chair behind his large mahogany desk. Sitting behind a desk always added to his. sense of power. He was a small man, conscious of his smallness, but slender and straight for his sixty-five years. A maroon tie was the one splotch of color against his dark, tailored suit, pale face and iron-grey hair.

The tires of the blue convertible crunched on the loose gravel outside, and he heard Jonathan's quick steps on the veranda.

Jonathan strode into the room, a broad-shouldered man of thirty. His sun-reddened face, touseled blond hair and tweed sports coat seemed oddly out of place among the morocco-bound books and highly-polished furniture of the room. He laid a brief case on the edge of his father's desk. His eyes appeared troubled, and he shifted his feet awkwardly like a young boy before a schoolmaster.

Parthon Rowe studied his son's face for a long time before speaking.

"I hope, Jonathan, that you've come here to tell me you didn't seriously mean what you said over the telephone last night."

Jonathan's large hands clinched at his sides. "I can't tell you that. I'm going to marry Kay Hammond now and leave Huntsville for good. It's silly as hell that a thing like this ever became a personal issue between us. But you're the one who has made it that. And it's still not too late for you to back out . . ."

Parthon Rowe took a long, thin cigar from the lacquered box on his desk and carefully clipped the end with the gold knife on his watch chain.

"I have never made a practice of backing out of anything," he said slowly.

"I know that—not even when your obstinacy meant ruining someone else's life."

The older man laughed softly. "Ruining someone else's life? Melodrama. I'm only trying to appeal to your reason. If you have any."

"I wasn't talking about my life—or Kay's."

Jonathan's eyes rested momentarily on the briefcase he had brought. "I hope I'll never have to tell you."

Parthon Rowe flicked his cigar ashes into a tray, walked around to where his son stood and put a hand on his shoulder.

"We're not getting anywhere, Jonathan, and I've got to go to the bank. Think this over. Talk to Miss Hammond and try to make her see reason. I've no objection to the young lady personally. But she's put me in an embarrassing position. I can't change my mind without making a fool of myself before everyone in Huntsville. Can't you see that?"

"No, I can't."

Rowe shrugged. "Well, Son, think things over today. Meet me here for dinner—and bring the young lady if you care to . . ."

"Yes, Dad, I'll meet you, but I won't change my plans—and I doubt that Kay will come."

It was five miles from Parthon Rowe's home to the business section of Huntsville, down in the valley, and every mile reminded him of his forebears. Just ahead, over his chauffeur's right shoulder, he could see the red barns and white frame house that marked Valley View farm where his grandfather had settled after the Civil War. He remembered boyhood summers spent there after his own father had built the big Colonial house in town. On the left, a mile further down the road, was another farm which his father had acquired on a mortgage during the panic of 1907. He remembered the old man saying, "You'll pick up many bargains in life, Parthon, if you have cash money when other people haven't." Both farms were run now by overseers.

Straight ahead, on the edge of Huntsville, he could see jets of white steam rising periodically from the Rowe Compress Company where 50,000 bales of cotton were reduced each fall to the size of bales of hay for shipment to the New Orleans docks and the overseas trade. He wasn't satisfied with the way Jim Dealey was running the place. He'd have a talk with him soon. And with Bob Trainer and Harvey Haynes, his farm managers, too.

Parthon Rowe sighed. There were so many things to think of. The bank, the farms, the compress, his rental properties, the Chamber of Commerce, the School Board, of which he was chairman. He needed help, and Jonathan. . . . Lord knows, he had tried to prepare Jonathan to take his place. Harvard. Yale Law School. A year in Europe. The boy was brilliant in his own way, but with no head for business.

He had given Jonathan plenty of rein, hoping in time he would find himself. He had not objected—well, not much—when the boy wanted to leave the family home and have his own apartment in town. True, Jonathan never asked for money. He had a few thousand a year from his mother's estate. Perhaps a little more from his desultory law practice. He seemed to care no more for money than for responsibility. If only . . .

But they'd been over all that time and again. He seemed to lack any feeling of — what was that French expression? *Noblesse oblige?* For three generations a Rowe had been the leading citizen of Huntsville. The privilege carried a responsibility. But Jonathan couldn't understand that. . . .

They were crossing the bridge over the Green River and the town loomed just ahead.

And now . . . that Hammond woman.

He wished he had never accepted that place on the school board, although it had seemed fitting for the town's First Citizen. But it was a trial to serve with such fools as Walter Mainwaring and Jim Haverford. That Hammond woman with her trim, lithe figure and glib tongue had taken them in completely with her radical ideas about a course in Preparation for Marriage in the high school. It had left him in an isolated position where he either had to throw his weight around or succumb to her crazy notion.

He remembered the afternoon she had come into his office at the bank, after he'd opposed her plan at the board meeting. He could understand Jonathan's infatuation for the woman, as much as he disliked it. Those friendly, intelligent brown eyes, set in a finely-chiseled oval face, did something to a man. One less accustomed than he to firm decisions might have yielded to their appeal.

"I felt, Mr. Rowe," she had said in that soft, precise

voice of hers, "that if we sat down and talked over this course I proposed—with the principal's approval, of course —you might understand better what I am trying to do."

"I understand it well enough, Miss Hammond. You want to teach these high school boys and girls—mere children—the facts of married life. And I say teaching of that kind hasn't any place in the public schools. Those are things they should learn from their parents at home, or from their churches."

She smiled at him encouragingly, as she might have smiled at one of her pupils who failed to grasp a difficult problem. She was almost patronizing, it seemed to him. A Yankee, with a master's degree in education from Columbia, she assumed everyone else was a fool. Well . . .

"That would be well enough, Mr. Rowe, if the churches and homes did the job—but most of them don't. Did you know that for every five marriages in this state last year there were two divorces? Many of these involved very young couples. You know better than I that many of the girls here marry when they are in their 'teens or early twenties. They drift into marriage blindly without knowing anything of the facts and responsibilities of married life. That's why there are so many divorces. These girls aren't prepared for marriage."

Parthon Rowe adjusted his glasses and looked at the teacher sternly.

"Miss Hammond, I have known three generations of young women in Huntsville, and I think their mothers have done a pretty good job of bringing them up to be respectable, God-fearing women. And they have done this without the benefit of any of the theories you learned at Columbia University."

He could see her cheeks flush, but she went on.

"Mr. Rowe, you have known women of your own— your own social class. But what do you know about the daughters of the laborers in your own compress or in the new textile mills? Most of them come from ignorant families. Any knowledge they have of the physical side of marriage is picked up haphazardly. They get inaccurate information that gives them a distorted point of view that can ruin —"

"Miss Hammond, if I've got to use blunt words, I don't

think the public schools are any place for sex education."

She looked at him evenly. "I disagree with you there. Anyway, that would be a very small part of the course I'm proposing—a slight extension of the physiology course we already teach. What I have in mind is much broader. We want to teach these girls how to budget a small income, how to care for children and keep house efficiently, how to develop mutual interests with their husbands so their lives don't become stale and barren, something of the qualities that go to make a desirable husband, something—"

Rowe raised his hand to interrupt her. "Things a girl should learn from her mother. They're out of place in a public school, supported by the taxpayer's money. . . ."

"I understand," the girl said, "that Mr. Mainwaring and Mr. Haverford disagree with you. Doesn't that show my idea has some merit?"

"In the next few days, Miss Hammond, you may find that Walter Mainwaring and Jim Haverford have changed their minds. And if you want to stay on in the schools here next fall, I'd advise you not to agitate this matter any further." He drummed on the desk. "You've been a very satisfactory teacher in most respects until you brought up this—this radical idea. I wouldn't like to ask for your resignation."

Well, she'd taken it like a thoroughbread, he recalled, standing straight and looking him coolly in the eye, even managing to smile a little. "I understand you perfectly, Mr. Rowe. You may get my resignation without asking for it. Good-bye."

There had been another meeting of the school board that night, and on the question of Miss Hammond's Preparation for Marriage course Walter Mainwaring and Jim Haverford had outvoted him two to one. He disliked using his financial strength to force issues, but this time, he felt, it was necessary. If radicalism got a hold in the schools, God knows where it would stop.

So the next day he had talked separately with both Mainwaring, the hardware merchant, and Haverford, the cotton buyer. To the former he indicated some doubt that the bank could renew even part of his $10,000 note which would fall due in June. He told Haverford he didn't believe the Rowe warehouse, the only one in town, could store his cotton the following fall. At another meeting of the school board that night both men had reversed their positions. And Miss Hammond, hearing the final decision, had resigned.

Jonathan had come to him next day, flushed and angry, accused him of being a "czar." That was the first time he had known how deeply the boy felt about this Hammond girl, although he had heard they were often together.

This was June 1, the last day of school, and Miss Hammond, Jonathan had said, would return to her home in Philadelphia tonight.

The car turned a corner and the tall, white Ionic columns of the Huntsville National Bank came into view.

AT dinner time Parathon Rowe sat in his library waiting for Jonathan. He felt very old, tired and lonely. During the day he had learned that Jonathan's threat to leave Huntsville was not an idle one. Looking over the bank's notes he had found one for five thousand dollars, discounted by Jonathan. It had been given him by Hess Streighter, the cattle buyer, for a herd of blooded Jerseys the boy had pastured on the south farm. Then a teller had called his attention to a fifteen hundred dollar check Jonathan had cashed. Drawn on a local automobile dealer who had bought the boy's convertible. Obviously he was getting together money. To marry Kay Hammond and go back to Philadelphia with her?

A deep melancholia enveloped Rowe like a fog. The thought of facing old age here in this vast house without his only son overwhelmed him.

He would agree to Jonathan's marriage to Kay Hammond, he decided, if only they would stay here. She was young—about twenty-five, he imagined. As Parthon Rowe's daughter-in-law and one of Huntsville's young matrons, she could forget her radical ideas. And, aside from her Yankee accent, she was charming. He was not blind to that.

He glanced at Kathleen's picture on the mantelpiece and wondered what she would have thought of Jonathan's behavior. Then, with a rush of self-accusation, it occurred to him that in her life-time he had never asked what she thought about any matter of importance. He alone had made the decisions. But always in her best interest. He was sure of that. . . .

On the driveway now he could hear the crunching of gravel, and glancing through the window he saw the lighted triangular sign of a taxicab. He heard Charlie open the front door, heard the sound of voices, one of them feminine. So she *had* come, after all.

She stood in the doorway, tall, slender, queenly in a black sheer dinner dress, relieved only by a single strand of pearls around her throat, her shining blonde hair piled high on her head, her cream-colored skin warm and glowing in the firelight.

Jonathan was carrying the same brown leather brief case he had brought there earlier in the day. He laid it on the grand piano and Parthon Rowe, centering his attention on Miss Hammond, thought no more about it.

Dinner over, they were back in the living room, sipping coffee and brandy before the fireplace, with Parthon Rowe sitting in a large wing chair, Jonathan and Kay on a small love-seat opposite him. True to his obligation as host, the elder man had kept away from controversy at dinner, had encouraged Kay to talk of her family, her early life, her college days.

He lighted a cigar and smiled at Kay benevolently. "Jonathan has told me that you have consented to marry him. I am happy to welcome you into the family."

Kay flushed and smiled. "I appreciate that, Mr. Rowe. I was afraid that after our talk at the bank you didn't think very highly of me."

"Nonsense, my dear. We had a little disagreement over a—a matter of principle. That didn't keep me from admiring you as a very charming young woman. After you've lived in Huntsville a while as Jonathan's wife, you'll understand our point of view. As for your resigning, that's just as well. As Jonathan's wife you will have certain social obligations. You couldn't have continued to teach school anyway."

"But, Mr. Rowe, we intend—"

He raised a hand and smiled.

"Now I've been doing some thinking this afternoon.

The idea that a young man should struggle for his place in the world is all very well — when it's necessary. But in Jonathan's case—his place is already made. As my only child he will, of course, inherit — everything. I want him to begin now to train himself for the position he will ultimately fill.

"This old house has been very lonely since Jonathan's mother died. I recognize a young couple's desire for privacy. I shall move downstairs, and you and Jonathan can have the upper floor as your own apartment—to do with as you like. I'll arrange for an architect and an interior decorator to meet with you tomorrow and—"

"Father," Jonathan interrupted.

"Just a moment, Jonathan. I shall give you Valley View Farm as a wedding present. And stock in the compress and bank. That, together with whatever you make from your law practice, should allow you and your wife to live on a scale fitting your place in Huntsville's social life. Now, what date have you two set for your wedding? I don't believe in long engagements for young people who know their own minds and have no financial obstacles in the way of their marriage."

Jonathan stared down at the pattern in the rug, shifted his position uncomfortably. He glanced at Kay, and her reassuring smile seemed to give him courage.

"Dad, I don't want to seem ungrateful. I know damn well there're a million guys my age who would feel awfully lucky to step into the easy life you offer. And a million girls who would think me a fool to turn it down. But Kay and I are different.

Parthon Rowe laughed. "All young people think they are different. . . ."

"Sorry, Dad, if I sound like a sophomore. What I mean is that money and social position just don't mean too much to us. We both have personal ambitions. . . . To Kay teaching school isn't just a way of earning bread and butter. She has some ideas about education she wants to test out. I never wanted to be a lawyer. I became one because you wanted me to, and because in my early twenties I didn't know what I wanted. Now I know. I want to write. I've a book nearly finished."

For the first time since his youth Parthon Rowe felt
fear—the fear of being old and alone.

"If you are determined on a different career from the
one I hoped you'd follow," he said, "you could follow it
here—here in Huntsville." He felt the futility of his plea
and added weakly, "I'm sure your mother never thought
you'd leave the family home."

Jonathan shook his head slowly. "No. Kay and I
could never lead our own lives here. We would always
be Parthon Rowe's son and daughter-in-law. Even if you
really wanted to leave us alone, Dad, you couldn't do it.
The habit of running the lives of everybody around you
is too deeply ingrained."

He smiled in an effort to take some of the sting from
his words. "Kay and I are leaving on the midnight train.
We'll be married at her home in Philadelphia. We're going
up to a camp in the Pocono hills for the summer while
I finish my book. I'll write to you from there."

Parthon Rowe stared into the empty fire place.

"Jonathan, I won't ask you to stay for my sake. But
you were so devoted to your mother—I'm sure this isn't
what she would have wanted."

Jonathan walked across the room and opened the brief
case he had left on the piano. He took from it a small
book bound in blue pin-seal leather.

"Dad, this is Mother's diary. She gave it to me before
she died. I've never shown it to you because I felt some
things in it might hurt you. But it may be the only thing
that will make you understand."

He put the book in his father's lap, then laid a hand
on his father's shoulder. "You've done a lot for me, Dad,
and deep down I love you. If you ever really *need* me,
I'll come back. But you won't—you have your kingdom
of Huntsville and everything in it."

FOR TWO HOURS after Jonathan and Kay left, Parthon
Rowe sat in the lamplight reading Kathleen's diary.

"Feb. 10, 1927—I am going to have a baby! Parthon
is overjoyed and insists it *must* be a son. He has even
mapped out in detail what schools the boy will attend,

what positions he will fill here. He reminds me of a king expecting a crown prince."

"July 15, 1932—I saw a cerise dress at Miller's today. Had it sent out on trial. It was lovely! But Parthon said it was 'much too flashy' for a 'woman in my position.' I had to send it back. I wonder what it would be like to have a little freedom, even in small things. Since the day we were married I have been a prisoner—kept in luxury, but still a prisoner."

"Dec. 10, 1954—Jonathan is home from the service, and my nights are no longer filled with anxiety. The boy was hardly home before Parthon began pushing him into the pattern he had cut out for him in advance. Will he be strong enough to break his father's golden chains?"

Parthon closed the book. The embers in the fire were dead now. Far in the distance he heard the faint whistle of the midnight train.

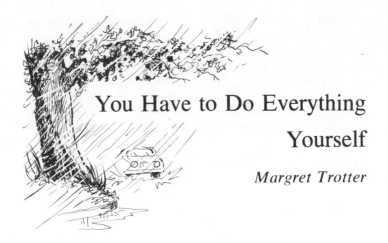

You Have to Do Everything Yourself

Margret Trotter

A S she turned into Mrs. Anglin's street, Miss Whitstone saw looming through the rainy night the huge old oak tree that leaned dangerously in the vacant lot on the corner. She compressed her lips and moved the steering wheel in an efficient turn. She did not approve in general of things that leaned. She sat or stood upright herself, and expected other organisms, whether animal or vegetable, to do likewise as far as possible.

She put her car in the garage, locked the door, and let herself in the house. Her landlady, Mrs. Anglin, was standing in the living room among her bric-a-brac: a little woman with dark hair and dainty little head, feet, and hands. She was wearing a pink quilted duster.

"Hey there, Alice," said Mrs. Anglin. "I was fixing to start worrying about you. Friday night and the weather. like this is no time for a woman to be out by herself. Just listen to that rain on the window."

"I had to go down town after school and get a battery. I was afraid the car would conk out on me," said Miss Whitstone. She was a tall woman, forty to sixty-ish, with long tan hair done up in a plain knob at the back.

"You must be wet and cold. Come in and have a cup of good hot coffee," said Mrs. Anglin invitingly. "I just finished my little bit of supper."

"I'd like a drop this once, Clara Mae," said Miss Whitstone. She felt sorry for Mrs. Anglin, home all day by herself. No harm in letting her talk for a little while. "I ate down at the Dixie Buffet. The specials are always good, nourishing, plain food."

Her landlady had set out a plate of sticky, crumbling fruit cake and began to pour their coffee. "You're mighty lucky, Alice, to teach chemistry all day long and to have something to think about. Some days I just can't stand it here. I messed around some in the yard before the rain and tried to find if my bleeding hearts were coming up yet. Do you think I could see one of them? I reckon they've withered away, just like my poor little old heart."

"Need fertilizer probably." Miss Whitstone drank her coffee. "This is good," she said. She tried to be fair at all times.

"There ain't a thing here that don't make me think of Sugar," Mrs. Anglin went on. "When he was in the hospital I carried that percolator down there and made coffee for him, but he couldn't drink it. Said he was too tired."

"It makes right good coffee," said Miss Whitstone. She ate some cake and tried to unstick her fingers.

"Here, I'll get you a napkin." Mrs. Anglin went into the kitchen. Her footsteps were quick and floppy. She was wearing those mules again, the ones she said her husband always used to tease her about. Sometimes she talked to Miss Whitstone about the mules and his teasing, giving Miss Whitstone the curious feeling that she was being invited to tease, too, but she never brought herself to do so.

Mrs. Anglin sat holding the warm coffee cup in both hands. Her black short hair was tousled, and her small face looked young for fifty. She put the cup down. "I'm glad you had you a good supper," she said. "*I* don't half eat, but how can I? There's a big knot right here." As she pressed her small hands to her diaphragm the diamonds on her fingers glittered. "Seems like after Sugar and I had been together thirty-two years, ever since I was seventeen, we just couldn't be separated. You don't have a notion what it's like, Alice, just lying there at night feeling your nerves jerk."

"Dr. Layton could give you something," suggested Miss Whitstone. "He fixed me up when I couldn't sleep after flu last fall."

"Doctoring never did me much good," said Mrs. Anglin. "Once they wanted me to go to the hospital, but I wouldn't leave my little old house and my Sugar; so he took care of me. Sugar was a real good worker. We both thought a heap of our house and all our little bits of things."

"It's a pretty little place, Clara Mae," said Miss Whitstone. She thought of the picture of Mr. Anglin which stood in a silver frame on the widow's bureau. After rooming here for five months she still remembered it with surprise: a picture of a big, homely, hearty man in shirtsleeves and suspenders standing in front of a freight engine. He and the engine looked out of place in Mrs. Anglin's bedroom, which was dainty, ruffled, sweet-scented, and rose-tinted.

Mrs. Anglin sighed. "Well, there's just me to care for it now," she said. Her voice got hard. "Last month, for the first time in my life, I even had to pay an insurance premium for myself. I tell you, when you're a widow you have to do everything yourself. The railroad won't even give me an annual pass, like they did when I had Sugar. I have to write in now for a trip pass every time I go someplace. It looks like as hard as Sugar worked I ought to get an annual pass."

"I guess so," said Miss Whitstone. She did not want to show her pity in her voice. "Listen to that wind!" They could hear it blowing outside. "I'm glad I put the car up."

She helped dry the coffee cups and then went to her room to knit and listen to a news analyst on the radio. As she was the oldest of six children and all her brothers and sisters had families, she had an endless series of birthdays to prepare for. She generally gave substantial sweaters or mittens made by herself. Tonight Mrs. Anglin was on her mind. The poor thing! So unable to cope with life!

Presently she heard Mrs. Anglin take a bath and go to bed, no doubt lying in the dark with her nerves jerking, and Miss Whitstone took a bath and lay reading a mystery until she was sleepy.

She was about to put out the light when she did not have to. There was a deafening explosion outside the

house, and almost simultaneously, with an ominous thud-
ding sound, the lamp went out. Miss Whitstone found
herself standing by the bed in the dark, wearing her robe
and slippers. There were two more explosions.

"It's not an atom bomb," she thought, and then, "I'd
better see about Clara Mae. Her nerves must really be
jerking, whatever this is." She felt her way into the other
bedroom. She was beginning to smell smoke. There was
another explosion.

"It's all right, Clara Mae. It's just me."

She heard a light snore from the direction of the bed.

"Clara Mae!" She found a shoulder and shook it.
"Something's happened."

There were five explosions in quick succession this
time. She could feel Mrs. Anglin sitting up. "We better
get set for whatever it is," said Miss Whitstone. "Here's
your robe."

Mrs. Anglin yelped, "Lord have mercy! The extension cord's afire. What'll we do? Oh!"

The cord was curled under the dresser like a glowing
snake. Miss Whitstone felt her breath come back. "An
overload on the house wiring, I expect," she said, annoyed
because her mouth was suddenly dry. "Must have burnt
out some things. Where do you keep your candles?"

"On the d-d-dining room b-buffet." Mrs. Anglin's
teeth were chattering. "Wait! Don't you leave me alone,
honey."

"Come on, then."

There was a loud detonation outdoors, Mrs. Anglin
screamed, and Miss Whitstone got the candles lighted.
She looked around the whole house. The air was thick
and acrid in the basement, but she did not see any flames.
She went to the front door. In the street, lit by the glare
of headlights in the rain, there was a tangled mass of ruin.
The immense old oak had fallen, as any sensible person
might have expected, taking a telephone pole and a mess
of wires with it, which lay across the asphalt, now and
then exploding in blue fire when they touched the wet
street.

Miss Whitstone gave a brief resume of the situation.
"Men!" she said. "Too late of course."

"I wish s-somebody would help us," breathed Mrs.
Anglin. "I'm so scared!"

At this minute a knock sounded on the door. Miss Whitstone opened it and looked sardonically at a big man in a glistening raincoat. "Howdy do, ma'am," he said. "We just had a little trouble with the electric line out here. My crew's working on it. Transformer knocked out. You folks all right?"

"Probably, except for the thermostat and the fuse box and whatever else was in the way when the voltage came through," said Miss Whitstone.

Mrs. Anglin spoke, trembling a little still. "I wish you would come in, Mr. Dillard. It is Mr. Dillard, isn't it? There's not anybody but just us two ladies, and if you wouldn't mind looking around some—"

He gazed down past Miss Whitstone at Mrs. Anglin, little and frail in her quilted pink robe, and said very gently, "Why, ma'am, sure, I'd be glad to."

The women, Mrs. Anglin pattering in her mules and Miss Whitstone erect in navy flannel and kid slippers, followed while he lumbered about flashing a light and checking things. "I said to myself as soon as the call come in, that old oak on Fairmount has finally gone and fell. We've been looking for it to, any time," he remarked.

"Why didn't you cut it, then?" said Miss Whitstone. "It was just waiting."

Mr. Dillard didn't seem to hear. "All you need's a new fuse box," he told Mrs. Anglin. "I'll call the electrician for you myself in the morning if you want."

"I'd appreciate it. My husband always used to tend to these things."

"I know how it is," said Mr. Dillard. He had a warm bass voice. "I'm glad to help you, ma'am. I used to know your husband in my lodge. He was a mighty fine fellow. Well, I have to get on out there." He still stood in the doorway, shifting his feet. "You just call on me if you need anything, ma'am."

As an experienced teacher, Miss Whitstone knew when she was broadcasting on the wrong frequency. "Goodnight," she said, and made her way to her room, where she composed herself for sleep. It had been an exciting evening, and so she began counting sheep at once.

The tenth animal to leap over the fence in her imaginary pasture was a blood-red lion, and Miss Whitstone was disturbed until she realized that as she was probably now dreaming, there was nothing to do but let him be a lion.

He vanished, and Mrs. Anglin was standing in the doorway, holding the candlestick, looking like one of her own dainty little china pieces. "Are you all right, honey?" she said. "I just wanted to be sure."

"Perfectly," said Miss Whitstone, "thanks."

There was a pause. "Mr. Dillard's gone," said Mrs. Anglin. Miss Whitstone did not answer. "He lost his wife two years ago, and his sons are both married. Poor thing! He lives alone with just a woman to come in and clean and wash and iron for him once a week. He was telling me about it. A man's really so helpless." Her eyes were shining.

"I guess he is," said Miss Whitstone. Her lips relaxed, and she could feel herself smiling. Perhaps it was because as a teacher she was pleased by the truth, whatever it was. And too, there were all those little nieces and nephews she knitted for. A woman who could be as devoted as that—

"Don't be worried if you see a light burning a while longer," said Mrs. Anglin. "My hair's so straggly I thought I'd roll it up. Mr. Dillard's right nice, isn't he? He's coming back tomorrow to make sure everything's all right here."

Pyramids Are in Egypt

William Virlyn Farr

SOMEBODY left the magazine at the store, and the General give it to me. It was one of these magazines that show how to build things—a mechanic's magazine, it was.

On my way home I tried to figure out how to build something. They had these pictures in there and they'd put numbers all over them. The idea was to put the numbers together so that you'd come up with a work bench.

The advertisements made more sense. An important-looking man held a roll of money in one hand, and with the other he pointed a finger in my face. *Can you draw?* he wanted to know. *The Success Art School will teach you how to make BIG MONEY*. Well, now, I could draw a star, a box, and a cat facing backwards.

I read on. *Do you have talent?* That was a interesting question. Ever'body's got talent of one kind or another, I figure. Learn what kind you got and you're bound to get rich. I couldn't make head or tails of the pictures showing how to build things; but I could draw and that's who makes money, the magazine said.

I read on. *Take our talent test*. And they had drawed this block there in the magazine, and they said you could take a ruler and draw a block like it. Once you'd drawed it you could put a cross in it and you'd have four little blocks. And they done it right there in the magazine to show how it's done. *We teach you by pictures. You observe the way we do it, then you do it.*

They had drawed this picture of a pretty girl and had put one of these blocks over her head. You could look at it and tell where the lines hit her eyes and nose and mouth, then you'd know where to put them when you drawed that block.

I read on. *Pay only two dollars now.* You could pay two dollars a month for the next twelve months, till you'd paid $24.00, and all this time you'd be making money selling the pictures you draw. *A taxi driver in New York sold a cartoon for $75.00 after five lessons. A housewife in Chilly Falls, Texas, completed the course and began work in the art department of an advertising agency. Can you deny yourself these opportunities?* I had $2.00— truth is, if you won't say I'm bragging, I had $3.00. I figured I'd be rich enough to pay it all off by time to make the second payment.

I read on. *You cannot enroll unless you pass our talent test.* And then I was afraid I'd flunk the test, they wouldn't take me, and I'd never be rich and famous. But the test didn't look too hard. They had drawed eyes and noses and mouths for you to copy. You mail them the test and they write back saying if they think you can become rich and famous by taking the course.

I walked faster. I cut across the field, knocking cotton blooms off right and left and almost run to the house. I drug my feet through the grass outside the door to get the mud off, and then I went to the tool box and got a ruler.

I took the ruler and figured out how much a inch is, and I got a piece of tablet paper and drawed a inch this way and a inch that way and got me a block like the one they had in the magazine. Then I put in the eyes and nose and mouth, like they done, and first thing you knowed I had me a pretty girl. I put it all in a envelope and put a stamp on it and mailed it.

I didn't tell Ma or Pa or the younguns. I knowed they'd laugh. Unless I got rich.

A week later I got a letter from the school, and when I got it this is how it read:

Congratulations!
You passed the talent test with flying colors.
Your future as an artist is assured. All you need
do is complete our course. Fame and fortune
await you!
   It will be a pleasure to work with a student
having your talent.
   Enclosed is a contract which you are to sign
and return before we can send your first lesson.
You will pay us ONLY $2.00 a month for the
next twelve months. We will work hard to make
you the successful and rich artist you have every
right to be.
   Don't forget to send in your $2.00 no later than
the first day of each month. We know that we
can count on you!

   I could answer all the questions on the contract but
one, and that was, *Are you a minor?* I asked Pa what
the word meant and he said something not important.
So I answered that question *no.*
   When the first lesson come it told what all you had
to have to get started: an apple, a cylinder, a cone,
a pyramid, and a rectangular object.
   I didn't know what some of these was, so I took off
for the store to ask the General. He ain't really a General.
I call him that because there's a sign over his store that
reads *General Merchandise.* And his name ain't Merchandise, either. It's McLenney.
   I like to go to the store. You hear funny stories, about
this traveling salesman, and drink Coca-Cola (Coca-
Colas ain't like beer or anything like that; even preachers
drink them) and you can ask a question and somebody'll
come up with a answer near about ever' time.
   When I opened the screen door and went in, the
General was swatting flies off of the counter. "Come in!"
he hollered. He always hollers, and then he laughs like
he said something funny, not just loud. And I laugh, too.
I always laugh when somebody else does.
   I set down on a nail keg. "What can I do for you,
"Private?" He had took up calling me Private because
I call him General.
   "I been reading . . . "

He laughed. He bellowed. He roared. "Whatcha
come up with this time, Private?"
When he asked the question he lifted up his eyebrows
and looked down at me. It made me laugh just to look
at him.
After awhile I quit laughing and got serious. "It's
what I didn't come up with, General . . . "
And he started whooping it up again. I laughed till
I got tired and then quit and waited for him to stop.
When he did, I said, "I run up on something I never
heered of. Something real peculiar."
"What now, Private?"
"It was a *pyramid.*"
"A pyramid? Uh . . . let's see, I seen a picture once,
in a book it was, a picture . . . in Egypt, pyramids are
in Egypt; they bury dead people in them."
"Egypt?" I said weakly. I knowed I couldn't go to
Egypt. I didn't know where it was but I knowed it wasn't
this side of Patesville, and maybe it was further away
than Atlanta, and Atlanta is way gone to yonder.
"You sure?" I said.
"Sure. They go up like this." He brought his hands
together like he was gonna pray.
I hoped you could learn how to draw without using
pyramids. The lesson didn't mention Egypt. What'd you
want to draw things you bury people in for, anyhow?
"Well, what's a rectangular object?"
"A *which?*"
"Rec-*tang*-u-lar object."
"Never heard of 'em. You wear 'em or eat 'em?"
He laughed his big belly laugh. I tried to laugh, and
did a little.
He stopped laughing and scratched his head and
stared at the floor. I didn't say nothing. I waited. In a
minute his eyes lit up and his mouth started to open.
I knowed he had the answer.
"I know. I know! It's sorta like a monkey, only
bigger. More like a baboon. I seen one in a zoo ten-
twenty years ago. The man said it was—whatever you
said, what'd you say it was?"
"Rec-*tang*-u-lar . . . "

"That's what the man said, all right. I'm proof-positive."

"It said rectangular *object*."

"That don't mean nothing. They just throwed that in there. Ever'thing's a object. You're a object, I'm a object, that thing's a object."

I told the General I'd be seeing him. I went home and wrote the school that I didn't want to be a artist, after all, if that was all right?

And they wrote me:

We thought you were sincerely interested in becoming an artist. You signed a contract and we reserved for your use all the facilities of our institution.

We have our bills to pay. You have yours . . . whether or not you avail yourself of the services for which you contracted.

If it meant what I thought it did, they expected me to pay for something I didn't get, and that made me mad. It made me so mad I didn't answer their letter. And a week later I got another, and the week after that I got two. They kept coming, and they got nastier and nastier.

It got to the place I couldn't sleep or eat, so I had to tell Pa what'd happened. He cussed me out for sending them $2.00, and then he laughed and said, "Why, they can't do nothing to you. You're a minor!" Still, I couldn't see what that had to do with not paying for the art course.

I reckon it was a month later. I was setting on the front porch and this car drove up. A young man got out. He was wearing a suit. "I'm looking for Chuck Bentley," he said.

"I-I'm him," I admitted.

"Oh, no!" he cried. "You're a minor!"

Him, too. It'd got to the place ever'body noticed right off I wasn't too important. I started to tell him he didn't look important hisself, but it would a been a lie. He looked right important.

"I drove twenty miles from Atlanta to get here," he said, running a hand through his combed-down blond hair, messing it up.

I felt right sorry for him. "You had to," I said.

"I *had* to?"

"Sure. It's twenty miles to Atlanta. You had to drive that far to get here."

He looked me in the eye. "Did you enroll for a course with the Success Art School?"

"Y-yes."

"And you're a minor?"

"Maybe where you come from; but round here, least ways, I figure I'm about as important as most of 'em. But I can't go to Egypt and there ain't no zoo here. We bury people in the ground, and we ain't got no animals but dogs and cats and things."

He come closer and looked at me. He didn't say nothing. He squinted his eyes like the sun was hurting them and just looked at me.

"Son, do you want to be an artist?"

"Sure," I said. "Who don't want to be rich and famous?"

"Then tell me why you think you can't be?" And he was real concerned about the whole thing, I tell you.

"Well, I aint got a pyramid or a rectangular object."

He turned and walked round the yard till he found a block of wood, and he picked it up. "Here you are," he said, "—a rectangular object!"

I looked at him. He didn't *look* no different, but that poor man had flipped his lid, for sure. I thought I'd better not upset him no more.

"Why, thank you, sir," I said. I petted it like a puppy dog. "Look at that tail! It does look a little like a monkey, don't it?"

He looked at me suspicious like and I tried hard not to laugh, and didn't. In a minute he said, "Why, yes, it does at that."

He started walking down the road. "Come on," he said. "We have to find you a pyramid." Now I begun to get scared. Should I go to Egypt with this man and him out of his head? But he didn't get no further than the barn. He went under the shelter and come out with a funnel Pa had made out of a piece of tin. "A pyramid!" he said.

I took the funnel and said, "So it is. A little old pyramid! Never knowed we had it." But any fool could see that you couldn't bury nobody in it.

"Now, you have everything you need to get started," he said, real pleased with hisself.

"Sure," I said, looking round before I laughed in his face.

"There's one thing more. Your father has to sign that contract before it's legal."

I told him I didn't know about that, and he got excited again. It was absolutely necessary, he said. I was afraid he'd flip his lid again, so I went in the house and asked Pa to sign it.

"Sign *what?*" he said, looking up from the kitchen table where he was crumbling cornbread in buttermilk.

"The contract," I said. "It wasn't legal when I signed up for the art course. You have to sign the contract to make it legal."

"I say make it legal!" He got red in the face and jumped up from the table. "Give that thing to me!" Pa is a big man and when you see he's mad you get out of his way. I got out of his way.

"Listen," Pa said, throwing the contract at the man. "I don't know what kind a racket you run, but I ain't signing nothing. That youngun didn't get nothing out of you, and he ain't giving you nothing. But you're giving me something—if you want to ride back to Atlanta in that automobile—you're giving me back the $2.00 he sent you."

The fellow had the door open. He reached in his pocket and counted out $2.00. "I-I'm sorry, sir . . . "

"Yeah! I know. Now, get off of my property."

This last I don't think he heard. He had pushed the starter and the car had crunk up. I moseyed through the house and out the kitchen door. Pa could have the $2.00, I decided.

I took off for the store. Half way there I looked down and saw the block of wood still in my hand. I was glad of it. The General sure would have hisself a laugh when he heard that fellow thought it was a rectangular object.

We're Beholden to You

William Tate

MOLLY and me has always lived near Sharp Top, called that away cause it's pinted, and we ain't been much even to Jasper, which ain't fifteen miles away, except I go down in my wagon for my store goods. We's seed Atlanta several times and a fair and circus there, too. I was borned right here, and Pa and me farmed this creek bottom until we sold some timber, and he gave me part to start store-keeping here at the cross-roads by Orr's Mill.

When I sits here on the porch, I can see all I aim to see—that mill wheel a-turning with the water splashing and the mill rocks rumbling, and Old Man Orr coming and going with meal dust white on his clothes, and his customers sitting around with their wagons hitched waiting their turn for grinding, or coming over to my store to pass the time a-day or buy some Brown Mule chewing tobacco. And far away is the Blue Ridge Mountains with haze and fog on them, or a summer rain, or just blue-green with the sunlight on them trees so far away. And when the wind is right I can hear the train whistle at Jasper.

Sometimes Molly walks down from the house, no piece away, and helps me take in eggs and hens and trade out thread and coffee and sugar and salt to the women folks, while I'm a-dealing with the men. She was from Glasper's Cove, just beyond Sharp Top a-toward Pine Log Creek.

We growed up knowing each other, and we sorter eyed each other from the start, then we married and set up housekeeping here nigh thirty years ago. We are still sitting here, but the kids have grown up and left. Martha's man fires the L & N train from Atlanta to Knoxville living at Fairmount; but Bud—he's my boy going on twenty—is in France fighting Kaiser Bill. His ma shore worries.

The first Christmas he was in France, she took the flu and cause she was worrying in her mind so much about Bud and maybe him being kilt, it turned to pneumonia. Doc Rogers from Ludville come by. He'd done give up his automobile on our slick winter roads and was riding his buggy again. Molly was real ailing, with it freezing cold at Christmas. When Doc was a-leaving after giving her some pills and bottled medicine, he said to me, standing on the porch, "Henry, she ain't doing well, and I'm going to get a nurse. They're scarce as hen's teeth, with all this sickness and they're hard to find for love or money. Your wife needs more now than her sister can do, and we better do something different quick."

It was mighty gloomy. Molly was weak and white-like, and I knowed her sister hovering around made her nervous, and she coughed lots at spells. She looked real tired and wore out, and I feared she was a goner.

But the next day Eddie Tate's boy came up in the buggy with a woman, "Miss Turk," he said, a nurse that Doc Rogers and his ma found in Calhoun. She agreed to come because Doc said it was a matter of life and death, so Eddie's boy took her off the train and fetched her up.

She was small but pert and quiet, but she took holt, and I shore mean it. Midge, that's Molly sister, cooked and sot by the bed while Miss Turk cat-napped. She and Molly took to each other right off. Molly was peaceful and slept lots; but her fever, hit was high, and she coughed fitten to die at times. Sometimes she talked about Bud like he was a baby, and him in France and her asking if he was dead. Doc was worried, too, cause he come by nearly every day, a-talking low to Miss Turk.

Christmas time came, but I kept the store locked mostly, with a sign about sickness. Old Man Orr's girl helped me

there with the trade, but I mostly set at home. Miss Turk
kept things dead quiet. Once I put some wood in the stove,
and slammed the door, cause I had a coffee pot heating up,
and Miss Turk came in mad like a wet hen and said, "I
done got her asleep, and you woke her up. She's asking
what air you doing. Now you git quiet or go stay at the
barn or store."

After that I stayed mostly in the parlor room, across the
hall from Molly, but I couldn't sleep for worrying. Molly'd
been my wife nigh thirty year. I kept a pot of coffee on
the hearth there and heated it on the coals, and I had
sugar and cream in that blue set Molly set so much store
by. My grandma did her cooking on a hearth fire, so it
was natural.

I was fidgety. I'd sit by the fire-hearth and stir the
embers with poking tongs, or I'd step up to the store and
help that Orr girl with the customers. Sometimes I'd
saunter out to the barn and see how the horse and cows
and hogs was a-doing, or I'd be feeding Molly's chickens,
all inside the shed cause of the freezing weather. Generally
I'd step out on the porch to get a breath of fresh air, with
the trees bare and naked against the stars, but somehow
I couldn't rest my mind none.

It shore seemed needed that Molly get well. In her way,
without no ruckus or hullabaloo, she was happy a-living,
and it was hard and unnatural to think of her as put away
in the ground, I reckon up at New Shiloh Church, with
our folks.

I'd be gone and sorter done for withouten her. She sot
on the store porch lots with me, and she was pert in showing our store stuff to women. I thought about her coming
across the yard with eggs in her apron, or setting with me
in church going to sleep kinder and nodding, or rattling her
pots and pans in the kitchen, or just being around somewheres. It all sets a man to thinking about his wife being
dead.

One night I was a-setting by the hearth close on to daylight, when Miss Turk come, flopped down in the chair,

a-setting so she could watch Molly thru the door, and she
said gruff-like, "Give me a cup." I knowed she had been
up plumb through the night, and I could see she was cross
as a setting hen, maybe worried some.

I handed her the cup, fixed with cream and sweetening.
She drunk the coffee sorter thinking to herself, and then
said, "Maybe the Lord is going to save her. Her fever is
broke a little, and maybe she's turning better. She's sleep
now." That heartened me much, and I said, "I know it's
nip and tuck. The Lord may be helping, but you're shore
doing your part." I didn't add no more, and Miss Turk
finished her coffee without speaking more; then she eased
back into Molly's room.

The fever it broke. Doc came by and sorter grinned and
said she'd be like a spring chicken in no time if she took
care of herself. And after that she did mend fast, maybe
partly because she heard from Bud. Miss Turk figured she
might as well go home since Molly's sister Midge could do
the nursing. And she spoke of a settlement, which she
ain't mentioned before cause Miss Eddie give me a good
name for paying, twelve days at ten dollars for nursing.
round the clock, she said.

It did set me back, cause I didn't know no woman was
asking ten dollars a day, let alone worth it; but I had the
money, and she shore did her job jam up to the beam.

After we rode down to Jasper, I called "Doc" at Ludville
on the phone, but his boy said he'd gone to Salacoa Valley
on a call; so I called "Miss Eddie" about that ten dollars
a day, and she told me plenty. She ain't never minced
words none. "You pay her right up, and no more words nor
grudging of it. Doc Rogers and I talked her into coming,
when your wife was at death's door. I told her you needed
her bad, and you and your wife was genuine folks, the salt
of the earth. She's worth every dime of it, you stingy
horse-trader." Then she put me off the subject by asking
about Molly and atelling me to take care of her.

I counted the money out to Miss Turk in the waiting
room at the depot, cause I kept store and carried some

extra in my money-purse for the Christmas trade. It was a heap of greenbacks for a woman's work, not a full month neither, just shading two weeks.

And the train come, the "Short Dog" we called it cause it wasn't anything but the engine and a baggage car and one passenger car. I toted Miss Turk's bag to the steps. She shook hands and said, "Write me about her, and maybe I'll be through your section some day, or I'll come for a real visit. She's had a close call, but she's safe now, with resting and taking it easy."

And the train was fixing to start, and I said to her, "Much oblige to you. She'd be gone withouten you, cause you pulled her back from the grave by a-tending her, She'd be pleased to have you come by, or maybe visit with us for a spell. Thanks for a-helping, and we're beholden to you."

$2500 Reward

William W. Lewis

"WAL, I reckon I better be gittin' down to see about the mail," and Constable Eph Werts emitted from between clinched teeth a thin ocherous stream marvelous for its carrying power.

"Number 5 is just pulled out. Don't reckon there's been time to put the mail up yet," suggested Lem Watson, Marshville's weak wit and the Constable's admiring satellite. "Reckon there'll be 'portant mail for you, chief," he continued.

"Wal, I dunno, I don't get important mail on ever train," Eph modestly confessed as he disentangled his spindly legs from among the rungs of his chair which was titled back against the guardhouse wall, its customary position. "I right frequent get information about desprit crimnals that there is a big reward for capturin'. By Golly, I could use a reward right now. The old car's about done and I need a new one bad."

The Constable saw no reason for admitting to anyone that the thought of a real criminal sometime disturbing the peaceful tranquility of Marshville was a constant nightmare to him.

"I reckon Sam has about got the mail up now," and Eph ambled down the street to Sam Purdy's general store in which was also the post office. The Constable had really been waiting for the mailtime crowd to gather in the store as he enjoyed making his entry with all the dignity and

impressiveness his six feet and sixty years of utter worth-
lessness would permit. Marshville was a quiet, law-abiding
village and its citizens had for years given Eph Werts the
job of constable because he would inevitably be a charge
upon the town in some manner, and because the emolu-
ment was so small that no one else coveted the empty
honor. Eph was a joke which only he could not see. As
he entered the store he was greeted with the usual facetious
questions and remarks which he always accepted as serious tribute to his high position. But on this particular
morning he swelled visibly when Sam Purdy called out:
"Hey, Chief, must be something important. Here's a
letter for you with a airmail stamp on it. It's post-marked
New York. Know anybody up there?"

Eph took the letter, examined the envelope carefully
back and front, and finally tore it open. He cleared his
throat loudly and set himself to read the letter aloud as
he was in the habit of doing with the police circulars which
formed the bulk of his mail. But before he had begun to
read, one sentence seemed to leap out and smite him in
the eyes. He turned white and began to tremble, and before
anyone could ask the trouble, he turned, bolted through
the door, and made all possible haste to his room over the
jail. He locked himself in and sat on his bed. It was some
time before he could control his breathing and read the
letter carefully.

> New York City Police Department
> Office of Chief of Detectives
> May 16, 1957.

Chief of Police,
Marshville, Ga.

Dear Sir:

This is to inform you that one Edward White, alias
Bill Birch, alias Slick Sample, etc., who is badly wanted
here in connection with a brutal murder is thought to be
making his way to your town. We understand he has a
brother living in that vicinity and he will probably seek
aid from him. A description of Birch follows: About 33
years, 5 ft. 11 in., 160 lbs. slender build, dark complexion,
brown hair and eyes. Probably well dressed, may be

wearing tortoise rimmed glasses, he is believed to have
left here in a late model black convertible. Has probably
switched license plates. He is desperate and dangerous
and also clever. We are sending one of our best men to
Marshville and he should reach there about 9:30 P.M.
Thursday. There is a $2500.00 reward for the capture of
Birch.

Very truly yours,
Michael J. O'Brien,
Chief of Detectives.

Constable Werts read and reread this communication
several times but could find nothing therein to give him
the slightest comfort. He couldn't get away from the fact
that a dangerous murderer might arrive in Marshville at
any moment, might even be already in the neighborhood,
and he, Constable Eph Werts, would be expected to arrest
him. His mind was working madly, seeking some scheme
which might let him out. Thinking was a little practised
art with the Constable but fear spurred his brain. Finally
he hit upon the idea of asking for a vacation. He had
never had a vacation, nor needed one, and he realized that
the request would be taken as a joke, but it was the only
chance and he could claim that he was sick, an excuse
which would also explain his precipitous departure from
the post office a while ago. And he was sick, deathly sick
with fear.

Having reached this decision he unlocked his door
and set out to locate Mayor Watkins. He peered carefully
out of the guardhouse door, looked up and down the
street, and, discovering with great relief that there was no
stranger in sight, startedly boldly up the street toward
Watkins Drug Store.

As he started across Simpson Street a black convertible with Georgia license plates rolled up beside him
and stopped. At the wheel sat a tall, slender man in a
dark blue suit. His hair and his eyes were brown and he
wore tortoise-rimmed glasses. The Constable shrank back
and seemed to shrivel as if he were seized with an attack
of the ague. The stranger spoke in a pleasant voice.

"What's the trouble, Chief? Did you think I was
going to run over you? Don't worry. I saw you coming

and I am very particular in my treatment of police officials. By the way, Chief, can you tell me where a fellow by the name of James Birch lives around here?"

As there seemed no immediate danger Eph managed to muster enough strength to point down Main Street and mumble, "'bout two mile straight out that way. White house on the other side of a patch of woods."

He stood transfixed and staring for minutes after the stranger had spoken a pleasant "Thanks" and rolled on out Main Street. He was brought out of his trance by the voice of Ed Simpson, Marshville's amateur detective, asking who the stranger might be.

Suddenly an idea was born in the brain of Constable Eph. It was too late now to ask for a vacation and besides that stranger was worth $2500.00, provided he could be caught and held, and with the menace of his immediate presence removed the Constable's cupidity got the better of his cowardice. He could deputize Ed and promise him $500.00 if they caught the murderer.

Eph took Ed by the arm and with sundry indications that there was a matter of great import to be discussed led him to the privacy of his room over the jail. Eph told Simpson of the letter and its contents, (omitting only the amount of the reward), and of his suspicions concerning the stranger.

Ed was eager for the trail. "I remember hearing tell of Jim Birch havin' a brother that run away from home a year or two 'fore the Birches moved up here. Come on, Chief, let's get out yonder and get that feller before he gets away."

The Constable was not so precipitate. He replied, "No, I got a scheme. I figger he ain't had nothing to eat and no sleep since he left New York and he likely aims to hide out at Birchs' till after dark and rest up 'fore he goes on. If we go out there now in broad daylight they'll see us coming and we might have ter shoot him. We better wait till after sundown and maybe we can slip up on him and grab him without no fightin'. I don't like to hurt nobody if I can help it."

After some discussion their plan was laid along this line, and about dusk Ed and Eph climbed into the Con-

stable's old car, tossed a small bundle of cotton bagging
into the rear seat and started for the Birch place. The
nearer to Birch's they got the more Eph hoped they would
be too late. Never had the old car rattled as she was rattling
this evening, and never had the road been so deserted.
Eph imagined his approach was being heralded miles in
advance, the car seemed to shout: "Here comes the Constable. Here comes the Constable." It was only by keeping
the thought of that $2500.00 constantly before him that
Eph kept headed in the right direction. As they came to
the patch of woods just before their destination, dark had
settled down in earnest. There was no moon, but the
Constable could see vague shadows flitting about from
tree to tree and his front wheels began to tremble and
wobble violently. At last the edge of the wood was reached
and the car brought to a stop. Eph's last feeble hope died
as he saw the house about a hundred and fifty yards away.
A light burned in the front room and in its beams they
could see the convertible out front. Had Eph been alone
he would have turned back and gladly said goodbye to
the $2500.00, but with Ed along he would not admit his
terror. He forced himself to follow Ed and they crept
silently toward that lighted window. When they had almost
reached the house a dog barked suddenly in the back
yard. The Constable's heart leaped to his throat in time to
choke back the scream which started involuntarily from
the depth of his abdomen. By some chance the dog did not
repeat the alarm nor did he come around to investigate.
After a few moments Eph and Ed recovered sufficiently
to creep up and peer in the window.

At a small table in the center of the room sat the
stranger with his back to the window, across from him was
Jim Birch and at his hand lay an ugly automatic. They
appeared to be in heated conversation, but the window
was closed and the officers could not hear what was being
said, until their quarry suddenly rose and shouted angrily,
loud enough for the listeners to catch the words: "Well,
I'll have to see if I've got gas enough to make the next
town."

Luck was certainly with the Constable and his deputy.
Their entire plan hinged upon grabbing the suspect when

he left the house alone. Now he was coming out and his
pistol was still on that table in the room he had just left.
Eph and Ed hastily stationed themselves, one on each
side of the front door, the length of cotton bagging which
they had brought along held between them at arms length
above their heads. Breathlessly they awaited the exit of
their man, and as he stepped out of the door they brought
the bagging down upon his head, wrapped it around him
quickly, tied it on with a stout cord, and, grabbing the
prisoner's arms, they set off at a run for the Constable's
car, dragging the suspected murderer behind them. This
happened so quickly that their captive had no chance to
voice his protests until they were half way to the car.
When he did commence, his language was a liberal education and a Masters' Degree in plain and fancy profanity,
continuing throughout the rapid ride to town. All of which
troubled Constable Eph not a bit. He was blithlely dreaming dreams of $2500.00 checks.

Arrived at the jail, they lifted their bundle across the
side-walk and into the building. They cut the wrappings
and shoved the noisy prisoner behind the bars, snapping
the lock shut. For the first time they were willing to
listen to his protests, and protests came thick and fast. The
unwilling guest turned back his coat and displayed a
shiny star on his inside pocket.

"You dumb fool, hick cops," he shouted, "let me
out of this. I'm a detective from Atlanta. We got a wire
to be on the lookout for Bill Birch, wanted in New York
for murder and I came up here to pick him up."

Eph's spirits and his jaws began to drop as the stranger
continued: "I knew he had a brother up this way and I
figured he would stop by there and I'm right. I'm sure he
was in that house up-stairs when you rubes made your
dumb play. He's probably heading west now in my car."

The Constable could feel the $2500.00 slipping away.

His prisoner rattled the cell door frantically. "Oh, you
fools, get me out of this and gimme a gun before it's too
late. We've got to get on his trail quick. Do you think
Whitey would have let you take me if I was Bill Birch?"

Eph was dolefully fitting the key in the lock, looking
like a man who had lost the only $2500.00 he would ever
have in this world ought to look.

Just as the lock clicked open Ed Simpson spoke:
"Hold on a minute, Chief. Jim Birch ain't been called
'Whitey' since he was a kid at school. Don't reckon no
detective from Atlanta would of known that name for him
and besides it seems sort of unnatural like for a detective
to of left his gun on that table if he were huntin' a desprit
criminal."

Before Eph could follow the drift of this, another
stranger pushed through the crowd which had gathered
and striding up, snapped hand-cuffs on the prisoner.

"Well, well, Slick," he laughed, "You look funny in
this coop."

Detective Clancy turned to Eph: "Chief, it's a good
day's work for you all right. I'll take charge of this lad now
and there'll be a nice check in the mail for you in a day
or two."

"All right, Clancy," said the prisoner, "it's all up now,
but if you had been ten minutes later I would have talked
this old coot into turning me loose."

Constable Ephriam Werts inflated his narrow chest
and answered belligerently:

"Turn you loose, eh? Why you durn rat. I was just
gonna let you out here and whup you half to death for
them names you been callin' me."

Mrs. Bass

Elizabeth Russell Mack

"WHEN Mr. Bass died, all he had in this world was the quarter in his pocket. I took it and bought me a veil to wear to the funeral."

Mrs. Bass bit off her thread and stuck her needle in the little cushion she wore pinned to the bosom of her dress. Handing the blouse on which she had been sewing to Nell, she said, "Here, try this on."

Nell slipped the garment on and then let out a wail.

"Mrs. Bass! One of these sleeves is the wrong side of the goods."

Mrs. Bass adjusted her glasses and took a look.

"Oh well. It looks almost like the right side. As I always say, it will never be noticed on a galloping horse."

We children loathed having Mrs. Bass make our clothes.

Our family first became acquainted with her when she rented the house from Mama. It was a miracle she had any money to pay down. But that first payment was practically the last. Year after year she lived on in the little house on the railroad while the rent bills mounted. And when Mama finally sold the place and the hard-hearted corporation that bought it for later industrial use refused to take the promise to pay for cash on the barrel head, Mrs. Bass came to Mama and borrowed the rent money.

Mama had a naive notion that it embarrassed Mrs.

Bass to have to admit she was unable to pay. Actually she was not at all abashed. She just made the simple statement: "I ain't got it."

That threw the whole matter back in Mama's lap. The implication was clear. If I ain't got it, how can I possibly pay it?

So Mama, to save face for her tenant, and against the protests of her daughters who had to wear the clothes, agreed to let her "sew out the rent."

During the time she rented from us she laid waste a mighty yardage of material. We children had a nickname for her, "Mrs. Guess," because she had a genius for guessing wrong as to the length of dresses, size of waists, depth of hems. However often she measured, however carefully she jotted down her figures, the completed garment practically always turned out to be a dismal misfit. Often it could not be worn, or, if worn once, was then relegated to the back of the closet, to hang there until outgrown.

If we children exclaimed despairingly when another favorite piece of material fell a casualty to Mrs. Bass' scissors, Mama would reprove us.

"Mrs. Bass is a good woman and there's not a lazy bone in her body. She is perfectly willing to work if only she could find the work to do."

This willingness to work had not been inherited by the bachelor son who made his home with her. Jory was chronically out of work.

Fourteen-year-old Sandy used to prod Mrs. Bass about Jory's employment status, much to Mama's distress.

"Mrs. Bass," he would inquire brightly (as though he did not already know the answer) "has Jory found work yet?"

"No, seems like Jory just can't find anything. Anything congenial, that is."

Sandy, brought up in the Horatio Alger tradition and himself always busy, after school and on Saturdays, at numerous paying jobs, in addition to the paper route he carried, was of the often expressed opinion that to Jory no work was congenial.

Mrs. Bass was never seemingly annoyed at the questioning, but there wasn't any doubt but that, to her,

Jory's allergy for work was but an evidence of an aristocratic temperament. In her eyes his tastes and proclivities contrasted quite favorably with our mundane, money-grubbing outlook on life.

Once, on one of his infrequent spells of employment out of town, his mother had written him a letter and, having neither an envelope nor the necessary stamp, had given it to Sandy to mail for her.

At our house where nothing was ever wasted, there was a stack of old envelopes, garnered from here and there, which were used for paying bills and such purposes and it was in one of these that Sandy posted the letter to Jory.

When she received his reply Mrs. Bass proudly read us the part that said: "Mother, don't ever send me another letter in those cheap yellow envelopes. Here is a dollar. Go out and get yourself some decent writing paper, for heaven's sake!"

Besides Jory there was only a young grandson, Jason. The other son had years before taken off for parts unknown. His mother actually didn't know whether he was living or dead.

"Wherever he is, though," she said, "I know he's having a good time. Moody was a great one for fun. He sure didn't have no use for folks that wasn't ready for a good time. If there wasn't any excitement around, Moody'd stir some up."

This happy-go-lucky philosophy was a Bass tenet of faith. On those rare occasions when the family received an unexpected windfall—if Jory had a job for a little while, or some other lucky circumstance brought a little ready cash into the family coffers, Mama often tried to dispense some good advice.

"What you want to do now, Mrs. Bass, is to buy a sack of flour and put in some potatoes, oatmeal and side meat."

Mrs. Bass would listen politely and maybe even agree. But the next day she would be over to borrow some flour or potatoes.

"We sure saw us a fine show last night," she'd tell Mama. "And had us a good steak dinner downtown."

She was determined not to grow old. To her naturally wavy silvery gray hair she applied a poisonous concoction

that made it come out a greenish-reddish-brass color and
gave her a hard and somewhat weird appearance. The
only time we saw her hair in its natural lustrous beauty
was when she could neither beg nor borrow the money
for dye.

I don't know if she ever told us the exact circumstances—whether she crashed the gate at an inaugural
ball, or what—but one of her proudest and most often
repeated boasts was of "the time I danced with the Governor of Kentucky."

However closely bad luck might dog her footsteps,
she was never dour nor downcast.

Among her reminiscences, freely shared, was of the
time when "the boys burned the furniture for firewood
when I was sick in the hospital. But then," brightening,
"they did leave me my bed."

For in every evil circumstance there was always some
good. And there was always a rainbow around the corner.
Like Mr. Micawber she lived in the confident faith that
something good was sure to turn up.

And in the end her faith was, to a degree, justified.

Came World War I, and Jory was caught in the draft.

He served only a brief time and upon his death (from
causes having nothing to do with his military service)
left war insurance which gave his mother a small monthly
income and, more important, something which was a
miracle and a glory to her for the rest of her days—
fifteen hundred dollars in cash.

Great as was this windfall, it was of course soon spent.

The family had now moved to a small town in Mississippi, and while the twenty dollars a month was enough,
in those days, to sustain life after a fashion, Mrs. Bass
dreamed of the days spent in the little house on the railroad and invested them with the nostalgic glamor of the
long ago and far away.

Particularly she remembered a visit she had made to
the State Fair; the sights along the midway; the thrills
of the roller coaster; the noise, and color, and life. It was
October and in some newspaper she picked up she read
that in our town the State Fair was soon to open. Mrs.
Bass decided to pay us a visit.

Of course there was the problem of railroad fare. Never one to let a little matter of that kind stand in the way of pleasure, however, she canvassed the charitable and civic groups of the town until she found one willing to advance her fare. She achieved this by telling them of her near-destitute condition and assuring them she had friends back home who would care for her if only she could get money for a railroad tcket.

We had not heard from her in some time on that day when the telephone rang and a familiar voice said: "Miss Nell, I'm here at the railroad station. Come get me."

She was well past seventy now. But Mama never dreamed that it was her plan to spend the rest of her days with us where, she thought, she could have her twenty dollars for just the frosting on the cake of life, with the necessities freely given. So Mama persuaded Nell to double up with one of the other girls and give the visitor her room.

As time went on, Mrs. Bass recounted over and over the glories of the days just past.

"Maybe you won't believe it, but right in this hand— *in this very hand!*—I held fifteen hundred dollars! Fifteen—hundred—dollars!"

And where was it now?

"Why, we bought us a big car. Second hand, but a big one. And we rented us a big house. I tell you, for a while there, me and Jason was *somebody! Fifteen hundred dollars!* Right in this very hand!"

As the visit went on and on and days lengthened into weeks, weeks into months, Nell became tired of being deprived of her room and Mama was prevailed upon to convey to Mrs. Bass the suggestion that she go back to Jason and his wife in Mississippi.

Our guest took no offense at the reluctantly proffered hint. After all, she had been to the Fair. Besides, she rather looked forward to the train ride back. She agreed to go if Mama would provide her fare.

So Mama bought her a ticket and gave her money for food on the return journey.

On the way to the railroad station Mrs. Bass called to Nell, who was driving:

"Miss Nell, stop at this next corner. I want to go

to the drug store."

"What is it you want, Mrs. Bass?" Nell inquired. "I'll get it for you."

"I want to get me some of that wrinkle cream I saw advertised in the paper. It's guaranteed to take ten years off your age."

"But you haven't any money for wrinkle cream."

"Oh, yes'm, I have. Your mama give me some money for my lunch. But, Miss Nell, when those folks on the train open up their lunches and see that I've got none, you know they're not going to go ahead and eat without offering me some."

The first of her letters to Mama after she got back to Mississippi indicated that the wrinkle cream had worked its anticipated magic.

"Caught me a beau on the train," she wrote triumphantly. "A little old for my taste. But still spry. We're corresponding."

Mama had a letter or two after that. Then we ceased to hear.

I often imagine Mrs. Bass as she must be in heaven. I'm sure she's doing nothing so static as playing the harp. As I visualize her, she's dancing away on the arm of the Governor of Kentucky, waving a check for fifteen hundred dollars, her hair red and resplendent in a really good dye job.

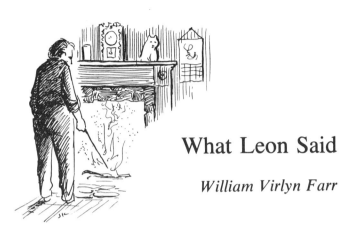

What Leon Said

William Virlyn Farr

"**U**SEEBUS! Come here . . ." He did not move from his rocking chair until he heard the door open, and then he stood up and began to poke the fire.

"Didn't you hear me?" his wife demanded, closing the door behind her.

He hung up the poker. The room was almost dark but the fire lightened his red face, which twisted into a frown, then a smile. "Uh, I had to fix the fire."

"You didn't touch that fire till you heard me, but I ain't got time to argue. That was Cap Whitlock, wasn't it? What'd he want?"

Usebious Jones was standing on the hearth, his back to the fire. It was roaring now.

"Look at you! You don't have to get *in* the fire. You gonna burn you'self up one of these days. Cap Whitlock, wasn't it? What'd he want?"

There was dough on her hands, he noticed. She would have to go back to the kitchen and cook supper, and he would have to stay in the living room and keep the fire going. If she wanted to argue, it would have to be quick. Perhaps if he approached the thing in the right way . . .

"Mary Kate . . . don't get excited now. It might not work out, and it wasn't my idea at all." He chuckled, then continued: "I'm not even sure I'll go along with it, or you either. You'll see how crazy it sounds."

He looked from her to the brindled cat that had taken his chair. He brushed the cat aside and seated himself.

"Take your time, Usebious. I got all the time in the world. It ain't that I got supper to cook or anything like that. . . . I don't know what does make you take so long to tell something. Anybody else will say what they mean, but you—oh, you . . . "

"Now, Mary Kate," he drawled, setting himself easily into the rocker, "I got to start at the beginning. I never was one to jump in at the middle of anything, and you ought to know it by now. I got a right to start at the beginning so you'll understand it wasn't my idea at all. I wouldn't think up something like this out of a blue sky, and—"

"You want any supper tonight? That dough will be hard as your head by the time you get around to what Cap Whitlock come over here for."

"Let me ask you something. You know Bumblehook ain't incorporated? Legally speaking, it ain't a city?"

"Or any other way of speaking. No more'n a hundred people at the most lives here. Is that what Cap Whitlock come all the way over here to tell you? I coulda told you that myself."

"Yeah, matter of fact, he did. And he said it's a law that the state has to pave the sidewalks of any legal city they pave a highway through.

For the first time, Mary Kate expressed more interest than curiosity in the purpose of Cap Whitlock's visit. Talk had it for a long time that the highway would be paved through Bumblehook, but no one had mentioned paved sidewalks in the bargain.

"You mean for nothing?"

"They have to, according to this law. But we ain't incorporated yet. We got to elect a mayor."

"I *say* a mayor!"

Usebious nodded.

"Well, I reckon it'll be Leon," said Mary Kate. "Looks like he has his way about everything round here."

"Oh, I don't know about that. It ain't the way Cap looks at it . . . "

To his relief, Usebious saw her smile. He had won the first round, he knew, when she started for the kitchen without another word. At the door she turned and said, "I don't think it's such a crazy idea, Mr. Mayor."

THE building may be unpainted and weather beaten, thought Usebious, as he approached *Whitlock's Gro. & Gen. Mdse.,* but it's a store. There was a porch where a man could sit and pass a summer afternoon, and inside there were nail kegs around a hot stove in the winter time.

Cap should have sense enough to retire after running a store for thirty years, people said. And it was true that he did little business now that Leon Maddox had opened a bigger and better store. Even Usebious traded with Leon now and then, just to keep on his good side. But now he was ready to fight the devil himself in order to be the first mayor of Bumblehook.

Cap was playing Pood Harris a game of checkers when Usebious came in.

"Gentlemen," Cap said, turning to Pood, "I want to interduce at this time the next mayor—the first mayor of the new corporated city of Bumblehook, none other than his honor, Mayor Usebious Jones!"

Pood applauded vigorously and said, "Hear! Hear! . . . Or should I say, Speech? Yes, Speech!" He was a little dried-up man wearing a black derby hat, who had been county ordinary for twenty years and more.

Usebious smiled and waved his right arm.

"Thank you gentlemen. On this solemn occasion, I want to say, uh—thank you. And I thank you!"

"Hear! Hear!" said Pood.

"And I want to say there ain't *one man* big enough to say who's gonna be mayor of our city. Am I right?"

"Right."

"Right."

"And I say right. It's anonymous!"

Pood lifted a hand. "Your honor, I have a question. What qualifications do you bring to the highest office in this metropolis?"

"I'm glad you ask that question," said Usebious, beaming. "It's a question that ought to be asked on this solemn occasion. Now, who's got a answer?"

"Never mind," Pood said. "The question is beside the

point. You don't need qualifications. You need votes. How many do you have?"

"What you say, Pood? Don't you know we ain't had the election yet? I just started running today."

Pood shook his head sadly. "You mean to say you've decided to run for public office without counting the votes? What idiocy! Cap, will you get me a pencil and some paper?"

Cap handed him a pencil and note paper and he started figuring.

Five minutes later, Usebious read the result:

	Maddox	*Jones*
Tenants _____	16	9
Debtors _____	8	0
Relatives _____	6	10
Friends . _____	0	2
	30	21

In question: 10

Usebious handed the paper to Cap and said, "I hadn't thought about it like this." All the the votes in question would not go to him, Usebious knew, and it wouldn't help if they did.

He was a defeated candidate before the race had begun.

"I guess Leon's got it in the bag," he told Pood. "Mayor Leon Maddox. Don't that get you, though?"

"You're wrong," said Pood. "Do you know what happened when he moved to Bumblehook? His folks all but disowned him. There's something funny, if not disgraceful, about living here. Suppose he should go back to town and say, 'I've been elected mayor of Bumblehook.' Don't you know they would laugh? Oh, no. Leon will never run for mayor."

"But the votes!" Usebious protested. "You counted the votes and said—"

"Leon still has the votes to do with as he pleases. And don't think he won't use them in his interest. All he needs is a puppet to nod yea or nay, depending on the way Leon crooks his finger."

Cap had studied the paper carefully and now he handed it back to Usebious. There was no question as to its accuracy. Pood had been county ordinary for over twenty years. He knew how to count votes.

"How about councilman?" Cap said. "I hear there'll be two . . ."

Usebious sneered. "I got my pride. I won't be no councilman under Leon's mayor."

"Look," Cap said solemnly. "We been kidding ourselves. Nobody's got a chance without Leon's say so, and I'll tell you the truth. I wanted to beat him in the election the way he beat me in business. I hate to say it, but it's the honest truth. I knowed you could do it, Usebious, if anybody could." Then, turning to Pood, "Seems like Usebious ought to have enough votes to say something about who's gonna get councilman, and we got to think about Bumblehook. It'll build up with this paved road running through here. Business will move in. Folks will build here and yonder, all over the place. We need an experienced man in there, Pood, and you was county ordinary for more'n twenty years. Maybe if we talked to Leon—"

"I decline the honor," said Pood. "I'm an old man with old ideas. If it's the fate of Bumblehook to grow, it'll have to be without my help. Leon has the votes. Let him decide what to do with them. I'm tired and if you gentlemen will excuse me, I'll go home and to bed."

Usebious sat there another thirty minutes, thinking. No one came in. Nothing was said. Then he picked up the sheet of paper and started to leave. "I'll see you," was all he said; and, "Yeah," was all the response he got.

"IT'd be bad enough if Leon was born here," Mary Kate told Usebious later that evening. "But he's just lived here ten years, since he married Sally. It'll be a long time before I set foot in her house again. Her and her airy ways. And them younguns, stuck up as she is. Things have come to a pretty pass, I tell you, when one man can say who's gonna be mayor. It ain't right. It just ain't right, any way you look at it. I wish there was some way we could get together and give this community a dose of good old-fashioned democracy. What was it Lincoln said?"

Usebious did not answer. He had read the *Atlanta
Constitution*. Now he was absorbed in the *Greer's Almanac*.

"U*see*bus! I said what'd Lincoln say?"

He looked up, puzzled.

"Lincoln was all the time saying one thing or another,
Mary Kate. Just what occasion was you thinking of?"

"You ain't been listening to a word I said, have you?"

"Oh, yeah, I have," he insisted. "You been saying
what a fine man Leon Maddox is and how lucky we are
to have a educated man like him to show us dumbbells
how to run our business. How Lincoln got in there is
beyond me."

"Aw, he said something about government by the
people and for the people, didn't he?"

"Yeah, I think he did, now that you mention it. But
he didn't live in Bumblehook. It's what Leon says that
counts here. . . . It's a pity I can't afford to buy me some
more farms. I'd show him who's boss around here."

"Who do you think he'll put up for mayor?"

Usebious hadn't thought much about it, his own disappointment had been so great. "Oh, I don't reckon it
matters one way or the other," he said. "Anybody he can
twist around his finger will do."

"It's a pity you can't afford to buy a couple of his
farms. That way you could take away from his votes
and add to yours at the same time . . . oh, I know you
can't and Leon wouldn't sell or he'd jack the price way
up. He'd know what you was up to. That sneak. Or
snake. A snake in the grass."

Finally she was quiet and had begun to knit. Usebious
was asleep and dreaming, he thought, when he heard the
door open and Mary Kate say, "Usebious, Leon is here."

"U*see*bus! Wake up! Leon's here . . . "

He opened his eyes.

No one would take Leon for a political boss. Now,
as always in the winter time, he wore a leather jacket
over a white shirt and tie. "How're you getting along,
Usebious?" Leon did not look him in the eye. He spoke
softly, not much above a whisper.

"Oh, I been doing all right for a old man. Ha, ha!

Been thinking about you, Leon. You getting along all right, I hope?"

Mary Kate scowled and went about her knitting, ignoring them both.

"Sit down, sit down," Usebious offered.

"No, I don't have time," Leon protested. "I have to be getting back. I just stopped by to tell you about our new sidewalks. Have you heard?"

"Is it a fact? I heard but I wasn't at all sure it was the truth. We going to get them, sure enough?"

Leon assured him that it was indeed the truth.

"Before they pave the sidewalks, though, we have to incorporate the city and elect a major. That's why I came to see you. You've got quite a few relatives and you own some property. Now, your kinfolks and tenants would go along with you when it comes to an election, wouldn't they?"

"I reckon so, Leon, if I was to ask them. Yeah, they would."

"Well, Usebious, we need a good man for mayor. I'm not running myself. To tell you the truth, several people have approached me about running for county commissioner next year. I'll need a mayor I can count on. . . . Let me get to the point. Would you be interested in the job, Usebious?"

"Me? . . . Why, I—" He laughed haltingly. "I hadn't thought about it. . . . You think I'd make a mayor, sure enough? Mayor Usebious Jones. Hey! Sounds pretty good, don't it?"

"I have to go," Leon said. "There won't be much to the job, actually, and I can help you out anytime. Of course there will be an election, but I'm sure the people will go along with whoever we pick. You did say you'd take it, didn't you?"

"Well, if you put it that way . . . I mean if I'm nominated and elected . . . Well?" He smiled.

"There'll be two councilmen. I haven't decided who to ask. Do you have any ideas?"

"Me? Why—why, no. I'll go along with anybody you decide on."

Mary Kate had dropped her knitting. "How's Sally?"

she asked Leon.

"Fine," he said.

"I've been wanting to get over to see her," Mary Kate said. "Tell her I've been so busy lately that I just couldn't get off, but I'll be over in a day or so. You will tell her?"

He nodded.

"Thank you, Leon. I've always thought so much of Sally—and the children, too."

Usebious opened the door and followed Leon to the car. It was cold out and he had forgotten to wear his coat, but he stood there and waited for Leon to leave. "I want you to know I appreciate this, Leon. I'll try to make the kind of mayor you'll be proud of."

"I know you will. And I like your attitude," said Leon.

Women Don't Understand
About a Goat

Beatrice Jefferson

"**M**AMA, I'VE GOT to have a dollar." The demand came low and urgent from behind Rogers' two enormous front teeth. He stood in the kitchen doorway, his arms thrust back like chicken wings and fists clenched and quivering.

Martha Russell lifted a plate from the dishpan, handed it to her daughter, and turned. "What for, son?"

"Mama hasn't got a dollar," put in Annie Mae, who was well-grown for thirteen, as tall as her mother. "We've only got sixty cents left till Grandpa's check comes next week."

Ignoring his sister, Rogers wedged himself between them and, looking up at his mother, whispered. "Wash will sell me his billy-goat for a dollar."

Mrs. Russell sighed. "I'm sorry, Rogers. I'd give it to you if I had it, but that load of wood took the last money I had. Wait till next week, and we'll see."

"I can't wait. They're packing up right now. Wash's father didn't make a crop and the fertilizer man says he's going to have the sheriff after him. They'll be gone if I don't hurry. Please, Mama, *I've got to have that dollar.*"

The desperate desire behind his blue eyes stabbed her heart. She wiped her hands and put her arms around the little boy, holding him close. Tears filled her eyes.

"Shame on you, Rogers," Annie Mae scolded, "Making Mama feel bad. I wouldn't let her give you a dollar for an old goat even if she had it."

Annie Mae had assumed a grown-up way ever since their father had drawn her to the hospital bed after his accident and said, "Be a good girl and look after your mother and little brother for me." Trying hard to keep her promise, she had grown bossy.

Rogers nuzzled his head against his mother's apron, and without looking up, answered his sister, "Then you give me the money in your missionary box. If Mama has sixty-cents, maybe that would be enough."

"Why, Rogers," Annie Mae was horrified, "You wouldn't ask me to take from the Lord to buy a *goat*. That would be a sin."

But no argument could dent the armor of his desire. He looked at his sister with begging eyes. "If *you* asked Grandpa for the money, he'd give it to you. Please, Annie Mae."

A loud thumping on the floor in the next room interrupted her firm refusal. Mrs. Russell called out, "That you, Grandpa?"

"Who do you think it is?" was the querulous reply, "Come here. Come here, all of you."

Arthritis had not improved the disposition of the old man who sat by the window in a Morris chair with cushions of faded olive green. He was hunched over in a hugging position as though he were trying to hide inside his own skeleton. One knotty hand gripped the stout homemade walking stick with which he continued to summon his daughter-in-law and grandchildren. He resented their dependence on his pension without realizing that his own helplessness made it necessary for them to continue living with him. He blamed his son, Henry, for getting himself run down by a car with no insurance. Martha's quiet resignation irritated him. Rogers' noisy play made him more conscious of his infirmities. Only Annie Mae could soften his voice and bring a smile to his set countenance, and that not often.

Annie Mae came first and stood in front of him. "What is it, Grandpa? Oh, you dropped your pipe." She stooped to pick up the pipe that lay beyond his reach.

"Leave it be," he barked, "What's all this about a goat?"

"Don't worry, Grandpa," Annie Mae replied, stroking his yellow-white hair, "Rogers knows he can't have a goat."

"Shut up, girl," the old man snapped his false teeth so sharply that Annie Mae jumped back. "Speak up, Rogers. Don't go hiding behind your mother."

Rogers, accustomed only to abuse from his grandfather, took two timid steps forward. Fear tied his tongue, but after several gulps, desire loosened the muscles of his throat for the words to tumble out. "You remember Wash, Grandpa? The colored boy on Mr. Jackson's place? He's got a billy-goat, and he only wants a dollar for him. Goats don't eat much, and I won't let him bother anybody."

"You needn't tell me anything about goats," the old man retorted. He tapped Rogers lightly on the leg with his cane and pointed under the bed. "Reach for that carpet slipper. Feel in the toe."

Rogers dropped to his knees. He ran his hand into the frayed slipper, drew out a soiled dollar bill and held it out to his grandfather.

"Take it," commanded the old man, "Go buy your goat."

For a second Rogers stood in a daze of disbelief. Then a toothy grin spread over his face. "Oh, thank you, Grandpa. Can I get him right now?"

The old man nodded. "And bring your goat outside my window so I can see him." He waved his cane in dismissal.

Rogers was out of sight before Annie Mae could protest. "That was your medicine money. You oughtn't to have given it to him. How'll you get by?"

"Leave me alone," growled the old man, "It's my money and my pain, and I'll thank you to mind your own business. Women don't understand about a goat."

Annie Mae followed her mother into the kitchen and began to sprinkle the pile of clothes waiting to be ironed.

Her mother noticed what a heavy hand she was using with the water. "Don't pay any attention to him. This must be one of his bad days."

"But he never hollered at me like that before," sniffled the girl.

"He didn't mean anything," reassured her mother,

"There's always been something about a goat that . . . " She completed her sentence with a sigh.

It wasn't long before Rogers' voice could be heard down the road. "Here he is, Grandpa. Come on, goat."

The old man shifted his position with effort in order to see out the window. A smile triumphed over the grim furrows fixed in his face by pain. He tapped his cane with approval as Rogers jerked an unwilling and unhurried goat at the end of a line compounded of plow share, old leather harness and twine.

"Can you see him, Grandpa?" Rogers shouted, as he urged the emaciated animal into a reluctant trot and came alongside the window. "He's a real goat, isn't he?"

Grandpa's body started to shake slightly, and gradually his amusement was voiced in a high-pitched "Hah-hah-hah. He just is, son. He just is." He took out his teeth. It was easier to laugh without them.

The goat lifted his head and gave a nearsighted squint down its long nose in the direction from which the sound had come. Then it replied, "Hah-hah-hah."

"Hah-hah-hah," piped the old man again. "You're the po-est critter I ever laid eyes on, and you must be most as old as me."

"Hah-hah-hah," the thin bleating of the goat echoed.

Rogers was overjoyed. "You can talk goat language, can't you, Grandpa? Did you have a goat when you were a little boy?"

"Did *I* have a goat? Of course, I had a goat. The finest black and white goat you ever saw."

"What was his name?" Rogers picked a handful of grass and thrust it toward the goat who was sampling the bark of a maple tree.

"His name was General Beauregard. That was the general my Pa served under. He was a beauty, too," he added ambiguously.

"Then I'm going to call my goat General Beauregard," stated Rogers.

"No you don't." Grandpa was jealous of his memories. "Not that skin and bones. Don't look like he ever had a square meal. But we'll find him a name. Just give me time."

"We could call him Billy," ventured Rogers.

"That's no name for a goat. Just means he's a he-goat, same as nannie's a lady goat." The old man shook his head.

"How about George Washington? That's who Wash was named for, and he was Wash's goat. That would be a good name, wouldn't it?"

Grandpa chuckled as he looked at the animal whose thin coat of brown and white was dirty and matted. "Somehow the name 'Wash' don't seem to fit that critter. Give me time. I'll hit on a name bye-and-bye."

"Wash mostly called him 'Preacher'. He said he looked just like their preacher at Mt. Zion, but I don't think Annie Mae'd like my calling a goat 'Preacher'."

Talking about Wash reminded Rogers of something. He rooted in his overall pocket, stood on tip-toe beneath the window and whispered: "I most forgot. Here's your dollar, Grandpa. When I got to Wash's house, they'd gone. I guess they couldn't take the goat in the car. I couldn't leave him there to starve, could I? Wash wanted me to have him. He told me so." He reached up to hand the wadded bill over the window ledge. The goat, who had been rhythmically munching Martha Russell's chrysanthemums, without warning lowered his head and thrust forward with direct aim at the seat of Rogers' pants.

The boy struck the weatherboarding of the house with such force the wind was knocked out of him, but he twisted and avoided a second collision. He grabbed the rope and shortened it around the tree while Grandpa laughed until the tears ran down his cheeks.

"Mr. Archibald *Butt*. That's the name for him," Grandpa declared when he was able to speak. "Don't know how that name happened to come to mind. Mr. Butt was a gentleman who went down on the *Titanic* back in 1912. Don't know much about him, but it seems like the name just suits your goat."

Rogers' injuries were slight enough for him to laugh, too. He caught the goat by the horns and looked him in the eye. "Mr. Archibald Butt, you didn't mean to hurt me, did you? You're going to be a good goat, and I'm going to make you a wagon, and we're going to have lots of fun."

"You'll have to feed him up before he can pull any wagon," commented Grandpa. Then, lowering his voice he beckoned to the boy, saying, "Here, take this dollar. Go down to Mr. Gibson's and get a sack of feed. Needn't say anything to your mother or Annie Mae. And when you get back, hide it in the cow shed."

Rogers' eyes danced with the joy of conspiracy as he whispered in reply, "I won't say a thing. Thank you, Grandpa. You look after Mr. Butt while I'm gone."

"If you know what's good for you, you'll get out of those flowers," Grandpa warned Mr. Butt who was systematically obliterating the last flowers in the yard.

"Hah-hah-hah," retorted the goat.

"You sassy old buzzard," laughed Grandpa, thumping his cane, the signal to bring Annie Mae from the kitchen.

"See your brother's goat?" he demanded when she stood before him. "He's a goat all right." He pinched his nose with two knotty fingers.

Annie Mae gave one glance and walked back to the kitchen without comment. After a long silence she said, "Mama, that's the most awful looking animal you ever saw. What Rogers wants with a dirty old thing like that. It—It—"

"Smells." Her mother completed the sentence for her, "And Rogers will smell, too, just being around him. But there's not a thing we can do. I remember my brother, Bob, had a goat once."

"But Grandpa acts like he doesn't love me any more," Annie Mae complained with injured pride.

"Play like you don't notice it," advised her mother, "When a boy, or a man, for that matter, gets a goat, it's like a new sweetheart. You have to stand by till the excitement wears off." Martha set her broom in the corner. "And it doesn't pay to be jealous, either."

"Jealous? Me, jealous of that thing?" Annie Mae tossed her head in scorn. "But I'm surprised at Rogers. He knows how things are around here, and he's old enough to help instead of spending Grandpa's medicine money for a goat."

Martha Russell sighed as she hung up her apron. There were so many things that Annie Mae, being a woman, would have to learn. The way a boy felt about a goat was only one of them.

Grandpa refused to leave the window and go to bed for his afternoon nap. He let Annie Mae lower the metal bar on his Morris chair. Occcassionally he would doze, but most of the time he kept up a running conversation with himself, with Rogers, or with the goat. Mr. Butt's presence acted like a magnet to draw from his store of scrambled memories long forgotten people and events which pushed the ever-present pain out of his consciousness and replaced it with scenes of his childhood from which all hardship and sorrow had been magically extracted.

Rogers went into somersaults of delight at his grandfather's story of General Beauregard eating the roses off the schoolteacher's hat the day she came to tell his Ma he had played hookey.

"But that wasn't the worst whipping I got," Grandpa admitted, "There was really something doing around our house when my goat et Pa's elastic-seam drawers off the line."

This kept them both laughing a long time. When Mrs. Russell or Annie Mae would approach, all talk abruptly stopped, and Rogers sensed that he was being initiated into a masculine brotherhood with revelations unsuited for feminine ears.

"Grandpa," questioned Rogers, "do goats really eat tin cans?"

"Not to my knowing," the old man replied, "Guess that's the way folks have of saying a goat ain't particular. Never heard of one saying, 'No thank you' to anything to eat. You can't fill a goat up."

"I'm going to fill you up, Mr. Butt," Rogers assured his pet, happy in the knowledge of the large sack of feed hidden in the shed. "I'm going to give you all you can eat."

Martha Russell came to the door. "The wood box is empty, Rogers. Do your chores; then you can go back to playing."

Her eyes fell on her flower bed now reduced to stubble. Mr. Butt was masticating the last stripped stalk with deliberate satisfaction. The red and yellow zinnias that had been so pretty were all gone. She had tried so hard to have something blooming the way it had been at home. She felt like crying until she looked at Rogers. The unspeakable joy on his dirty freckled face as he tied the goat's line to the tree was more than compensation for a few fall flowers. A wave of gratitude surged through her heart with the realization that this child of hers was as happy at that moment as it is possible for a little boy to be. Tears blurred her eyes and instead of scolding, she turned and went hastily into the house.

Next morning Martha was stirring the hominy grits when Annie Mae appeared for breakfast already dressed for Sunday School.

"Where's Rogers?" her mother asked.

"Out with that old goat, I guess. He got up early," said Annie Mae, sliding carefully into a chair to keep from mussing her starched skirt.

"Goodness, I hope not," said her mother, "He'll have to take another bath before he puts on his good clothes. Go call him while I get Grandpa to the table."

Annie Mae went to the door and called. No reply. She hated to soil her shoes, but when a series of louder calls failed to get a response, she tipped through the chicken yard toward the old cow shed. The sagging door was open and she peered into the semi-darkness. Rogers was not to be seen, but on the ground lay the goat, its uppermost side distended like a football, its legs pointing stiffly outward, and neck thrown back at an unnatural angle. Close by lay a crumpled feed sack with big red letters on it.

"Goat," Annie Mae called, transferring her annoyance at Rogers to his animal. But even as she spoke she saw beyond a possibility of a doubt that the goat was dead.

She darted back to the house, forgetting to keep her shoes clean. "Mama," she panted, "Roger's goat is dead." And then as Grandpa appeared in the door, she added with satisfaction, "And your medicine money's gone."

"Shut up," shouted her grandfather, "Where's Rogers?"

"I don't know," she answered, "I didn't see him anywhere."

Grandpa picked up his cane and started toward the shed, waving Annie Mae aside. "Stay where you are,

both of you. Eat your breakfast and go on to Sunday
School. You can put us something up. I'll handle this."

The fierceness of his command prevented any offer of
assistance in his difficult walk toward the barn. When he
had at last reached the cow shed, he saw that Annie Mae
had been right. The half-starved animal had emptied the
entire sack of feed and had literally eaten himself to death.
The old man leaned against the door frame. From the
adjoining tool room came the muffled sobs of a broken-
hearted boy.

"Rogers," the old man's voice was sharp. "Come out
here. Do you hear me? And bring the long handled
shovel. You've got to bury this goat."

"Oh, Grandpa, I can't." The wail came from the boy
flung face down on a pile of sacks. "I just can't."

"Can't my eye," shouted his grandfather, "Don't tell
me what you can and can't do. You march yourself out
here this minute, and bring the shovel with you. You don't
aim to throw him out for the buzzards to pick, do you?"

The fear he had always felt for his grandfather returned
and spurred Rogers to obedience. He came slowly from
the tool room, dragging the heavy shovel, his head down
and face streaked with dirt and tears.

"Please don't make me bury him," he begged. Fresh
tears were in the making.

"You don't expect me to do it, do you? Or your
Mother or Annie Mae?" was the reply.

"Rogers," called Annie Mae, "it's time for Sunday
School."

"Leave her be. Don't answer her," ordered his grandfather, "I told them to go on without you."

"I'm never going to go to Sunday School again,"
sniffled Rogers, "God is mean to kill my goat."

"I've no use for a baby," snapped the old man. "A
baby kicks and whines when things don't go to suit him.
But a man takes what comes, especially if it's his own fault.
Don't go blaming the Lord for putting the feed where the
fool goat could get to it."

"But you said a goat never got enough to eat."

The old man did not answer, and Rogers, between
sniffles, continued: "I come out at bedtime and gave him
a little more feed so I could fatten him up in a hurry.

He must have seen me put it on the shelf and jumped up
and knocked it off. He was the smartest goat in all the
world."

"Well, he wasn't smart enough to know when to stop
eating," stated Grandpa, "And crying won't change matters. You've got a job to do. I had to help dig my own
Father's grave when I wasn't much bigger'n you. Now pick
up that shovel, and go dig a good deep hole in the corner
of the garden."

With a grunt and a groan Grandpa eased himself onto
a box and waited with closed eyes until he realized Rogers
had returned. "Now, catch hold the goat's legs and pull
him to the garden. No need to stand back. He's the same
animal you were playing with yesterday afternoon. Just
because he's cold you needn't be afraid. He won't hurt
you."

Rogers winced, but dared not disobey. He grasped the
goat's front legs and tugged the body after him. The old
man followed. With his stick he helped guide the dead
animal into the hole. Each spade of earth brought tears,
but no words from Rogers. When the last shovelful of
dirt was mounded over the grave, his grandfather spoke
in the voice Rogers had heard for the first time the
previous afternoon: "I clean forgot how much company a
goat can be."

He pulled out a rumpled handkerchief, gave a vigorous
blow and put the handkerchief back into his pocket. Then
he put his gnarled hand on the boy's shoulder. "Here, son,
help me to the house. We'll get us another goat—somehow
or another. Won't be like General Beauregard. Won't be
like Mr. Butt. Might even be a nanny, for all I know—
but it'll be a *goat*."

Hoodwinked

Leon V. Driskell

WHEN the first shot was fired, Jake dropped to the ground and flattened himself against it, squirming ever so slightly at the contact of the heavy vines against his belly and moving his head slowly from left to right to determine, if he could, from which direction the shot had come. He could see nothing in the darkness, and he cursed (as only a farm boy can curse) the impulse which had sent him and his two best friends, Henry and Lew, out on a mission of this sort in the dark of the moon.

He'd heard a cry — shrill and piercing — immediately following the report of the shotgun. Old man Youngblood's shotgun. Jake imagined, dully, that the cry he had heard had been made by Henry, and he searched his memory to determine whether he had also heard a body fall to earth. Or had he only heard the thud of his own body against the dirt and vegetation?

Henry, Henry, Henry. His mind kept repeating the name, and Jake was more nearly in tears than he had been since the death of his father five years earlier. Henry, the one lad of the three who had not wanted to come. Had begged the others not to come. Had given in at last only because of his (Jake's) urgings and ridiculing. Henry who had insisted over and over that he was not afraid but that what Jake wished to do was wrong. Henry who had become so excited over the night's adventure (once he had given in and had agreed to the plan) that he could not keep his mind on his work, had grinned openly at Jake whenever he felt Jake's eyes on him, had been so infectiously delighted at what lay ahead that Jake feared the boy would give everything away before the time came to act.

Jake himself was young — young even by the standard of the hill country where boys became men when they could hold the plow lines and girls became women when they could reach the top of the wood range to cook—, but he was older than Henry, and he always thought fondly of Henry as "the boy." Henry was his cousin, and since Henry's father (like Jake's) had died leaving a large family to make its own way as best it could, Jake had always befriended the boy. They had tramped the mountainsides together, had fished along the clear, cold streams, and had worked side by side in the corn fields, and, more lately, Jake had arranged for Henry to work part-time in the mill where he was employed. And it had been at the mill, during the dinner hour, that tonight's adventure had been planned; for two days Henry who had always before followed Jake's lead in everything, had said "no" and on the third day he had said "yes."

Now, perhaps, Henry was dying, or (and Jake swallowed hard) perhaps he was already dead, lying face down in the Georgia dirt.

Grimly Jake began to inch himself along the ground toward where he suspected he would find Henry's body. He tried to move silently, for he knew that somewhere nearby was Mr. Youngblood with his shotgun. Moving silently was next to impossible, and he was making little progress, for it was necessary to make wide detours around huge, mountain-grown watermelons lying in his path. He hated the melons and cursed them individually, the very same melons which he had described so enthusiastically that day at dinner.

Jake had had his eyes on the big green-striped watermelons in Julius Youngblood's field for almost a month; he had to pass the Youngblood place to get to the mill, and each time he passed the melons looked better to him.

"As big as a washpot," he had said, holding up both hands to indicate the size of the watermelons to Henry and to Lew. "Dead-ripe, right now, and that ole' skinflint's gonna let 'em rot in the fields 'fore he'll sell 'em for market price."

It was true that Mr. Youngblood's melon patch was the prettiest one around, and Mr. Youngblood—a combination farmer, preacher, and school teacher—had been heard to say that the price for watermelons down at the farmer's market didn't make it much worthwhile to haul them into town. Had Jake really wanted the melons, he probably could have bought them from Mr. Youngblood, and the old man might even have given Jake one free had the idea occurred to him. But far more delicious than the watermelons—to Jake's mind at least — was the idea of hoodwinking the old man, getting into his patch and selecting the very biggest and best of the melons and hauling them off while Mr. Youngblood slept a short distance away. So well-known was Jake for devilment and mischief that he knew Mr. Youngblood would suspect him at once should the patch be robbed, and he knew that most of the people in the community would assume that he, Jake Wilkins, had been behind the spiriting away of the melons, and that too would be part of the fun.

"The day after," Jake had giggled to Lew, "I'll go up to his front door, big as life, and ask 'em if he's got any melons to sell; he'll be so all-fired mad he'll most explode in my face, but I'll act real goody-goody and kinda' like I don't know what he's fumin' about. No matter what price he gives me, I'll look like it's too much and say I figger I know where I can get melons for a whole lot less."

The three conspirators had laughed together at the imagined visit of Jake to torment Mr. Youngblood, for the old man was hardly popular with the younger set of the settlement. For one thing, Mr. Youngblood had taught most of them English and mathematics in high school, and he was one of the old-fashioned teachers who could and would administer a sound whipping to a misbehaving boy—even if that boy happened to be seventeen or eighteen years old. And, for another thing, Mr. Youngblood was part-time preacher at four or five small churches (all of them churches which could not afford a full-time minister), and he kept the boys' and (worse yet) the girls' families in a constant state of evangelical zeal. He preached well, and whole families would walk miles on a Sunday afternoon to hear him, but brevity was not one of the virtues of his sermons. He seldom stopped talking short of two hours, and when he finished talking, all of the women and most of the men would be crying unabashedly. Even then, however, the restive younger generation would not be free, for Mr. Youngblood would invite the sinners to give their "testimonies," and that would require another full hour. More than one young farm lad had, as a matter of fact, found himself prodded to his feet by a parent at one of Mr. Youngblood's meetings, and once on his feet had seen no alternative but renouncement of his previous ways.

None of this would have been so bad in itself had it not been for the fact that Mr. Youngblood did not always wait for sinners to become repentant on their own, and he was capable of getting quite personal in his sermons; he had been known to name names from the pulpit and to censure openly youthful activities of which he did not approve. And the list of things of which Mr. Youngblood did not approve was no short list. Most of the farm mothers and fathers adopted in blanket form Mr. Youngblood's views, and there was nothing their offspring could say to alter their minds. Mr. Youngblood approved no more of automobiles (he still drove a buggy) than he did of lipstick and rouge or of the movies which were shown in nearby Gainesville.

"Young folks," he said, "should be devoted to the Lord, and they can't do that if they're gallivanting all over three counties."

Everyone (even Jake) had to admit that Mr. Youngblood was a good man, and everyone said that he could be elected to the State Legislature if he would but run. He worked hard at farming, he knew the first names of practically everyone in the county, he knew (or most people believed he did) every single word in *The Bible,* and besides, he was known to be liberal with his wordly goods when folks were really in need. Despite being a scholar, Mr. Youngblood got along well with folks, and he was often called upon to give advice to farmers and even merchants of nearby towns.

For all of his virtues, however, Mr. Youngblood was not a man liked by young folks. He believed in a stern and exacting God, and to save a soul, he did not mind striking terror to a young heart. Taller than most men, Mr. Youngblood was lean of stature and sandy of hair. His eyebrows jutted out over eyes that were so blue that few men were comfortable looking him straight in the eye. He was never seen outside his own house unless his worn dark suit was perfectly clean and pressed and his face freshly scrubbed.

Jake, like all of his fellows, had been frightened by Mr. Youngblood's sermons, and he had considered the old man cold and exacting to a fault, but it had never occurred to Jake that old man Youngblood would be mean enough to shoot at a fellow for getting into his melon patch. Jake's eyes were smarting from the strain of looking so fixedly into the darkness, and he itched all over, but, doggedly, he crawled on looking for Henry. He was aware suddenly that he himself was in considerable danger from the cold, hard man lurking there in the shadows with a shotgun in his hands. Jake was on the point of calling out to Mr. Youngblood; he would confess everything and say that it was all his idea, and he would beg for the safety of his friends. He had just raised himself to his elbows to call out when the second shot was fired, and, for one horrible moment, Jake thought that he himself had been hit.

"Owww! Run, Jakey, run for your life. He got me!" someone shouted from the far side of the melon patch, and hysterically, Jake leaped to his feet and began to run. A third shot was fired, and, then, Jake was standing in a pool of light cast from a lantern which Mr. Youngblood was holding aloft, and he heard other shouts — not of fear or of pain but of laughter. And he saw Henry, not at all dead, leaning weakly against Lew, and the two boys were whooping with merriment. The lantern light was dancing about crazily, for the hand which held the lantern was shaking convulsively. The shotgun was propped against a fence, and Mr. Youngblood had one hand held tight against his stomach as if to forcibly restrain his own laughter. The preacher was attempting to look stern, but Jake could see that his too blue eyes were watering and his mouth kept twitching upward.

Without speaking, Mr. Youngblood laid a heavy hand on Jake's shoulder and then the four of them — Henry, Lew, Jake, and the preacher — were holding onto each other and laughing without control.

But with one arm around Henry's waist and the tears of relief and near hysteria running down his cheeks Jake was thinking, "Hoodwinked by Henry, Henry, Henry, and I always befriended the boy."

But he did not stop laughing.

Somebody for Someone

Walter Swift Richardson

A NEATLY typed envelope lay at the bottom of a stack of mail which I had begun sorting upon my return from a three-day vacation. The small, modified printing of the name, "Harold Foster," written in the upper left hand corner immediately set in motion the wheels of memory. I opened the envelope with some care and reverence, to find a letter which began:

> "Despite my protest, the Editorial Board of the Jepson Review has decided to accept your story, 'Somebody for Someone,' for publication in its Summer issue.
>
> "It was, and is, my opinion that this narrative is ineptly written, grossly contrived, and astonishingly lacking in good taste, but the majority of the Board members have voted to the contrary, so it is to them that you are indebted for this opportunity finally to see your name in print."

What the hell has happened to Hal? was my first reaction.

It had been seven years since I had seen Hal and almost that long since I had heard from him. His last attempt at communication had been a Christmas card from a midwestern university, where he was working for a master's degree. That was two years after we were discharged from a navy base in Virginia.

Because of a slight limp, Hal had been denied application for a commission but was finally drafted and given a specialist rating. Most of the specialists in the navy did nothing. Hal did even less. He was assigned to the library. His duties began every morning when he arose at nine o'clock, put a pot of coffee on to boil, and went back to bed. Thirty minutes later, with the agility of an ailing elephant he bounded from his sack and, attired only in his shorts, walked the full length of the hundred-foot library to open the front door for business. He then strolled leisurely back to his elaborate quarters, pulled on his dungarees and, with coffee pot in hand, came out to a small desk to await his first customer.

The first customer was usually an officer's wife who arrived about eleven to return a book on contract bridge or to see if her name had come up on the waiting list for "Forever Amber." By then, of course, the work detail had been in from the boot area to swab what was referred to as the deck and his two assistants had come aboard to lend a helpful, if not intelligent, hand to the few seekers after culture. Hal, meantime, languished in a modified contour chair, read whatever suited his esoteric taste and now and then answered a rare or ridiculous question. The afternoons and evenings brought a few more interruptions but by nine-thirty, when he ceremoniously locked the front door, he had read at least one novel, spent two hours on research, and insulted half a dozen people.

Back in his elaborate quarters, Steve and I were usually two drinks or two beers ahead of him, but he caught up on his drinking as easily as he did his reading.

Steve worked in the commissary warehouse, so we usually had all the food we could manage on a two-eyed burner and, through my connection with the supply department, we always had enough beer on hand to supplement the whiskey we bought on weekends. The whole thing seemed quite admirably arranged and we felt pretty smug sitting there in Hal's private suite, privileged among the underprivileged, yet believing we were bound by a common cause.

Some of our best discussions were, perhaps, of twentieth century American writers and what, if anything, the big war would do for literature. Scott Fitzgerald's "Crack

Up" had just been published and we easily agreed that this was the stuff a really good writer is made of. We wondered also if a twice-lost generation would not be twice as difficult to write about. However, our conversation was not limited by our enthusiasm for literature. There were always sex and politics and the cause and effects of wars, heredity versus environment, music, art, economics, and sex.

As I have said, it was quite cozy and we could laugh at each other and ourselves, which is the only salvation for the disciplined mob.

Then, one bright summer's day, the Waves came. Despite the fact that we had waited two years for their heralded arrival, each of us pretended it was still only a rumor and, for the first ten days, they were never mentioned at our nocturnal soirees. Finally, Steve was the one to complain about the unreasonable regulations which were now imposed because the stupid females were abroad. From then on they became the object of our witticisms and with sadistic joy we went about making life as unpleasant for them as possible. Actually there were less than a hundred assigned to the base and only six with whom we had to work. It was about these six that Hal and I decided to write the great war novel. We spent our nights plotting and replotting until we realized that there was really only one plum among them, so we began again and planned our narrative around her. She was indeed, as our plagiarized title said, "The Beautiful and Dumb." She came from a small town somewhere in the deep South and, since Steve was a Mississippian, we designated him as an interpreter in order that none of her naivete might escape us through lack of a common language.

We changed her name from Ida Belle to Maggie, which seemed a sacrifice, and we described her beauty with the finest prose we could borrow, for she was indeed beautiful. The rest seemed fairly easy, for it was simply a matter of creating inane situations to fit the riotously stupid dialogue which she daily furnished us. Nobody would believe it, we said, but we stuck to all the straight quotes. After all, truth is funnier than fiction. By then the war was over and we spent most of our waking hours trying to make Maggie appear as funny on paper as she seemed to us in person. She was apparently never aware that the witness was being led although at times it seemed, even to me, that Hal displayed unnecessary cruelty.

Then suddenly the point system was changed and Hal was discharged. The Waves were transferred during the same week and two months later Steve and I were civilians again. I heard from Hal now and then but, without our living model before us, the chisel grew dull and our great monument to literature was lost in a new and changing world.

It was quite by accident that I came across it six months ago and decided to change the title and try it as a short story. It still somehow seemed funny to me and I sent it out with some other stuff which I was trying to write during that elusive period known as spare time. It came back with accustomed regularity until, one day, I decided that it might be better suited for one of the college quarterlies.

My mind returned to Hal's letter and I picked it up again with a deep feeling of nostalgia and affection.

"It has been my pleasure," the letter concluded, "to serve as a member of the Jepson faculty for the past three years and I thought perhaps you might be interested to know that the young lady whom you so vividly describe as Maggie enrolled here two years ago and last summer became my wife."

Father's Ghost

Elizabeth Davenport Plant

SOME weeks ago the Sunday papers carried three widely separated news items. One was the story of a family on Long Island whose house seemed to be haunted by a poltergeist — that mischievous type of spook given to playing supernatural pranks. Another story concerned a castle owned by the Queen Mother of England that is haunted by a ghost of great dignity and antiquity. The third item told of a building boom in Bainbridge, Georgia.

As these three stories converged in my attention they reminded me that we once had a family ghost. It was not a Yankee Ghost scuttling around in the New York area, nor a royal ghost sequestered in a Scottish castle. It was a cozy, homespun Georgia ghost, and its favored locale was a house in Bainbridge. Its manifestation occurred years before I was born, but I have heard the story often enough to claim a few vicarious goose pimples.

At the time the ghost walked, my father, Thomas Edwin Davenport, was a young Methodist minister not many years out of Drew Seminary in New Jersey, who had come back to his native state and entered the South Georgia Conference. With his young wife and baby daughter he had just been moved from a circuit-riding appointment to the post as pastor in Bainbridge.

Back in that era one of the tenets of Methodism—or so it seemed to the ministers' families—was to make it easy for a preacher to renounce the vain pomp and glory of the world by giving him very little pomp and glory to renounce. Possibly in observance of St. Paul's dictum that pride was the worst of the seven deadly sins, parsonages at that time frequently were in such states of obsolescence that the most calcified sinner could have taken no pride in them.

Countless ministers' children may have reached maturity before they learned that wall-papers destined for parsonages were not deliberately designed with intermittent patterns of brownish stains and brighter patches of almost-matching motifs.

Father, to whom a call to the ministry perforce meant a call to sacrifice, never entertained a thought of disapprobation. But Mother, who had not been called to preach, but merely to fall in love with an inordinately handsome young preacher, may at times have felt a more earthy yearning for the flesh-pots of her ancestral home.

On arriving at their new appointment they were met at the railroad station by members of the Board of Stewards of the Church, and ushered to a waiting surrey. When they turned in at a driveway and stopped, Mother and Father looked at each other in puzzled amazement. Could this be the parsonage? This lovely old house? True, it was somewhat dilapidated, and the paint was peeling in orthodox parsonage style, but the house itself was gracious and stately.

Inside, the walls in places showed some traditional early-parsonage ravages near the roof line, but they hardly mattered against the time-mellowed softness of the beautifully textured wall-paper.

The furnishings, instead of the usual conglomerate accumulation of articles just a shade too good to burn (considered appropriate for parsonages, since preachers should be just a shade too good to burn) were in keeping with the house. It was as though a connoisseur had simply walked out and left the place *in toto*.

The furnishings of the kitchen even included a cook who had been working for the former incumbent. If the phrase had been current at the time, Mother and Father might have said that the whole set-up was "out of this world." And perhaps it was.

The cook, Lutie, smilingly informed them that she

would have to be away from the house well before sundown, and they cheerfully agreed, thinking she probably had small children at home who needed her.

Several days after they were ensconced the Chairman of the Board came to call. "Are you comfortable?" he asked. "Does anything — er — bother you at all?"

They expressed their appreciation of his solicitude as an evidence of the thoughtfulness and generosity of Father's new flock.

A few days later Mother, having ascertained that Lutie had no small children after all, asked her if she could stay with the baby that night, so Mother herself could go out.

"No'm," said Lutie unequivocally. "Don't you remember I tol' you I had to git away f'm this house befo' sundown?"

"But why?" Mother pressed her. "We will see that you get home all right."

"Lawsy Mussy, Honey," exclaimed Lutie, "don't you know this house ha'nted? Won't nobody live here but just preachers."

Mother went to find Father in his study and told him with delighted amusement, "Do you know we are living in a haunted house?" Then she added, "Even though I don't believe in ghosts I certainly approve of them. Think what a nice house they have provided for us!"

One night shortly after that the weather was cold and misty, and Father built up a big fire in their bedroom. This room was at the end of a long corridor, off which opened other rooms and Father's study. The baby was asleep in her crib beside the big double bed. Because the night was chilly father had closed all the inside doors to avoid drafts. He and Mother sat cozily before the hearth, a student lamp on a table between them, Mother re-reading one of her favorite Dickens' novels, and Father absorbed in the current issue of the *Wesleyan Christian Advocate*.

Suddenly they heard footsteps coming down the corridor. Heavy footsteps, as though there were two pairs of feet walking in clumsy boots. Instinctively Father reached for the stout fire poker.

The steps came to the door of their room, turned and walked back down the corridor. Father jumped up and

opened the door. He saw nothing at all. He came back
and got the lamp. Carrying it high above his head in one
hand, the poker in the other, and with Mother close behind
him, he walked down the corridor. There was nothing.
Only shadows advancing and retreating in the light of
the oil lamp.

The house that had seemed so invitingly spacious suddenly became cavernous and sepulchral. While Mother
went back to the bedroom to stay with the baby, Father
tried every door and went in every room. He could find
no evidence of anything's having been disturbed.

He went back to the bedroom. "I guess that's Lutie's
'ha'nt'," he said.

Mother picked up her book. "I'm glad I'm reading
Pickwick Papers instead of *Marley's Ghost*," she said.

Father discarded his *Advocate* and took up a *Life
of John Wesley,* leafing through to find the place where
the elder Wesley had the altercation with a poltergeist.
Methodist though he was, I'm not too sure he didn't recall
with more than Anglican fervor the lines from the ancient
Scottish Litany:

> *"From ghoulies and ghostes and long-leggedy beasties,
>   and things that go boomp in the night
>   ` Good Lord, Deliver us!"*

With the sun shining brightly the next morning, things
going boomp in the night seemed pretty ridiculous to
both of them.

"But I could have sworn we heard something," said
Mother.

"We *did* hear something," Father said. "The thing
to do is to find out what. And I have a theory. There's a
carpenter who lives two doors down the street. I'm going
to talk to him."

A little later he dropped in for a pastoral call on the
carpenter. "Do you ever do any work at night?" Father
asked conversationally. "Any nailing, or hammering?"

"Not me," the carpenter asserted emphatically. "What
I can't get done in daylight don't get done. When night
comes I go to bed."

"Here endeth the first theory," Father said to himself.
No more was heard of the footsteps for a week or

more, so he decided to dismiss the whole thing from his mind.

Then again on a cold, misty night, he had just gone to bed. The lamps were out, and only the light of the flickering fire wavered on the walls. The last log burned through and fell, sending a jet of sparks and an upspurt of flames over the charred wood. Just then the footsteps were heard coming down the corridor. They came to a spot outside the bedroom door, and stopped.

Father crept out of bed and over to the door. Silently he turned the knob and flung open the door. There was nothing. Nothing but the dim light of the fire flickering on the closed doors of the corridor.

He came back and whispered to Mother. "It may be somebody or something on the veranda. Listen carefully for any noise while I go and look."

The pallid light of a thin moon struggling through the mist was hardly brighter than the darkness inside the house, but from a bay window Father could see dimly the entire length of the porch. Nothing was there, and in the fine mist that overlay the floorboards there was no sign of a footprint.

When he reported this to Mother she laughed with not much amusement. "I think I'll start going home with Lutie befo' sundown!" she said.

Father put his arms around her, and she shivered. "Is it making you nervous, darling?" he asked.

She looked about the pretty room with the firelight glinting on the carved walnut furniture, and giggled a little hysterically. "Not as nervous as some of those other parsonages have made me," she said.

Father hated having an unsolved riddle lying around, particularly in his own corridor, and he began to evolve other theories, and to discard them after investigation.

One cold, damp night just as he and Mother were drifting to sleep the footsteps came again. "Let 'em walk!" said Father. "I'm not getting up from here."

The steps sounded for a while, up and down the corridor, up to their door and back, and then they stopped. Once, on waking during the night, they heard them again.

The next morning Father was more than ever determined to try to find some cause for these mysterious promenadings. The day was gray and misty, much as the nights had been when the ghost had walked. He began making a systematic search of the neighborhood, ready to test any theory that might present itself. He looked up on the roof of the house, speculating on the possibility of noises coming from a loose lightning rod. But the lightning rods were firmly attached, and besides, practically every house in the area had lightning rods—and no ghosts.

In small towns at that time most of the houses were set on large, deep lots, with stables, gardens, or chicken runs in the rear. Back of a group of houses in what would roughly correspond to a block, there were a good many acres of field or service property in the center.

Father started exploring this area behind his house, not knowing exactly what he was looking for. As he approached a clump of overgrown bushes and honeysuckle he heard a noise. Not footsteps, but a resonance, with the broken cadence of footsteps. He waited until the sound stopped, and then, stepping silently on the soft, moist earth, he pulled aside the overgrowth and discovered an abandoned cistern, half of its corroded metal buried in the ground. He hit it with the palm of his hand and it gave off the same dull, resonant vibration. He hit it several times with his fist and recalled the laws of transferred vibration, and a theological anecdote about a musician striking a piano key until the vibrations caused a crystal chandelier to shatter.

A good theory for a starter, but what was to cause the cistern to vibrate? There were no footprints of man or beast in the vicinity, and anyhow, who or what would want to spend a cold, dreary night beating on an old tank?

Could it be possible that a sound from somewhere else might resound in the cistern and be thrown into the corridor? It hardly seemed likely. Reluctantly he abandoned this theory and went on his way, hoping for more rewarding clues.

As he crossed the stable area back of one of the houses a delicate little bay mare stood looking at him over her paddock fence. Father loved horses and had rather regretted giving up his post as Circuit Rider because he had enjoyed driving a horse and buggy to visit his parishioners, or ridng horseback where country roads were impassable for wheels.

Now he walked over to speak to the mare and to pat her velvet nose. Obviously she was a thoroughbred, and was cared for as a thoroughbred should be. Her glossy coat showed signs of regular grooming, and she was stabled in equine luxury in her own two-room stall. One side was a lean-to shelter over the bare earth. The other was a box stall with a stout wooden floor.

As Father reached out to pat her she tossed her head, turned on her slender pasterns, and walked with dignity under the lean-to. She curved her neck to regard him for a moment, then stepped into her box stall like a lady stepping into her carriage and ignoring a too-familiar subordinate. She walked the length of the stall and back, and then stopped, looking disdainfully out of the window, up and over Father's head.

When her hoofs sounded on the wooden floor of the stall Father recognized the cadence of footsteps that had become so undesirably familiar.

With the excitement of prediscovery he hurried toward the nearby house. "Brother Clark!" he called. "Brother Clark!" (Father called everybody 'Brother'— even Baptists.)

When Brother Clark came out Father said, "I want you to help me lay a ghost."

"Now, now—" Brother Clark began soothingly. "Don't you let what people say about your house—"

"But if you will help me for fifteen minutes," Father interrupted, "I think I may be able to find that ghost."

"I had just started to town—" Brother Clark hedged, but Father pulled out his fat gold watch and flipped open the lid.

"It is now a quarter of eleven," he said. "Give me ten minutes to get home. Then will you lead this horse around in her box stall for five minutes? That is all I want you to do."

With relieved alacrity Brother Clark agreed. He took out his watch and they synchronized their timing. Then Father took off across the fields more like a miler than a cleric.

He burst, panting, into the house. "Come here! Quickly!" he called to Mother. "I think I've found something."

They closed all the doors to the corridor, went into their room and sat down. Father took out his watch and began ticking off the minutes. The mist muffled the house in silence except for the crackling of the fire.

At five minutes of eleven they heard heavy footsteps in the corridor, walking toward their door. Up and back, for exactly five minutes. Then they stopped.

With a satisfied smile Father snapped his watch shut.

Mrs. Swartz and the Postmaster

Frances Greene

M RS. SWARTZ'S accent was thick and a little for-
bidding, but her face, rosy red from the chill of the
December air, was kind and soft. She stood just inside
the door of the mountain store and asked at the window of
the small post office if her "lett-urz" had come.

John Eliot shook his head. He had just finished putting up the mail that Roy Abercrombie, the carrier, had
brought by buggy from the valley some fifteen miles away,
and Mrs. Swartz had received nothing.

For a moment, she tilted her head, and her eyes became large as if she wanted to repeat the question, but
then she wet her lips slowly and smiled. "Tomorrow,
maybe. Yes, tomorrow, I hear."

She turned abruptly, not once looking back as she
made her way down the steps and along the lane, her
legs moving slowly but steadily as she began her three
mile walk past the clearing with the one room, red school
and then across the branch. now swollen with rain, past
the Carter's farm and then the Smith's and to the little log
cabin where she lived with her daughter, Sophia, and son-
in-law, Josh.

This was "the mountain," as folks called it, and it
never occurred to them or to their Tennessee neighbors
on the right or their Alabama neighbors on the left that
anybody could question, "Which mountain?" As far as
they were concerned, there was only one: Lookout Moun-

tain. And it curved and rolled for miles upon miles from its point in Chattanooga to its less publicized cliffs in Valley Head, Alabama. In the meantime, it wandered and twisted through a part of Georgia, and its rich, rolling land was cultivated to corn and wheat and tobacco, and its pastures fattened registered cattle which were herded to market once a year.

The land, sold originally by lottery in the 1830's, was rarely resold. Sons and daughters inherited it, and with each new generation virgin timber was sawed, more land cultivated, better farm equipment added and homes improved. And the little band of people became a community and built a church and started a school, leaving the hiring of the one teacher to "Aunt Mary" who volunteered to keep the young lady in her great big house a little beyond the general store with its post office department. But the folks, too, left more than the hiring of the teacher to the woman and her son, John Eliot. They brought their problems to the store; their hopes and their dreams. And they left feeling better for having talked out their worries or sharing their joys.

But Mrs. Swartz was new to the community. To her the people were strange; their ways were strange. She attended the all day meetings in the little church and she dressed in her best and went to the socials in the school house, but her eyes, though soft and gentle, were far away; perhaps even a little dreamy as if she were remembering other socials, other gatherings in a country across the water where now Mr. Swartz was scrimping and saving "fare money" to join her in this land that was rich and plentiful; a land that had given their daughter, Sophia, so much after the desolation of a terrible war.

But she was lonely. Though she helped with the chores in the little log cabin, crowded now with the arrival of Sophia's second baby, she was so dreadfully lonely for "her man." And it was nearly Christmas and somehow her Christmas would be brighter if there were only a letter from him .

John Eliot shook his head thoughtfully, but with a sigh he went through the mail again, just to be sure the "lett-urz" were not there.

For a moment, the sun shone through the store window, and Roy, clapping his hands to warm them, wished aloud that it would shine day and night for a month. A six day cold rain had made the road up the mountain slick and treacherous and he was already dreading tomorrow's trip down.

"Another day like yesterday and even old Doc Dawson wouldn't try to get up the mountain," he added. "The bend is washing out again — something fierce."

The two men walked to the store porch. John Eliot latched the door behind him; if customers wanted supplies or their mail, they had only to ring the big dinner bell or walk down to the house. For an instant, each paused and looked at the sky. The sun had become a faint blur; a haze of clouds moved in slowly and it was almost as if one could reach out a hand and bring them to the earth.

By mid-afternoon, the mountain was still and quiet. Nothing stirred. The limbs of the tall pines, the branches of the giant oaks were motionless. The dogs lying on the porch, appeared lifeless except for the alert movements of their eyes. Only the smoke from the big chimney drifting upward to dissolve into the haze marred the stillness of the afternoon. And then the large snowflakes began to fall dropping slowly, lazily to the ground. Christmas was yet three days away but Christmas on Lookout would again be a white one.

Ten inches fell during the night but the flakes had stopped by dawn and the thermometer began to drop steadily. John Eliot had the mail pouch ready for Roy to take to the valley, and he also asked him to bring back a hundred pounds of sugar; the store was running short and the snow was apt to stay for weeks.

Mrs. Swartz was waiting when Roy finally returned three hours later than usual. "I sure won't be taking the buggy any more," Roy said as he warmed by the stove. "Might not even be taking the horse."

But the little old lady was not listening. Her eyes were on John Eliot as he went through the mail carefully, sorting it slowly, putting the letters in the boxes.

"No?" she asked finally. But her face, pinched from the cold, was eager, hopeful.

John Eliot shook his head. "Mama wants you to come

by the house for a cup of coffee. She baked a fresh cake," he added hurriedly. "Chocolate."

"Tomorrow, maybe. Yes, tomorrow," she said firmly. And with a smile, she moved quickly to the porch and down the steps, her head turned toward home.

But "tomorrow" was a terrible day. The snow was a thick crust and more snow was falling. Roy picked up the one sack. He planned to walk down and up the mountain, leaving his horse in the Johnson's barn, and the trip would be long and tiring.

When he was out of sight, Aunt Mary rang three longs and one short and lifted the receiver. She asked everybody on the mountain to pass along the word that the mail would be late. She asked Emma Smith to notify Mrs. Swartz.

Roy did not return until after the supper dishes were put away but John Eliot lighted a lantern and went to the store and put up the mail. There were a few cards and one package for the Carter child from her grandmother in Atlanta. Nothing else. And tomorrow was Christmas Eve.

The morning dawned clear and cold but the rolling hills and tumbling land on top of Lookout were covered with a blanket of impenetrable white. Landmarks were camouflaged with sheets of ice; trees leaned gracefully toward the ground; fence posts were like toothpicks jutting from a frosted layer cake. The narrow, steep road to the valley was impassable.

Over steaming bowls of oatmeal and plates of hot biscuits, Aunt Mary discussed the day's chores with her family. A Christmas tree had been cut earlier and was now in the big barn; cranberries were in the pantry ready to be strung; the grandchildren could pop corn while the older ones could go upstairs to the storage room for the decorations.

John Eliot's face was long. Everybody in the big house was preparing for a merry Christmas but somehow the day had lost its flavor for him.

Aunt Mary sent him to the cellar for apples and onions and sweet potatoes; she sent him to the smoke house for a ham and out to the chicken house for more eggs. But he performed each task quietly, thoughtfully.

"All right," she said finally, "what is it?"

John Eliot had the idea completely worked out in his mind. He could take barrel staves and he could loop them to his shoes with bands of rubber or rope, and then with a sturdy stick in each hand, he could get to the valley. He could pick up the mail sack. It was, he added quickly, his duty.

"The woolen scarves are on the bed," Aunt Mary said quietly. "But somebody will have to watch the pies in the oven while I help you with the staves."

In less than an hour, he was on his way, and though Aunt Mary went back to her baking, she kept one eye on the sky throughout the day. She also informed the mountain people over her telephone that John Eliot would be needing a cup of coffee to warm him up. But never a word did she mention about the hazardous journey to the valley; never a word about the accident last year when old Mr. Jamison went over the cliff at the bend. She continued her preparations for Christmas Day, filling the kitchen with the yeasty smell of rising dough; the spicy odor of mince-meat and potato pies.

The hours went by slowly. Ordinarily the house would have been filled with neighbors who tracked in snow and filled the rooms with laughter and good will, staying just long enough to eat a bite. Ordinarily the children would be outside building snowmen and having battles and racing to the barns. But the weather was too bitterly cold. Lookout was not having an ordinary Christmas.

As dark settled over the mountain, Aunt Mary lighted the big gas lamps that hung from the ceiling, and built up the fire in the kitchen stove. The phone rang two shorts and the house was suddenly quiet. Aunt Mary replaced the stove lid and, wiping her hands on the white apron, she walked quickly to the telephone.

"Thank you, Ella," she said finally. "And a Merry Christmas to you."

With a relaxed smile on her face, she set about pre-paring supper. John Eliot was on his last lap home, Ella had said. He would be coming up the lane past the apple orchard and then through the big gate in about thirty minutes. He had made the trip to the valley and back, and he was safe. But more than that, he was carrying an empty mail pouch now. There had been only one small envelope addressed to the community on the mountain, and John Eliot had delivered it in person to the little woman in the log cabin three miles back. Mrs. Swartz had finally received her "lett-urz" and she would spend a very merry Christmas.

John Eliot, on his barrel staves, was spending one, too.

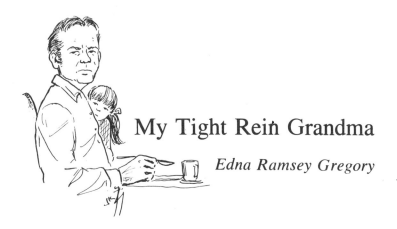

My Tight Rein Grandma

Edna Ramsey Gregory

WE WERE AT breakfast when ma said, "It's going to be a nice day for the wedding."

Pa snorted, "Babe, don't you mention such a day to me. I hate it."

"Now, Silas," grandma said, "don't you start breathing fire and brimstone again. It's my wedding day—a day I've long wished for—and I'll thank you not to hate it."

I stopped eating to watch pa's face hoping to see the fire and brimstone I had heard mentioned so often lately. Grandma set her coffee cup down in its saucer with a loud clatter and sailed out of the room. Then she banged her room door shut so hard her cup rattled in its saucer again.

Pa bellowed, "Mary Belle, what are you so goggled-eyed about; eat your breakfast and then leave the table."

I went out to play and I had not more than got my mud pies ready to bake, when there was ma calling me to come in. "I declare, Mary Belle," she said when she started washing me, "when you make mud pies, do you have to make them in your ears too." She plaited my hair and then said, "Come let me put your wedding dress on you."

Then pa started again. "Don't you call that child's dress a wedding dress. She's not getting married, though sometimes I wish she were instead of grandma."

"Now, Silas," ma said in her soothing voice, "your ma is old enough to know what she wants to do. She has always held a tight rein on you, and you know it. It's too late for you to buck her now. Mary Belle," she admonished, "go sit quietly somewhere and don't muss your dress."

I went and sat in the hammock on the side porch and crinkled my nose at the sweet scent of the early summer flowers drifting in from the garden. A bird was making a happy little noise out in the chinaberry tree near the kitchen, and I felt happy too, and all peaceful like, as I swayed gently to and fro in the hammock.

But there was no peace inside our house. I could hear ma and pa as their voices rose and fell. "I say," ma repeated, "she's always held a tight rein on you—it's too late to buck her now."

"Nobody's ever held me down," pa vowed.

"Well you stayed and worked the farm when you really wanted to go to college because she said stay. And you never got drunk but once."

Ma honeyed up her next words. "She's been good to us, Silas. She let us live in this old home with her all these years; even when she moved into her new home, we stayed right here, and she never charged us any rent, either. And remember all the good crops you have raised here, and you have not even had to pay the taxes on the land."

"Yes, I know all that is true," pa admitted, "but that scoundrel is just after her money."

"Well, Silas, be that as it may. But you remember when your father died and you insisted that she not stay alone in her new home, she reluctantly agreed to come here. All women want their own home, Silas. She's no different from the rest of us."

"Yes, Babe," pa agreed, "I knew she really didn't want to come here to live, but what could I do but insist. I could not sleep nights knowing she was alone. Well, I guess I'll have to shave, but don't be surprised if you find me on the floor with my throat cut."

All the time the sun was getting higher and higher in the sky. I was getting sleepy sitting so still trying not to rumple my dress, but my hair was plaited so tight I could scarcely close my eyes, so I just sat staring at the heat waves that were beginning to shimmer on our white sand yard, listening to grandma as she rummaged in her room and to ma and pa as they argued.

Although the wedding wasn't until ten o'clock Dr. John, the groom, had already arrived. When pa saw the two bays he drove coming down the road he exclaimed, "Well, old mustache doesn't aim to miss it, does he!"

"Now, Silas," ma cautioned, "mind your manners and go on out and greet him."

"I'll be danged if I will," pa declared, but not suiting his actions to his words, he put on his shoes to go out. At the door he turned and said, "I believe it was his waxed mustache that took grandma's eyes. I'd like to yank it out and," he hesitated a moment before delivering the final words, "I may do just that."

Sammy, our yard boy, unhitched the bays and now Dr. John and grandma were in the summer house down in the flower garden. This was the garden she had planted as a bride. Grandpa, who had come from the old country where land was scarce, had thought it a waste to plant such a large place with flowers when it could be used to grow corn, but grandma always said, "I just held a tight rein on him." The tight rein had also gotten her the summer house, which was no house at all but just a roof with latticed sides. It was covered with climbing roses and there were two benches inside, and I must say it was a sweet smelling place.

I tried as I waited to remember all the events that had led up to my new dress and tightly plaited hair. It must have been a little before Easter that pa came back from town one day where he had gone to buy some nails, and delivered himself of a bit of news. "New man in town," he said, "though come to think of it, I don't think much of him being a man after what I heard in Alex's Drug Store."

"What was that, Silas?" ma asked.

"Well it seems that man claims he is an eye doctor. There were some men talking in the drug store and they said, 'eye doctor, ha! ha! He's got an eye for women with money. He's already inquired around if there are any rich widows in town'."

All the next week our party line was kept busy. Mrs. Walker called. "Babe," she asked, "heard about the new eye doctor? He's been in trouble with some woman in the city and is hiding out here." Ma was never one to gossip, so all she said was, "You don't say."

Then Mrs. Wilson called. "Babe," she said, "did you hear that new eye doctor was drunk the other night? Somebody picked him up off the street, and you know what, that mustache he's got ain't real. It fell off when they picked him up."

"Well, well," was all ma said.

Then an astonishing thing happened. Grandma, who had always had such good sight she could see me doing something I wasn't even thinking of doing, got up one morning and called pa. "Silas, come here and see if you can find anything in my eye. I don't seem to be able to see very well." Ma held a lamp while pa looked and looked, but he couldn't find a thing. He put a flax seed in her eye, but that didn't help either. "You hitch the horse to the buggy about ten o'clock and take me to town to see the eye doctor," she told pa.

"I'll be swiggered if I'll do it, ma," pa said. "I'll get you to the city if there is anything wrong with your eyes."

"I am not going to the city. I am going to Dr. John, like I said. You are not going to tell me what to do."

Every week after that Sammy had to hitch the horse to the buggy and, no matter how busy pa was, he had to stop work and take grandma to town.

Then it was Easter and everybody, even if they hadn't been to church all year, was there. That is everybody except Dr. John.

"Guilty conscience." pa said.

"Nonsense," grandma replied, "he's really a good man. All he needs is for someone to hold a tight rein on him."

When Dr. John first began driving up to our hitching post with his two bays, we thought it was just a family visit and gathered in the parlor trying to be polite, that is all except pa. He just sat in a corner and scowled. Then one night Dr. John brought grandma a bouquet of flowers. I never thought grandma would be so unladylike as to giggle, but the sound she made when he handed her the bouquet sure sounded like one to me. This bit of information I laid up in my mind to bring out when next she lectured me about giggling. After that we didn't bother to come out when we saw the bays coming down the road and Dr. John and grandma took to riding off in the early evening.

One day pa said, "Babe, I'm going to the city to see if I can find out anything about this Dr. John. He's just too pat in his answers when anyone asks him a question. And if there's anything I hate, it's a dandy, and he's dandified as all get out. Sure makes me think there's something dead up the creek." But when he came back he had no news. "Couldn't find out a thing. His name isn't in the telephone book. It's not even in last year's book."

Grandma had ordered herself a wedding outfit from a catalog and when the mail carrier delivered it, we all gathered round to see it. Pa said, angrily, "I tell you ma, everybody knows he is just after your money."

"Humph, everybody," grandma said, "just a lot of gossip, and don't you dare raise your voice to me, Silas."

"Why in heaven's name, if you must marry, there are plenty of bachelors and widowers around here that would be happy to move into your nice home and put their feet under your table—people we know."

"All sticks-in-the-mud," grandma said, beginning to fold up her outfit. "Yes, they'd like to put their feet under my table, and the table is as far as they'd ever see. I like a man who is daring, one that has just a pinch of the devil in him. You take your pa—he was courageous and daring. Coming here from the old country without knowing a word of our language and without a cent in his pocket; I never spent a dull moment with him. He may not know it, but Dr. John is both courageous and daring, or he wouldn't want to marry me, and he doesn't have a cent either."

"Well, he's not a first rate doctor, I'll wager, or he wouldn't have come here. He isn't even what I'd call a second rate doctor. I might take my dog to him, but I'd never even let him look at my eyes."

Pa dried up then but he would, when he thought grandma was not watching, look at her in the queerest sort of way, and one day I heard him mutter, "She's riding for a fall," but I couldn't see her riding anything at all.

And now here it was her wedding day and ma was calling me to run down to the summer house and tell grandma that the preacher had come. Which I was glad to do, and had been wanting to do ever since I had seen the woman hired for the day go down there with two tall glasses of lemonade. I went up to the back of the summer

house and peeked through the latticed sides. Dr. John's
back was turned toward me and he was saying, "I'll always
take care of your eyes." And I saw grandma's face and
saw her eyes snap as she said, "There's nothing wrong
with my eyes, Dr. John, and you know it."

They went on up to the house after I had told them
what ma had said. I stayed behind to drink the lemonade
they had not touched. It had gotten warm and made me
feel a little sick, or maybe I should not have drunk both
glasses. When I felt a little better, I went on up to the
house. Someone was playing a sad thing on the organ and
ma was sniffling into her hankie and saying, "Mama, are
you sure? Oh! mama, oh! oh!"

Grandma scolded, "Stop your crying. This isn't the
end of the world. Go powder your nose."

Then the wedding was over and grandma was gone.
And all ma's pound cake was gone, together with her home
made blackberry wine. The only guest left was old man
Dillworth, who sat in one corner of the parlor snoring. Pa
got him up and started leading him out of the room. He
winked at ma and said, I told you it would happen—drunk
again."

Ma kept wiping her eyes when she thought no one was
looking. If we looked at her, she smiled one of those hard
brittle smiles that do not come from the heart. It was all
very sad.

We sat at supper and just stared at the food. Ma
said, "Dr. John smiled at you real friendly like before he
left, didn't he, Silas?"

Pa said, "Smile, ha! it looked more like a sneer to me."

And he just sat there stirring his coffee spoon round
and round in his cup. Finally he said, "Babe, did you ever
see anything like it? If I had not seen it with my own eyes,
I wouldn't believe it."

We knew what he was talking about. For when Dr.
John helped grandma into the buggy after the wedding,
grandma slid right over to the driver's side of the buggy
and picked up the reins. When Dr. John got into the buggy,
he had to take grandma's seat. The bays pranced off down
the road, grandma holding the reins tight.

"And as I live and breathe," pa said, "I never in my
whole life heard of a bride driving her own bridal chariot!"

Down the Aisle

Waldo Puckett

THE LITTLE church still stands in a grove at the cross-roads. Even today, one driving by in an automobile would look at the little white structure and instinctively remark that it must be called some Biblical name — it just looked the part. Thirty years ago everyone passing by knew its name and the modern traveler had surmised correctly. For, indeed, the little church was called Mt. Zion. And very little change had come to the church, it being off the highway — only a vast addition of white tombstones around the building, a silent reminder that most of the pioneers who blazed that trail to Mt. Zion had gone on, hopefully to the beautiful city of Zion.

In the late summer of 1901, BIG MEETING was going on at Mt. Zion. Crops were "laid by" and every-body in the community turned his thoughts from ma-terial things to the spiritual. All roads led to Mt. Zion. In addition to the old fashioned gospel, it was a reunion time, too. Maybe sister hadn't seen sister since the last Big Meeting and, then, all of them "knowed" if Sophrony Ellis wasn't there she was "plumb" down with that rheu-matism.

And so Wednesday night came. All the night meetings were deeply emotional, but somehow Wednesday and Sunday nights were the special times the elect spent on the lost ones. This night was to be a really sure enough night — for rumor, gossip and whisperings had it that

Sally was "gonna" join the church that night. It doesn't matter what Sally's last name was — when you spoke of Sally in connection with Mt. Zion, everybody in the county knew whom you meant. For Sally had come to be the main victim the Big Meeting prayed for, talked about, worried over and hoped to catch.

Old Bill Stevens could stay drunk most of the year, neglect his children and beat his wife, but everyone knew Bill belonged to Mt. Zion and would, during the first or second meeting, get up, cry and take on, get prayed for, stay sober and attend all the meetings with a sanctimonious look; no one worried over Bill (except Mrs. Bill and family). For, after all, wasn't Bill's name on the church roll and didn't that somehow keep Bill in the Fold?

Take Jack Pharr—although he gambled and was shift-less, yet, Jack at fourteen had joined Mt. Zion, and everyone expected Jack to raise his hand for prayer, take a new start and last for several weeks. But somehow Jack was in the Fold. Then there was Mary Dozier — true, it did go a little harder with Mary, for she was just a woman. Everybody knew about Mary's misstep — there was the living evidence always by her side. But Mary atoned, joined Mt. Zion, and the few hard-hearted sisters who wouldn't exactly forgive Mary and allow their daughters to associate with her except in a passing way — still somehow put Mary in the Fold, remarking that after all, Mary's Ma was a lot to blame.

But Sally — why, Sally was completely out of the Fold and no prayers, efforts or persuasion of former years had ever made Sally walk down the aisle. From the time Sally was fourteen (she was in her late twenties now) the entire membership had been concerned over her. Her Ma never missed an opportunity to ask all of the societies to pray for her. At Sunday School speeches were often made around a person whom all knew to be Sally. The pastor usually dropped a hint in his sermon that everyone knew was a plea for Sally.

Until Sally was about twenty, they worked with her personally — begged, talked, prayed, pleaded — mostly patiently but sometimes even firmly. Always when the doors of the church were opened, sly eyes glanced toward Sally. And during Big Meeting when the opportunity to unite with the Saints was given, her every move was

watched. Now the news was being peddled everywhere —
Sally was going down the aisle that night and put an end
to everyone's worries! Not that Sally had told anyone —
in fact, since she had become twenty, her church fate had
become a sealed subject with her and she had created a
barrier that not even Ma or her best friends dared approach.

It was Sally's Ma who started the rumor, for as Sally
had combed her hair that morning she had turned around
and said simply: "Ma, I think I'll join the church tonight
and I don't want any taking on." Ma couldn't get the
news started quickly enough and even without telephones
— there were none in the community — the news spread
like wildfire. And the settlement was deeply relieved for
they were to redeem their chief sinner! It didn't matter to
them that it was Sally who had helped her widowed mother
daily — cared for her brother's two children who had never
known any mother's love other than Sally's and Ma's —
made dainty dishes for any sick neighbor — sympathized
with and aided Bill's wife when he was on a spree. Her
every move was above reproach but to the folks there Sally
was a lost sinner, for she had, they said, stubbornly refused to join the church.

"Oh, the pain she's causing her ma," they would
whisper to each other. And Ma was grieved, too, just as
sincerely as the folks were on the surface.

Gossip had it further that the reason Sally was an old
maid today was because Lem Miller's boy couldn't afford
to marry a heathen — for was not Lem the chief deacon
of Mt. Zion — and no heathen-like person was wanted in
the Miller family. True, Sally probably could have told a
different tale when Lem's boy, after a long courtship — as
close a one as Sally would allow — up and suddenly
married Minnie Spinks. Sally's sacrificial love for Ma may
have figured in some way — but not with the settlement
folks — they just "knowed" Sally lost her opportunity to
get Lem's boy because she had not joined the church and
Lem's boy couldn't afford to take any chances. Through it
all Sally said nothing.

But now Sally had spoken — Ma heard her about ten
o'clock — spread the news at the morning service as worship broke up — crowds lingered to discuss it; there was

much extra visiting that afternoon and everybody said they
would be at Big Meeting that night — all their prayers
were at last answered — and they all felt they must be
there to give Sally the right hand of fellowship when she
took that step towards going with the Saints.

Big Meeting opened at seven o'clock and it was almost
an unpardonable sin to be late. But no one needed to con-
cern himself over such a matter tonight. Six-thirty
found Mt. Zion packed and folks sitting in buggies close to
all the windows and doors; people were standing on boxes
— all where they could watch the spot Pastor Lanes stood
when he opened the doors of the church and asked people
to come down the aisle. There were only two vacant seats
in the building; these on the bench where Sally and her
Ma always sat. These two were religiously and sacredly
kept clear tonight — but only children had to be told —
the elders would have sooner slipped some of the sacra-
ment wine than to have been the cause of any act that
would keep Sally back tonight.

At ten minutes till seven, Ma and Sally entered the
church and found their customary pews. The loud laughter
and talking preceding services fell to almost a hush as Sally
entered and seated herself. But if she realized anything or
suspicioned that she was the subject of all the conversation she gave not a sign by any outward expression or
movement. She simply opened her fan, proceeded to cool
her mother in her usually dutiful way, leaning occasionally
to say a word to someone about her. The "Hymn Hyster"
realized this was THE night of Big Meeting and he met his
duty by calling the service to open and start the first song.
(Now that Sally had arrived there was no reason to wait.)
With deep feeling, he nervously directed them in singing,
then quickly turned the services over to Brother Jones,
tonight's lay leader who told them his heart was too full
this night to say much and he would cut his talk short as
Pastor Lanes had an unusually appealing message for
them.

Presently Pastor Lanes arose and called for a song,
designated "For You I'm Praying" and then had a very
short prayer, said by himself, not trusting to Deacon Lem
tonight, as Lem was long-winded.

Without a pause Brother Lanes started his sermon,

announcing his subject, which, he apologized, was long —
"The Shepherd Has His Ninety and Nine — We Must
Safely Bring in the Hundredth." With deep feeling, he
spoke about the rejoicing of the Elect over a lost Lamb
coming into the Fold. But everyone, unless perhaps it was
Sally, seemed to notice that Pastor Lanes shortened his
sermon in his haste to give sinners the usual invitation.
Even at that, the moment seemed an eternity to all the
elected brethren and sisters.

But at last it came!

Pastor Lanes announced that the doors of the church
were open to receive sinners and the congregation would

stand and sing. All the folks sang deeply the first stanza, but, on the others, the volume decreased considerably, and the eyes wandered from the Hymn books, apparently at random, but somehow all ended toward Sally.

All the stanzas were at last sung and Brother Lem arose and asked Pastor Lanes to repeat the chorus — that somehow he felt they hadn't accomplished their mission that night. True, two had joined but somehow there had been no worry over them, and the rejoicing seemed to be saving itself for some other soul.

Next Preacher Lanes broke in, telling the congregation to continue the invitation by singing another hymn. The chosen song was "Oh, Why Not Tonight?" and one hearing them singing it would have known it was a plea to some special soul. Though all were singing or humming, many were almost gazing — almost towards one space — only conscious that the earth had not yet moved. They sang every verse but no one joined the church during the song.

The moment was tense as the last words were silenced — then Preacher Lanes called for a moment's silent prayer, imploring them to put their very All into it, then announced in a shaky voice that somehow he just couldn't withdraw fellowship until they had sung another hymn, and Brother Lem almost took the words out of the Pastor's and the song leader's mouths — in fact, all the congregation knew that the hymn would be "Almost Persuaded."

Surely the Angels in Heaven smiled as that hymn was sung — understood and felt the spirit. But in earthly Mt. Zion, only one eye was on the book — any who knew not the full words just hummed if they missed — in all the church only Sally's eyes were glued on the Hymnal. The last verse had begun—Ma cut her eye deeply, ever pleadingly at Sally, but Sally gave no sign of seeing. Everyone had now dropped his book to the seat or closed it, managing to glance at Sally during their movements.

And at last the song was over!

Pastor Lanes hastily received his two new converts into the Fold, announcing that due to the lateness of the hour, the right hand of fellowship would be extended the following night — led them in a short, nervous prayer of dismissal and Wednesday night's Big Meeting was over. Practically everyone stood glued to his place as Sally and Ma passed down the aisle out the rear door of the church building. Neither spoke to any one. No sooner had they reached the first step of the exit than a deep hum and buzz of conversation broke out in Mt. Zion.

Ma and Sally walked down the road towards home about a quarter of a mile when Ma broke the silence with — "Well, Sally —"

Sally broke in quickly with "Ma, that organ in the church sure needs tuning."

TWELVE years passed and it was 1913. Automobiles and telephones came into the Mt. Zion community. Preacher Lanes was no longer pastor of the church. The new preacher called himself their minister, nor did he wait for "laying-by" time.

One Sunday in May he announced that he would hold Revival Services two weeks from the next Sunday and that they would be of an Evangelistic nature. Such words didn't matter to Lem now, for he had gone on some years before. If, perhaps, some of the "old" folks wanted a real Big Meeting, a newer generation had come on who felt it perfectly proper that they be Evangelical services.

Fate had been kind to Ma and Sally. Both were in good health. All these years Sally had gone on daily in her routine life — mended clothes, if needed — hearts, if possible — nursing any who were ill — dividing milk with old Aunt Marthy whose cow had died — always being a God-send where needed.

Everything and most everybody had changed except Sally and Mt. Zion church building. Ma had aged some— — a few of the "die-hards" had said worry over Sally had caused it, but Ma and Sally had been faithful in attending Mt. Zion all of these years. It was Sally who decorated the church with her home grown flowers; made and kept fresh covers on the pulpit and tables. As the church modernized and organized and capitalized any opposition came from others than Sally. But could it have been otherwise? — for Sally was still out of the Fold!

Most of the deepest-grieved Old-Timers had either joined the Heavenly Saints or else developed ailments that kept them home. Those still within the age of attendance had somehow come to regard Sally a part of Mt. Zion, calming their misgivings over her being out of the Fold by just saying that everything would work out for the good of all concerned.

Revival Week arrived (to a few Old-Timers it was still Big Meeting) and the Reverend Donalds, now pastor, imported Doctor Emerson to expound some of his theories of Christian doctrines to his fellow creatures, admonishing them that it was a sacrifice to such a high evangelist to come to a small church like Mt. Zion and he would expect the Finance Committee to take good care of money matters, as his time all during the meeting would be concerned with souls. During the meeting, word came that Preacher Lanes, now feeble and practically retired, was visiting his daughter in the community and would be at Wednesday night's services. There was real gladness among all the older ones who knew him, when promptly, on Wednesday night Preacher Lanes came in the Meeting-House, aided by his cane and daughter.

Several modern hymns were sung, accompanied by the piano which several years ago had replaced the organ. The pastor sat down to permit Doctor Emerson to proclaim some of his theological doctrines and as Doctor Emerson retired to his chair to allow the Pastor to open the doors of the church, Brother Lem's boy, now filling his father's place, arose, interrupted the Pastor — begging his pardon for so doing — and announced to the congregation that he felt that the unusually large gathering had come, not only for spiritual reasons, but as a tribute also to Brother Lanes who for so many years had been Mt. Zion's leader, and he felt Preacher Lanes must have a message for them. The immediate bustle and stirrings of the congregation was a seal of approval and as Lem's boy accompanied Preacher Lanes to the rostrum, a hushed silence was noticeable.

In a voice deeply affected by the occasion as well as advanced years, Brother Lanes laid his cane aside, raised his voice and uttered: "Beloved, let's have a real Big Meeting here tonight — Let's praise God for all His Goodness." Shouts of "Amen" broke the tenseness. As Preacher Lanes spoke of past days, there were some tears — some sighs — more "Amens" — some laughed an emotional assent — ALL listened and all eyes were on Brother Lanes. It was as though the Holy Spirit had stepped in and blessed those ready to receive it!

And then former Pastor Lanes completely forgot himself and fairly shouted: "Let's open the doors of the church — Praise God from whom all blessings flow!" Before the pianist could strike a chord, Sally arose, bent over Ma and whispered: "Ma, I'm going DOWN THE AISLE!"

The Ghost of Tom Brewster

Lois Newman

THE CLODS fell with a dull rattle on the boards that covered the black coffin. A few people stood around in silence. Mostly farmers who lived in the settlement, a mile or so away. The sawmill crew gathered in a group to one side of the grave, where they took turns shoveling earth into the grave that now held their buddy and friend. Few tears had been shed, for Tom's folks lived way up in Tennessee somewhere. The old country preacher had spoken of the pity of dying so far from home. A song and prayer had ended the simple service.

The sawmill crew consisted of Mr. Chandler, who owned the mill and had come into this area of Georgia six months before from Alabama. Cal Benton, who was twenty years old, Charlie Wills, twenty, and Lester Mayfield who was sixteen had come with him. Others who made up the camp, were Joe Bass, Fred Hester and Paul Martin, who had just drifted in, and Tom Brewster.

Tom had been in the camp only six weeks. He was well liked by all the boys but he and Cal had become fast friends. Tom talked a lot about his folks at home and his new friends felt almost as if they knew them. He and Cal sometimes had sat outside the shack, at night after the others retired, and talked.

But now all this had changed. Everything seemed strange and out of focus. Tom had sickened suddenly and lived only three days. A doctor had come from the settlement but nothing had helped. Tom had died in spite of all they could do.

"Cal," Tom had said on that last night, "if I don't get better, you will write Ma, won't you?"

Cal couldn't believe Tom's illness was that serious, but he assured him he would write. And now Tom was gone.

The funeral was on Friday. On Monday evening the crew had finished with supper and were resting. There were no women in the camp, and the men lived in a large one room shack, equipped with bunks, a table, dishes, cooking utensils, etc. Rough benches made from lumber served as seats.

Charlie and Les were playing checkers. The others sat watching. Cal arose and announced that he was going to the settlement for some tobacco.

"Any you fellows want to go?" he asked, as he started to the stables for a mule.

"We got to finish this game," said Les. "It may take most of the night. You better go on by yourself."

The scent of turpentine, from the big stacks of new pine lumber, filled the air as Cal mounted the mule. He could hear the sound of steam escaping gently from the big boiler, as he rode away into the gathering dusk.

The road to the settlement led by the country church, where Tom was buried. The mule's hooves beat a steady tattoo. A katydid chirped in the grass by the roadside and a lone screech owl mumbled eerily in the distance. Cal kept thinking of the letter he was to write. It wasn't that he minded writing the letter, he just didn't know what to say. You couldn't just come out flat and say, "Your son is dead." He must soften it somehow. So he had put off writing.

He could see the church now, and the big oak at the side of the road. As he got closer, he was startled to see a man sitting by the tree. He sat with crossed arms resting on his knees and his head bowed on his arms. Cal's first thought was that some of the boys had probably had too much to drink, and had to stop and rest before getting on home. Then he remembered that they were all at the shack when he left. Anyway, it must be someone drunk or sick who might need a hand, so he approached and got off the mule.

"What's wrong, Mister? Need help?" He was close now, but the man did not answer or move. He stood wondering what to say next, or whether to go on and leave him there. Suddenly the moon broke from behind a cloud, and shone brightly on the hunched figure by the tree. The man slowly raised his head and looked at Cal. His heart dropped to the soles of his shoes. It was Tom Brewster!

Cal mounted and kicked the mule in the sides. He headed back to the shack forgetting where he had started. He didn't halt until he was at the door. He dismounted, dropped the reins and entered. Charlie and Les were still playing checkers.

"Quick trip," Charlie said. Then looking up he exclaimed, "What's the matter? You look like you have seen a ghost!"

"I have," said Cal, as he dropped on a bench.

"What?" They dropped the checkerboard and stared at him.

"Listen," said Cal, "I have saw Tom Brewster."

"But you couldn't have," said Les. "He's dead."

"I know, but he's sittin' up there in that church yard."

The shack was dead quiet except for the snores of the boys who had gone to bed. They just sat and stared at him. Finally, Charlie spoke.

"Let's go up there and see," he said.

"I've already seen," Cal answered, "and I don't want to see again."

"You want us to believe you, don't you?" Charlie asked. "Well, we sure ain't going to, unless we see for ourselves."

"Let's get the boys up," Les suggested.

"No. No use in bothering them," Cal said. "Let's go."

They went outside. Cal caught his mule, which was grazing near the door. They went for the other mules and rode off up the dark road.

Finally Les spoke. "My grandma used to say ghosts only came back when they were troubled about something. Say! Cal, you wrote that letter yet? ! !"

"Not yet," Cal replied. "But I aim to."

By that time they were near the church. They grew quiet. Soon Les stopped. "I ain't going no farther," he said. "You all can go on. I'll take your word for it. I don't want to see Tom Brewster."

They approached cautiously. The man still sat by the tree. Just as they came close enough for a good look, he arose and walked slowly toward the graveyard.

"Do you believe me now?" Cal whispered.

"Yeah," answered Charlie.

They mounted and rode back to join Les.

"Did you see him, Charlie?" Les inquired.

"Yeah," Charlie answered. "It was Tom all right."

Back at the shack a few minutes later, Les insisted on rousing the other boys. The exciting events of the night were fully discussed before they all got ready for bed.

As the rest crawled into their bunks, Cal drew a box from under his bed and got out pencil and paper.

"Aint you going to bed, Cal?" Les asked.

"Not just now," he replied. "Guess I better write that letter."

Born of the Blue Ridge

Catherine McKee

IT WAS twenty years ago or thereabout that this happened, but somehow a gray, drizzly day in December brings it back as real as if it were now.

I had sludged through the red North Georgia mud to Judson Powell's crossroads store at Hardscrabble, in the foothills of the Blue Ridge Mountains, thinking about the war going on and wondering how soon nineteen-year-olds like me would be called.

"It won't be as long as it has been, Charlie McClure," the man at the draft board had told me the last time I went to ask. "You may as well start gettin' your affairs in order."

But no sign of a call had come, and I was anxious to find out what was going on. I wanted to swap news with any of the farm folks who might be at the store. There'd probably be some, the weather being like it was. It was too rainy to work around the farm, too wet to gather corn and fodder still standing in the fields, and even too wet and sloshy to do good rabbit hunting.

Although it was only the middle of the afternoon, the inside of the store, whose wooden walls had never known paint, looked as if night·was already coming upon us. Only the glow from the four panes of isinglass in the door of the coal stove gave a cheery light. The kerosene lamps cast shadows that added to the dreariness.

There was something more than just the weather and

the half-darkness, though, that made the six or eight farmers somber and quiet. Right away one of them told me what the trouble was.

"Newt Holbrook's boy has been killed in the fighting in the South Pacific, Charlie. Word come to Newt this morning," Tom Pritchard told me.

I remembered the boy, but his image seemed to merge with that of the farmers around the stove, men whose mud-stained, worn overalls told something of the hard work they were in the habit of doing. The boy, too, had been a hard worker. He had been in school with me, a quiet, slim fellow two or three years ahead of me, but he had drifted out along about the ninth or tenth grade. After he left school, I hadn't seen much of him. He seemed to tend to his own business and live rather quiet around the farm.

His pa, though, was different. We all knew Newt and liked him, but most of us were kinda scared of him. Tall, gaunt, and raw-boned, he stood out in any crowd of folks hereabout. He had no mind to take any sass from anyone, his own young'uns or anybody else. The thing that always came first to my mind was that craggy brow, like an eagle's nest near a mountain peak, with those fierce blue eyes looking restlessly around, ready for a good fight any time.

"Reckon this'll just about kill Newt," worried Judson Powell, whose storekeeping trade kept him in close touch with folks. "Newt could be hard on his boys if need be, but he was plumb foolish about 'em."

"It'll just about kill him, if he don't kill hisself first a'rarin' and a-tearin' about it," replied Tom. "That's always been Newt's trouble. Remember what a buck he cut when the draft board first called his boy?"

"I do, for one," reminisced wiry little Will Moore, who had come in just ahead of me and was standing warming his back at the stove. "Sent word that him and his folks stood ready to fight with anything they could get their hands on, right down to bare sticks if need be, to keep the enemy out, but that him and none of his would go one step into the other feller's country. Told 'em the boy's blood would be on their hands if they took him and got him killed. They took the boy anyway. I hear Newt ain't spoke to ary one of the draft board since."

"That pitchin' and rarin' has always been Newt's
trouble," Tom went on. "He wears hisself out over everything the gover'ment does, or anybody else for that matter
that tries to meddle in his business. Makes no difference
whether it's the county gover'ment a-tryin' to put a new
road through his property or the federal gover'ment sendin'
out cotton stamps and tellin' a feller what he can raise
and what he can't, or a'sendin' out revenuers like they
used to do lookin' for a liquor still on his place. He don't
want none of any gover'ment interference."

Tom stopped a while, his eyes thoughtful in the glow
from the stove; then he added, "Now Newt'll say the
federal gover'ment took his boy and got him killed."

"But how can he blame the government?" I asked.
"A thing like this is too big to blame on any one thing.
It's maybe too big for our minds to understand."

Will unbuttoned his steaming overall jacket, cut a chew
of tobacco, and sat down. Stretching out his wet brogans
to dry at the stove, he leaned back, chewing, all set to tell
the rest of his story.

"I don't know how he'll figure it but I'd hate to be in
the shoes of our local draft board right now. You're too
young to know Newt like we do, Charlie. When Newt gets
his dander up, a body'd think lightnin' was strikin' amongst
these Blue Ridge hills.

"I knowed him once to have a run-in with the county
surveyors," went on Will, sliding his chair back from the
stove as he warmed to his story. "He was a fairly young
man then, not long married. Seems they wanted to cut a
road through his property.

" 'Ain't nobody gonna cut a road through this land,'
Newt told the surveyor. 'Me and my folks before me have
owned this place since the Indians left this part of the
country, and I ain't a-aimin' to have it bothered.'

" 'Why, Newt,' said the surveyor, kind of awe-struck,
bein' a college man hisself, 'It was in 1830 or thereabouts
that the Cherokees were driven out of North Georgia.
Your folks must have been on this land for about a hundred years.'

" 'I don't know about the date,' Newt told him. 'I
ain't had much schoolin.' But my family has had title clear

to this land ever since the Indians left, and I aim to keep it that way.' "

I couldn't help breaking in at this. "Didn't Newt have sense enough to know that the road would make his property more valuable?" I asked.

"Sure he did," chuckled Will, "but he didn't care about that. 'My old cow goes across that path to the spring to get her drinkin' water,' he told the surveyor, 'and I don't aim to have no road interferin' with her right to drink. Now, git!' "

"Couldn't the county have condemned the property and taken it anyway?" I asked, feeling rather stupid.

"Sure it could," agreed Will, "but it didn't. Newt's last word was, 'I got me a shotgun and it loaded, I-grannies, and everybody in this part of the country knows I'll shoot. Now git! And tell the folks at the county seat I'll be waitin' fer 'em with it if they decide to come on.' "

Will spit tobacco juice and chuckled again.

"What finally happened?" I asked, not remembering any road through Newt's property.

"Nothing," said Will. "They fooled around for a while, and the next thing anybody knowed, they'd laid out a new road a couple of miles from Newt's place."

"Like his ma before him," recalled old Grady Nesbit, his red-apple cheeks reflecting the firelight as his eyes kindled with remembrance. "When her first young-un was born — she couldn't have been more than eighteen years old at the time — folks were standin' around the room to wait on her, the doctor, her own ma, and a neighbor woman. Doc had no idea her time was so near. It was a chilly night in early April, and Doc was standin' in front of the fireplace warming hisself.

"All of a sudden, her ma heard a baby's cry from the bed. 'Doc, you're needed,' she yelled. That first young-un had been born without a sign of help from Doc and without a whimper or groan from the ma."

"Aye, Law," said Tom Pritchard, "men was men in them days, and the womenfolks was near 'bout as strong."

"After that," concluded Grady, "as her other young'uns come along, she'd always say, 'Just throw me a plow line over the rafters and let me hang on. I'll make it all right.' And she did, when Newt was born and all the others."

The men about the stove sat silent for a few minutes, letting the well-known tale soak in again. Will got up, opened the stove door, and spit his tobacco juice into the fire this time.

"That puts me in mind of the time Newt had to let his family go on relief during the depression," recollected the storekeeper.

"How did that happen?" I asked. "I'd have thought he was too independent for that."

"He was," replied the storekeeper, "but he was a victim of circumstances. A man in my position can't afford to talk about his neighbors, but when I tell what I'm about to on Newt, I'm not trying to run him down. I glory in his spunk for the way he acted.

"Along in the fall of 1933," the storekeeper went on, "Newt got in trouble with the law and got sent to the chain gang for a year. Seems he was over at another feller's place on Hogwaller Creek when the officers came, found a still on the creek, and arrested the whole bunch. Newt never would say much about it. Plenty of folks thought he was framed somehow. He spent what little he made on his crop that fall, and it was mighty little, with prices as low as they were, trying to come clear. He got sent up for a year anyway.

"Not long after he left, his wife and two or three of the little ones came into the store one day with about a bushel of corn to trade for groceries. It was mighty sorry corn, some that must have been overlooked and left in the fields till the winter rains had nearly ruined it.

" 'Mis' Lucy,' I told her, 'I can't allow more'n fifty cents on this corn, even in trade. You'd be better off gettin' it ground into meal.'

" 'Maybe that's what I'll do, Mr. Powell,' she said, 'although me and the children are gettin' mighty tired of cornbread and no biscuit bread.'

" 'Why don't you and the children go on relief till Newt gets back?' I asked her. 'Plenty of folks better able to work than you are doing it.'

" 'I'd ruther not,' she said, 'if we can make out without it. Looks like a family that owned their own place could at least manage to eat without callin' on the gover'ment for help.'

"So she left with the corn. She and the children did what they could, trying to hire out for work. There was mighty little to be had that winter. Grown men were hiring out at a dollar a day, and some as low as fifty cents, when they could find work. People on the farm just didn't have the money to pay.

"One day Mis' Lucy came in and said, 'I've decided to go on relief, Mr. Powell, if you'll help me get on. My children have nearly all had the flu, and the youngest one might' nigh had pneumonia. It looks like they can't get their strength back until they can get enough to eat.'

" 'Of course I'll help you,' I told her. 'Does Newt know about it?' "

" 'Yes,' she said, 'and he's agin it. Said there wouldn't be no need of the gover'ment feedin' his wife and young'uns if they'd let him out of there and let him mind his own business. You know how he talks,' she ended, kind of apologizing."

The storekeeper paused for a moment, reflectively.

"She turned out to be nearly as independent as Newt," he chuckled. "The relief helped them through that winter, and, come spring, her and them little children planted the biggest garden you ever saw. Every time the relief woman went out that summer, they'd give her a mess of fresh vegetables, or the oldest boy would come a-runnin' with a watermelon.

" 'You've no call to give me this,' the relief woman would tell them, 'although I do appreciate it. But I'm only doing my job.'

" 'Somehow it makes us feel better,' Mis' Lucy would say. 'It rubs Newt the wrong way when we have to take help.'

"Late that summer, Newt got out of the chain gang a few months early because of good behavior. Then things started popping. It was layin'-by-time for the crops, with no work to be done in the fields until time to gather. Men all over the country had been lookin' for work or goin' on WPA. But not Newt. No, sir! The very next day after his release, he sent word to the relief woman that he could take care of his own now. Danged if he hadn't gone and got him a job driving a team of mules for the county!

Folks at the court house had found out while he was serving time that he wasn't afraid of work.

"And now this oldest boy of his, the one that used to go a-runnin' with the watermelon, has got killed," the storekeeper broke off, his voice choked with sorrow for the family.

Will Moore took another chew of tobacco. "That draft board will be a-hearin' from Newt in no uncertain words," he declared, "and I'd sure hate to be around when it happens."

I thought the situation over and said I'd like to go over to Newt's house to express my sympathy. Grady Nesbit thought that would be the fitting thing to do, too, but the others seemed to think it would be better to let Newt get over it in his own way. Scared to hear him rave and rant, it appeared to me.

There wasn't long to think about it, however. The rain had started coming down hard as the day grew later, but a noise louder than the beat of the rain told us that an old car had wheezed up. I wondered if I recognized the man getting out of the mud-splashed Model A. It was hard to tell, because the brim of his old felt hat was pulled down over his face and ears, near about meeting the turned-up collar of his overall jacket. There was something about the lean haunches that looked familiar, but the sag of the shoulders looked like that of an old, old man.

It was Newt, we saw as he pulled back the heavy wooden door and stood framed in the twilight, but not the Newt we had known. It was a Newt sagging and beaten, his sharp old eyes bleared with fog and cold as he tried to focus them in the lamplight.

"Better not mention that boy of his'n," Will whispered next to me, his whisper partly drowned by the closing of the door. "No tellin' what he'll say if we do."

But the storekeeper was not afraid. He waited on Newt, got up his groceries in silence, and then, as he took his pay, "Mighty sorry to hear about that boy of yours, Newt," he said.

All of us rain-bound idlers waited in silence for the lightning to strike.

"Yes, it's hard," said the old man. Then the piercing

look in his fierce old blue eyes softened as if a mist had rolled over his native Blue Ridge foothills. Newt wasn't old any more; he straightened his shoulders as he turned down his collar and took off the old battered hat; even his eyes looked young. Newt wasn't an old man! He couldn't have been more than forty-five or fifty at the most.

"My wife and younger children are taking it mighty hard," he admitted. Then the momentary softness in his blue eyes gave way to the old proud look as he added, "But I figure if it hadn't been my boy, it might have been somebody else's."

With a final squaring of his shoulders came his parting shot, "And I reckon I'm as able to stand it as the next feller."

The Mule Trader

Jannelle Jones McRee

I HADN'T BEEN around too long before I found that you had better not skin a Georgia mule dealer unless you are prepared to have your own hide nailed to the barn door.

A mule trader just naturally begins early. When Jed was twelve he bought what he considered a beautiful bull calf. I remember the great gleam in his eyes as he led his animal home. When he told Pa the price he paid, Pa said a little sad-like, "Son, you went too high." Jed straightened up to his sixty inches and said, "Maybe so, Pa, but he'll grow to it."

Jed had a white-faced Hereford that I wanted. I figured a little trading between brothers might pay off. I had a beautiful horse I wanted to get rid of. You see, she was a blinker. In case you don't know what that means, a blinker is a moon-eyed animal who has good eyesight at a certain time of the moon and poor vision at other times. So one day I asked Jed if he'd be willing to swap his cow for my horse. Jed was blunt.

"Bud, my cow won't suit you."

I finally convinced him that nothing could suit me better. "It's a deal, then," he agreed and we made the trade.

As he climbed on the horse and picked up the reins I said a little too casual like, "Jed, at a certain time of the moon you might watch your horse carefully. His eyes——"

Jed leveled a straight shot look at me. "Thank you,
Bud. And there's something I failed to tell you. If you
expect any cow juice it might be wise for you to get the
strongest oak timber you can find to build a stall. The
cow you just inherited is the world's worst kicker."

That finished me in the trading business but Jed
went on from there. Some liked him and some cussed him.

One night when Jed was eating supper someone
knocked hard on the door. When he opened it there stood
Jake Bellows. Jake's mouth was playing shake and
twist. Beside him stood a mule with his head aimed low.

"Jed Barker," Jake trembled, "you handed me a
dirty deal. I've had this mule a month and she won't do
a durn thing. What are you gonna do about it?"

The mule dealer pondered. He looked at Jake. He
inspected the mule. "Jake, I don't believe you quite
understand the full significance of your situation. By the
way, do you have a horse?"

"No," snapped Jake.

"Well, it just so happens that you are luckier than
most mule owners. You see, you've got what is known
as a high-brow mule."

"What the dickens is that?"

"It's when a mule becomes more than a mule. When
this happens there's no use trying to make him plow. He
wants to be a saddle animal, and I tell you that a
saddle mule is something your neighbors will talk about.
Think it over, Jake. You know my motto—'If you like
the mule keep him and pay off. If you don't, bring
him back'."

Weeks went by but Jake did not return. As far as
I know Jake is still riding that high-brow mule.

Ma didn't want Jed to bet with anybody, much less
Tom Simpson. Tom said Jed bragged too much. "Any
fool would know that all the mules you ever sold
wouldn't remember you," Tom argued.

"Why, Tom, not only do they recognize me but they
do what I tell them to do."

"All right, we'll make a trade," said the unbeliever.
"Let me pick out a mule you've sold and if he knows
you and does what you tell him to do I'll give you fifty
acres of the best bottom land in Elbert County. But if

you lose I want six of the best mules in your barn. Shake on it, Jed?"

"I'm willing," said the trader.

Well, they traveled all over Elbert, Hart, Wilkes, Madison, Lincoln, and Oglethorpe. Finally they found a 22-year-old mule that Jed had traded years before. Jed walked up to her and stroked her head. "Hello, Hattie. You're the best trainer of green mules I ever had. Remember when you had a sore foot? I nursed you for six months."

Hattie snuggled on Jed's shoulder.

"Humph," snorted Tom. "What does that prove?"

"Take it easy, Tom. Hattie," Jed said gently, "go to the branch, get some water, eat your dinner and come back to your plowstock at one o'clock."

Hattie obediently went to the branch, drank some water, ate her dinner, and at one o'clock she backed up to the right plowstock. Finding the right plowstock was something in itself since there were ten identical ones in the field.

Nobody thought Jed would ever find a woman. He didn't show them the proper attention. I would say he looked about as good as brothers usually do. All the girls liked him and the women folks too. When a woman buys a mule wouldn't you say she was interested in the dealer as well as the deal? Well, Jed sold more mules to women than any other dealer this side of the Mississippi.

His world went around in a spin the day Sadie Higgins moved to town. He bought a tailor-made suit and parted his hair on the other side. Some bet Jed wouldn't get Sadie but the folks who had traded with Jed figured he would win. He started dropping by to see Sadie and he'd sit till bedtime. Word got around that Jed proposed to Sadie one night but she turned him down. Sadie didn't seem to take much stock in mule dealers. It seems she wanted a professional man.

I believe Jed was cut up over Sadie but he buckled down and sold more mules. Ma and Pa advised him to slow down but their son had a mind of his own.

He didn't seem scared when Jim Limkins cornered him in the livery stable and leveled a gun at Jed and shot his hat off.

"Anything wrong, Jim?"

"You've sold one mule too many," Jim roared. "Just one ornery stubborn cussed mule too many."

The dealer in mules picked up his hat, rolled it around and inspected the hole. "Jim," Jed countered, "if a mule's master is sensible and intelligent, the mule is too. If the mule packs a mean wallop in its hind legs, he's only kicking up for his rights. Look in the mirror, Jake. What you see is what your mule is."

"What are you talking about!?"

"Just this. Whose footsteps can a mule follow but his master's? Watch your step, Jim. Your character might be showing."

With that Jim jumped on Jed and knocked him flat. Jed rose slowly. I've often wondered what would have happened if one of Jed's mules hadn't taken over and kicked the daylights out of Jim.

Jed might not have gone to Texas if penicillin had been discovered. He shipped fifty mules to Missouri and all of them died of pneumonia. Of course there was talk around the corner drug that half of Jed's heart was aching for Sadie and the other was grieving for the four-legged critters.

The old town didn't have the same feeling with Jed gone. Men grumbled and found fault with Preacher Wilkins, and Preacher Wilkins promptly brought their weaknesses into focus.

The first Sunday the new preacher came, I went to church and sat where Jed used to sit. Sadie Higgins looked around, hopefully, I thought, but when she saw me she opened her Bible and bowed her head. I had a feeling she was praying for the return of a dealer in animals that have no pride of ancestry nor hope of posterity.

The mule trader came home the next year, a little older and a lot richer. His tall tales turned a dozen men toward Texas, but Jed settled down to the mule business in earnest. He got to be such an authority on mules that he wrote a book about them called "Tips to Mule Traders," but that book didn't give away my brother's real trading technique.

One night Jed was invited to make a speech on brood mares. I have a feeling that Jed knew Sadie was sitting on the back row. "You ought to choose a brood mare," he said, looking carefully over the audience, "like you would a woman. There are four things to keep in mind: First, her blood; second, her frame; third, her state of health; and fourth, her temper."

You might say that was a right unique way to propose but it worked anyway. Jed and Sadie got married during a slack mule trading season. On their first wedding anniversary they exchanged gifts. Sadie presented Jed an eight-pound son who just might grow up to be like his father. And when Jed presented Sadie with a high-brow mule I knew for sure that specifications had been met and approved.

A Truly Remarkable Invention

William Virlyn Farr

FACED BY the awful knowledge that the sun had to climb to the top of the cloudless sky and go down again before rest would come, Huie Larkin wished to be anything but a human person . . .

A cow, for instance, grazing all day in the pasture or lying under a shade tree (but not a mule that had to take every step he did). Or a bird flying where it will, working never —

But a bird is shot, falls to the ground bleeding and dead.

A fish, then, swimming all day in cool water, something to drink always, never to walk in the hot sun, feet burning, throat dry, hands blistered —

But a fish gets caught on a hook that is jerked out leaving flesh torn.

What?

Calves get shot, rabbits knocked in the head, chicken necks wrung off, turtles stabbed with ice picks, snakes hit with rock (on sight), bugs stepped on, flies swatted, weevils poisoned, rats caught in traps. But people —

What awful, awful things happen to them! For instance, how many rot in prison or go to the electric chair for crimes uncommitted?

These weren't pleasant things to think about, and Huie took no delight in them; but there they were, facts about life to be considered, to be accepted somehow. How did it happen that he would be an exception? That he would, he had no doubt whatsoever. It might happen that he would be brought before a court of law and accused of some terrible crime, his picture on front pages all over the country with stories telling how he was on trial; but in the end, after the trial went on for months and months, some evidence would come to light at the last moment and headlines would declare: "HUIE FOUND NOT GUILTY!" And there his picture (for the thousandth time) on the front page with a statement: "I can't find it in my heart to hold this against them. They thought I was guilty; I wasn't. I'm glad it's all over and done with."

But it wouldn't be over with. Moving picture companies would offer him contracts and off he would go on a plane for Hollywood, California, to make pictures, and he would be on the front page again (he was getting a little tired of all this publicity), and when the picture was over he'd come back to Atlanta and get talked to on the radio, get asked how it feels to be a big moving picture star. Well, he wouldn't put on any airs about it: he would tell them he didn't feel any better than anybody else, that at heart he was a country boy still and, truth to tell, he'd just as soon be back home plowing a mule where nobody made much of a fuss over him. Yet, he would point out, it would be unchristian to hide his light under a bushel. Of course they would agree wholeheartedly, shuddering at the idea that he would quit making pictures, for how many moving picture stars came from his part of the country? Not many. Not any that he knew of.

But he would quit just the same and do something constructive, like being President. Oh, it would be a lot of trouble living in the White House, going to parties all the time, photographers snapping his picture everywhere, people crowding around so they could boast they'd seen the President (him), but he would go down in history books, his name the answer to test questions. What if war came, though, or a depression? He thought about this while he plowed two rows without coming to any conclusion. Of course he could call in his cabinet and they'd probably tell him the best thing to do — but what if one said do this and another said do that? All the people looking to him for an answer, to save the country, and him not knowing any more than any of them how to go about it! He could read the books and see what other Presidents had done, but if they hadn't been up against the same kind of situation, the radio announcer would say, "Ladies and gentlemen, the President of the United States . . ." and there he would be, the people waiting, and in all honesty he would have to say, "People, I don't know what to do . . ."

It would be pretty hard making a go at something else after you've been President, especially when you leave office under circumstances such as faced him. But had he become President (as he had become a moving picture star) not for the sake of helping people but for the glory? He would not make that mistake again. Next time he would become something truly worthwhile—a scientist, for instance. True, he didn't know much about science, and he wouldn't have time to go back to school after he'd been President and all; he'd just lock himself in a laboratory and start experimenting right off the bat. He wouldn't sleep, wouldn't eat (much), wouldn't see the light of natural day till the job was done and he'd invented something truly remarkable. It might be years later when he'd call up the newspaper reporters. And there he would be in the papers again . . .

Cotton fields will grow up in grass, for it won't be necessary to get cotton that way any more. Huie Larkin, once a big moving picture star and ex-president (United States) made the discovery in his laboratory early this morning at 3 o'clock while everybody else was sound asleep.

"I've sacrificed a lot," the scientist admitted, "but it's nothing compared to all the back-breaking labor endured in cotton fields since time began. Now cotton will be grown in factories—in the shade. There won't be no hoeing or plowing or picking or anything like that. I've made it unnecessary."

When asked why he did it, the famous scientist declared quite simply, "I wanted to do something that would help people. That's all. I thought it would be about the best thing I could do, and I did it."

Pleased with all he had accomplished, Huie became more aware of the heat, the dust, his scorching feet. He remembered the good old days before he was big enough to plow, when he had nothing to do but fill up the guano distributor and tote water to the field; but thinking about the good old days wouldn't bring them back again, and he made up his mind to concentrate on something that might happen in the future—rain, for instance. Now, if it would only rain, he could go home and lie on the front porch till supper time. If he could only believe that the sun was gone . . .

It was gone now, yes, it was gone. Clouds were gathering, rolling darkly across the sky, exploding with lightning and thunder. The air was cool, blowing off the clouds. Any minute the rain would fall.

Not for one instant did he doubt it.

Gone Are the Ways

Christine Gower Warthen

BACK in the late twenties and early thirties we still had a milkman, a yard man, washwoman, cook, chickens, barnyard with cows and plenty of meat in the storehouse at Broad Acres—our old plantation on the Ogeechee River. There were big patient mules, horses to ride, plenty of Negro families in the quarter and plenty of children.

The Negroes still came to the yard early each morning for job assignment for the day, which lasted from "can see" till "can't see." They knew the boss would always be good to them and let them use the big two-mule wagon for town and church and furnish them with calomel and quinine when they had malaria.

These were quiet times — no noisy tractors nor machines dispersing bad smelling insecticides — no washing machines, no screeching buzz saws in the peaceful woods.

There were Negroes on the place who had been born there as their parents before them had been—good ones, bad ones, honest ones, thieves who got caught and some who were never caught! They probably took the advice of an aged one who would say, "Chile, if yeh ain't got no education yuh jes got to use your brains!"

Their superstitions had been handed down from generations "far gone"—to hang up a new calendar before the "fust" or fail to have hog jowl and peas on that day was asking for bad luck! Their language was quaint and very expressive, full of wit and wisdom.

The colorful expressions and quaint sayings of Essie who stayed in our kitchen for twenty-three years are still quoted by our family and friends though she has been gone to her reward for more than twenty years.

Essie was a "geechee," almost a mulatto. Her family lived near the Ogeechee River, the boundary of our plantation. Two sisters lived there in two cabins. Essie's mother had fifteen children and her sister had nineteen. They were close kin but most of them had different fathers. They were a peculiar clan, very devoted to each other, even to the present day, as many of them are still on the plantation.

Essie was barely seventeen when she came to us and she was the only one of the girls who never married and never had any children. She was gentle, quiet and had a sense of humor and a deep loyalty to us. This we returned.

She had to get used to "white folks ways" and we had to learn what she meant by what she said. When asked if she had finished a certain task she always replied, "Yes'm, I'm is." If I asked where a seemingly lost article was, she would say, "De last time I seed it, it was on dat back shelf, but course dat don't represent it dar now." When asked about a broken dish, she reminded me, "I meet it broke," which meant it was broken when she first saw it. When asked if she liked oysters she replied, "I'm not humpback about dem." If you have ever watched a hungry cat eat you know what she meant.

Essie had many nieces and nephews and I asked her what she did when they had sore threat. "I goes to the woods, cuts me some red oak bark, (don't let it tech the groun') boil it with salt and alum and den let them gurgle it!"

They are usually very cold-natured. I asked Essie if she had enough quilts to keep herself warm. She said, "Long about November fust I gets into a *quile* and don't *unquile* till May." Usually healthy, she sometimes had malaria and was given quinine — but she reported she wasn't going to take it any more as it made her feel "more foolisher than common."

She hated snakes and was very good at destroying them. My husband asked her not to kill the king snakes as they were harmless and only ate rats. "Yes sir — but 1 don' trus' none of 'em." Once a large one crawled under her house which was quite low on the ground. She fixed a shovel of hot fire coals, sprinkled red pepper generously over it and put it under the edge of the house. Pretty soon the snake crawled out and she was ready with her hoe. From my porch I watched and heard her saying, "It's me an' you, snake, me an' you"—and she alone survived!

Since our back yard was quite large and contained the usual wood pile, fig trees, etc., it was often visited by rattle snakes. These were a hazard since so many children visited our son. I offered to pay a dime for each one killed in the yard. She announced next morning, "You owes me a dime! I'se killed a rattler with 8 rattles!" "Was he in the yard?" I asked. "No'm, not quite, but he was *a-headin'* that a way!" She got the dime!

Essie was very fond of my mother and when she came from North Carolina to visit me, we would sit on the back porch and sew and talk. She could hear us from the kitchen and observed, "You an' your mama talk lak she jes fust cum."

My mother was rather stout and when my brother came to take her home, being about her size, they were teased a lot as to which was larger. As they were getting ready to get in his car, I said, "Essie, now which do you think weighs more?" She replied wisely, "It's just tip and tap!"

All the colored people on the place were much interested in the two Carolinas and spoke of them as N. C. and S. C. When, one summer, I went to N. C. to visit my people, upon my return I at once asked if Sylvia's baby had come. Essie very promptly told me it had and was a boy. "Named him N.C.," she said. I was puzzled until she explained, "Named him N. C. for the place you wuz gone to." He is a grown man now and still called N. C.

One of her nieces decided to visit some of the kin who had gone North. So among them they made up the money to send her to New York. Months later I asked Essie how she liked it up there. "She dun fooled around up dar an' got herself a burden, so she dun cum home to her Ma." They should have called that one N. Y.!

Essie was a sincere Christian and always had the day off on her "preaching day." She loved her pastor and took a great interest in ours. Our spare room was always the home of the visiting minister during revival time and she waited on them very humbly. After many different preachers, she remarked to me, "I laks Brother S——— bettern' any—cause he allus makes his own bed." I couldn't resist telling the one just leaving what she said. It amused him very much and when he went to the kitchen to tell her good-by he said, "Essie, I'm sorry you don't like me. I never could make up my bed." It embarrassed her terribly and she muttered, "Shucks, white folks tells ever thing!"

One of the young Negro boys decided he was called to preach. Essie didn't think much of it. She explained, "He ain't ready, ain't studied none, ain't never been nowhere and ain't never suffered none." I gathered that she didn't think he would have enough sympathy for sinners. When the would-be preacher heard of the members' objections, he exclaimed, "Dar now, jest when I gits up spunksion to spound de gospel, yawl up and squshes me!"

The colored people enjoyed funerals . . . their sympathy was so real it kept them from being normal for days. When old Mandy died, they were especially moved and were marching up and down and around the coffin, some almost hysterical. The preacher was standing quietly in the pulpit. One asked, "Preacher, do you think the Lawd will let Mandy into Heaven?" He replied, "I'se not the one to say. I won't be standin' at de gate saying who can go in and who can't. I don't jedge Mandy." When I remarked to Essie that Mandy had so many children, though never married, she excused her by saying, "She was jest so kindhearted she couldn't fuse nobody."

During a gubernatorial campaign one of the candidates promised to do a lot for the colored people. She was excited over the outcome and the day after the election asked, "Well, who got the seat?" When told that the opposing candidate won, she was distressed, saying, "What's going to become of us po' colored folks?" She need not have worried—the other one couldn't have kept his promises.

One morning when she came to work she informed me that one of the Negro men had died. "What happened? Was he sick long?" "No'm—his job fell on him!" His job really had as the ditch he was digging had caved in on him.

Most of the Negro churches in the country had services in the afternoon to make it possible for all of them to go, as many had to get a big Sunday dinner so the white folks could go in the morning. They never carried their children and the yards were full of them singing as they played. I decided to bring Sunday School to them, using papers left over from Primary classes where I assisted in the mornings at my church.

The children and I cleared out an empty tenement house, put empty wooden boxes in a circle and began meeting each Sunday afternoon at three. More than twenty children came and we had a wonderful time.

They loved Bible stories and loved to "pretend" or "act" them. Especially did they like the story of the good Samaritan. A big boy always rescued the wounded man and carried him very carefully to the innkeeper, pretending to leave a coin for his care.

They were quick to memorize and learned many Bible verses. Each answered the roll with his favorite. One little five-year-old, rolled his big eyes around, stuttered, and then came out with his version of Psalms 122:1. "I wuz glad when they tole me . . . come on, les go to church."

They loved singing and how their faces shone when they sang, "Jesus loves the little children / All the children of the world / Red and yellow, black and white / They are precious in his sight / Jesus loves the little children of the world."

Another favorite was, "I shall not be moved—just like a tree that's planted by the waters, I shall not be moved." Only they sang it, "I shall not be *re*moved." It didn't matter if I sang it as in the book, they sang, "I shall not be *re*moved." So I quit trying to change it.

Essie was very proud of this little crowd and helped the parents see that they came—clean and in their Sunday best. The older people worked during the week and made a decent living for their families. They didn't wait for the "Guvment" to give them a handout — they did for themselves as long as they could and trusted the Lord and the owner of the farm, along with their children, to see that they didn't suffer for real needs.

They had their fun and were happy with their work, their religion and their beliefs in signs, etc. Essie always said, "If it rains when one is being buried, he's a good man and gone straight to heaven." They had strange use of words like *when*soever for whenever, and *atter* for after

—"I seeded him go by, right atter de down train."

Once a relative of Essie's had a chance to go to Macon for the first time. They all gathered around to hear her tell about the big store. "Never knowed there wuz so much cloth in de world—and den I got on de *cultivator,* went upstairs, and dar was more." They loved the sound of big words and one described a young man with a new car: "I tell you, he's tryin' to make an airplane outen dat car —he went thru' dat *intersession* like he wuz *self compelled,* didn't even stop for the clinkers." We hope he got where he was going.

A few lines from "Wishing" in John Charles McNeil's *Lyrics of the Cotton Land* (1907) describes the Negroes' feeling of aloneness and also their closeness to nature:

> *I wisht I wus a hummin' bird*
> *I'd nes in a willer tree*
> *Den noth'n but sumpn' wut goes on wings*
> *Could ever git to me.*
>
> *I wisht I was a snake. I'd crawl*
> *Down in a deep stump hole*
> *Nuthn' u'd come atter me down in dar*
> *Into de dark en col'.*
>
> *But jis a nigger in his shack,*
> *Wid de farlight in de chinks —*
> *Sump'n kin see him ever time*
> *He even so much as winks.*
>
> *I'd lak to sleep in a holler gum*
> *Or roost in a long leaf pine*
> *Whar nothin' u'd come to mess wid me*
> *Or ax me whar I'se gwine.*

White Oak's Midnight Ghost

Grady Jones

DO YOU believe in ghosts? Mister Jim didn't — *until!* - - - The old White Oak Church building, standing on a knoll of bleached, white sand, surrounded by scrub oak, is beautiful in its serene setting — so quiet and gentle in its ageless beauty — so much a definite monument to its founders and organizers who worshipped there. The quiet dignity of the neighborhood is enhanced by such refinement as only God can create. To many of the inhabitants living in the White Oak community, it stands out "as having always been, and probably *always* will be."

The surrounding countryside is made up of prosperous, well-to-do planters, owners of large plantations. Before the days of the automobile and farm tractors, most of the farmers used mules with which to cultivate the fields; and, almost every family kept a couple of fine blooded horses to drive and to ride.

Mister Jim, as he was known by everyone in the community, was highly esteemed and respected by both white and colored, and the colored people considered it a privilege to be employed on his big plantation.

Riding Ebony, a big, black, high-spirited stallion, Mister Jim was returning home at midnight, having been detained in Thomson by business, when, just as he neared White Oak Church and having three more miles to ride before he would be home, a heavy thunderstorm forced

him to stop and seek shelter. Knowing the doors and windows of the church were never locked, he rode up to one
of the windows, raised it, dismounted, threw his saddle into
the church, and climbed in behind it. After pulling the
reins in behind him, he closed the window just as the *fury
of hell* seemed to break loose in a heavy downpour of
torrential rain with piercing lightning and a cannon-like
roar of thunder.

The church building had no outside blinds at the
windows, nor any window shades. During the brilliant,
blinding flashes of lightning the sanctuary would be lighted
up momentarily, as though it were broad daylight. Although happy in the comfort of indoor protection and
shelter for himself from the heavy deluge, he regretted that
Ebony had to suffer the discomfort of the cold, downpour
of rain.

The heavy beat of rain on the roof caused him to feel
drowsy, and he permitted himself to enjoy a fanciful reverie
of the day's happenings. Suddenly, his reverie was broken
by a person's—a woman's—sobs coming from the pulpit.
Instantly, he was wide awake and standing on his feet. A
flash of lightning revealed a woman dressed in a long flowing, white robe, with her long, black hair falling loosely
over her shoulders, silhouetted against the pulpit, kneeling
as if in prayer. In his sudden perplexity, her sobs were the
most heart-rending, unearthly sounds he had ever heard.

"Am I *actually* seeing what I see, or am I dreaming?"
he asked himself. "Who is she—or *what* is she, and what
is she doing here at this hour of the night?" were his next
thoughts.

"Actually, for the first time in my life," he admitted
later, "I was mortally afraid; *BUT!* afraid of *WHAT?*"

With cold perspiration dripping from his forehead,
he wondered, "Can *this* be—?" He had never permitted
himself to believe in ghosts. At the moment, however, he
wasn't sure!

In a flash, the conversation he had overheard the day
before came back to him. "Big Tom," his lead-hand, and
several other farm hands were discussing the "hant" they
had seen here at this very church only the night before.
He recalled joining the group, and asking, "Big Tom,
what's this nonsense about you and Bill seeing a 'real, live

hant'?" Out of respect, Big Tom had raised his height to its full six feet and four inches, as he said, "Yas-sir, Mister Jim, me and Bill and Sam has done jes *THAT!* We had got to the fork of the road, and we's a-standin' there a-tawkin'. All to once, Sam grabs my arm—scairt plum to death—an we seen this here *she-hant,* a woman dressed in a long, white robe, come through the door, and it wuz *shet tight!* No, sir! She didn't open that there door, but she done come slap through it—an it wuz *shet TIGHT!*"

Even though Big Tom had already told his listeners the story, they became more excited as he had repeated it for Mister Jim to hear. "Then, Mister Jim, that there *she-hant jes* disappeared in *thin air* in the grave yard." And when he had said that, one of the women let out a blood-curdling shriek as she slumped to the ground in a dead faint.

After they had revived her Big Tom went on with his story. "Yes-sir! Mister Jim, before we could git oursefs ready to run, that there *she-hant jes* disappeared *in thin-air* in the grave yard, an' we ain't seen *IT* no more!" Big Tom had sensed that Mister Jim didn't believe what he was saying and asked him, "Law, Mister Jim! Aint y'awl never seen a *hant?*"

As Mister Jim was actually seeing the woman in the pulpit, and at midnight at *THAT,* Big Tom's story now took on a wholly new meaning. From the way he felt, it now hit him right in the middle of the pit of his stomach, as he recalled having answered Big Tom, "No, Tom, I never have — for there just aren't any such things as *'hants'!*" He'd even added, "When a person dies, if he goes to Heaven, he won't want to *come back* and if he goes to hell he *can't* come back!"

Right then, he thought to himself, "I'm not *sure* but that Big Tom could have been *RIGHT!*"

With his eyes fixed, in a steady stare, on the apparition at the pulpit, through a flash of lightning, he saw the woman rise from her knees and begin walking slowly toward him. He thought, "She *is* beautiful, but *who* or *WHAT* is she?" His instinct told him to run! To get outside, get on Ebony and get away from the church as fast as he could. He explained later that he was not sure but that he made an effort to follow his instinct; but, his feet seemed to have turned into lead, and seemed to have been glued to the floor; anyway, they were too heavy for him to move them.

Then, as the apparition walked slowly toward him, he just *knew* he had suddenly become bereft of his senses. On she came, and in his fright, it seemed like an hour before she came near to where he was standing. For some reason —he never could explain why—he reached out his hand to touch her, or *IT!* Just as he did touch her, through the lightning's glow, he saw that it was a real person, a human, and—he *recognized* her.

"What a relief!" he sighed.

Grabbing both her arms to prevent her falling—for he saw that she was walking in her sleep—he shook her and said, "Miss Mary, wake up!"

That caused her to awake, and she was as frightened as he had been. He helped her to sit down, and when she could speak she asked, "Why, Jim, what are *you* doing here—where are we?" By now she was fully awake and sobbing hysterically. He quieted her by assuring her, "Everything is all right!"

Before Miss Mary could explain further, Jim understood. Andrew, her husband, had died only the week before, and his death had so upset her, her family feared for her sanity. "Oh, Andy's death was *so terrible*—I loved him so much," she explained brokenly, through a new outburst of tears.

By the time Jim was able to quiet her the rain had stopped and only the low rumble of thunder and flickering flashes of lightning catapulted across the distant sky. Just then the moon came out from behind the clouds and to Jim it had never shone more brightly. Helping Miss Mary stand up, he told her, "Now, you go on to the front door and wait for me there, and I'll walk with you to your home." She made an effort to protest, but Jim wouldn't listen.

Raising the window, he placed the saddle on the sill and climbed out. After he had resaddled Ebony and given him an assuring pat, he began walking around to the front door, where Miss Mary was waiting for him. She lived only a short distance from the church and by the time they had reached her home she had regained complete control of her mental faculties.

Before he reached home, Jim began to ponder the wisdom of telling Kate, his wife, about his gruesome ordeal. "If I don't" he questioned his better judgment, "and she should later *find out,* it will make it even more difficult to explain." So he did tell her, omitting none of the details, and they both had a hearty laugh over the possibility of someone having seen them leaving the church at that time of night, and—"Just what would the neighbors have thought, and what would they have said?"

Several times during the next couple of weeks, Kate was awakened by Jim's moans from terrible nightmares, as he would yell out, "No, oh, no! It can't be!"

One night, about two weeks later, Jim had gotten out of bed during one of his nightmares and was *storming* around the room, when he suddenly ran into the door which was partly opened. The impact of hitting the door head-on awakened him as he slumped to the floor. By that time, Kate was awake, and she helped him back to bed and placed a cold, damp cloth across his forehead.

Several years later, while discussing his trying experience and nightmares with his friends, Jim expained, "My fight with the door cured me of my terrible dreams." And he added, "That terrifying ordeal at least solved the mystery of White Oak's Midnight Ghost!"

The Monkey Show

William Virlyn Farr

ANY OTHER time John Edwin would have been excited about his new shoes, but this morning no matter how much of an effort he made to keep his mind on them, it kept going back to the monkey show. He would have stayed home, wouldn't have made out he was going to school in the first place if he hadn't thought they would give him a quarter at the last minute when they realized he was going no matter what; but the last thing his mother said was, "I never seen a monkey show in my life and it ain't hurt me none;" and his father said, laughing, "What you want to see monkeys act like people for? You can see people act like monkeys for nothing."

John Edwin thrust his lunch into a hip pocket (half the time there wasn't a sack in the house—there wasn't this morning, and anything he couldn't stand it was to be seen carrying his lunch wrapped in a newspaper) when he saw Boon Gossett at the fork of the roads. Anybody he hated to be seen with it was Boon who wore dirty overalls.

"You going to the monkey show?" asked Boon first thing.

"I see enough monkeys," said John Edwin. "I don't have to be going to any show to see them."

Ignoring his come back, Boon said, "That man who was here? He said them monkeys is going to eat like people, with a knife and fork? And ride tricycles and

walk on ropes and I don't know what all. I'd give a
million dollars just to see it."

"Ain't you going?" asked John Edwin.

"I ain't got no quarter," said Boon.

Before he knew what was going on, after they entered
the yard, someone tagged John Edwin. Well, he didn't
care. Now he had a perfect right to turn away from
anyone no matter what they said; he could run like crazy
in the opposite direction and nobody could say a thing.
Only now, with the new shoes on that he wasn't used
to yet, he couldn't run fast, and he'd be *It* till the bell
rang. Just let someone ask him about the monkey show:
he'd tell them to their face to mind their own business.
But the bell rang before anyone got a chance to come
out with it.

There were four grades in his room and there would
be some time before Miss Clovis got to his. He had read
everything in the book anyway, so now he decided to
draw pictures for a while. He had been practicing Dick
Tracy—a good one to practice because it was so plainly
Dick Tracy that anyone looking at it had to say so.
Nothing hurt like showing someone a picture and then
having to explain who it was. Cindy in Smilin' Jack was
hard to draw: everyone said she looked like she had
the mumps. He knew she wasn't the same as in the paper,
but why did they have to laugh? At least he could draw
some and they couldn't at all, not even a cat facing backwards. It was a risk to draw someone from real life
who might not be recognized, but he did it anyway—now
he was drawing Miss Clovis.

She was on the fat side, and old, with straight hair
that was combed back and balled behind. Anybody would
recognize her right off, if he got her fat enough and old
enough. He tried from different angles. He liked the
head-on view best but sideways the balled-up hair made
it look more like her, and it was this resemblance that
he perfected, putting in details down to the tiny flowers
in her print dress. When the picture was finished, he
passed it down, and each time someone got it he heard
a muffled giggle. When it came back, he folded it and
placed it in his book to carry home. Even his father
who laughed at most things he drew would be sure to

recognize Miss Clovis: he got her head up in the air
just right.

When his turn came to read, he knew all the words
and after he finished, Miss Clovis said, as always, "Very
good, John Edwin." She didn't spend much time with
any one pupil this morning on account of the monkey
show. They wouldn't be much interested in their lessons
anytime, but this morning, because of the excitement,
most of them forgot half the words they knew. But there
wasn't much noise, and no spit balls thrown. Miss Clovis
could keep them from seeing the monkey show if they
didn't behave themselves.

The car with a trailer came at ten o'clock. The
principal went outside and talked to the man who brought
the monkeys and then came back and told Miss Clovis
that there would be a recess until the man got ready.
A partition had to be removed between the two rooms
making a big auditorium.

Everyone ran outside and, of course, straight to the
trailer; but the man said they could look much as they
wanted to after they bought a ticket. They played tag,
but their hearts weren't in it. Whoever was *It* didn't much
care if he got someone or not and those who might get
tagged didn't care either, for it wasn't often that a show
came to this school and the excitement was all but unbearable. The man took all kinds of things out of the
trailer including tricycles, chairs, swings, and some things
that nobody could figure out what they were.

After the bell rang and the principal told them to
line up and have their money ready so they could get
inside, John Edwin wandered across the yard and sat down
under an oak tree facing the sun. He wished he had a
book to read or some paper to draw on, but since he
didn't he picked up a twig and, smoothing out an area
in the sand, began to draw: it was of Popeye, the Sailor-
man.

He didn't know Boon was there until he heard him
laugh. Then, with one swift movement of his hand, he
erased the picture. Leaning against the tree and closing
his eyes to the sun, he wished that some people could
mind their own business and keep to themselves.

"I sure wish I could see them monkeys," said Boon.
"They must be really something."

"Oh monkeys," said John Edwin. "If there's anything
I'm good and tired of hearing about, it's monkeys."

Miss Clovis approached from behind the tree. "Now
boys," she said. "You can go in now. I asked the man
and he said it'll be all right."

"Oh boy!" said Boon, and took off running. But
John Edwin didn't move.

"John Edwin," said Miss Clovis in a tone she had
never used with him because he always had his lessons
ready and never spoke out of turn. "I asked the man
if you could go in and he said it'll be all right. Are you
going to sit there?"

It would be more fun than anything seeing the monkeys; then he could go home and say he'd seen them
after all . . .

"John Edwin, why do you want to be that way? You
know you want to see the monkeys like everybody else.
Why do you sit there?"

. . . but he remembered how he felt this morning,
how he forced one foot in front of the other, waiting
to be called back, and no one said a word. How could
he go now?

The first roar of laughter came from the school house.

Miss Clovis was saying, "You're always so good to
behave that I don't know what's got into you. Aren't
you going to say anything?"

Let her beg. He would sit there under the tree until
the school house rotted down, if the monkeys stayed there
that long. Never in his life would he see a monkey show,
either, no matter how much money he might have some
day. Even if he could afford to buy a monkey and keep
it in a cage, he wouldn't. He wouldn't have anything
to do with monkeys, ever. They knew how it'd be when
he left the house this morning, but did they care? They
let him go. *They let him go.*

He paid Miss Clovis no more mind than if she had
been a puff of wind. He wouldn't go now to please her.
He wouldn't go now if his mother came and handed him
a quarter and begged him on bended knee. He wouldn't
go for anything.

Miss Clovis stood between him and the blue sky.

Glancing up, he saw her hand run through graying hair which the wind blew loose. "Are you coming?" she asked.

He shook his head without looking up, staring at the ground to hide his burning cheeks, and said: "I don't want to see any monkeys."

"Well, it's all right with me," said Miss Clovis, turning around, "I just don't know what's got into you."

Her footsteps sounded across the yard and then drowned in a wave of laughter that came from the school house. Now alone he smoothed out an area on the ground and began drawing a picture, intending it to be of somebody, but it turned out to be of a monkey.

The Bell Rang Friday

Frances Greene

DAVIDSONVILLE, where I grew up, had three churches with tall, imposing steeples, and each steeple had its bell. Each bell, however, rang out with a different and distinct tone, and just by listening close, one could tell which of the three meeting houses was calling its members into the fold or which section of town was sending out the alarm, "Fire, a house is burning."

Whatever my mother was doing, when a bell rang she would pause for an instant and cock her head slightly, barely breathing. Though she did not tell my father and me to listen, we too would pause as we worked in our small garden or as we rushed to get dressed for Sunday School, and for a long minute we would stand quietly to hear the ringing of the bells.

In time, I came to know that the big iron bell in the Baptist Church up on the highway north of town pealed forth with a deep, gruff ring, a long ring that was spaced with a tinkling echo while the clapper lazily and indifferently swung to the other side. I came to recognize the truer, higher, quicker ring of the small brass bell in the Methodist Church on the south side of town down toward the river bridge, a ring that had a certain urgency about it—a frantic appeal as if warning the congregation to hurry, hurry, hurry. And then there was the bell in the big stone Congregational Church. The biggest church in town it was, built into the side of the hill looking down on Main Street which was either dusty or muddy, depending on the seasons, and the tone of its bell was loud and clear, its clapper leaving a resonant ring as if to proclaim to the world that its steeple was the highest, its church the grandest.

This latter one was Mama's favorite, not because of its grandness nor its sound of strength, but because each time she heard it she knew that young Benjie Hawkins was fulfilling his duty as the official toller. Mama had a special feeling for Benjie Hawkins. It took root on the Christmas Eve that she helped deliver boxes of food to the town's needy, and though the Hawkins family had been on the list ever since they moved from the mountains into the shanty across the creek behind the broom factory, Benjie had never gotten his fair share. Mr. Hawkins figured that ten bright children were enough to feed without adding a son who foolishly but happily frittered away his time taming chickens and cats and squirrels, not to mention skunks and raccoons. But between Mama and Reverend Lovelace, overgrown, pale Benjie was fed and clothed, and he rang the bell for a bed near the church furnace.

And so I, as well as most of the other children in Davidsonville, grew up knowing the sound of the bells. Our churches were never locked but not one of us ever dared to pull the ropes—even on Hallowe'en—and they were never rung except on Wednesdays for prayer meeting and for services on Sundays and for fires.

That's how Mama knew that a house was burning near our street early one evening as she bought groceries in town. Mr. McDonald had just finished weighing up the sugar and the coffee and the potatoes; the sacks were on the counter ready to be listed and charged and then loaded into the basket of my second-hand bicycle. But because Father was away at summer school getting his degree at the University, and because he was coming home for the weekend, Mama tilted her head and rashly ordered, "A pound of steak, please."

Mr. Mac was all smiles suddenly. He had been slicing liver and side meat all day, and now came along a woman wanting steak with it as high as it was and people as hard up as they were.

She watched him bring the beef from the cooler and throw it on the big, round, wooden chopping block. Mr. Mac smiled at her once and lifted a long, thin, sharp knife from the holder on the side of the block. He wiped the blade across his dirty apron and then held it poised delicately in his right hand.

The first, deep gruff bong of a church bell floated through the open doors of the cluttered, unswept store. Mama drew in her breath, holding it for a moment, her eyes going to the front where signs advertising fresh honey, fresh eggs, fresh bread flapped against the plate glass window. Mr. Mac held his knife steady, lifting his head to look at Mama but not really seeing her. Prayer meeting was night before last; Sunday was day after tomorrow.

The bell paused, bonged again. The Baptist Church bell was summoning all fire fighters in town. The sound brought men from their front porches, women from their kitchens. A house was burning. It was the third fire in a month. Folks said they came in threes.

Mr. Mac laid his knife on the chopping block. Untying his apron as he moved, he circled the side of beef, going quickly past Mama, past the long counter. We followed, stepping carefully along the oily floor spattered with sawdust.

Teen-age boys yelled, "Fire," as they ran up the street. A woman, strands of black hair falling from the knot at the nape of her neck, her face contorted with exhaustion from heavy breathing, half dragged her three year old daughter whose short legs jerked in a running motion.

The bell rang in a steady beat, not urgent, not insistent. But people began to fill the dusty road, all running now in the same direction. Mr. Mac was running too, leaving his store doors open, eager to reach the fire in time to lend his experienced hand.

Mama's eyes darted quickly to the sky beyond the post office across the street. The first trace of black smoke was rising slowly and her face paled as she too began to run.

"It's your house," a woman gasped, turning toward Mama.

"Yes," she answered. Her face showed pain and fear mixed with disbelief. Her breathing was heavy and hard, and she slowed a little at the corner before turning up the long hill.

"It's the Barker house, all right," a boy shouted. His long legs moved more swiftly and his eyes were bright with excitement.

Mama slowed to a walk. She had to catch her breath. Her hands trembled; her legs felt weak; her heart hammered much too fast. Past the neighboring houses we walked, the barn-like Smith house, Miss Mamie's small cottage, the Johnson's house with its cluttered front yard. Mama could see the people standing in the road not venturing any closer to the heat. She could hear the piercing crack of Father's shot gun shells, the explosion of glass-canned fruits. We could see the flames spouting from the windows, the doors, the roof.

Mama stopped at the edge of the crowd. Men walked on the lawn, carefully avoiding the flower beds, the young trees and shrubbery, scorched now from the heat. Women talked in muted voices. Glass shattered. A child screamed.

"They say she was in town," a bystander said to her companion.

With a heavy thud the roof collapsed; the chimney shuddered once and then righted itself to stand alone.

Mama moved, her eyes closed as she drew a deep, trembling breath.

"Hold her. She's going in!"

Mama forced a smile to her thin lips. "I'm not going in," she assured the woman whose fingers firmly clutched her arm.

"How did it start, Mary?" Mrs. Johnson asked.

Mama shook her head.

"And you and Mark had done so much work on it. It was beginning to look right cute."

Cute? How could her house of blood and sweat be described as cute? But Mama said, "Yes," quietly, and she thought of all the pennies that she had saved from Father's small teacher's salary; pennies that she had applied on a new floor, book shelves, a trellis at the end of the porch, andirons for the fireplace. Small things but ever so many things for this house, this home, the first one that they had ever owned. "A place," Mama had often said with a smile on her lips, "to plant an apple tree and watch it bear fruit; a place to bring up children and cats!" And Father had borrowed money on it to go to summer school.

"They didn't save anything, Mary," Mrs. Johnson said. "But you ought to be grateful you weren't in it."

"If it'd happened in the middle of the night . . ." Mrs. Carter let her voice trail into a shuddering silence.

Mrs. Johnson agreed with a nod of her head. "It would have been terrible, calling Mark, telling him his wife and daughter. . . ." She closed her eyes with the horrible thought.

"We are grateful," Mama said automatically.

"Houses can be replaced," a bystander added.

The group was suddenly silent. There was a matter of a place for Mama to stay, clothes to wear, food. . . .

"You're coming home with me," Mrs. Carter said quickly.

"We have an extra room," Mrs. Johnson insisted.

"There'll be other nights," Mrs. Carter said. "We can take turns, but tonight she is staying with us."

Mama nodded once, made an effort to smile. People were trying to be kind. And she was grateful and thankful and . . . she wet her dry lips. "If you don't mind, we'll be along in a little while."

The teen-agers were leaving, their laughter brash in the silence that had settled with the darkness. The tangy smell of rich burning pine, the heavy odor of burned leather, the cloth, the sickening sweetness of cooked jellies and fruits, the stifling smell of cotton batting. All this filled the night air that had always been so fresh, so wonderful late of an afternoon as Mama sat on the porch and read. But now there was no porch; there was nothing but charred lumber and smoke.

In a moment, the Carters, the Johnsons, all the others walked slowly to their homes, leaving Mama alone in the road. Only the chimney was left of our house, a place of memories, little memories like a geranium on the window sill, bookends shaped like a ship, a bud vase. . . .

"She's lucky," a voice floated and settled over the stillness. "It could have happened in the middle of the night."

"And they're young. They can start over. Not like being an old couple with nothing left."

Mama heard, and for a brief instant she closed her eyes.

Out of the shadows the tall, lanky figure of Benjie Hawkins moved haltingly. His long hair clung to his perspiring head; his shirt was damp and dirty, and he wiped a blackened hand across his mouth. He came slowly toward Mama and when he reached her, he extended his cupped hands in which a small furry kitten slept soundly. "For you," he said. "This'un was all I could save."

Tears streamed from Mama's eyes and wet her cheeks but she accepted the little bundle and cuddled it to her. The cat had been on the back porch. The kittens were in a box. And suddenly the sobs came to replace the tears and her body shook.

Benjie cried too, not loud, not loud at all but a deep, moaning kind of cry that is sad to hear. And for a long moment, they stood there, each crying for all things lost, each giving way to the hurt inside that each of them knew. In spite of their gratefulness for the things they did have, in spite of kindness and generosity and friends, at this moment they could give way to their hurts, their grief.

For Mama, tomorrow would be the beginning of a new day. Time then to pick up the pieces and start over. Time then to be brave, to be grateful for life itself. But tonight was the time for crying, a time when only tears could express the deep pain.

And Benjie Hawkins was offering the only thing he had to give: a willingness to share her grief.

A Cotton Pickin' Story

Jane Cassels Record

NOT SO long ago I read a piece by a Yankee lady who on recently moving south suddenly discovered that her youth had been, in at least one important respect, misspent.

"You mean to say that you never *picked cotton?*" her new Arkansas friends asked.

When she confessed that she not only had never picked it but had never even seen it growing, except in the medicine cabinet, the looks on their faces made her feel so inadequate that, the very next time a harvest season rolled around, she went out and hired herself to a cotton farmer, for what turned out to be a gruesome, endless day.

Now, the only white southerners who would admit to having picked cotton — much less brag about it — are those who obviously never *had* to pick it. I smiled when I read the story, for I could just picture the lady's taunters, sitting on the country club terrace, julep in hand, conjuring up memories of their prowess in the fields; and I knew that in their youth they had no doubt picked about as much cotton, and in about the same way, as had I.

South Georgia is a rancher's landscape now, but when I was growing up there during the 1920's and early 1930's, the August fields were white with ripening cotton bolls, and whole families of colored workers passed up and down the rows from dawn to dusk, dragging long, heavy pick sacks behind them. Though it was rare to see a white person doing field work, there was something about those big wads of white fluff hanging from the brown pods, just asking to be plucked — to say nothing of the camaraderie of the pickers — which drew almost every child like a magnet.

The summer I was seven my five-year-old sister and I spent the latter part of the school vacation on my grandfather's plantation, and from the moment we arrived, we started plotting to get into the fields. My grandmother, who, like many other southern grandmothers of French descent, was called Bigmama — a literal translation of *Grand-mére* — thought we were too young for such things. I agreed with her about my sister, but I could scarcely have been expected to understand her misgivings about me.

After much wheedling by both of us, Bigmama, who was permissive before it became fashionable to be so, finally said yes, provided we picked only in the cool of the day, watched out for snakes, and stayed close to Ada, the cook, who was picking in her spare time.

After the first few moments of elation we went into a fury of preparation. Since it was unthinkable that we would drink from the communal bucket and dipper which the regular field hands used, or share a container between the two of us, for that matter, we had to find a couple of bottles or jugs. Scavenging through the pantry, we came upon just the things: two half-gallon fruit jars of the old-fashioned sort whose glass tops were held in place by spring clips. We also had to have something to put our cotton in, and Bigmama sent Ada out to the commissary to cut enough cloth from the heavy bolt of Osnaburg — pronounced Awsingburg locally — to make authentic miniatures of the big sacks carried by the colored pickers.

It took us the rest of the day to assemble our equipage. Early the next morning we set out for the fields in new straw hats and overalls (Western blue jeans had not yet crossed the Mississippi), with the smelly, scratchy pick sacks slung over our shoulders and the brimful fruit jars held tightly in our arms. To get to the cotton patch we skirted the stables, cut through the "quarter," where the shacks of the colored hands were strung out in a row, and came out onto the field road, whose black, fine, dry dust oozed deliciously between our bare toes with every step. Soon we reached the place where Ada and her friends were picking, and, after greeting everybody and setting our water jars under a shade tree, we got down to work on the separate rows which we insisted on being assigned.

Attacking my first stalks enthusiastically, stuffing handfuls of cotton into my new sack, I had progressed about ten feet when an elderly woman a few yards away called to me.

"Get the bolls cleaned out good, now. Hear?"

Looking back I saw that the stalks I had already worked had little flags of white fluff sticking raggedly in the corners of many pods.

"But I can pick a lot faster if I don't have to worry about all those little pieces," I answered, with irrefutable logic.

"All right, but I'm sure going to tell your grandpa that you was on that row, so's he won't be getting on nobody else about it." I pretended not to hear her.

Soon my sister came over and started working on one of my stalks. When I told her to get back where she belonged, she said, "There's a bug on my row." That settled that.

Though the sun was not very hot at first and we were not particularly thirsty, the novelty of drinking out of the jars caused us to run back to the tree every few minutes and, after unclipping the lids, take a few swallows. By the end of the first hour we were beginning to feel water-logged. Furthermore, by then the sun was starting to make itself felt, the bolls were becoming more and more contrary about giving up their treasure, and we were beginning to itch and sweat. Where the strap pulled against my shoulder, a wet stripe had formed on my shirt. Worst of all, the ends of my fingers were raw from contact with the dry, abrasive pods. We began talking about dinner, which rural southerners had in the middle of the day.

"Dinner?" shouted Ada. "Jesus Lord, the sun not nowheres near noon high and these children already talking about wanting to eat. It's a good two hours yet before I got to go back and start cooking."

The other pickers, most of whom had known us all our lives, saw our discouragement and, thinking that they might boost our morale, contributed handfuls of cotton to our sacks as they passed us by on their own rows. That was not enough, however, to offset the growing heat and scratching bolls. The enchantment had worn thin. When we reached the end of our row, I told Ada I thought we ought to keep our promise to Bigmama and go on home, now that the cool of the morning was over.

A COTTON PICKIN' STORY

"Maybe you better," she said.

Our fruit jars still had a lot of water in them, and, since there was no point in lugging it all the way back to the house, we started to pour it out. One of the younger men suggested, with a big grin to the others, that our cotton would weigh more if we poured the water into our sacks. That sounded like a wonderful idea, and we drained the last drop; then we started home with our wet cotton.

"Why don't you just leave your sacks here, being's you'll be coming back this afternoon?" asked old Jordan, the colored field boss.

"I'm not sure my grandmother wants us to pick any more," I said, clutching my cotton to me and backing toward the road.

"Well, leave it here anyhow and I'll have it weighed up when the scales come by. No use toting it all the way to the big house," urged the old man. "I'll keep a good eye on it and see to it that it's weighed just right," he added when he saw the hesitation on our faces.

Each of the regular pickers had a large burlap sheet into which he emptied his sack periodically during the day. Near sundown the overseer came by with a beam-type scale, weighed the piles of cotton, and had them tossed into a high-boarded wagon to be hauled off to the gin. I did not want to let go of my cotton; somehow I did not relish the idea of its being mixed in with the rest and losing its identity. Besides, if I took the field boss's suggestion, I would have to wait until dark to find out how much it weighed.

"We might as well take it on home with us now," I said. "We've got a scale there."

As I remember it, the going rate for cotton picking that year was sixty cents a hundredweight, but my grandfather solemnly contracted with my sister and me for five cents a pound. When Bigmama had first said we could pick, I had figured out I could gather at least two hundred pounds if I worked early morning and late afternoon every day for a week. That would mean ten dollars. I was practically rich.

My picking ardor had been considerably dampened by the first morning's experience, however. I was not sure I wanted to work any more; certainly not until I had rested up a few days. So what I now had in my sack might have to do. All the way home, as the hot dirt road burned into the bottoms of my bare feet and the load on my shoulder got heavier and heavier, I tried to guess how many pounds I had. Maybe as many as thirty; the sack certainly felt like it. Better not count on more than twenty, though; that way I would be pleasantly surprised. My sister told me she was sure she had picked at least fifty pounds, and I smiled at her naiveté.

"You got back early," called my grandmother from the side veranda as we crept up the back steps. It was wonderfully cool on the porch after our walk in the sun, but though I was tempted to flop down in a Brumby rocker, I disciplined myself and asked Bigmama to weigh our cotton right away.

She went into the house, got out the big kitchen scale, and helped me balance my sack on the platform. The pointer swung around to eight and a half pounds and stopped. We put my sister's bag on the scale and the hand came to rest at five and three quarters.

Seeing our faces Bigmama asked, "Well, for goodness sakes, how much did you *think* you'd picked?"

"I thought I had about ten pounds," I said, quickly recovering my poise. My sister didn't say anything.

Bigmama nodded wisely, her usually snappy brown eyes softening. "Forty-three cents is nothing to turn up your nose at, you know, especially your first morning. And remember, you earned it yourself."

That I certainly had done. With my own two work-reddened hands and the literal sweat of my furrowed, feverish brow.

The Cowbells

Mary Roxie Edwards

DADDY Jesse was cleaning the carriage harness in the shade of a chinaberry tree out in the broad backyard. As the Little Boy approached, he began to talk: "Here yo' come now, lickin' yo' fingers. I know yo' been pesterin' yo' ma to death an' she done loaded you off on me! If you ain't been eatin' de icin' off de cake! Child, don't you know no better?"

"They hadn't put it on, Daddy Jesse!"

"Don't make no diffunce! Never was too much icin' fer any cake, an' dis·one is sho' a big cake! La! La La! Just ter think, Little Miss is twenty years ol'!

"It don't seem no time since dey called me in to see dat precious baby! An' didn't dis ol' nigger feel proud when yo' gran-ma say to me, "Daddy Jess, I'm goin' to let you name her!"

"A lump come up back o' my mouf an' I had ter swaller fas' ter keep fum cryin' — I was so happy!"

"Did you name her, Daddy Jesse?"

"Honey, don't yo' hear me comin' to dat very pint? 'Course I named her! Says I — when I got de best of dat lump—'Missus, I'm goin' ter name her for yo' sister, de bes' woman de good Lord ever made, an' fer de state whar she was borned!'

" 'I knowed you was,' says she, laughin' fit to kill hersef; an' dat's de way Little Miss Virginia got her name! But I done fergot! — What yo' gran'ma send you out here fer besides gittin' rid o' you? Ax me, ax me, an' move erlong!"

"Daddy Jesse, she said you'd tell me why Mr. Middle-brooks put bells on all of his cows."

"Oomhoo! Curisority agin! You got mo' curisority than anything on the plantation 'ceptin' dat coon what Miss Ben catched in her henhouse awhile back.

"But dat sho is de way to fin' out things—ax an' keep on axin'! You say yo' gran'ma sont you out here fer me to tell you 'bout dem cows?

"Well, come erlong an' set down here on de harness box, 'cause I never could talk to folks far off. An' don't you lay hands on nothin'!

"I got to git dis harness shinin' fer to meet de quality folks what's comin' over fum Macon to Little Miss' party termorrer. If you so much as lay a finger on a strap or buckle, I'm done with dat cow story for good!"

I won't move a thing, Daddy Jesse."

"I knows you won't, honey, ef it's nailed down or drove in de groun' — whar was I?"

" 'Bout the cows—"

"Sholy! I was erbout ter ax you is you ever been down to de cowlot of a Christmas mornin' an' see all de cows down on dey knees a-prayin'?

"No, Daddy Jesse, I didn't know that animals knew how to pray."

"An' raised right here on dis place! You sho mus' move aroun' with yo' eyes shet! You must suttinly have a heap to learn!

"Well, dey do pray on a Christmas mornin', which is more dan a lot o' folks do! But, as I was sayin', ol' Henry, Mr. Middlebrooks' man, went down to de cowpen 'bout de crack o' day las' Christmas an' all de cows was down on dey knees 'ceptin' Betty, de bell cow.

"Henry come erlong back an' tol' Mr. Middlebrooks dat dey all look up at Betty, an' up in de sky, with dey mouths a-workin'; dat dey kept on a-lookin' an' a-lookin' till he sot de milk bucket down on de groun' an' went erlong back.

"He tell Mr. Middlebrooks he got to have a bell for ev'y one of dem cows — a bell like ol' Betty's — for dey was down on deir knees an' prayin' for bells. Mr. Middlebrooks look at him hard an' say:

" 'What crazy notion done hit you now, nigger? What
does we want wid six more cowbells? One makes fuss
enough, goodness knows!'

" 'It ain't no crazy notion, Marse Waldron,' says
Henry, ' 'cause I'm jus' fum de cowlot, an' ev'y one of
dem cows was a prayin' fer a bell like Betty's, an' dey
is got to have 'em if I has to sell my Sunday coat an' Monday britches to buy 'em! When po' dum' cows pray fer
any little thing like a bell on Chrismus, dey sholy mus'
git it.'

"Well, de upshot of de case was dat Mr. Middlebrooks'
big heart landed him an' Henry at Mr. Berry's store 'bout
de time he got de front do' open.

"When Mr. Berry hear 'bout dem bells an' de prayin'
he laugh hissef 'mos' into a fit, but it didn't make no
diffunce to Mr. Middlebrooks. He come along back with
Henry, a-bringin' six new cowbells an' six new leather
collars.

"When he got out at de front door, he says to Henry,
says he, 'Henry, seein' as how it's too late to put de bells
an' collars in de cows' stockin's, the bes' thing you can
do is to slip down to the lot an' hang 'em on their necks
with a howdye for 'em all!" They do say that nigger
fairly shouted, he was so proud.

"Erlong, about breakfus, here come Henry up fum
de lot, drivin' dem cows. All de white folks was on de
front porch, just a-laughin'. Old Betty was in de lead,
an' all de other cows strung out behin'! My, but dem bells
sho did play a tune!"

"What tune did they play, Daddy Jesse?"

"Old Henry said it was de tune dey always sing in de
church after de prayin' is all done, called de Sockdology—
'praise God fum whom all blessings flow!'

"But all along the road the people would run out of
de houses to see what was comin', an' de chillun thought
it mus' be a circus.

"When dey got to de bend in de road whar ol' Miss
Sykes' pastur' is — whar Mr. Middlebrooks kept his
cows — Henry says de church bells broke out fer Chrismus an 'de cows all stop to listen, an' ev'y las' one of 'em
shook her head an made her bell jine in de racket!"
Daddy Jesse gave an imitation of a cow shaking her

head, much to the Little Boy's delight.

"But nex' day," he continued, much pleased with himself, "ol' Miss Sykes come a-pitchin' down to tell Mr. Middlebrooks he must take dem bells off dem fool cows or take de cows out of her pastur', for dey almost run her crazy. Mr. Middlebrooks say he can't do dat, for it would break old Henry's heart.

"Miss Sykes up an' say then, 'If dat's de case why not hang 'em all on Henry?' Dis sorter got Mr. Middle-brooks' blood up, an' he called Henry an' all de hands together an' took a piece of his own lan' down by the swamp whar there was water an' cool, dark shade, an' whar de grass was long an' green, an' dey run a fence aroun' it fer de cows.

"An' that's what come of de cows prayin' on dat Chrismus mornin'. Henry says de good Lord give 'em more dan dey axed for."

A Lesson in Judgment

Hubert B. Owens

I REALLY had nothing against George Mayfield. In fact, I would have given him one of the highest grades in the class if it hadn't been for an error in judgment. But let me start at the beginning.

It was May, 1928. I was teaching my first class in landscape architecture at the University of Georgia. It was my long-awaited opportunity to pass on to students four years younger than I everything I had learned about life in general and landscape gardening in particular. This is how I met George Mayfield.

George was a good student who showed genuine interest in all phases of horticulture — fruit and vegetable production, floriculture, and the growing of ornamental plants. He had even spent the previous summer in North Africa studying the life habits of the microscopic wasp which pollinates the fig.

George was also interested in the propagation of Camellia Japonica. At that time this handsome shrub was scarcely known and little planted except in a few of the older gardens of the Deep South and in conservatories. When George learned that I had never seen the ancient twenty and thirty-foot specimens, he insisted that I drive to Savannah and inspect these remarkable plants in his cousin's garden.

Toward the end of the first quarter he renewed the invitation and it was agreed that we would make the trip in his Ford roadster the third weekend in November.

Athens and northeast Georgia had an abnormally heavy rainfall that year. It rained continuously, day and night, the week prior to our departure. Nevertheless, we decided to depart Friday morning and return on Sunday. Since there were few paved roads, we had to allow a whole day for what is a five-hour trip today.

It was against my better judgment to depart at the stipulated hour in a heavy downpour that Friday morning. Each day the papers had published stories about approaching flood conditions in some of the less hilly areas of the state. Besides, as a result of the prolonged cold and dampness, I began to notice symptoms of a sore throat.

My hesitancy served only to fire George's enthusiasm. The first few hours — through Oglethorpe and Wilkes Counties — saw slow but steady progress, despite the fact that the miles of unpaved sand-clay roadway were a continuous series of mud puddles, interrupted very infrequently by narrow ribbons of pavement.

Early in the afternoon we encountered our first real obstacle. We reached Little River, between Washington and Thomson, to find this stream was no longer a little tributary of the Savannah River. Instead, it was a turbulent, red clay-colored torrent, which had risen high enough to submerge the floor of the bridge under two feet of water that morning.

A few farmers had gathered in the rain to witness the spectacle. Even bouyant-spirited George could see that it was impossible to make a crossing in the roadster. I proposed that we return to Athens, but my companion would hear nothing of it. He inquired for directions to Thomson and the assembled natives outlined an exceedingly devious route which, they assured us, would keep us on high ground all the way.

We set forth. After traversing most of the back roads of western McDuffie County in a continuous downpour of rain, getting stuck in mudholes several times, we arrived in Thomson just before dark.

We ate supper at the Knox House, an old-fashioned small town hotel which served delicious meals family style. Sad to relate, a few years ago it became a casualty of the fast-moving order of things. My only memory of our brief sojourn at this extinct oasis is the welcome meal and the awe-inspired manner in which we were regarded by the regular patrons when they learned we had driven there from Athens that same day. How, they asked, did we do it when all the roads in the Thomson-Augusta area had been declared practically impassable?

This information sounded ominous. I, who was George's senior by four years, felt it was my duty to recommend that we remain at Knox House for the night. I admitted that I was getting a cold. By this time, however, George was warming to the challenge of adventure. He assured me that we had already covered the worst part of the journey; that it was not far to Waynesboro; that he knew a shortcut which would make it unnecessary to go through Augusta; and that if we could reach Waynesboro that night we could easily get to Savannah the next morning. I acquiesced.

The short stretch of pavement leading toward Augusta from Thomson was soon behind us. Ahead of us were long stretches of unpaved road. Now we began to make detours in order to stick to high ground. The details of that part of the journey are not clear, but I recall that when we left Thomson we also left the clay lands behind and the soil became a kind of soggy sand. We traversed miles and miles of cotton, corn, and peanut fields in the rain, and got stuck innumerable times. Despite my raincoat, I became thoroughly soaked each time we hunted for pieces of timber at farm houses or pine boughs in the woodlands to get the roadster out of mudholes.

I can well remember being stuck in a beauty of a puddle in a place where our little-traveled trail in supposedly high ground emerged from a pine woods and entered a cotton field. The rain persisted, after a long, unsuccessful struggle to extract the roadster, we saw an approaching light in the forest.

It turned out to be a truckload of corn whiskey a bootlegger was running through from the mountains of North Georgia to the prohibition desert of Macon. In addition to his approximately 100-gallon cache of white lightning, the bootlegger had brought along six strong men who could literally lift the large truck from any hole or raging stream.

Since our bogged-down roadster was in their path, these

laborers were directed to transport our vehicle to safe ground. Needless to say, George was delighted, and from this point enjoyed the jaunt more than ever. He made certain that we kept in front of the caravan of contraband with its muscle men. They assisted us for several miles, each time we got stuck in an overflowing brook or one of the endless puddles. Unfortunately, about 10 p.m. when we reached a small town called Blythe, our ways parted.

By this time I was practically exhausted, and George did not put forth any resistance when I insisted that we get a place to spend the night. The only accommodations we could find in the heavy downpour was a large upstairs room over a combination grist mill-store-filling station at the intersection of the two main roads. The owner told us he had no beds available, but that there was a large rug stored in the room on which we could sleep. This we tried to do — in our soggy clothes, doubling half of the large rug back over us for cover.

Shortly after settling down, we became aware of one other minor inconvenience. Our refuge was situated beside a small mill pond on a stream. The rains had saturated all the ground around the pond and flooded most of the nearby area. As a result the service station's large underground gasoline storage tank was washed up. Although still anchored to its pump, the flowing water caused it to beat against the building all night.

The rain ceased some time before dawn. When I arose from my couch of dusty rug, I realized that my tentative symptoms of the day before had developed into a full-fledged sore throat and headache. But encouraged by the fact that it had stopped raining, we pushed ahead. We traveled for miles over water-logged plantation roads through peanut and cotton patches, pine woods, and pastures, and finally arrived at the small town of Hepzibah at noon.

By this time the sun was shining, but I felt miserable because of my ever sorer throat. After eating a sandwich, I purchased a box of aspirin at one of the few red brick stores in Hepzibah. The owner directed me to a hydrant at the sidewalks where I could get a drink of water to chase down the tablets. I was standing there when a large Buick, completely covered with mud, drove up in front of me. Out

stepped a young man dressed in once-white knickerbockers, a once-white shirt, a dark sleeveless sweater, and high boots. His ensemble was almost as bespattered with mud as the Buick.

"This is a hell of a note," he announced without any preliminaries. "At this very moment I am supposed to be in Waynesboro at a party celebrating my own wedding which is scheduled for tonight."

Our new acquaintance then explained that he had started the 30-mile trip from his home in Augusta to Waynesboro that morning. The back seat of his wire-wheeled 1928 Buick sedan was piled high with boxes containing a bride's and several bridesmaids' bouquets. (The local Waynesboro florist was unable to get the flowers stipulated by the bride because train service had ceased three days ago, he told us.) Clothes, including the wedding tails, were hanging from hooks. Two pieces of beautiful new luggage in the front seat next to the driver contrasted conspicuously but glamorously with this muddy car on the unpaved Main Street of Hepzibah.

This accidental meeting with the romantic traveler from Augusta — whose name I cannot remember but whom I shall call Ted — transfigured George into a state of absolute exhilaration. While we ate lunch, before Ted's arrival, I had practically succeeded in discouraging him by firmly announcing that I was no longer the least bit interested in seeing camellias at Savannah, but that my best judgment dictated that I stop at the first half-way decent hotel and put my ill self to bed.

George assured me that when we got to Waynesboro — which was "no distance at all" from Hepzibah — we would contact Sidney Cox, a cousin his own age who lived there. We would then inquire about the condition of the highway to Savannah, and, if it was impassable, we would spend that night with the Coxes. I did not like the idea, but the thought of a bed in Waynesboro seemed like a haven in the disrupted world around me, so again I agreed to proceed.

Ted joined the caravan, with George and me leading the way in our roadster with the top down. The sun was shining brightly by this time and the sky, the trees, the goldenrods and asters along the roadsides, the miles of cotton plants with their abundant, unharvested bolls of rain-damaged white fleece and even the pools of quiet water standing in all the low places along the road took on the appearance of calm which inevitably follows a storm. Although my intermittent dosages of aspirin improved my spirits to a degree, this sudden look of innocence which nature assumed made me vaguely uneasy.

The journey went fine, though, for the first few miles. Then we encountered water on the highway again. Several times Ted, the only member of the threesome with boots, had to walk slowly hundreds of yards through large ponds in the road to guide our conveyances. George drove his car and I drove Ted's Buick. After countless detours at snail's pace, we reached the village of McBean.

At this point we learned that the Briar Creek bridge was completely inundated and that no traffic had crossed it that day. McBean's inhabitants doubted our ever reaching Waynesboro because, as one individual put it, "the remainder of the way to Briar Creek is full of mud holes and anybody would be stupid to try to get there in a little car, much less a big new Buick."

Ted therefore decided to leave his car with a farmer in McBean. At George's urging, he transferred his essential and non-essential wedding gear to the roadster and the three of us plodded on.

Dusk was arriving when we reached the north side of Briar Creek. It was indeed a raging torrent, at least a fourth of a mile wide. A lone man who had spent the afternoon watching the moving water and other sightseers, happened to be departing for his home as we arrived. He looked us over and said, "Do any of you happen to be the fellow who is supposed to get married?"

"I am that very person," Ted said as he jumped from the car. (He, George, and I had long since removed our footwear and rolled our trousers above our knees. We were covered with mud.)

"There's been a gang of young people waiting for you on the other side of the creek all day," said the old man.

"How on earth can I get to the other side?" asked Ted.

"A fellow with a bateau who lives on the other side has ferried a few people across today," the man replied, "but he just quit for the day."

By this time the sky had become overcast and dusk had set in. Except for the swirling, rapidly flowing stream before us, a wet stillness had settled over the Briar Creek swamp. Only a dim outline of moss-draped trees could be seen on the opposite shore through the mist.

"I've simply got to get to Waynesboro at once," Ted said, "and I hope you can help me find some kind of boat."

It was clear that the elderly man in overalls already knew the circumstances and did not need to hear more. He turned, walked to the water's edge, and without any words of warning let out a terrific yodeling sort of howl the like of which my ears had never heard.

Between brief pauses, this same prolonged, unearthly noise was repeated a few times. Shortly, a similar idiomatic yodel was faintly heard from the far shore. Our new-made friend then began shouting something incomprehensible to the Briar Creek boatman. Apparently he understood, for it was not long until we saw him descend the sloping south bank and launch his two oar-propelled craft.

While we waited for his arrival, George reluctantly arranged to leave his Ford with the north bank farmer. George and I also agreed that Ted's mission rated top priority and that he should be the first to make the crossing.

Despite the fast-moving current, the boat was dexterously maneuvered through the swirl pools and brought to a safe landing where our road intersected the creek. When it was secured, the agile middle-aged boatman walked up the slippery rise, greeted us and, with a diamond-in-the-rough type of sincerity, expressed his sympathy to the bridegroom.

Ted lost little time loading the craft with his cargo of paraphernalia. The suitcases were placed in the bottom of the wet boat, then several large paper boxes of flowers, and topping off the pile were evening clothes, a woolen business suit, and a pair of tweed knickerbockers. He mounted the narrow front seat. The boatman in the rear seat paddled the light craft in the direction of Waynesboro. This was the last I ever saw of Ted.

After a while the boat returned. I felt worse than ever, and knew that my cold had developed into a substantial case of flu. No urging was necessary for George and me to embark. After we had passed midstream and were approaching the south shore, I commented that we were now passing near the top end of a telegraph pole which protruded only eight inches above the water.

"Yes," said our pilot, breathing deeply between oar strokes. "If you had been near this spot this morning you would have seen a shoe salesman drownd-ed."

"How did it happen?" asked George.

"A washed-up tree came floating down the creek and looked like it was heading for us," he replied. "The current was strong and I knew I could miss the tree, but the salesman got excited, stood up in the boat, lost his balance, and fell into the creek.

"Nearly turned the boat over," he continued, "and he sure was grabbing after them sample shoes when he went under. Ain't found the body yet."

The gruesomeness of this tragedy, heightened by the impersonal manner in which it was related, did not boost my spirits. But George and I were soon safely deposited on the south bank of Briar Creek, where we bade our oarsman goodbye. In a short while some accommodating soul drove us to Waynesboro where we were brought to the home of the Coxes.

I do not recall whether Sidney was at home, but his mother, father, and sister, Ria, could not have been nicer. I was not only embarrassed at finding myself an uninvited guest in the home of these hospitable strangers, but also chagrinned that my cold made me a contagious intruder.

Mrs. Cox did not seem at all disturbed, however. She took my temperature, conferred briefly by telephone with the family physician, and prescribed that I go to bed immediately. This I did with profound relief, while adventurous George excused himself. That same evening, I learned later, he hitch-hiked to Savannah.

A day of rest rendered me sufficiently recovered to return to Athens, although it took another week of bed rest to regain some perspective on who or what was responsible for this remarkable misadventure. But as soon as I was on my feet again, I was forced to abandon this provocative but fruitless line of thought. I had to plunge immediately into the work which had been piling up during my illness.

My most pressing task was the evaluation of design plans submitted by my landscape gardening students in lieu of a final exam for the first quarter. As I looked through the plans I realized that the most surprising two weeks of my life were to end in yet one more surprise. George Mayfield, one of my best students, had committed a serious blunder. His design showed what I considered an inexcusable error in judgment — a whole row of camellias set much too close to the house. Reluctantly, I gave him a failing grade.

The Day Off

Walt Stephens

I T could have been the silence after the last notes of the
Whip-O-Will's song, or maybe the final challenge of the
great horned owl that woke the boy from his dreams. He
sat upright and looked out the window. Two thoughts that
had been in his mind last night were the first to enter this
morning: tomorrow would be Ma's birthday and he had to
hurry to the river or the bass would have stopped their
morning feeding.

He jumped out of bed, danced lightly about the floor,
then pulled on his overalls. Slipping into the kitchen, he
picked up the lunch his mother had packed, and paused,
listening to his father's snores. Outside, the sun was beginning to filter through the trees and lift the cool dampness
from the piney air. He breathed deeply and smiled — it
would be a pretty day, and likely the sunset would be
bright orange — but by that time the day would be over
and his day off from work would be only a memory.

Spring plowing was finished Friday, and all day he had
followed the mule, stopping once in a while to bust a clod
of the black bottomland and catch the worms to put in his
front pocket. At the end of the row he dropped each into a
can thinking, "Might be, you'll catch Old-Big."

Last night at the supper table, he had asked his father
about Old-Big. It seemed that everyone near the Okefenokee Swamp had hooked the monster bass and a rare
few had almost touched him before he broke the line or
straightened the hook.

"Yep, son, three years ago, 'bout this time, I was down there where the water goes round the big cypress stump. Baited up with a shiner, and throwed it in at the first calm water. Well, when the minner sunk, Old-Big grabbed it up and busted straight out into the river. He jumped one time, and when he did, I near swallowed my terbacca. Must of weighed 10 pounds. He jumped that one time, then just flat went deep and even my wading in didn't keep him from busting the line."

Later when he had pulled up the covers, his dreams filled with a bent fish pole and a line — knotted in the middle — swinging taut. Then his imagination conquered the fish and changed to a vision of Mr. Johnston's round eyes and sagging mouth as the fish was weighed: these eyes narrowed and the mouth turned to a frown when he handed over the prize. Probably, just before dawn, he saw his mother, hands trembling a little and eyes shiny, as she untied the ribbon and slowly opened the box — being careful not to tear the paper.

Sunlight was bouncing off the roof of the woodshed as the boy found his sack of hooks, line, corks, the can of worms and, most important, the shiny store-bought cane pole.

This was the first real fishing pole he'd ever owned. Usually a long reed cut from the swamp near the river with a bit of line tied on was enough — but not today. Today he had a pole just like Pa's.

Saturday morning three weeks ago he had bought it at Johnston's General Store. It was like something wished for that had turned to real life. He had saved ever since Christmas, but the saving hadn't been hard, only slow. He had enough left over for a few hooks and a red and white cork.

Going down the sidewalk, he was watching its varnished surface caught in the sunlight, when he saw his mother, one hand holding a bag full of groceries, staring into the store window, looking at something blue with black fringe on it.

"What're you lookin' at, Ma?" he asked as he came close.

"That hat in there, I don't believe I ever saw a prettier one."

"Well, why don't you get it?"

She turned and looked at him, smiled faintly and said, "Now you know there are a hundred things that we need more than I need a hat; sides, don't believe I'd know what to do with one as pretty as that if I had it."

She was right. There were things they needed worse than a hat — worse than a fishing pole. He'd thought about nothing the whole week; only fishing equipment — not about things that other folks might want — might need — only about himself.

"Look, Ma," he burst out, "I'll take this pole back into the store and get my money and then you can buy that hat; I'll even trade back the hooks. I don't need them."

"How you carry on, child; don't be thinkin' such things, you done saved for three months now, and I'm not gonna take it away from you."

"But I want to."

"No, that's final, besides, the hat would cost more than you and I put together could spare."

The boy looked at the pole this morning the same as he had done that day. "I shouldn't of bought you. She wanted that hat — if I hadn't been so selfish I'd of got it for her. But that's past; I'll just fish real hard and hope."

Soon he was in the pine flats where gallberries, broken only by clumps of palmetto, grew thick on each side of the road. Unseen swamp critters watched him, then scurried to hide making rattling sounds in the leaves. Ahead a doe, silent as fog, crossed the road, and disappeared into the brush.

In a tall pine, a blue jay lit, and started to shuffle along the branch, making pieces of bark fall to the ground.

"You're just the color of that hat Ma wanted," he said to the bird, "cept it had fringe around the front."

Last week when he had gone into town to get the mule harness repaired, he had wandered back into Johnston's store.

"What do you need, boy?" Mr. Johnston had said, looking up from lighting the pot-bellied stove.

"How much is that spool of fishing line over there?"

"Now boy, you don't want that line; it costs too much, besides it's stronger than you'll ever need."

"How much is it?"

"What're you figuring on doing, catching a whale?"

"Might be. How much is it?"

"You fool country boys always got something wild on your mind — always trying to outdo everybody else."

"Could I see it just a minute?"

"You figuring on buying it?"

"No sir — I just wanted to look at it."

"Well, look from where you are. Now what'd a boy like you want with a line that was nigh on to 30-pound test? Maybe you're figuring on catching Old-Big — huh?"

"Could be."

"Ha, tell you what — you catch Old-Big and I'll give you that line — free."

"Instead, would you give my Ma that blue hat in the window for her birthday?"

"See what I mean about these farm boys, always starting something they got no business trying? Something there ain't no hope in the world for them to do?" He was talking to a customer who had just walked into the store. "I just offered him a roll of line to catch Old-Big — but he ain't satisfied and wants that blue hat yonder in the window."

"Well, you afraid to bet with him?" It was Mr. Toms, vice-president of the town bank.

"No, I ain't afraid — boy, you catch that fish, then the blue hat in the window is yours. Mind you, though you gotta catch him and bring him in here."

THE jay cried once and flew to another pine, leaving a vacant branch and hollow dreams. "There ain't no use even hoping. I couldn't catch Old-Big If I had a hundred-pound test line and a year to do nothin' but fish," the boy said to himself.

When he rounded the last bend in the road and could see sunlight dancing on the river, he began the awkward stumbling trot that only a 10-year old knows.

He stopped in a few yards and looked at the last clump of palmetto. Wild hogs had already been here this morning and had dug shallow trenches looking for acorns. Their heart-shaped footprints led through the palmetto and down the bank.

"If them scoundrels have been in the river they'll have ruined the fishing for sure."

He crawled through the fringe of brush. A ribbon of

mud still trailed downstream from where the pigs had
wallowed and drops of the river trickled in filling their
footprints.

The easy water behind the big cypress stump showed
no sign of fish, much less Old-Big. He would have been the
first to go when the hogs came. In the slack area near the
opposite shore, a bream struck. That wasn't Old-Big,
though. He probably wouldn't come back till after dark.

The boy wrapped a strand of black cord around the
tip of the pole. The line was old and weak now, knotted
in the middle where it had once broken. He tested it and
the knot easily separated in his fingers.

"Foot, that won't do a'tall. What if Old-Big had been
on? That wouldn't have been enough pull to even set the
hook," he said, looking again at the trace of muddy water at
the hog wallow.

He retied the knot and tested it to his satisfaction this
time. Wrinkling his forehead, he mashed on a sinker and
tied a hook onto the line. The cork was snapped on and
now no finer fishing gear could be found in any of the
stores in Waycross, Brunswick, or even in Atlanta.

After kinking his biggest and juiciest worm onto the
hook, he eased down the sandbank till he was squatting,
feet in the water. With a smooth motion, he swung the
pole to let the bait drop behind the cypress stump.

The instant the cork settled and the faint waves from
the splash started outward, it disappeared. His heart made
a mighty jump, then sank when a struggling warmouth
came from the excited water.

"Ah, come here, you little fighter. You'll shore be good
to eat," he said aloud, trying to outtalk his disappointment.

He fished with a concentrated intensity while the sun
climbed its ladder in the sky and then prepared to come
down. By then, the warmouth and bream had quit biting
so he laid his pole aside and crawled into the shade.
Settling against a tree he unwrapped the sandwiches and
brushed off a couple of black ants.

At first he didn't recognize the grunting sound he heard
in the distance, but now it was close enough to have some
meaning — somewhere back up the road, the group of wild
hogs was coming back to the river.

The boy jumped up and ran toward the sounds. "Git,

git you scoundrels, you come back down here and you'll
ruin everything!" he shouted.

The black sow stopped, ears perked forward; a single
commanding grunt silenced the four little ones. She was
frozen, head lowered — then the sound came again. "Git
outta here, you hog!" She whirled, grunting the scattering
signal, then ran back into the woods. They would have to
find a new place to wallow in the river.

The boy returned and finished his sandwich, then settled
back to his station beside the water.

The midafternoon sun brought out moisture beads and
these turned into small rivulets which ran down the neck,
then dropped onto the sand. The river was dark and cool
looking like the shadows in a cave when seen from the outside, but the boy did not dare lay down his pole to strip his
clothes and jump into the inviting shallows. He might be
in the river the exact moment Old-Big decided to return, or
his moving about might scare the fish. The moist heat and
silence burned his thoughts away so that he sat staring
but not seeing the cork and line drift too close to the base
of the cypress, then remain in one place, not floating down-

stream as usual or upstream against the current, when it hit a swirl.

He mechanically lifted the pole to swing the bait into a new place, but couldn't; it was caught on a root. He tugged lightly, careful not to move quickly or put too much strain on the knotted line, but for no use. He would have to move downstream and pull from a different angle. As he moved slowly a breaking wave and the racing shadow of a huge fish marked the path and place to which Old Big had returned and again fled.

"He's gone again," the boy thought. "Probably figured I was another hog come to the wallow. Probably'll be dark 'fore he comes back or more'n likely won't come back a' tall."

He pulled the hook from the root, then looked again at the cool water. It would be all right to swim, since the fish had left. But he would try as hard as he could and fish his best; he might be beaten, but he would not give up.

THE sun was sliding down rapidly now. First the shadows crawled across the river, then the sand bar and finally the trees on the east side. The last worm was gone — gradually dissolved by the nibbling of small fish which were so dainty the cork had not even trembled.

The last of his day off was nearing. But it had not been wasted; he had fought hard and the solitude and the murmuring river which granted an occasional bite were adequate rewards for the hours spent. If no big fish had found the worms, that was all right, too, because they would be there another day.

Stiff in the knees, he stood and held against the red fading sunset the small string of fish. Old-Big would have been a good end for a fine day, and a prize for his mother. It would have been the only thing he could give her, but he had known the chances were too small in the beginning. When the day was new, he had dared a hope. But now he saw how foolish his hope had been. Maybe Mr. Johnston was right; maybe a country boy was always starting something he couldn't finish and therefore ought not to begin — yet if no start were made he might as well have been one of the swamp hogs, beginning here and ending where he had begun; never improving — just remaining the same. At least he had tried.

At the top of the bank he stopped and looked back toward the base of the cypress tree. A minnow skipped across the surface and then another. Something below had frightened them.

He was suddenly staring round-eyed, his mouth open.

"Pa said last night that he used a shiner to get Old-Big to strike; I wonder —," the boy said.

He selected the smallest fish from his catch, hooked it under the top fin and again tested the knot in the middle of the line. Crawling back down the bank, he dropped the bait just behind the stump exactly as he had done at first this morning.

He could barely see the line swerving with the current, and then felt rather than saw it grow taut and the tip of the pole bend, almost cracking.

"I got you now! I got you now!" he cried. "Please don't go into that tree and get off."

But Old Big was surging toward the open river, making the water roll from the powerful strokes of his tail. The boy followed, trying to ease the strain on the line. Then the fish turned back toward the tree and dived.

The line trembled as the fish fought with its head down trying to dislodge the strange thing which stung its mouth. The tension slackened and Old-Big exploded out of the depths, seeming to hang motionless for a second, the bristling fins and huge tail beating the air.

"Don't break this line; I never seen such a fish in all my life. I gotta catch you now."

Old-Big circled away from the tree and out toward the middle of the river, but this run was not as powerful as the first one.

The boy eased toward the bank to draw the fish in closer so that he could catch him behind the gill and lift him out of the water.

The boy and fish were in the shallows. Old-Big lay sideways, its tail fanning the current. The boy waded toward him and with nervous hands tried to find the gill plate, saying "steady now — steady, boy," as though talking to a horse.

When he touched the great fish, it gave a mighty heave and rushed back toward the cypress. The boy saw the water splash, felt the pole bend, then heard the sickening twang as the line parted at the knot.

He stared at the base of the cypress, fighting back something that glazed over his eyes. But there was a great white blur, hardly noticeable in the early dark, a few feet below the roots where his line had tangled earlier. It was strong one moment, then grew weaker, like a dream, as it sank. He carefully waded into the water; it was deep here, first at his waist, then chest. As he came closer, the blur was very weak. Below the root, he found the line, broke it loose and gently pulled. The big fish offered no resistance; it had given its utmost for the last battle and had won, until the line tangled on a root, and then it had suddenly lost, and now it could fight no more.

Back on shore, the boy lay beside the fish on the sand, breathing quick — not believing.

Somewhere in the brush, the Whip-O-Will was starting its evening call.

In Time for Christmas

Frances Greene

CHRISTMAS, to Mama, was a season that began in July and ended sometime during the afternoon on Christmas Day. She started her preparations with crochet needles, balls of thread, yards of material, embroidery hoops and determination, and by Thanksgiving she had "pillow slips" decorated with pink French knots, aprons appliqued with oranges and apples, hemstitched luncheon cloths and pot holders. These she happily, though carefully, boxed and labeled for her in-laws and friends, and then she placed them on top of her hat boxes in the clothes closet where she could mentally catalog her accomplishments each time that she opened the closet door. She also switched labels at least a dozen times before delivering the gifts, always wondering aloud if Cousin Amelia would prefer pillow slips to a luncheon cloth or was it Cousin Amelia who skimped on her housework by eating off a bare table?

Gifts for Mama's immediate family, which included Papa and me, were quite another matter. She saved these presents until the last possible moment with the fervent hope that she could buy them rather than make them. Cash money at our house was scarce. Papa was a brilliant young science teacher in a small college but he was a poor one.

"Sometimes," Mama complained now and then with a toss of her auburn head, "a man can be too dedicated to his profession."

Papa agreed that a man could, but he kept right on teaching under the same arrangement; money, to him, was relatively unimportant. His needs and the needs of his family were provided. Practically all of his salary was on a trade-out basis. This included a small, square table set for three in the large school dining hall over which thin, little Miss Etta fluttered from six in the morning until nine at night; a four-room apartment on the first floor of the boys' dormitory with a porch all its own; clean clothes from the school laundry; medicine from the school infirmary; quail hunting on the school farm that supplied beef, vegetables and milk for Miss Etta's charge; gas for the car from the school garage, and good books from the school library. Man does not live by cash alone, Papa believed.

Mama, however, was never able to find a school commodity that she could wrap and place under the Christmas tree for her family, a fact that rankled her into resolving every Christmas Eve, "This time next year, I am going to have a job of my own. And no trade-outs."

To which Papa always replied, "Ummmmmmmmm."

Mama tried. She investigated a few leads but either the jobs were filled or they were not exactly suitable. After all, Papa was a college professor, and though Dean Lowndes would not frown on her cooking or waiting.tables in Miss Etta's dining hall, he would not approve of her taking orders and slinging hash in Mac's Cafe — not even for the month of December. Consequently, at least until employment reached the peak that Congress predicted, Papa was going to receive another half dozen handkerchiefs and a monogrammed night shirt. Only this year she would use blue thread instead of yellow. If Papa were not so persnickety, she would really fancy it up by sewing some of her crocheted lace around the bottom. In spite of his complete disregard for the material things in life that only money could buy, she loved him dearly, and nothing was too good for him.

With Christmas only a few weeks away, she set to with vim and vigor. She spent an entire morning cutting out yards and yards of pieces which she ran up on her machine, and took the almost completed nightshirt to the porch where she could do the handwork and enjoy the Indian summer sun at the same time. The day was quite peaceful.

The maples were shedding their yellow leaves; splashes of red on the dogwoods waved in the slight breeze. With a sigh of well being, Mama threaded her needle.

The late model car stopped at the curb. She lifted her eyes and then moved her head a little in order to see through a gap in the vines that Papa had planted and strung on wire from the bannister to the ceiling. At the sight of a strange man bouncing up the walk, she carefully folded Papa's gift and tucked it inside the basket.

The man moved quickly, and now he was flashing a friendly, disarming smile. "Your name was given to me, Mrs. Ramsey. Understand you're an energetic young lady, a go-getter." He propped a foot on the bannister, balanced his brief case near the knee and opened it to remove reams of paper.

Mama wet her lips and watched the man swiftly leaf through the papers until he came to the copy he wanted. "I am not a salesman," he interrupted her thoughts hurriedly. "I sell my services to newspapers. Your local weekly was delighted to sign on the dotted line. I am," he paused to smile at Mama again, "going to put this town on the map. I am going to have the STAR in every home in this county and in every county in this state. AND YOU'RE GOING TO HELP ME."

Mama blinked. She was already a subscriber — or at least the paper came to Papa because he wrote a science column once a month.

"We're having a contest, young lady. It's never been tried in this town before, and YOU'RE going to win.

"We're getting the prizes right here in town so everybody can see what he's working toward. And," his eyes sparkled at Mama, "there's nothing to buy at all. All you have to do is sell subscriptions to the paper. Easy? Easy," he answered himself. "See for yourself, little lady. Look at these prizes, will you."

Mama glanced at the list. She could never hope to win first place; anybody with any sense and money could invest some cash to get the new car. She did not want the bedroom suite and she certainly had no use for a building lot — not unless the school started a lumber yard, and French knots she could make without a sewing machine.

"Wouldn't any one of those prizes look fabulous, simply

fabulous, under the Christmas tree?" He winked and smiled again. "Everybody wins something. Whether you sell one subscription or 1,000 subscriptions, you HAVE TO WIN SOMETHING."

Mama nodded once, not really hearing him now, but studying the fifteenth prize. "It this a real bird dog?" she asked.

The man looked at the list. "As real as rain, young lady. I seen him myself at Bud Anderson's kennels."

Mama wet her lips again. Papa would be completely overwhelmed; he would still be gasping for joy on New Year's day. "My husband always wanted a bird dog," she explained simply. "He hunts at the college farm, and he always has to take me along to shoo the quail from the haystacks."

The stranger coughed and cleared his throat. "But that's number fifteen . . ."

Mama nodded. The perfect Christmas gift had suddenly presented itself. For the first time in her life, she could really give a store bought present unless . . . "There isn't a rule against setting your goal is there?" she asked quickly.

But the man had found the contract, and though he made an effort to force a sparkle to his eyes, his voice was not too enthusiastic as he handed her a pen. "Sign here, please," he told her. "And good luck."

Mama's invasion of the fourth estate began that night at the dinner table when she casually mentioned to Papa that she would need the car every afternoon in order to canvass the county for subscriptions. He nodded once and grunted, "Hmmmmmmmmmmm."

Miss Etta, who stood at his elbow to make her usual check on the silver and water glasses, winked slyly at Mama. She was in on the secret. How else could Mama wangle sandwiches and a thermos of coffee to carry along for her lunch?

For the first two weeks, subscriptions to the paper sold well. Horace Abercrombie was in number one position with the new car practically in the bag. Elvira Leatherwood ranked number two, and she had already selected a fringed bedspread to go on the bed that she was sure to win. But by the fourth week, both contestants and subscriptions were slowing up. And Mama was forced to take to the hills — a

section of the county with rutted red clay roads that mean-
dered through fields and woods and across creeks and gully
washes. Mama drove the car into places where wagons
feared to tread, and once she spent two hours in a barn
dodging a pitchfork loaded with hay only to have the old
man pause finally, lean the fork against the side of the
stall and scratch his head thoughtfully. "Iffen I could read,
chile, I'd surely take your paper," he assured her.

Nevertheless, Mama's spirits were high. She had a goal,
a purpose. She was going to give Papa something that he
had always wanted and could not afford; he would now
have a sporting chance with the birds. After all, he could
control a dog.

Papa was quite aware of her labors but completely un-
aware of her motive. Shaking his head and ignoring the
glances and giggles that went on between Mama and Miss
Etta, he wondered silently how he and the thin innertubes
would hold out?

Neither held up very well. By five o'clock on the last
day of the contest, Papa was pumping two flat tires in
order to get to town in time for the festivities. Mr. Roberts
was resplendent in his policeman's uniform that he wore
only twice a year, and he stood at the corner of the highway
and Main Street to stop all traffic. A platform, bearing
red crepe paper streamers, had been erected in front of
the newspaper office, and suddenly the entire town seemed
to converge onto the intersection at one time. Mr. Roberts
happily lifted and waved his arms and hands as if he had
been born to his job.

"Does he know?" Miss Etta whispered to Mama as they
stopped next to the post office door. Naturally she meant
Papa.

Mama shook her head, all the while watching Jim
Carter, the auctioneer, look over the list handed to him
by the editor.

"Shhhhhhh," a woman hissed at Miss Etta. "Can't hear
nothing if everybody decides to talk," she complained to
her companion.

Jim Carter lifted both arms. "PU-LEESE," he begged.

The crowd hushed; necks craned.

"I'm going to ask all the contestants to come right up
here on this platform with me. Every last one of you . . ."

"You gonna drive that new car home, Horace," somebody yelled.

Mama quietly took her place on the platform. She felt
the bumps of excitement popping to her arms; her breathing was fast.

"Number one winner: Mr. Horace BU-ROUN," the
auctioneer shouted.

Car horns blew; Mrs. Brown screamed; folks yelled
and whistled.

Mama lifted her eyebrows indifferently.

Elvira Leatherwood won the bedroom suite. Prizes
three and four were awarded. The whistles were scattered.
Women began to pick up their children, push their way
through the crowd wanting to be the first ones to leave.

Mama listened to the names of the winners. She was
impatient now. It would have been better if she had just
asked the editor to give her the bird dog puppy that afternoon. She could have kept it hidden until Christmas morning.

"Prize number fourteen, a beautiful wrist watch. And
it's yours." He whirled, smiling broadly as he pointed a
finger at Mama.

She opened her mouth to protest. She did not want a
watch. She wanted prize number fifteen.

"You are Mrs. Ramsey, aren't you?" Jim Carter asked.

Her face paled but she walked forward stiffly. Tears
streamed from her eyes.

"Now, now . . ." the auctioneer cooed. "You deserve
it, little lady. You worked hard. A big hand, folks . . .
How 'bout it?"

Mama accepted the watch but she turned abruptly
and moved quickly down the steps. She wanted to go
home. She wanted to go right this very minute and she
wanted Papa to take her.

"Congratulations," he said, ignoring her tears.

He took her arm and propelled her to the corner. He
was always awkward when Mama could not talk, especially
when he did not know why she could not talk. "You'll enjoy the watch. I know it must be a good one."

Mama burst into tears.

"Like I said," Papa repeated, turning to look at Miss
Etta, "you need a watch."

Miss Etta reached for her handkerchief. "Men," she snorted. Her tone implied that the male species was the exact reason why she had never married.

Mama sniffed. Papa licked his dry lips. Miss Etta burst into tears. "All she wanted was the dog. For YOU," she sobbed.

Papa slowly rubbed his hand across his eyes, over his nose and along his mouth. He had never been very good at expressing his real feelings to Mama; somehow she had always understood without his having to struggle with the right words. But now Mama was not in any condition to understand anything. Words were necessary, And he said them. "Laura," he paused; his eyes were sincere, earnest. "Believe me, I had much rather have you in a haystack. Honest."

Mama sniffed. Wiping her eyes with the handkerchief, she stole a glance at Papa's face. And she knew exactly what he was trying to say. Honest.

When Somebody Cares

Cliff Sewell

IT happened in a Georgia country school years ago, the kind with black blackboards in long rooms furnished with rows of nailed down desks, a fat, round wood-burning stove at one end and a teacher's bulky desk at the other. Tall wide windows welcomed the winter sun and, on warm days, the summer breeze. On bleak dark days old-fashioned pull-shades were rolled to the top to accommodate every possible ray of light.

On a certain Monday morning in one particular grammar school classroom, forty pairs of boy and girl eyes gazed expectantly at the new teacher. With a minimum amount of confusion roll call was accomplished and the first lesson of the day, Arithmetic, was started. Ten pupils at the boards worked busily on long division, the chalk making thin squeaky noises as they figured, when a tall blue-eyed boy, several sizes too large and several years too old, stood up and ambled over to the door.

"Where are you going?" teacher asked.

"Just out and around," the boy shrugged broad shoulders.

"You forgot to ask permission."

"He goes when he wants to," the class chorused. "He can't learn, but he hasta come to school."

Joe, the boy at the door, hitched up his blue overall strap and spoke with heart-breaking indifference, "Nobody expects me to do anything. Nobody cares what I do."

"I care," teacher stated firmly.

"You do?" The blue eyes lighted a brief instant, then dulled again like headlights in a fog. "I can't do anything good," he muttered with a sort of defiant pride, "read or spell or write. I bet you can't read my writing," he challenged.

"I bet I can. At least we'll find out after written spelling today. Now go back to your seat and work the first arithmetic problem," the teacher added briskly.

The boy obeyed. He worked the problem correctly so the teacher knew the mental ability was there.

But Joe's reading was pathetic. He mispronounced simple words, stumbling and mumbling in singsong fashion, with the teacher supplying the correct pronunciation. "Now try again," teacher encouraged. "Begin at 'Harvest time—' "

"I already read," Joe squirmed.

"If at first you don't succeed, try, try again." The worn old adage rose unbidden to the teacher's lips followed by the thought, "Can't I think of something new to help this boy?"

However, Joe's second reading was considerably better.

At lunch time teacher learned from the harassed, overworked principal of Joe's harsh farm life; for years an ill father, many mouths to feed, Joe's help a necessity, weeks of absence. Now his father was well, home conditions vastly improved. But Joe had gotten so far behind he felt there was only one reprisal left to life's unfairness, desperate indifference.

This showed on his spelling paper, a triumphantly illegible scrawl which he blamed on being left-handed. To his apparent chagrin the teacher could identify all but one word. Fifteen out of twenty were misspelled.

"Most left-handed people write quite well," teacher remarked casually. "I think if you'll work slower and make larger letters your penmanship will improve, Joe."

"I can't spell," the boy insisted. But his eyes registered hope.

"You can if you study and try harder," teacher said. "If you really wanted to you could even make a hundred."

Joe looked stunned and the class appeared amazed.

One pert young miss whispered audibly, "That'll be the day!" Everyone laughed.

Several days later they regarded Joe with interest and respect when he made seventy in Spelling.

That afternoon he lingered after school, ostensibly to fill the wood box, then he stood hesitantly by teacher's desk. "Can I — I mean do you think," he winced and blushed as he inadvertantly stubbed his toe on the desk leg, then blurted, "you think I can learn?"

"I know you can." The answer was confident. "But you have to try and keep trying and not be discouraged or give up."

"Bout Spelling. You think I could make a hundred sometime? And, uh, did you mean, uh, do you really care?"

"Of course you can and I do care. I'm a teacher, Joe. If I didn't care I wouldn't be here. Ask me about anything you don't understand, keep working and I'm sure you'll improve."

Joe did improve in every subject. Along with teacher the class took him on as a project, encouraging him and helping him to study. Somebody cared, so he cared, and eyes alight with purpose, applied himself diligently.

The day finally came when Joe actually made a hundred in Spelling. His writing was still difficult to read, but legible and clear enough to show he deserved the grade. He carried the paper home with the pride of a college graduate holding a diploma, and it was a question who was happiest, Joe, the class or the teacher.

I was his teacher.

All through the years I've remembered Joe; and my discovery that each time an old adage is used it becomes a new concept because of its eternal truth. "Somebody cares." "Try, try again." "God helps those who help themselves." These ancient platitudes and maxims bring comfort and hope and *results,* for they are really prayers by which people live.

Kathy's Christmas Gift

Ann Dickinson

K ATHY was home for Christmas. Sure, she could stay only three days but, when you lived the rest of the year in the Children's Hospital for Crippled Children, three days was a long time. It was long enough to store up enough love or hate to last a full year ahead. And, when you were eight years old and had cerebral palsy, you knew more about love and hate than eight year olds who could walk and talk with ease.

Last Christmas Kathy had stored up hate. Nurse Margaret at the hospital had a terrible time with her after she returned from her short visit at home. It wasn't easy explaining to a little girl that her mother loved her as much — or more — than she did her other two children, Alice and Jerry. Just because Alice got skates and Jerry got a bicycle when Kathy could not use either — did not mean, not in the least, that Kathy was not loved.

It was Nurse Margaret's idea for Kathy to make this NEW Christmas the best one yet.

"You will have to give your mother a BIG PRESENT, though," Nurse Margaret explained.

Kathy cried when Nurse Margaret said that. How could *she* give anything? She couldn't hold anything in her hands — and she couldn't walk to go buy anything. She couldn't even wipe away the tears from her cheeks — except by rubbing her face against the pillows!

But — that was last Christmas! A whole year had
passed and it was Christmas morning again. Kathy smelled
bacon cooking. It was a wonderful smell! In the hospital
you didn't have time to smell food before eating. Someone was always there to start feeding you before you had
time to enjoy the smell.

Alice, Jerry and their mother all helped to get Kathy
out of bed and into her special chair. They went to the
small living room where a big tree took up most of the
room in one end. Alice gave out the gifts and they all
opened their gifts. Of course, Kathy's mother had to open

Kathy's gifts for her but this time — Kathy did not mind. She kept thinking about HER big gift!

After what seemed an eternity to Kathy, they were all seated around the breakfast table. Jerry, the man of the house, said the blessing. Then Kathy's mother reached for Kathy's glass of orange juice. She wanted Kathy to have her orange juice at the same time as Alice and Jerry.

"NO," Kathy said, "NO!"

Her mother moved her hand from the glass. Kathy had wanted to say, "No, please," but every word, big or little, was so hard for her to say.

Kathy looked at her family. Then she took a deep breath. Suppose she couldn't give her gift! But — she had to! Nurse Margaret had said that she could — and Nurse Margaret was always right!

With a slow, painful effort Kathy gripped the glass with both hands. Then, WITHOUT SPILLING A DROP, she lifted the glass to her mouth and drank the orange juice. NOW! IF she could only put it down without dropping it, she could tell Nurse Margaret that she had kept her promise!

AT LAST — the glass was safe on the table!

"Mer—ry Chris—mus," Kathy said to her family. She did fine with the words, too. She was so glad that she had practiced for months to say those words.

Nurse Margaret was right. Her gift WAS wonderful! Kathy knew! Her mother cried. Jerry said, "Gee, look at Kathy!" Alice said, "I'll bet Kathy can ride a bicycle NEXT Christmas!"

And Kathy thought, "I just might."

We Blowed It

Frances Greene

BY profession, I am not a little old wine maker. I spend my days at the local newspaper office getting copy for the weekly edition, my nights at home getting caught up with housework, and serve at both locations as Billy Nichols' perfect patsy. The churn of fermented muscadine grapes that blew up the cedar chest in the guest room closet was simply a by-product of the three careers.

The explosion was terrific. It rocked every picture and vase within a radius of thirty feet and shook Grandpa's treasured Confederate muzzle loader over the mantel in the den. Friends now tell me that I should have known better. Billy Nichols tells me that it couldn't be "holped." I prefer to believe Billy Nichols; I am his favorite customer and he would not tell me wrong. He also knows about fermentation and such things.

Billy Nichols found the muscadine vines on top of Tally Mountain. He was a wart of a little codger who moved to our small southern town along with his mother and six sisters from the range of hills in the distance. With him he brought an extra pair of breeches, a stubborn pride and a sixth sense for finding buyers like me, the "paper woman" whose husband, the "paper man," he at first eyed suspiciously until he turned his dark brown eyes in my direction and asked solemnly, "He yore true love?"

I nodded, and to show that he approved my choice of a mate, he let me purchase the bunch of wood violets that he carried in his grubby hand. Since that day, I have found a use for every thing from rusty pipes that he picks up at the garbage dump to smooth stones that he gets out of the creek. His prices are reasonable. Actually, they are "real cheap, being who 'tis," and I managed to acquire the prettiest, rustiest lavatory ever seen in our section for the nominal sum of nineteen cents, the cost of a new "ink pen."

Being who I was, and there was a high school football game at the athletic field and the admission of students — even warts of students — was fifty cents, I came by a half bushel of muscadine grapes gathered that very afternoon. As Billy Nichols pointed out, I could not get 'em much fresher than that or much cleaner either. He added that they was worth every dime but if I could see fit, he'd like a little extra to buy a hamburger at the concession stand, since he had spent the better part of a day gettin' 'em and his Ma had probably throwed his supper to the dogs already.

I saw fit. I even saw fit enough to add an additional few cents for a soft drink. It is not every fall afternoon that a paper woman gets a half bushel of fresh, clean muscadines.

But Billy Nichols would not dast leave me standing in the middle of the entrance hall holding a cardboard box full of grapes while he hied himself to the ball park. He remembered that an old churn was in the basement behind the furnace. "Just the thing to hold 'em," he announced with a nod of his tousled head, "after I wash 'em down a mite."

That was worth two bags of popcorn to go with the ticket, the hamburger and the soft drink.

I would have made jelly from those muscadines; I would have spent the better part of next morning boiling, straining and measuring but the sugar cannister was empty and rain beat against the windows, and suddenly it was too late by some five days to do anything with the beading product in the churn.

"They wasn't easy to pick," Billy Nichols said as he watched the swarming gnats.

I agreed that they were not.

"If Pa was home, he'd do somethin' with 'em. He's not a wasteful man, my Pa."

I did not know his Pa but I was sure that he was not a wasteful man.

Billy Nichols sighed heavily. "I had to kill me a snake before I got to 'em. He could've bit me but good." His dark eyes clouded over with disappointment and condemnation. "When you stop and think of it, you was down right unthoughty."

To be unthoughty in Billy Nichols' estimation was not good. To be wasteful was not good either. But a churn of fermenting muscadines?

"You ever drunk any of the juice?" he asked suddenly.

"I never have," I answered with a shake of my head, "but Aunt Lily made scuppernong nectar to use in fruit-cakes . . ."

If True Love had any qualms about grapes on the bead, then he should have tasted my Aunty Lily's zesty cakes. I thought as I searched through the file of her "Southern Family Dishes."

In precise handwriting, Grandpa's only sister had declared that the scuppernongs were to set in a churn, crock or jar covered with a clean towel for nine days. Strain. Add three pounds of sugar for each gallon of juice, return to churn, crock or jar for fourteen days or until the beading stops. Bottle and cork.

Billy Nichols' eyes regained their sparkle as I found a clean towel.

On the ninth day, I dragged the churn from the back porch into the kitchen. For two hours, I dipped, poured and strained.

"You sure are turning everythin' purple," Billy Nichols said candidly, reaching for a doughnut on top of the bread box.

I measured the juice into bowls; I measured the sugar into pans. I washed out the churn and returned the whole of it from whence it had come.

"You ruint your floor, too," he commented as he jumped the purple puddle in front of the sink on his way to the back door. "See you tomorrow when I bring that pretty little old holly tree that'd look real good in yore back yard," he called over his shoulder matter-of-factly and much too quickly for an answer.

I was left with a churn of nectar and nowhere to put it.

By rearranging umbrellas, the vacuum cleaner, two rolls of surplus wall paper and a beat-up golf bag, I found the space in the entrance hall closet and sat back happily for the beading to cease. And it suddenly occurred to me that I really had something going: inside my crock was the perfect answer to the people-who-have-everything Christmas list. They definitely did not have nectar from the Greenes' hall closet.

Visions of bottles tied with gay, red bows flitted through my head.

Along with the holly tree from the back yard came the question, "Hey, what's that that's smelling?"

It could have been a gas leak or the exhaust of a stray transfer truck, but it was "Muscadines, of course. You know . . ."

Billy Nichols knew; he knew enough to shrug and sigh deeply. "Sheriff Dunson raided Pa's place on the mountain," he said, wandering into the den. "Denamited it, he did," he called, bounding toward the television.

By the end of the tenth day, the pungent, tingling odor of nectar was spreading to the front lawn. A good high wind could take it to town.

On the twelfth day, my True Love said to me, fighting his way through the heavy air, "I don't like this."

I agreed.

"Ya nectar done yet?" Billy Nichols asked at his heels.

I shook my head.

Billy Nichols sniffed loud and long. "Ya ought to set you up a place on the mountain."

Ready or not, I removed the churn. Not having a funnel, I made one of a sort out of aluminum foil.

"Humph," Billy Nichols said, "Pa pumped his juice through an old car radiator."

I began to pour the liquid into bottles.

"Pa used fruit jars," Billy Nichols pointed out.

"Now see here, young man," True Love sputtered, "this is nectar for fruit cakes."

But Billy Nichols grinned slyly.

True Love's face reddened. He swallowed hard. He looked directly into my eyes; his voice was firm. "Out," ha said. "Every last drop."

I nodded. But what True Love did not know would not hurt his conscience. I had the perfect place for the bottles, a place that even Billy Nichols could not find. Who would ever think of looking in the cedar chest in the guest room closet?

On the twenty-first night, my True Love said to me during a tense TV drama, "What in heaven's name was that?"

I T could have been an airplane breaking the sound barrier; it could have been a train wreck; It could have been rolls of thunder hitting head on. But it was none of

these things.

"Yore nectar blowed up," Billy Nichols said matter-of-factly from the sofa, never lifting his eyes from the screen. "It blowed all by itself."

I nodded dumbly. The whole deal had blowed as far as I was concerned.

But I was Billy Nichols' good friend; I recognized his contempt for charity, wastefulness and unthoughtiness, and I nearly broke my back planting his trees and carrying his rocks. He was on my side.

"I know where there's an apple tree," he said simply. "Onct Pa made some cider . . ."

By profession I am a "newspaper lady." By necessity I am one of the best jelly makers in our small town. And as Billy Nichols pointed out. "To my nohow, jelly ain't ever blowed yet."

I Remember, I Remember

Joyce Flint Holland

"*C* HRISTMAS *doesn't mean a thing anymore —
Christmas is so commercialized"* — When I hear
those oft-repeated words, I pause a moment, caught up
in a tiny perfect memory that flashes across my inner eye.
I am suddenly once again very small, lost in a misty
memory of those long-ago and faraway Christmases when
we were very young, life was simple, and the stars were
not so far from earth.

I can remember strong arms lifting me high, the heady
feeling of being taller than the grownups — and then I
glimpsed it — reflected in the convex glass of the old Seth
Thomas clock on the mantel was a tiny image of the
shining Christmas tree across the room. All the mystical
wonder of Christmas seemed to me caught in that little
reflection, stretching backward through the glass into what
magic worlds. There was laughter at my fascination with
the glass; I stretched out my hands, already dimly knowing
that you cannot grasp magic; you cannot hold wonder. You
can only remember.

For five stair-stepped children living in a rambling old
frame house high in the mountains of North Georgia, life
was a continuous adventure, culminated each year in the
almost unbearable happiness of Christmas.

These were the grim, bitter days of the Great Depression, but no one had ever thought to tell us that we were
economically deprived or labeled our little village a pocket
of poverty, and to us life seemed abundantly rich.

Our little town of Mount Airy, perched high in the North Georgia mountains, had once been a famous summer resort, with wealthy visitors from Atlanta and the seacoast coming to spend cool summers. But when hard times came a-knocking, it had become for us a last resort. Our drafty old house, once a summer home, was designed to catch mountain breezes; unintended for winter living, it now invited all the icy blasts yowling off Yonah Mountain. We children coped nonchalantly with unheated bedrooms and ice-coated toothbrushes in the morning, glorying in the fact that we had two chimneys, allowing Santa Claus not only access, but the luxury of a choice.

WHEN the first chill winds of fall blew through the pine trees, the early frost ripening the persimmons, we raced through the *Winesap* air, vowing we could already feel Christmas in the air. We began gathering hickory nuts and pecans, spreading them to dry on the kitchen roof, in preparation for our Christmas baking.

Thanksgiving was scarcely past before Christmas preparations began in earnest. The hoarded nuts were carefully cracked and the fruit cake baking began. For days we chopped citron, sifted flour, tasted batter for the final glorious, spice-tinged all-day baking of the cakes in the old wood-fired iron kitchen stove. Big tube cake pans nestled with pound size Morning Joy coffee cans of batter in the oven, and a steady vigil was maintained to chunk in the right amount of stove wood to keep the temperature even. The cakes would be our Christmas gifts to friends and kin folks and the love and thought baked into them was almost as tangible as the currants and walnuts.

Giggling and whispering, we scurried about with scissors, flour paste, crayons, needle and thread, making and hiding away gifts for each other. Crossword puzzles and cartoons clipped for months from newspapers and magazines were carefully pasted on brown paper and sewn together to fashion books. Bumpy, lumpy hats and bootees were inexpertly crocheted for each other's dolls, and clay from the banks of the creek was fashioned into lopsided, highly decorated pots and vases.

There was the high excitement of dragging down the huge wire frame from the attic, trooping to the Big Woods for holly, mistletoe, boughs of nose-tingling cedar for the enormous wreath our mother made each year for the front door, gaily proclaiming that Christmas was really near.

But, to me, Christmas really began the day The Dolls arrived.

Each year college girls up North where my mother had gone to school, dressed a collection of dolls and sent them to be given to children in the mountains — children who otherwise might never have owned a doll. The dolls arrived in a big wooden box by railway express, clear from Boston, Massachusetts, a place as remote and mysterious to us as the North Pole. We three little girls stood in big-eyed expectation as the box was carefully opened and the dolls inspected after their perilous journey. We gazed in admiration at this wondrous array of dolls, loving each one at a distance, finding them more precious because we knew they would never belong to us but were on the way to other homes. By today's standards of lifelike elaborate dolls, these identical-faced, cheap little composition babies with their painted-on hair, would seem rather pathetic, but each was dressed with such painstaking care and imagination that it had a personality of its own, and to us they seemed unbearably beautiful.

THE WINTER days grew shorter and colder and excitement mounted higher and higher. When two of the Advent candles had been lit, it was time to put up the Christmas tree. We searched with complete absorption through the frosty hills for the very perfect tree, which was chopped down and dragged home through the biting cold to the accompaniment of Christmas carols, sung loudly and tunelessly.

Bumpy, mysterious packages from Sears-Roebuck were hustled into the house and disappeared into closets that had suddenly become secret forbidden caves of hidden treasure.

One whole snowy, giggly, tongue-biting afternoon was spent writing our letters to Santa Claus. We gathered around the fireplace to send our letters flying, smoke borne, up the chimney to be whisked away to the North Pole.

All five of us children earnestly and devoutly believed in Santa Claus and each tiny reindeer, but with the practicality of childhood, we automatically relegated Santa to our own

income bracket. It would never have occurred to us to ask for bicycles, electric trains or wrist watches. In truth, we not only didn't ask for them, we didn't miss them. But when you have your own creek to catch muddy crawfish in, your own private telephone line made out of two baking powder cans and a long string, two brothers to fight with and adore, and two sisters to play dolls and whisper secrets with — well, who needs a bicycle? Our Christmas lists were modest but earnest wishes for water color sets, paper doll books, a few new clothes (a brand-new union suit with all the buttons on at one time was indeed elegance), and always, by some magic, there were the wonderful magic carpets of new books to be read and treasured throughout the year.

Word went out through the hills and down under the

mountain that the dolls had arrived and were waiting for their new mothers. Busy as elves at Santa's workshop, we bustled about importantly helping mother fill the little brown paper pokes with bucket candy from Kimzey's General Store, a small toy for the little boys in the families, an orange for each child, a few raisins and a balloon. With the doll, this would most likely be all these children would know of Christmas gifts. The skimpy little bags weren't offered in any Lady Bountiful manner, for tiny though they were, they represented skimping and saving all year for my parents and were given only in love and the joy of sharing with friends.

Sometimes walking four or five miles over the frozen red clay roads, our visitors began to come — long-time, dearly loved friends. All of these women were desperately poor if you count only dollars as the treasures of life. But they were kingly-rich in wisdom, dignity, and humor. These were mountain people of fierce pride and loyalty, not beholden to anybody. They came as friends, each bringing us a gift — a Mason fruit jar of huckleberries back-breakingly picked and canned during the summer, a little dish of tongue-burning homemade sausage, a pat of country butter. Some could bring only armloads of holly or a bundle of pine kindling gleaned from the snowy woods. With elaborate casualness, they declared they were much obliged for the doll baby and 'lowed as how the young-uns would be pure tickled over the Santy Claus. But their eyes, caressing the cheap little doll, and the careful way they tucked the paper sacks under their thin coats betrayed their happiness that they would be filling stockings on Christmas Eve.

UNBELIEVABLY, it was Christmas Eve. The days that dragged by agonizingly slowly now had melted into that one busy, frenzied day before Christmas. There was much to be done — the brave and the bold helped Aunt Sarah kill and pick the fat turkey gobbler who had been stuffing in his backyard coop for weeks. The more timid helped take down and wash the fragile, mismatched "good" dishes for our tomorrow's feast. Each piece had its own legend and story — "Your great-grandmother's gravy bowl. I do believe it was a wedding gift from the Halls," "Cousin Faye's sugar and creamer," Aunt May, Great Aunt Julia . . . the impenetrable line between the living and

dead seemed to fade and these long ago people seemed to hover very near and dear in an atmosphere of love.

The anemic winter sun disappeared behind Yonah Mountain, a few bright stars shone and it was, at last, that most magic of all times, the night before Christmas.

With the long cotton stockings hung from the mantel, out into the night we trooped, across the chill, starry dark of the backyard, past the smokehouse, down the path lined with fig bushes, to the barn where we gathered an arm-load of fodder to place on the hearth for the reindeer. (The fodder was always gone on Christmas morning; did the reindeer really eat it?)

Lulled into a temporary quiet by singing carols, we sat close around the crackling fireplace while Mother, the smallest child snug in her lap, read the Christmas Story from the Bible. Every year we each vowed we would stay awake until midnight to see if it was really so what Aunt Sarah told us, that the cow would kneel down at the stroke of midnight in worship of the Christ Child. But somehow, we always fell asleep before twelve, one ear cocked open for the sound of reindeer hoofs.

Christmas morning found us awake long before dawn, snug under our quilt, giggling and shouting from room to room. But we couldn't come downstairs for the stockings until Aunt Sarah arrived from her little house clear across town. Ancient, wizened, grumpy, beloved old Aunt Sarah. She had been a part of the family since my father's babyhood. Christmas couldn't begin without her.

Just as the sun burst over Currahee Mountain, we heard her coming down the hill singing lustily,

> Go Tell It On The Mountain,
> Over the Hills and Everywhere,
> Go Tell It On The Mountain,
> Jesus Christ is Born.

We ran to meet her, singing at the tops of our lungs until the very hills rang with the news. It was Christmas.

WHEN you groan and tell me that Christmas is such a bore; it is so commercialized it has no meaning, forgive me if I seem not to hear you, if I stand very quietly gazing past the gaudy plastic decorations. For a magic moment I am once again very small; there flashes across my inner eye the image of that tiny, perfect Christmas tree crystalized forever in the face of an old Seth Thomas clock. I stand, lost in a misty memory of a time of love and gentleness, a time when we celebrated the birthday of a Saviour with such simplicity and pure joy that perhaps for a tiny sliver of time we caught a glimmer of

Thy Kingdom Come, On Earth As It Is In Heaven.

The Man Who Hated Details

William Virlyn Farr

MR. Moreland liked to talk about how long he had worked with Dock Tompkins, but that was a fanciful way of putting it. For a long time, it is true, Dock Tompkins had handled his financial affairs, rented his property, and looked after the cotton gin and warehouse, but with little assistance from Mr. Moreland who was now in his advanced years. All Mr. Moreland wanted to know was how much money he had in the bank at the end of the month; how it got there didn't interest him.

This evening Mr. Moreland was lighting his tenth cigar when he finally got around to the purpose of his visit. "Doc," he said, "we've been working together for a long time." He paused, gazing at the open fire, then asked: "How long has it been?"

"Oh," said Dock. He had slumped deeper and deeper into the old rocking chair while Mr. Moreland carried on the conversation single-handed. His khaki shirt had worked its way out of his pants — a fact that had not escaped the attention of Mr. Moreland who made it a practice to maintain a neat appearance himself. Now he was wearing a plaid gray suit and a snappy bow tie.

Dock sat up straight. "Let's see now. Twenty? I'd say it's been twenty years."

"Twenty years," said Mr. Moreland as if amazed. "And to think, in all that time I didn't know you. I didn't know you at all. Here I left everything in your hands for twenty years, thinking you could be trusted. It's more than I can understand."

Dock said nothing in his defense. Mr. Moreland snapped his fingers. "Are you going to leave me just like that?"

"I told you, Mr. Moreland, it's nothing personal."

"I sure take it personally when the man who's managed my affairs takes it in his head to quit. Why, I've told everybody in the state of Georgia that you can handle details like nobody's business. And you know how I hate details."

Mr. Moreland had to be sure that he was making himself clear. "I depended on you, Dock, I counted on you. What do I know about details?"

He lit another cigar and puffed furiously. "Why can't you think of *me* for a change? After all I've done for you, it does look like you could do that."

"I don't mean to be ungrateful," said Dock.

"That's *precisely* what you are. Ungrateful." Mr. Moreland decided against reminding him of the Pig 'n' Pickle fiasco at this point. During the course of his employment Dock had failed him only once. That was a few years ago when he let O. J. Hammock get into the barbecue business ahead of him. O.J. had put up a roadside cafe called the Pig 'n' Pickle which caught most traffic passing through Rock Station. Pig 'n' Pickles had sprung up for miles around like crabgrass in the springtime.

Mr. Moreland thought it best to take a positive approach. "Why," he said, "I'm the first to admit that I have you to thank for the fact that I'm pretty well off."

"You can get someone to run things," said Dock, and then added, "if you pay them enough."

IT was true that his admiration for Dock had not manifested itself in the form of excessive compensation, but this slap in the face hurt too much for him to speak of a raise in salary just now. "Dock," he said in a conciliatory tone, "I've been thinking about fixing this place up. I know Effie would like to have it painted. Maybe I'll even put some of that imitation-brick siding on the house. Of course I wouldn't charge any more rent, since you work for me and all."

Dock threw another lump of coal onto the fire and watched it blaze up.

"I know Effie would like that," said Mr. Moreland. She had complained many times about the rundown house. Mr. Moreland hadn't paid her much attention, but he was willing to fix it up if that would hold Dock. He looked around at the unpainted walls adorned here and there with a calendar. "I wonder how this room would look with wallpaper? I think it'd look fine. Wallpaper all the rooms!" Dock showed no interest in the proposed renovations. Afraid he was going a little far, Mr. Moreland said, "Does it need a new roof? Put it on!" Dock had come to him time and time again about the leaking roof, but now he didn't say so much as thank you. "Fix up the kitchen," Mr. Moreland went on, "get a new sink, cabinets — some of this modern stuff."

He might as well have been talking to a post for all the response he got. "Is Effie asleep?" he asked. "I'd like to tell her right now." He waited for an answer, which wasn't forthcoming. "Dock?" He waited, then asked testily: "Is your wife asleep?"

"Well . . . she went to bed."

What insolence! Never in his life had he expected to hear Dock Thompkins address him in such a manner. He had half a mind to dismiss him on the spot . . .

Then he remembered that he was here to get Dock to stay on.

"Why, you can't quit," said Mr. Moreland. "How'd you get along? You'd better think about that. Yes, and think about your health, and think about Effie, I've been meaning to advise you to slow down. Have you seen a doctor lately? Go round to see Dr. Pemble in the morning and have him send me the bill. Maybe what you need is a vacation. Take one of the trucks and drive down to South Georgia next weekend — see the Okefenokee Swamp. Get out and see the world! I've always enjoyed traveling myself, and it might do you some good too."

Mr. Moreland was speaking with such enthusiasm, thinking of ways to make Dock's situation more attractive, that he could not stop. "Put somebody in charge of the gin," he said, "and somebody else in charge of the warehouse. Take some of this load off your back. Say, I've been meaning to raise your salary. Let's see now. Five dollars a week, no, ten. Why, that'd put you up to eighty a week,

wouldn't it? I bet you never dreamed you'd be making that kind of money. But, like I say, take care of yourself. If you don't look out for yourself in this world, who will?"

Considering all he had promised — the renovations, the trip to the Okefenokee, the raise, and less responsibility — Mr. Moreland was afraid that he had gone too far. He might have tried one thing at a time.

"Say, Dock, you know that brick house going up out on Highway 22? Go by there tomorrow, take a look at it, and see if you think it's a good buy. You'll have to be quick, mind you. They snap these houses up soon as they're built. Everybody wants to 'own' their home these days. 'Own' my foot. They go head-over-heels in debt, is what they do."

Dock was looking at him as if he had been deprived of his reason. "What's the matter, Dock? Don't you think it'd be a good investment? Of course if you don't think so . . ."

"Mr. Moreland," said Dock firmly, "I don't work for you any more."

"Come, Come! I thought we settled that. Haven't you been listening to me?"

"I heard you," said Dock without enthusiasm, and paused. "I got a new job, I thought you knew. I'm going to

be looking after the Pig 'n' Pickles."

"The Pig 'n' Pickles! So it comes to that, does it? You go behind my back and get another job, with O. J. Hammock, of all people, when *I* might have owned those Pig 'n' Pickles. Such selfishness! Ingratitude! But you forget one thing: I have friends in this town. I have influence. Don't you know I can keep O. J. Hammock from taking you on?"

"He already has."

"Before he had me to deal with. Just wait. Don't you realize that I could tell O. J. anything? I could tell him you aren't reliable. I could even tell him you've been doing something — illegal. I can put a stop to this nonsense one way or another. And don't think I won't!"

"Look what time it is, Mr. Moreland. I ought to be in bed." The clock on the mantel was striking twelve.

"Sit down!" ordered Mr. Moreland. "We're going to have this out here and now. "Why, you couldn't stay on in this house, the house I've provided all these years. If you don't change your tune, Dock, I'll have you out of here so fast it'll make your head swim. So sit down and let's talk this over like gentlemen."

"You look tired, Mr. Moreland. You'd better go home and get some rest."

Mr. Moreland sprang from his chair, grabbed his hat, and shoved it onto his head at a jaunty angle. "All right, Mr. Tompkins, what do you want? Tell me and get it over with. Is it more money? Is that it? All right, I know when I'm beat. I'll pay you eighty-five a week, and that's final, not a penny more."

"I've never asked for a raise, Mr. Moreland. I've just done the best job I could and never asked for anything."

"Until now, that is. What are you holding out for?"

"Nothing. It's like I told you. I'm going to be looking after the Pig 'n' Pickles."

Mr. Moreland had opened the front door. He turned back and said, "You just think you've got another job. We'll see about that, Dock Tompkins. We'll see."

NEXT morning Mr. Moreland phoned O. J. Hammock and asked if he intended to have Dock Tompkins running the Pig 'n' Pickles. He did.

"I don't recall that you asked me," said Mr. Moreland. "Now listen here, O. J. There's something you ought to know." His voice took a serious, confidential turn. "I hadn't mentioned it to anyone, but I was thinking about letting Dock go."

"Then there'll be no hard feelings. I'm glad of that, Mr. Moreland. I was a little worried, tell the truth."

"O. J.? I have reason to believe that Dock has been — O. J.? You know I wouldn't be saying a thing like this if it wasn't the truth." His voice was barely above a whisper. "O. J., I caught Dock stealing."

O. J. Hammock laughed into the phone.

"Uh," said Mr. Moreland, taken aback. "Now look here, O. J. Hammock. How much do you mean to pay him?"   "In a manner of speaking," said O. J. Hammock, "I don't. You see, I've decided to make him my partner. Who you think's responsible for all these Pig 'n' Pickles round here but Dock? Anything he touches turns to gold. I'm sorry, Mr. Moreland, but, like the fellow said, business is business."

Mr. Moreland slammed the receiver down. He had never thought much of O. J. Hammock anyhow.

He dialed the realty office that was handling the house out on Highway 22. No matter what Dock thought, he was convinced that it would be a good investment. Besides, it seemed that he would have to handle his own details now and he might as well get started. "WHAT?" he screamed a moment later.

"It's sold," a girl's voice said.

It seemed that everyone in this town was out to get the best of him. "Who bought it?" he demanded.

"Is that Mr. Moreland? I thought I recognized your voice. It was an employee of yours, or should I say 'former' employee?"

"It couldn't be . . .

"Dock Tompkins," the voice said, pleased with itself. "The house will be ready for him to move in when they get back from Florida."

"Florida! What's he gone to Florida in?" said Mr. Moreland, thinking he would have him arrested if he had gone off in one of his trucks.

"Why, in that new automobile he just bought. Mr. Moreland. Whatever else would they have gone in?"

Stunned, Mr. Moreland let the receiver fall into its cradle. Then he eased himself into the most convenient chair. "Details, details," he muttered. He simply hated details, and would rather do anything than handle them.

There had been a phone call, he seemed to remember, but what it was all about he could not get straight in his mind. Had he referred the party to Dock Tompkins? He couldn't be sure, but, thinking how fortunate he was to have an employee like that taking care of details, he certainly hoped so.

Such Things as Love

Frances Greene

THE world of music will never know how close it came to being blown off its axis and literally sent into another orbit altogether. The near catastrophe was blamed on me but I would like to make it clear that I had an accomplice: a mite of a lad by the name of Edward William "Billy" Nichols.

True Love, an innocent bystander in the whole affair as well as the man who married me, will accept no excuses. He reviewed the incident with an open mind and then voiced a closed mind opinion that an adult, meaning me, should have known better than to meddle in other people's lives anyway — especially the life of young Billy Nichols. To emphasize his feelings on the subject, he proceeded to liken my association with the skinny little codger to molten lava that bubbles, rumbles and boils, and whether or not it ever erupts, it still scares the blue blazes out of everybody living around it.

He exaggerates because he does not approve altogether of my Billy Nichols projects. He figures that they always cost him money one way or another, and peace of mind either way. And he is a thrifty man with both.

I am willing to admit that, now and then, I do come up with some pretty good thoughts about the young fellow's future, but what I am actually doing is for Billy Nichols' own good. I figure that if his abundance of energy can be channeled in the right direction, there will be no stopping him this side of the White House; if his ability to learn is challenged with more than the basic school subjects, he will be the most well rounded lad of his generation. And, since he already knows about such things as making a good minnow pond out of an old hot water tank cut in half and buried in the ground, and conning and charming his teachers into passing English, and training a squirrel to eat out of his hand, I feel it my bounden duty to broaden his education.

I tried once. I tried by introducing "the arts." I even had a plan, such as it was. I thought to start with a library checkout card followed by a tour of a few local clothes-line craft shows, a band concert and maybe a little theatre production. I believed and still believe that any one of these arts, especially music, is something to everybody, and to my favorite skinny, wide eyed, young friend who wandered the woods for beauty that he was not even aware of seeking, it could be comfort, companionship, happiness.

True Love said that I was wasting my time.

Billy Nichols acknowledged the invitation to attend a musical recital with the announcement that when they lived back up in the hills Pa had played an old saw onct but all it sounded like was a trembling bong.

"I could try picking something," he suggested. "You ever seen a git-tar that plugs in?"

True Love quickly interjected the thought that to know a squirrel tamer was to know a rare, unusual person, and why was I getting so steamed up all at once over a cultural program? After all, there were boys and boys and boys. There was only one Billy Nichols, he insisted. "Already he is getting more out of life than three-fourths of the adults I know," he added. But the firmness in his voice did not completely hide the envy.

He could have had a point but neither of us will ever know. Love, it seems, works in wondrous, mysterious ways, and Cupid reared his curly head and shot an arrow straight through Billy Nichols' full, oversized, unselfish heart. He discovered a girl. Whereas one day there was a thrill in skipping stones across the pond, the next day there was Sharon with hair the color of jonquils just bursting into bloom and eyes the color of wood violets. Not only that, she could pitch a ball so hard and fast that it burned your hands to catch it and she made A's in English and taught her dog to walk on his hind legs and played the flute because she had the lips for it and was, wonders of wonders, the "onliest" girl he ever knew who liked just mustard on hot dogs.

"Not even catsup," he confided, and his voice was filled with amazement, awe, admiration.

True Love immediately pointed out that it was spring, the one time in every year when a young man's fancy always turns to blondes.

Since he was a male and knew all about things such as seasons and fancies, I did not argue. But since I was a female and knew all about such things as feminine wiles and flattery, I meddled. I suggested quite subtly that if Sharon played the flute, then she must be in the Junior Band; if she were in the band, then she knew the director. "Perhaps you could go to practice with her one afternoon and maybe try out for an instrument," I tossed off casually. "And if you have any talent . . . why, who knows?" I shrugged.

True Love's eyes indicated that he knew exactly; he would end up buying a git-tar that plugged in.

Billy Nichols did not answer. Standing at the door, his eyes stared unseeingly at the bird feeder attached to the limb of the pine tree beyond the kitchen window. His mind was faraway — maybe on the setting sun or the slight, warm breeze or the floating clouds overhead; maybe on the beautiful days to come or maybe on Sharon with the lips for a flute.

"See you" he said finally. And he gently closed the door behind him and slowly descended the back steps.

True Love and I ate our sandwiches in silence. Our friend was growing up.

But Billy Nichols did not "see us" for three long days. The girl with the jonquil hair and wood violet eyes had replaced chocolate chip cookies and milk.

His sudden appearance, then, in the middle of a school day morning was frightening; only an emergency or illness could interrupt classes. It could not be the latter. His face shone like a star, his lips curved in a pleased smile, his excitement was as noticeable as the belly button exposed by the gaping shirt.

He stuck out his lower lip, blew upward to dislodge the damp hair on his forehead. He drew in his breath to control the short gasps. "I'm in the talent show," he announced triumphantly.

True Love walked to the desk. I closed my mouth.

Billy Nichols lifted his tired shoulders, squared them off, looked down his snub nose. "The director signed me and Sharon up to sing in the PTA talent show." His voice tried for matter-of-factness, even his eyebrows strived for an aloof arch.

I swallowed hard. The youngster could no more carry a tune than he could fly. Time, he could keep; words, he could learn. But notes? He had never even whistled on key.

"But that," Billy Nichols said, "ain't all."

That, True Love's expression said, was enough.

The tousled head bent forward, retrieved the sack on the floor, turned it upside down. A red coat trimmed in white braid and a wide belt spilled onto the desk in a wrinkled pile. Slowly, carefully, he slid one arm into the sleeve. He paused for a long moment, reluctant to relinquish this feeling of ecstasy. Time was willed to stand still if only for a golden second as the lovely, beautiful memory was folded and tucked securely in his file of treasures.

With a sudden, satisfied sigh, he completed his task of trying on. The shoulder seams struck the vicinity of his arm muscles; the dirty knees of his jeans peeped from beneath the bottom. I found a paper of pins, folded back the sleeves, turned under the hem, lapped the sides.

"If your mother is too busy . . ." I offered hesitantly.

His eyes brightened. His ma was a hard worker and he loved her but there were some things best left to others. "She's busy," he said. And his long look silently explained that he would really like to kiss me but he was, after all, Billy Nichols, and Billy Nichols did not show gratitude with kisses. He shared gifts like a golden rod in a broken pickle jar and Maypops and frogs.

He blew at the strands of hair. He cleared his throat. He opened his mouth and sang the first few bars of whatever he thought he was singing.

The sound was terrible, and I knew then with a sickening thud how Lot's wife must have felt when she glanced over her shoulder. "As time goes on . . ." I said, evading his questioning eyes.

He nodded understandingly. "We got plenty of it. The show don't start until eight tonight."

I wet my dry lips.

With a grin, he bounded toward the door. "You're gonna get the surprise of your life," he promised. And he was gone.

True Love said that he was sure we would. But he could not understand why a director wanted a duet in the talent show — especially if Billy Nichols were one-half of it!

I could. Talent shows were for raising money; the more entries, the more people who attended; the more people, the more gate receipts. Whether or not a child could sing was irrelevant even though the judges, bless them, were sincere and fair and selected the best performers in the three age groups. The band director had been given the job to round up entries. He was grasping at straws.

But explaining the whys and wherefores was not getting a coat in shape, and armed with thread, needles, pins and hope, I set to with trembling fingers and sweating palms.

The stitches were long, uneven, angry looking. Three times I started to the phone to call the band director; three times I vowed to speak my piece on the unfairness of putting a child on the stage to make a spectacle of himself and three times I broke the thread and spent fifteen minutes trying to find the eye of the needle again.

"They'll laugh at him," I exploded to True Love when he came in from the office. "Children are cruel. Oh . . . they're cruel." I shuddered.

He shrugged a what's-done-is-done shrug. He opened the refrigerator, searched the shelves for something to eat. Nothing appealed to him; he closed the door.

The clock over the stove ticked. The coat was finished and pressed. My stomach churned nervously; I was taut, upset, mad.

True Love poured two cups of coffee. The sun was down, shadows played across the table, a bird fluttered to the feeder and pecked silently at the grain.

A spoon slammed to the table. Sparks spit from the flashing eyes of the man I took for better or for worse. "Just what," he asked heatedly, "will those women do with all that money anyway?"

I shook my head. The molten lava had bubbled but now it was rumbling. He had never liked the PTA even without talent shows.

He stood and opened the refrigerator again. He closed the door and paused, his head cocked. Both of us heard the carefree whistle, the bounce on the back steps. True Love sat quickly, picked up the cup of steaming coffee.

Billy Nichols' eyes went immediately to the coat across the ironing board. He turned to face us but the sparkle, the smile were gone. He ran his tongue over his lower lip; he chewed at it for a long moment. "You sure did work," he said finally, quietly.

I nodded. Maybe he had stage fright or something.

He shuffled slightly. His shoe lace was untied again and he studied the dirty strings as if he had never seen them before. He sighed heavily, squared his shoulders and drew in his breath. "I ain't gonna wear it after all," he admitted reluctantly.

He was not dressed to go on a stage without it. The

shirt was the same he had worn this morning, his face was smudged with dirt. "She'd ruther sing with somebody else," he explained quietly.

The clock ticked, the motor of the freezer in the basement came on with a roar. I could offer chocolate chip cookies and milk; I could even suggest a nut sundae at the Drive-In, but neither would alleviate the pain behind this horrible admission.

Billy Nichols lifted his tousled head. He had to make me understand, make me see it like it really was. He looked long and deep into my eyes. He blinked once. "I was only doing this," he said slowly, "to make you proud . . ."

For an instant, time stood still again twice in the same day as the second was folded and tucked away in the treasure chest of a middle aged woman, her middle aged husband. And suddenly, cookies and milk sounded good. Maybe a hamburger would hit the spot, too. After all, we were not going anywhere; we had all night to eat if we liked.

True Love suggested that we go all out and eat in the den; a good show was scheduled on television. He would be glad to take orders if someone would go along to hold everything . . .

"A hamburger?" he asked me.

The nervous stomach had settled. I was hungry and I held up two fingers.

Billy Nichols smiled, a sly, small grin that twitched at the corners of his mouth and crinkled his eyes. "Catsup?" he asked.

I returned his grin. Who could ever trust a mustard eating woman again? "Catsup," I repeated.

And everything was on the way to being right again. Not quite yet, but on the way.

Roxana
and
the
Pension

Edith Beckner

I F you're under forty you don't remember paychecks without
tax deductions or farms without subsidies. Chances are
you wouldn't know about bread lines or bank failures. When
you take a job you want to know how soon you'll get a pro-
motion, if the company gives free insurance policies, and
what the pension plan is.

Don't misunderstand me. Like thousands of others, I
have come to accept these shock absorbers against poverty
in old age, sudden unemployment and crop failures. But
every once in a while when I get a printed slip from the
company telling me how my retirement income is adding up
and I begin to feel pretty smug about the future, I bring
myself up short and remember Grandma Roxie, who lived
and died with serenity if not security.

Her name was Roxana, and you'd call her an old-time
Southerner — a fanatic, a die-hard. But, wait — let me tell
you about her.

When I was six I'd heard about the time the Yankees stole
the last of the family's big fat ducks. I knew all about the
confiscation of the horses by the Confederates. With the
slaves gone and the men gone, there was no one to farm,
horses or no horses. Roxana's folks nearly starved. But you've

heard all that, of course, in truth and in fiction.

If Roxana was prejudiced and biased, we simply let her be. No one ever argued with Roxana. We humored her. We knew she'd lived through some pretty tough times, and we felt if someone had stolen our last duck we might feel the same way.

Roxana had married a sickly veteran of the War, borne eight children in a poverty-stricken South. Widowed at forty, she continued to fight hardships like the rebel she was. The older children worked in the factories which were then creeping into Georgia and the South. Even so there were times when they had little to eat except biscuits and molasses. When the youngest child was out of diapers she began to keep boarders. This had put better food on the table, but there was rent and clothes and shoes for many feet. . . Somehow or other she had survived it all, and at the ripe old age of eighty-one she had even outlived six of her children.

IT was on a bleak day in December, 1931, that Bill Baines, an old acquaintance of the family, came by with an affidavit for Roxana to sign. With him was his mother, who at seventy-nine was deaf as a doormat and on the witless side. I noticed Bill wore no overcoat although the day was bitter with flurries of snow, and his mother's black outfit, which bagged on her shrunken and witchlike figure, looked more than just a little rusty.

I was somewhat embarrassed as I ushered them into our chilly living room where Grandma Roxie sat with a shawl around her shoulders and a light afghan across her knees. Six months before, our bank had closed its doors, and three months later Joe, my husband, lost his job. Stouthearted, Grandma hadn't complained of our skimpy heat and sketchy meals. She was taking the depression in her stride. With the air of a queen she held her silver pompadour high as she nodded and smiled at our visitors. Wrinkles of happiness gathered around her mouth and eyes.

When I had Mr. Baines and his mother comfortably seated, I went down and poked up the furnace a bit with a sidewise glance at the small heap of coal in the bin — enough for two or three days at most. Grudgingly I opened the drafts, put on two shovelfuls of coal, and went upstairs.

I hadn't seen Bill Baines for several years, but I remembered him as plump and fortyish. Now he seemed really old — thin and gray and stoop-shouldered. Deep furrows crossed his forehead and lined his sagging cheeks. His naturally sallow complexion grew pink with excitement as he

explained his mission, punctuating his remarks now and then
with a hollow laugh.

"It's a lotta red tape," he began as he pulled some papers
from his seedy coat, "but you run into that when you deal
with Washington, ya know." He hesitated, laughed uneasily
and squirmed a little. "Seems Ma can't get her pension unless
she can prove she rilly is Pa's widow. You remember the
county courthouse burned in '72 and all the records was
lost, so they want somebody who was at the weddin' of Pa
and Ma to swear that they was rilly married." He reddened
and tried to laugh again. "Seems foolish after all these years.
But Ma recollected that Bob and Roxana Holland stood up
with her and Pa, so that's why we brought the papers over
here. If Miz' Holland will sign, I'll go fetch a notary and get
him to come over."

"What sort of pension is it, Mr. Baines?" I ventured to
ask.

"Well, it's because she's the widow of a Union soldier."

Grandma Roxie lifted her chin higher than usual. "A
Union soldier?"

Bill Baines floundered a moment, then settled back on the
sofa and told the truth about Mr. Baines, senior. He was
captured late in the War by Union soldiers and put into
prison. A country-bred youth, barely seventeen, he grew more
and more despondent as the months crept by. Behind the
prison walls there were only rats, vermin and ragged fellow
prisoners to keep him company. One day some spoiled beans
made him frightfully ill, and he thought he was going to die.
If he could have died the glorious death of a hero on the
battlefield . . . but to die like a rat in a hole . . .

When the Captain offered each prisoner his freedom, a
clean U. S. A. uniform and currency to boot, in exchange
for an oath of allegiance to the Union, young Will Baines
and some of his companions compromised. They had begun
to think they would never again walk on green grass or feel
the Georgia sunshine on their faces. Right was right, and
loyalty was loyalty — but how could anyone say for sure
who was right and who was wrong? What good were you
to your country if you rotted in a stinking prison? News by
way of the grapevine had leaked through to the prisoners that
the Cause was already lost . . .

The boys were uniformed and sent to Western posts where
forces were maintained as a defense against possible trouble
with the Indians. That was the understanding — that they
would not be asked to fight against their homeland.

Mr. Baines said his mother had never considered a

pension before as she hadn't needed it particularly, but now with the depression and all, well, forty dollars a month was not to be sneezed at.

I thought of the dwinding pile of coal in the basement, of my half loaf of bread in the kitchen, the dab of margarine, the sliver of cheese I had saved for our supper. *Forty dollars a month!*

"Goodness, that's wonderful!" I congratulated.

"Well, it'll help keep the wolf away from the door." Bill Baines gave his cheerless cackle again.

Grandma Roxie was silent. To draw her into the conversation I said jokingly, "Grandma, don't you think you could dig up some family history somewhere and find that Grandpa was a Union soldier at the end of the War instead of a Rebel?"

Grandma gave a little toss to her head, and her black eyes snapped. "If you think you're funny, Edith, I can tell you, you aren't." Then turning to Bill Baines she said, "And you ought to be ashamed of yourself to tell that story about your father, let alone taking Federal money that way."

Bill colored. "Well, if Federal money was good enough for Pa, I guess it's good enough for us."

For a moment I thought Grandma wouldn't sign the paper. But she did. "If that's what you want," she dismissed the matter loftily, "I'll sign. It's *your* business, not mine."

We ate the bread and margarine and a slice of cheese around for supper. I didn't even fix a cup of tea for Grandma. There wasn't a quarter in the house for the gas meter, and I knew there was scarcely enough gas to cook a little oatmeal for breakfast . . .

WE didn't starve that winter, but we did sell the guest room furniture. Joe picked up a few odd jobs, and I got fifty cents an evening now and then as a "sitter." A year later, Joe (he's a certified public acountant) got a full-time job as school janitor.

Grandma Roxie lived to be eighty-six and she *didn't* die of starvation. Her heart had been bad for a number of years, and she passed away quietly in her sleep. Joe had gotten a job as bookkeeper then, and we saw that she had a real nice funeral.

A few days after the funeral I looked over the letters and papers in Grandma's old trunk. At the very bottom lay a faded yellow document — the honorable discharge of my grandfather, Robert Jethrow Holland, from the *United States* Army!

The Biggest Hillbilly of Them All

William Virlyn Farr

I WAS drawing a bucket of water, and no matter what anybody says, it wasn't my time. What had Otis and Dewey
and Joe Joe done, not to mention Corrie Lee and Trudy
who could do something round here, it looks like? Otis thinks
he ought not to do nothing cause he has to plow, and I
may be older than Dewey but I ain't much bigger, and they
won't make Joe Joe do a thing cause he's the baby. I'd
slopped the hogs and milked the cows and fed the mules and
toted in I don't know how many turns of wood — and it
Satday, after hoeing cotton all week besides. Anyway, I
was drawing water, where it was my turn or not (which it
wasn't), and had it to the top of the curb, the bucket leaking
every which way, when I heard a car coming up the hill.
Not giving a durn the water would be gone by time I got back,
I run across the yard holding a hand to keep the sun out of
my eyes so I could tell if it was the mailman or not. It was.
So I'd get the mail for a change! We take the *Atlanta Constitution,* so there's always something, and sometimes there's
something else.

I beat him to the box, and he handed me the mail out
the window. The rest of them come running around the house,
and I waved a letter at them, saying, "We got a letter from
Loudora!"

Loudora, that's my oldest sister who went off to Griffin
and got a job in the mill. When she comes back (with a

permanent wave, wearing high heels), she's all the time talking about streets paved with brick and ice-cold Co-Colas and a radio program she listens to at that boardinghouse called "Swing and Sway with Sammy Kaye." She makes out like she can't stand the kind of music you hear round here, the kind Uncle Wash plays on his fiddle, and won't admit she ever did — but don't you know she listened like everybody else when we had a Victrola before the records got broke?

I found Mama in the shed room. She come on in the kitchen; and when everybody gathered round, she read out loud: "Dear Mama and all—how are you? Fine I hope. I'm doing pretty good. Next Sunday Pete Penson is going to take me home, and we're going to eat dinner with you all—" Mama looked up from the letter to say, "Law me, that's tomorrow," and then went on: "I want you to have something good to eat, I mean something *besides* peas!"

We'd never seen Pete Penson, but she'd been writing about him for a good long while. He worked at the same mill with her and was making payments on a car.

"Law me," said Mama, putting the letter down. "We got to get started. Trudy, you get to sweeping up. Corrie Lee, take down them curtains in the front room — when was they washed last? Dewey, you go to the branch and get some white mud. Billy!" She give me a hard look. "Didn't I tell you to get me a bucket of water? Get it! Get two buckets. Fill up the reservoir, fill up a tub. And put some fresh shucks in that mop." (You see what all I have to do round here? No mention of what I already done did this morning, and hoed cotton all week besides.) "Joe Joe, find yo papa and tell him to fix that front step. Corrie Lee, shell these here butter-beans."

"Mama! You told me to take down the curtains," said Corrie Lee.

"Dewey, you take down them curtains."

"You told me to get some white mud!"

"Now do like I say! We got to get this place looking decent."

"Why don't you make Otis do something?" I ask.

"Young man, didn't I tell you to get me some water?"

So I made haste back to the well.

WE didn't get to bed till I reckon it was nine o'clock (slow time). Mama kept changing the furniture round and putting anything that might embarrass Loudora in the barn till we had it full and the house nearly empty. I was wore to a frazzle, let me tell you, and by time I laid down to sleep that night I didn't have no more use for Pete Penson than I did for the man in the moon.

Mama was in the kitchen all morning long Sunday, putting the big pot in the little one, and every time she caught sight of me I had to do something else. She had me pen up the chickens so none would get in the house. Then she had me run the clock up an hour so we'd have the same kind of time as they do in town. So it was really eleven when they got there, though the clock said twelve. Well. Loudora was wearing nylon stockings and high heels, her hair all frizzled, and Pete Penson he was wearing sunglasses and smoking a pipe. Well! Everybody said how glad they was to make his acquaintance and Mama apologized for the house being in such a mess, but Pete Penson said not to mind him on account of he wasn't nothing but homefolks. It was too bad we hadn't had no time to straighten the house up a little, I put in, but didn't nobody pay me any mind.

"You sure got a big house," Pete Penson said when we got to the kitchen.

It's true. We've got five rooms and a hall besides, not to mention the shed room.

At the table Loudora didn't put on as many airs as you might expect — she's all the time saying "idn't," you know, afraid to come right out and say "ain't" when that's what she means. Well. There was fried chicken and ham besides (what do you think of that?), corn on the cob, butterbeans, no peas, stewed sweet potatoes, and two kinds of pickles: peach and cucumber. Pete Penson said "sir?" to Papa and "ma'am?" to Mama, and I knowed after they was gone, we'd mock him. "Sir?" we'd say to Papa, and laugh. "Ma'am?" we'd say to Mama, putting on.

I don't know how the subject of music come up, but when it did Mama says to Pete Penson: "I reckon you like this swing and sway music they have these days?" He just looked at Loudora and sort of grinned and went on to talk about something else.

When Mama said she had a surprise for dessert and set a box of corn flakes on the table, Loudora looked like she could dig a hole and crawl in it, I don't know why. First thing she managed to say, she ask Pete if he hadn't ruther have a half-moon peach pie, which looked mighty good to her. But no, said Pete, just a-grinning at Mama, nothing would suit him better than a bowl of Post Toasties. They was good, and that's a fact. I hadn't had them but once or twice before, and don't you know Loudora wound up eating them too?

We'd just about et all we could hold when we heard a truck coming up the road, backfiring to beat the band and coughing like it was going to give out of gas. Everyone of us younguns run out the door and across the yard and down the road till we met the old truck and jumped on when it slowed down enough and rode to the house like we always done when Uncle Wash come to see us. Mama was standing in the door looking like it was a hearse that rolled up. Uncle Wash is about a hundred years old, I imagine, and a big embarrassment to Mama: he will take a drink of liquor and don't care who knows about it. Well, he said how glad he was to make the acquaintance of Pete Penson, who he'd heard tell of, and then he sat down and commenced to eat what we'd left.

Pete Penson seen the stobs out in the yard and said he'd play me a game of horseshoes. The truth is we don't have horseshoes, account of we don't have horses: we have mules. That makes the game all that much harder, cause mules have real narrow feet. Anyway, we played, and what do you know? I beat him. I said it was most likely an accident, maybe he wasn't in practice, and he said we'd make it the best two out of three, and I beat him the next time, too, but the third time he skunked me good. So then we went on round to the front porch where everybody else was.

They was talking about folks who lived a long time ago: who they married, where they lived, if they was Baptist or Methodist, what they died of, where they was buried, and when. None of it was very interesting, to my way of thinking, so when I got a good chance, I said: "Uncle Wash, did you bring yo fiddle?"

That was the wrong thing to say. He had brought his fiddle and nothing else would do but he play us a tune. If looks could kill, I wouldn't be here to tell this story. The way Mama looked at me! And what if Pete Penson did find out we wasn't nothing but a bunch of hillbillies? We ain't nothing else in the world. Well, if that's the way they wanted to be, I wouldn't listen to no music. I went in the house quick as you please and moseyed out to the barn and then all the way to the woods.

By and by I come back far as the barn and peeped just to see what was going on. They had took chairs to the front yard. And such a crowd! I counted 4 cars. Uncle Wash was playing one of his prettiest tunes: Golden Slippers. And that wasn't all: Pete Penson had a yellow gettar, and he was picking it like nobody's business. Well. I run fast as I could, scooted up close, setting on the ground, fixing my eyes on them singing:

Go dig my grave both wide and deep
Place marble at my head and feet
And on my grave place a turtle dove
That the world might know that I died of love

If that don't get you, I don't know what would — the way they done it, holding onto the high note when they got to "grave," putting so much into it, and the fiddle coming in there so sad. Soon as they finished a piece, argument set in as to what they ought to do next. Some called for square-dance tunes, but others considered them kind pure devilment and wanted to hear gospel singing all the time. Everybody named their requests — *Dance All Night, Gold Watch and Chain, Get Along Home, Mary of the Wild Moor, Dust on the Bible, Life's Railway to Heaven,* on and on, till they heard them all. I got them to do *The Wreck of Old 97* two different times!

Well. Sometimes they sung and sometimes they just picked. The crowd was still there when the sun commenced to fall behind the pines.

I hadn't give Loudora a thought till Pete Penson was singing,

I wish I was a little sparrow bird
I'd never build my nest on the ground
I'd build my nest in my true lover's breast
And there I'd lay my head down

and then it was to wonder when the *funeral* would be. Now Pete Penson had turned out to be the biggest hillbilly of all, don't you know she'd die a natural death?

Where in the world, I ask Loudora who was sitting in a chair behind me, where'd all these people come from and how'd they know we was going to have string music? What she done, she had wrote post cards telling them all, even Uncle Wash, but hadn't let on cause she wanted to surprise us. You see, Pete Penson hadn't lived all his life in Griffin where the streets are paved with brick and everybody has a radio: he was raised on a farm and didn't give a durn who knowed it.

"Loudora," I ask, "are you going to marry him?"

"That's for me to know and for you to find out," she says, watching him sing *Little Darling, Pal of Mine,* her foot patting, her lips moving right along with his.

Shucks, she wasn't studying no swing and sway music.

A Letter from Uncle Sam

William Virlyn Farr

LEM Kimble was taking a nap in the swing on the front porch when the screen door slammed and woke him up. "What's this here letter?" said his wife, a little woman whose hair shone silvery white in the afternoon sun.

Lem sat up and yawned. "What letter is that you're talking about, Fannie Mae?"

"Aw!" she said in a manner which indicated that he knew full well what she meant.

He had brought the letter home along with the groceries, but he hadn't bothered to ask the postmaster to read it. "Hit ain't nothing but another one of them advertisements. I don't know whut they keep a sending them to us fer, no more money'n we got. You can throw hit away."

"*Humph*," said Fannie Mae, who believed in having their mail read no matter what it was. She opened the letter and examined it every which way as if she could somehow comprehend it. Lem kept assuring her it was nothing that would interest them.

"Whose picture's this?" Fannie Mae asked, and handed him the letter.

It pictured an elderly gentleman wearing a strange-looking suit of stars and stripes in red, white, and blue. He was pointing a finger like a preacher might in the middle of a rousing sermon.

"Why, I don't know who that is, Fannie Mae." Lem removed a plug of Brown's Mule from the pocket of his overalls and cut himself a chew. "Some of the younguns ought to be here Sunday, and they'll know who hit is."

"Aw, it ain't but Wednesday. I'd worry myself sick by time Sunday gets here. With the war and all, L. M. and Jumbo off in the army . . ." Fannie Mae sneezed. "Them old ragweeds," she explained. "You know they give Liza Gazaway the asthma, and Gus he had to cut everyone of them down in *their* yard."

"I never put no stock in what them Gazaways said."

"It was the *doctor* who said it. When aire you going to do something about them old ragweeds, Lem?"

He was lying down again. "I'm going to take me a nap," he said.

"Ain't you going back up yonder and get this letter read?"

"Huh?" said Lem, and dozed off.

He slept until it was time to eat supper and Fannie Mae called him to draw the buttermilk out of the well where it had been cooling.

Fannie Mae didn't eat anything. She just sat there staring at her empty plate.

"What's the matter with you?" said Lem.

"I don't know what that letter says," she murmured.

"I don't know neither."

"And *you* don't care," she said, and choked up.

"Now, Fannie Mae . . . now. I'll go back up yonder in the morning and get Ike Roseberry to read hit. All hit says is how much this and that's selling fcr, like I done told you. That's all they write letters about anymore."

Next morning Lem found Gus Gazaway and George Roper playing checkers outside the store. He only nodded to them and hurried inside. Ike Roseberry was putting up mail in a corner of the store where he kept the post office. Lem handed him the letter. "Whose picture's this?"

"Why," said Ike, adjusting his spectacles, "that's Uncle Sam."

"Uncle Sam who?"

"*Uncle Sam!* The United States government, that's what it amounts to. That's the picture they use when something real official goes out of Washington, D. C. You better watch out when you get some mail with this picture on it — that means it's official business."

Lem began to get a little worried. "I didn't know that," he admitted. "What does hit say?"

"Let me see. It looks like your number came up." Ike removed his spectacles. "The army wants you, Lem."

"What the deuce you trying to say, Ike? You know I'm too old fer any army."

"Well," said Ike Roseberry, placing his spectacles in his shirt pocket, "I didn't write the letter, I just told you what it says. You see, Uncle Sam here's saying, 'I want you,' and down further it explains where he wants you — in the army."

"When have I got to go?"

"It doesn't say. That probably means they'll come after you."

Gus Gazaway and George Roper had followed Lem into the store. Gus pulled off his hat as if someone had just died. "I sure hate to see you go, Lem."

George nodded his head in full agreement.

"Aw, I ain't going nowhere," said Lem. "I ain't fit to be no soldier. I can just barely hold out to do a little now and then round the house, resting along."

"They're scraping the bottom of the barrel," said Gus. "That's what it looks like."

"I hear the news over the radio," said Ike Roseberry, "and the other night I heard somebody say — I forget who it was — he said this is a 'desperate' situation, and 'desperate' situations call for 'desperate' measures."

Everyone laughed, for that was certainly a hifalutin way to put it.

"Ike," said Lem, "I ain't ask you to write me no letter in I don't know how long."

"Why, anytime, Lem. Who're you thinking of writing?"

"The gov'ment. Say I can't go, cause I — well, I can't sleep. Ever' night I lay awake hours at the time, is what I do."

"That don't make no difference," said George Roper who had been in the army himself and knew what he was talking about. "If you can't sleep, they put you on guard duty."

"Now listen here," said Lem. "I done got too old fer the like of that. "Why, if them furriners come after me I couldn't run at all."

"That's the kind they want," George Roper pointed out. "You can't run, you'll have to fight.' '

Lem was halfway out of the store, and he turned back, hoping to see them laughing, to hear them saying it was just another one of their jokes that they liked to play so well. But he had never seen such solemn faces.

On his way home, Lem got used to the notion that he would have to go to the army. He just hoped they wouldn't expect him to keep up with the younger fellows.

Fannie Mae was sitting on the front porch. She came down the steps and across the yard to meet Lem. "Now, Fannie Mae . . . now. You got to hold up, hit looks like this war's done got a whole lot worse. . ."

"I knowed it was bad news! What is it? What's happened?"

"Well," said Lem, making an effort to appear cheerful. "The army's done got me, Fannie Mae. I been drafted."

"*You?*" Fannie Mae laughed.

"This picture," said Lem, taking the letter out of his pocket. "This here's Uncle Sam, and he's saying, 'I want you.' They'll be coming after me before you know hit."

"Is that what Ike Roseberry told you?"

"He read the letter to me, is what he done. Hit's from Washington, D. C."

"I never heard the like," said Fannie Mae, looking at Lem intently. Then she laughed. "You can think up excuses aplenty when *I* want you to do something, I guess you can think up one for the army."

Lem cut himself a chew of tobacco, and said, "Whut you can't get in yore head, Fannie Mae, is that hit's the whole United States Army after me. There ain't a thing I can do. I could go up in the hills or to the bottom of the creek, and they'd find me."

Fannie Mae took the letter from him and pursed her lips as if trying to keep from smiling.

"You'll see," said Lem. "They'll come after me, and then you'll change your tune."

He started up the steps to take his nap.

"Wait a minute, Lem," said Fannie Mae, her voice in earnest now. "You so used to taking a nap half the morning and another one half the evening, and I don't imagine they'll let you do that in the army. What you better do is get you'self in shape. Them old ragweeds, it'd do you more good'n anything to dig them up."

Now Fannie Mae was taking the army seriously, and Lem had to admit she had his interest at heart. He said yes, of course, he would dig the weeds up right away.

Two hours later, just when he had the yard clean, Fannie Mae came to the door and said: "Looks like the beetles is going to eat them 'taters up. I sure wish you'd dust them with some arsenic."

He dusted the potatoes.

Then Fannie Mae said, "I don't know what I'm going to do with them petunia boxes, look how rotted they is?"

Realizing that he would soon be gone and wouldn't have the opportunity to do that kind of thing for his wife, Lem said that he would build her some new boxes.

He didn't take a nap all afternoon. He kept busy until suppertime, and soon afterwards he went to bed and slept soundly. Fannie Mae woke him at sunrise with a reminder that he would have to get used to rising early. At breakfast she mentioned a number of things that needed doing, and Lem agreed to get as many done that day as possible, for he didn't know when the army might come after him.

"You think they'll get here in a day or two?" asked Fannie Mae.

Lem shook his head. "I don't know," he said with a sigh. "I sure wish I did."

"We better work in the garden first, get that grass dug up."

Lem was in the garden all morning. He was going to take a nap in the early afternoon, for it was hot and he was tired, but Fannie Mae said: "I wish you'd haul some rock in the wheelbarrow to that gully yonder where it washes across the yard everytime it rains."

Lem hauled the rock. He was sitting in the wheelbarrow resting when Fannie Mae came up and said, "Lem? You see that piece of loose tin up there on top of the house? It rattles everytime the wind blows. I wish you'd get up there and nail it down."

Lem nailed the tin down.

Just as he stepped off the ladder, Fannie Mae said: "You reckon you'd have time to build a new pen for the chickens before the army comes after you?"

"I can start hit," he said.

They were at the supper table when Fannie Mae saw someone coming down the road. "What you looking at?" said Lem, and leaned over so he could see out the window. He saw a soldier coming toward the house, and sank back. "There they come!" he said.

"Aw, that ain't nobody but L. M." said Fannie Mae.

L. M., their youngest boy, who was stationed at Ft. Jackson, had come home on leave.

"Won't be long now till I'll be in one of them uniforms," said Lem as the boy seated himself at the table.

"What in the nation are you talking about, Pa?"

"I been drafted, that's what!"

"But they wouldn't have you. You're too old."

"That's what I kept telling them."

"Telling who?"

"Ike Roseberry. Everybody at the store. I kept telling them I'm too old to fight in no war, but they said I'm the kind they're taking these days."

L. M. rared back in his chair and roared with laughter. "Don't you know they were teasing you?"

"But I got a letter from Washington, D. C. Fannie Mae, get that letter."

L. M. glanced at the letter that his mother got from the dresser drawer. "Pa, do you know what this says?"

"Like I done told you, Ike Roseberry read hit to me. Uncle Sam there says he wants me."

"But do you know what it means?"

"I been drafted."

"It doesn't mean any such thing. It's nothing but an advertisement. It's trying to get you to enlist — not you personally, but anybody they'd have. What'd Mr. Roseberry tell you?"

Lem was so overjoyed at this turn of events that he couldn't remember what Ike Roseberry had said. "You mean I ain't got to go?"

"Of course not! Ma, you know how Mr. Roseberry likes to tease him. Why didn't you tell him better?"

"I couldn't tell him *nothing*. Besides, you ought to of seen what all he done since he got that letter."

Lem got up from the table in a hurry. "Hey!" said L. M. "Where're you going?"

"I'm going lay down and take me a nap. I got a whole lot of sleeping to catch up on."

The Gift List

Frances Greene

IN spite of the generation gap, my young friend, Wiliam Edward Nichols, and I do not lack for communication — not when it comes to free enterprise and Christmas. Both of us are firm believers in each.

On the first count, we have, in the course of our friendship, raised a calf on a bottle and sent him to market (barely breaking even), and gigged frogs in the dark of the moon because there was a man "who'd buy all we could git" (which was one). As for Christmas, we get the spirit of gift giving and receiving along about Thanksgiving, and reluctantly, even sadly, yield to the New Year in the middle of January.

Actually, there is no connection between these two lines of communication. We never make any money in our business deals, and even if we did, we would spend it before the twinkling lights, the plastic stars and tinsel hit the store windows.

However, being the "newspaper lady," as Billy Nichols calls me, and being the wife of "True Love," the middle-aged newspaper publisher, gives me a definite advantage money-wise over my young friend's financial condition. The proud little fellow is not only the head of his family composed of Ma and four younger sisters, he is the sole provider of those little extras that their small monthly check will not allow. Billy's Pa, it seems, is away for a spell. And the law men who dared to invade "that pretty little old place up on the mountain was about the most unthoughty folks in this neck of the woods." According to Billy, "They was not happy jist to pour out the mellowest moonshine ever to run through copper tubing, they denamited every last one of them cookers."

Though the towheaded lad did not condone his Pa's occupation by any means, he violently reacted to wastefulness in any form. And them cookers could have been used for something — maybe even an outside bathtub, he confided, as we tramped through the woods that Sunday afternoon before Christmas in search of mistletoe.

But before I could answer, he was off through the rhododendron toward the sound of squirrels in a tree.

The youngster, I remarked to True Love, was at heart a pack rat. To which he replied that our house had turned out to be the perfect hidey hole.

He had reference, of course, to the dime I paid for the ten pound, lead pipe door stop for which I was still trying to find a door that needed it. In other words, I was Billy Nichols' made-to-order, gullible Patsy. But I was also his friend; I respected his inbred conviction that something should never be taken for nothing, and I got what I paid for.

T RUE Love, though a smart man, does not understand completely how and why I get sold on so many of Billy Nichols' ideas. He, too, believes in man's right to make a quick dollar but he does not believe that the youngster and I should go to such lengths to test the privilege; he believes in glitter and "Jingle Bells" and big packages tied with red ribbon but he does not believe in getting too involved. He points out clearly, concisely and a bit grimly that I should make a gift list, fill it and then be through except for wrapping and labeling. He adds in a positive tone of voice that I should not meddle in our skinny little friend's annual shopping spree at the local *five and ten* where he selects in rapid succession six silver capped bottles of colored toilet water — four for his sisters, one for the name he draws in school and one for his teacher.

I promised. I promised that I would neither suggest scents nor exchange colors. And so it was that Christmas in the newspaper office and at home had the earmarks of being calm, peaceful and merry. But True Love and I had forgotten that life's problems cannot always be solved with a half dozen containers of 29 cents rose water; we had forgotten that sooner or later every young man bounces, skips, runs and then walks straight into the crossroads of dreams and reality. And Billy Nichols trudged tiredly, heavily, listlessly to that point of no return. His route stopped at my desk where he stood for a long moment, searching for the words to explain what he had to do.

"I reckon," he said finally, his dark eyes wandering over the stacks of letters, "that I'll jist stay out of school after the holidays."

Carefully I removed an unfinished news story from the typewriter. The announcement was unexpected, baffling.

"If I go in debt, it'd take full time to pay out."

I swallowed hard.

"And there jist ain't no other way." The skinny little shoulders shrugged; a heavy sigh started at his unbelted breeches and went all the way to the thin lips.

I looked at the other desk quickly, wanting True Love's help. "You could get a job now," I offered casually, stalling for time.

He picked up a pen idly, unseeingly; drew a mark on an envelope. And for a long minute, he did not look up, but he shook his head slowly. "I jist thought you ought to know," he said finally.

I was glad that he told me; maybe we could find a way . .

"There ain't an answer." He had never appeared more dejected, more despondent; he was completely, utterly defeated.

I glanced at True Love but he was no help. Christmas, I decided, was getting out of hand, it was not the gift that counted — only the thought.

"You know that, Billy Nichols," I said firmly. "You know as well as I do that your mother had rather have something you made just for her."

But his eyes stopped me; large swimming, heart broken eyes that begged me to be quiet for just a little while. And he reached into the skimpy jacket and ever so slowly removed a folded sheet of tablet paper. He did not look up again but the hopelessness was there in the bent touseled head, and his voice was low when he spoke. "Why," he whispered, "don't you try telling that to Missy?"

Throwing the letter on the desk, he turned quickly, slamming the door behind him.

In block letters, the penciled printing overflowed one line into the next but any Santa worth his salt could see that the letter was to him. The request was simple: "I want a warm, red coat and candy for my sisters. Please." And it was signed "Melissa, 6 years old."

True Love gently lifted it from my hands. I hit a typewriter key. "I saw one yesterday," I mused aloud.

But True Love knew Billy Nichols; he knew his stubborn pride, his disdain for charity. The Nichols were honorable folks in spite of what the law men thought. To Pa, his occupation had been a family inheritance, an art, a gift like painting or singing.

"We have a lot of trash," True Love broke the silence.

I cleared my throat. "There are three more. How could just one red coat help?"

True Love smiled. "We could have a direct line to Santa," he reminded.

But Billy Nichols would not have accepted that, not in his present state of mind. He was not accustomed to miracles, only hard work. He would not, as he often said, "be beholden."

"He is," I insisted to True Love the next morning as our young friend eased silently around the office, broom in hand, "going to be sick. Why does he have to have so darned much pride?" I complained bitterly, throwing more trash on the floor.

"That," True Love reminded gently, "is all that he has left." His voice implied that if I were a real friend to Billy Nichols, I could not take that away from him. And I had only one day left to round up all the trash I could find.

I WAS glad that the phone rang then. I was glad that people started coming in and out, wanting poster board, renewing subscriptions, giving them for presents to relatives out of town. "Jingle Bells" tinkled over the record player from the Music Shop up the street; a group of girls peeped through the window and waved. Silently, Billy Nichols sharpened the pencils, straightened the papers on the counter, wandered into the back shop. He avoided conversation; his eyes were clouded over, not really seeing, not really looking.

"You are taking this too hard," True Love cautioned over coffee. "There will always be six year old Missys in this world. . . "

I had to agree but all of them were dependent upon a snub nosed, skinny little boy who could find a use for everything but could not come up with red coats. I had promised not to meddle but the promise had not included a loan that would be payable next summer when I needed rocks for a walk. I could make it legal if necessary; I could have it notarized.

"We may be moving," Billy Nichols answered curtly. "If I don't go back to school, I could make a crop on the mountain . . . get ready for Pa and all." He looked at me steadily, daring me to argue.

"You're being sort of unreasonable." I took his dare.

His thin lips were like two lines. He lowered his eyes to the floor. "I spoke to Mr. White already," his voice was belligerent, bitter, "He's gonna let me pay monthly."

The little codger was actually serious about going to work; he had already made arrangements about purchasing the gifts. Why, I wondered, did True Love always have to be busy or out in town getting ads when I needed him most? How could one little old codger, no bigger than a minute, spoil a holiday season by being so stubborn?

The fire siren across town wailed in the stillness; there was the screech of brakes beneath the stop light. And uptown, shoppers were going in and out of stores, rushed, but a gay kind of rush that was contagious in their cheery greetings.

The holly wreath on the door bounced. The briskness of the wind showed on True Love's cheeks, in his clear eyes as he closed it behind him. "Merry Christmas." His voice was teasing but his smile was warm.

Under ordinary circumstances, Billy Nichols would have added, "Happy New Year." But these were not ordinary circumstances. The youngster got busy behind the counter.

"Something has to give," I exploded that night as we sat in our silent house, a plate of uneaten cookies on the table. "You know and I know that we will deliver a box Christmas Eve."

True Love sighed.

"This is the season to be happy and" . . . my voice was rising.

True Love stood, yawned. "And who was preaching faith last week?" He ambled off to bed.

Maybe I preached it but it was not helping Billy Nichols now. And I stalked into the kitchen to whip up a batch of fudge. At least I could supply the candy.

I TRIED to get to the office early since we would close for the holidays when the last run was made and the papers were addressed. But the big press was already roaring and the mail was on the desk. The weatherman had predicted snow flurries; I did not even bother to tell my young friend.

The penciled letter to Billy Nichols was on top of my typewriter. He had never, to my knowledge, received mail in all his life, and I tried to decipher the post mark before carrying it into the back shop where the youngster was catching papers off the carrier.

He accepted it quietly and tore it carefully at the end. He unfolded the sheet of tablet paper and read. His eyes brightened; his face broke into the most beautiful smile I had ever seen in my life. He had heard from Pa, and clipped to the sheet was the most gorgeous twenty dollar bill ever to be printed by the treasury department.

For a long moment Billy Nichols could not move. He swallowed hard. And two large tears slipped out of the dark eyes and rolled ever so gently down the pinched cheeks.

The big press had stopped; even the phone was not ringing, and from the Music Shop next door we heard voices lifted in "Silent Night."

"I guess," I said slowly, rubbing my nose matter of factly, "that you should go shopping."

He grinned then, a wide Billy Nichols grin that brought light and happiness wherever it was aimed. He hitched up his breeches, gave a short carefree sigh. "I reckon," he agreed. He rubbed a dirty hand across his damp cheeks. "I'd be mighty beholden if you'd go help me."

I rubbed a hand across my wet ones. I could think of nothing better that I would like to do.

But first, I had a mission at the linotype where the middle aged publisher I married some thirty years ago was busy setting a line. I did not have to ask now why he had slept so well; I did not have to ask why we had a straight line to the North Pole.

I ambled to the big machine and placed my hands on his shoulders. "Merry Christmas," I whispered. And then because there are some things that he does that I don't understand, I kissed him.

He did not look up. After all, somebody in the family has to make a living — not just a pick-up dollar, but say about twenty or so?

Round 'im Up,
Herd 'im In

Frances Greene

THE trend, these days, is to "tell it like it is." And I am
more than happy to play along if for no other reason than
it relieves me from having to find plausible explanations for
my involvement in the projects sponsored by young Billy
Nichols.

Actually, I use the word "sponsored" loosely. The truth
of the matter is that my small, skinny, towheaded friend had
more promotions up his faded, plain sleeve than, as he puts
it, "a sow's got pigs.'" And every last one of his ideas requires
the steadying hand of a middle-aged newspaperwoman: mine,
and the financial backing of a middle-aged newspaper publisher: True Love's.

However, in all fairness to the little fellow, I have to add
that he is by no means a juvenile con artist. He sincerely and
honestly believes that his business ventures will work, and
if they do, he unselfishly spends the profit on his mother and
three younger sisters. At this stage in his life, his primary
objective is to "hold Ma and the girls together 'til Pa gets
back."

True Love adds that this will be a snap if I live so long.

But without me, Billy Nichols would find a way. He is not
only unselfish, he is enterprising and energetic. We have the
best swept office in town, the sharpest pencils, the emptiest
trash basket and the prettiest rock paperweight "you ever did
see." His stubborn pride, however, is something else again. He
refuses "to take somethin' for nothin' "— an attribute that is
vexing and nerve-wracking considering that it would be far
cheaper to write a monthly check for Ma's vittles and far

more restful and relaxing to just sit and rock instead of trying to grow and raise 'em. Both of which we have tried, and this brings on the telling of the calf project like it was.

Billy Nichols, in his wandering around the countryside, ran up on the "prettiest little ole bull a cow ever had, and the farmer didn't really want 'im 'cause he raised only them that gives milk." We could, it seems, get that calf real cheap and we could raise him. We also could double our money and even if we could not do that, we could always butcher him and have a freezer full of hamburger.

And so it was that I found myself at noon of a beautiful spring Saturday trying to sneak down the driveway past True Love on his riding lawn mower, in a rattling, belching, burping pickup truck loaded with a six day old frightened, bawling bull. We—the driver, Billy Nichols, the bull and I—were headed in the general direction of our small, faded red barn with a gate that also served as the entrance to a big, tree shaded pen that had been occupied, in the past, by a pet deer.

At the sight of us, True Love and the mower headed straight for the prize azalea bed. But I was not the one, at this point, to shout a warning. He would not have heard me anyway.

Billy Nichols' face, as he jumped out of the truck to direct the driver, was like the sun after a forty day rain. His eyes danced and his feet jiggled, and he held one grubby hand at half-mast as the pickup backed slowly between the pines.

I glanced nervously up the knoll toward the mower. It had choked out; pink blooms hung from the engine. True Love was wiping his forehead.

The driver was telling me something about sterilizing the bucket and nipple after each feeding and that it was best to set a schedule.

"After a few days, you won't even know he's around," he assured me.

I believed him. I honestly and truly believed him, and I marveled at the ease with which he then maneuvered the little wild-eyed, homesick noisemaker into the shed, removed the rope, looped it around his arm and crawled back into the truck.

"Good luck," he said with a smile. And he was gone, leaving me with half a hungry bull, a sack of dried milk and a bucket with a nipple. I looked helplessly at Billy Nichols, wondering just what he planned to do with his half!

I could have been looking at the moon. The youngster had stars in his eyes. He had owned many things in his lifetime, including a "real to gosh rod and reel" and an old, white, shaggy dog, but never had he owned anything of such value. This was real—this was better than an oil well, a gold mine, a truck garden. This was sort of like the ark with a fresh start toward filling the world with animals; this was the beginning, the father of a future herd. And he glanced unseeingly in my direction as if to say that he sure was glad he had thought of starting us off in the cow business; in fact, he wondered how he ever managed to come up with such a breathtaking idea anyway!

I stole a nervous look at the azalea bed; True Love was gone.

"Ya ever fed one before?" The starry eyes condescended to meet mine. I shook my head. I had never been closer to a live cow than a fence allowed.

"It's easy," he assured me. "First you mix warm water and powder, then you jist cram that thing in his mouth and he takes it like a baby."

I volunteered to walk up the knoll to the house and make the formula.

"Ya got to be careful." The thin shoulders had a tilt of importance. "Too much feeding at one time and he'll get sick." I nodded as if I understood.

"But they got tablets, big ole yellow ones, to cure 'im," he added quickly. That was nice, I thought. Now I could set the alarm for medication.

The mixture, when stirred briskly, looked a little like milk; it smelled a little like milk. Maybe we had an ark after all.

"Don't you reckon," Billy Nichols suggested, climbing onto the gate to sit on the top board, "you better try feeding 'im first so's he'll know you?"

I reckoned that it was a pretty darned decent concession he was making, and I crawled into the stall with the six day old baby that was already bigger than I was.

But contrary to all that I had been led to believe, the pretty, little ole black bull definitely knew the difference between his Mother Molly and a sterile nipple. He lifted his heavy hooves, danced a wild jig, bawled, bobbed his head, rolled his eyes and snorted.

"Cram it," Billy Nichols shouted from his grandstand seat.

I crammed. The calf turned the nipple crosswise, chewed and drooled and snorted with a tremendous jerk, slinging the bucket and its contents to the rafters.

Billy Nichols swung his legs and shook his head in bewilderment; this was not the way it was supposed to happen.

I wiped the sticky stuff from my arms and legs.

"He's got to learn," Billy Nichols decided.

I began the walk back up the hill to the house. True Love was digging around his tomatoes and softly whistling something about being an old cowhand.

Billy Nichols had not moved an inch; he had not taken his eyes from the bawling calf. "I've been thinking," he admitted, "something is wrong."

That was the understatement of the day.

He leaned forward. "Maybe when he lets out another bleat, you could shove."

He had not stopped bleating but there was a fraction of a second when he drew his breath. I shoved.

Black eyes flashed; nubs went up; milk splashed.

"We got a problem," Billy Nichols said, sighing tiredly.

I could hardly see how he was suffering with fatigue but I nodded.

At the tomato patch, a voice softly trilled, "Yippee Yi Yo . . ."

Billy Nichols watched silently as I changed my approach with the new, fresh, warm mixture. I cooed and crooned; I made soft mooing sounds as I eased the nipple forward.

The boy on the rail was captivated but the bull was scared stiff. He snorted, jiggled and bawled. I felt the milk running down my legs and into my shoes; my toes squashed.

"I'll jist be . . ."

I cleared my throat; I drew in my breath. Billy Nichols did not like my expression; he was worried, worried sick. "I could make up a new batch," he offered. "I know how . . ."

I picked up the bucket; it took energy to give a shake of the head.

The tomato patch was no more than a landmark; the man with the hoe was not more than a figure to be ignored. "Yippee," the ignored voice said casually.

Limping into the barn again, I leaned for a moment against the stall.

"Ya don't have to cry," Billy Nichols comforted. "There's got to be a way if I can jist think of it . . ."

There was. The farmer could have him back for free with a bucket and a sack of feed thrown in to boot—not to mention a youngster full of directions to sit on a stall gate.

"I was figuring . . ." Billy Nichols said thoughtfully.

I was too, on bull hemlock.

But the boy had jumped to the ground; his eyes were bright again. "Pa straddled his. I remember now." His voice was louder, excited. "Jist try it . . ."

By nature I would not call myself a bull straddler; I am, quite frankly, a bit awkward, but if Pa straddled his bulls, then I could straddle this one.

I put the black head between my legs and dared him to bob. I planted two firm hands beneath his chin and pulled upward with brute force. I held fast and yelled at Billy Nichols to pop the nipple in the open, drooling mouth. I clamped it shut. And suddenly there was a clink, a beautiful, melodious clink of milk's leaving one container and going into another. The calf was swallowing.

In the failing light I looked at Billy Nichols. He grinned. "We done it," he said proudly. "We really and truly done it."

We might have done it but I was still riding herd; it had been easier to straddle than it was now to unstraddle. To slide forward, I gave the bull's head a downward push. Billy Nichols dropped the bucket and opened the gate. The gate hit the bucket, the calf lifted his back legs, I bounded forward on the run.

A pine tree broke the dash. And for a long moment, the youngster did not speak. He was struck with a mixture of fear and admiration over the one point landing. He waited respectfully until I lifted one leg.

"It broke?" he asked solicitously.

I shook my head.

He closed the gate, walked over to the tree and sat on the ground beside me. His brown eyes were clouded over; the idea had been a good one but it was doubtful that his middle-aged newspaperwoman friend would live long enough to see it through.

I sighed heavily. I was hot, tired, dirty, hungry and sore. I felt like used flypaper. I had been talked into a project that would require the acrobatics just performed twice a day, seven days a week for six weeks. And suddenly, I was ready to admit defeat; anyway who could possibly eat the hamburger that was now licking his lips in the stall?

The gate creaked; True Love cleared his throat.

Billy Nichols looked at the ground; his chin was not so strong now. I looked aimlessly at the branch just inside the back fence.

True Love cleared his throat again. "I had a calf once . . ." His voice died away, leaving an undertone of wistfulness.

Billy Nichols turned slightly, waiting.

"In the morning I'll show you how it's done," the newspaper publisher said matter-of-factly. "We'll have to get a bit of hay, too . . ."

The gate closed. I glanced at my friend; the brown stars were shining again; the ark had withstood the flood; the herd would make it.

"I was wondering," he said finally, "if maybe we oughtn't to name that little ole black bull . . ."

I nodded.

"I was thinking that—well—I jist sort of believe that he," he jerked his head toward the retreating figure of the man headed for the tomato patch, "might be sort of pleased if we named him 'True Love.'"

If I had thought for a century, I could never have thought of that; the idea was wonderful, positively outstanding. Imagine having a bull in your barn called TRUE LOVE?

"Yessir," Billy Nichols said, giving his head a jerk, "it jist suits 'im. So I reckon I'll go tell him now."

I went, too. That I had to see and hear.

Calamity in a Camper

Clyde W. Jolley

HUGH Dorsey Brown was bone-tired. He had worked the swing shift at the aircraft plant, packed the new camper on the pickup truck and got to bed at 2:30 a.m. His wife, Willie Belle, woke him at 4:30 because they wanted to leave their Canton, Georgia, home in time to get through Atlanta before the morning traffic rush.

They had stopped for breakfast at Forsyth and now they were tooling along Interstate 75, headed for the first real vacation they had ever had, what with raising the children and all. A whole week in Florida lay ahead of them and they were eagerly looking forward to the experience.

But Hugh Dorsey was worn out. He smoked a Tampa Nugget, hoping it would revive him, but fatigue and sleepiness had him beat. He pulled off the road.

"Willie Belle," he said, "I've had it. How about you taking over a while?"

"Okay," she said, then brightly, patting his knee, "Why don't you try out the bunk? You can take a good nap and I'll wake you up when I get tired."

He didn't argue but marched straight back to the new camper and climbed in, unbuttoning his shirt along the way. Hugh Dorsey couldn't go to sleep comfortably unless he stripped down to his underwear.

Just at the moment he stepped out of his pants Willie Belle let out the clutch and jerked into the I-75 traffic. Hugh Dorsey fell against the unfastened door and sailed through the air, landing on his rump on the concrete.

After the flight and fall he had just a split second to wonder if he were dead and another to get out of the way of the whooshing Florida-bound traffic. Safe on the shoulder he saw Willie Belle and the camper as a speck on the horizon. Willie Belle always had been a fast driver.

The watery April sun was in a stand-off against the chill mid-Georgia 'climate but the warmth radiating from Huge Dorsey's rear and the shame he felt at his state of undress made him hot all over. Car after car rushing by squealed their tires briefly then gunned away as if frightened by the strange apparition. Finally an old Chevrolet came to a screeching halt on the shoulder and four black men piled out, three of them apparently under the influence.

"That's the whitest man I ever saw," cried one of the drunks.

"Let's tie him to the back of the car and let him run along behind us," said another. "He's dressed up for running anyhow." "Fellows," Hugh Dorsey said, "I got thrown out of my camper. I'll give you fifty dollars if you can catch up with my wife."

"That makes sense," said the sober one. All of them seemed impressed at the mention of cash, but one kept muttering, "How can that mullet get fifty dollars out of that little bitty suit?"

They all climbed in. The sober one was the driver. They put Hugh Dorsey in the back seat between two of the drunks who immediately sprawled out with their feet stuck out the windows. The old Chevy leaped down the road and in a matter of seconds was doing ninety.

CORPORAL Tom Harrison and Patrolman Jake Rakestraw had just finished their coffee at the Stuckey's place in Unadilla and were pulling back into I-75 when the Chevy blasted by.

"What in the hell was that?" exclaimed Jake.

"Looks like the NAACP done caught themselves a nekkid white man," said his partner. "Let's go!"

With light flashing and siren at full voice they tore out in pursuit. The Chevy's driver heard the siren but kept floorboarding the gas pedal. He thought about his strange cargo and figured he had nothing to lose by trying to outrun the cops.

Tom and Jake finally overtook the Chevy at Ashburn.

"What in God's name is going on here?" asked Tom.

"We're trying to get this man back into his breeches," said the driver. "We ain't done nothing wrong."

"He's gonna pay us fifty dollars to catch up with his wife."

"He was freezing and we had to take care of him," explained the black men, all talking at once.

"That's right," said Hugh Dorsey. "These fellows are trying to help me catch up with my wife." He pointed helplessly toward Florida.

"That sure does sound crazy," said Tom, "but there's no doubt about it, you do have a problem. Tell you what, Jake, you drive their car and I'll take this nekkid fellow with me and we'll try to catch up with his wife. I don't want to turn these guys loose till we've asked them some questions."

The patrol car and the following Chevy whizzed through the warming south Georgia countryside past the big green signs proclaiming Sycamore, Sunsweet, Chula and Tifton, then on past Phillipsburg, Unionville, Fender and Lenox. As they approached Adel, Hugh Dorsey saw in the distance Willie Belle and the camper, its door still swinging in the wind.

Willie Belle had been driving nearly three hours. She had felt good and had enjoyed singing along with the radio. It was now playing "I'm Bound for the Promised Land" and she thought, "In a couple of hours we'll be in the promised land of Florida." Just then a siren's wail drowned out the radio and a patrol car crowded her to the shoulder.

When Corporal Tom and her stripped-down Hugh Dorsey jumped from the patrol car, Willie Belle felt she was having a full-blown nightmare. When the Chevy pulled up and another patrolman and four black men got out she fainted dead away.

Hugh Dorsey didn't even look at her but climbed in the camper, put on his pants and shoes, and shirtless, returned to find the troopers reviving Willie Belle.

After thanking them and paying the fifty dollars to the Chevy's driver he retrieved his shirt and pulled off leaving the two officers talking to the blacks at the side of the road.

"Hugh Dorsey," soothed his wife, "everybody is going to be all right. We'll be fishing in Tampa Bay this time tomorrow and you won't remember a thing about this."

Hugh Dorsey was not at all sure. His body ached all over and his spirits were lower than a mole. All he could say was, "For two cents I'd turn around and head back home."

"Let's get some lunch," said Willie Belle, "then we'll both feel better."

They stopped at Valdosta and went into a nice looking restaurant and ordered a good meal. As Hugh Dorsey looked down at the iced tea and roast beef and home fried potatoes he began to lose a little of the terror and embarrassment of the morning. Then when he started to spread his napkin he saw that his fly was completely open. He had overlooked this detail when he had put his pants back on.

He jerked the zipper shut and caught with it a corner of the red tablecloth. He jerked the other way but the tablecloth had become welded to his being. Willie Belle jerked too, but all they accomplished by their desperate efforts was to clatter the dishes to the floor. By now every eye in the place was on them and the waitress came over to survey the damage.

Hugh Dorsey was standing, the red tablecloth held in his hand like a bullfighter's muleta. "Miss," he implored the waitress, "how much for the tablecloth? Looks like I'll have to take it with me."

The waitress was kind. "Don't you worry about the tablecloth, sir. I'll fix you right up." She left and returned with the biggest pair of shears Hugh Dorsey had ever seen. She whacked him loose, leaving an eight-inch tongue hanging from his trousers.

Futilely trying to cover the remnant with his hands Hugh Dorsey paid the bill and they left accompanied by a chorus of raucous laughter from the assembled tourists. The story of the tablecloth and the zipper would be related for years to come in homes from Minnesota to Massachusetts.

Hugh Dorsey and Willie Belle climbed into the truck and pulled back onto I-75. They drove silently for an hour before Willie Belle noticed they were heading north. Even then she didn't say a single, solitary word.

Down
on
Cooter's
Creek

Jannelle Jones McRee

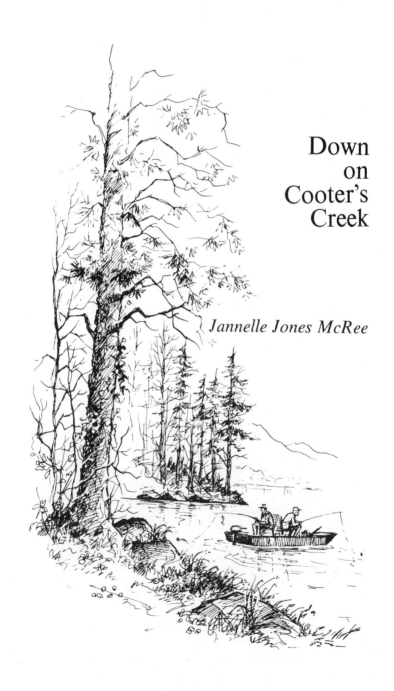

If a man's got the love of fishing in his blood, that love courses through his veins as long as he lives. And that's the way it did for Walter C. Jones and A. B. Crisp of Elberton as long as they lived. Just a few years ago, before they went on to a better fishing ground, they decided to go fishing on Clark Hill Lake.

In their early eighties the two needed cheering up. Mr. Crisp was despondent over his wife's recent death and said that he had lost his desire to live. Being hard of hearing didn't help his feelings either. Mr. Jones, better known as Uncle Walter, wasn't too happy over his failing eyesight, but they agreed on one thing. Fishing kept worry from edging up too close.

"I'll be your eyes, Uncle Walter," Mr. Crisp said.

"And I'll be your ears, Brother Crisp," rejoined his fisherman friend.

One bright spring morning in early April the two fishermen went down to Clark Hill, better known around Elberton as the Big Lake. Mr. Crisp had a small, lightweight aluminum boat with a motor attached. As was their custom they took their old folding chairs to sit in the boat while fishing. On this particular morning on Cooter's Creek, Uncle Walter got a hard tug on his line and stood up to pull in his fish. The light boat rocked and the two men were thrown out of the boat. As the boat spun round and round, the fishing line wrapped around Uncle Walter's legs. Eventually the fishermen were able to catch hold of the spinning boat and hang on.

"Hang on, Brother Crisp, hang on!" Fisherman Jones shouted.

"You do the same!" Fisherman Crisp yelled. "How are you making out?"

"I'm holding but the water's cold."

"Keep kicking, Uncle Walter."

"Can't," was the reply. "Legs tied up. You kick."

From the way those two fishermen reckoned they held on for over two hours. They agreed, though, they couldn't last much longer. Their arms and shoulders ached, their bodies were numb from the cold.

The little motor on the aluminum boat finally stopped chugging. The gasoline supply had given out. It was quiet now on Cooter's Creek. They were too tired to call out to each other, but they were not too worn out to do a lot of thinking and a lot of praying for somebody to come to their rescue.

And Somebody did. Suddenly a strong spring wind came up and started moving the boat. The boat obeyed the instructions of the wind and moved slowly to the very shore of Cooter's Creek.

It took some time for Brother Crisp to untangle Uncle Walter from the fishing line, and it took more time for the fishermen to get their shaking sea legs used to operating on solid ground. When they struggled up, they folded their old chairs, retrieved some of their fishing equipment, and Brother Crisp found his glasses and his false teeth in the bottom of the boat.

"I can tell you one thing for certain, Brother Crisp, you *have* been living right," observed his friend.

"You, *too*, Uncle Walter."

The fishermen finally crawled into the car and sat in silence and awesome gratitude. They sat awhile and drank a cup of steaming coffee from a thermos jug that Brother Crisp had brought. When their legs and hands stopped shaking so much they cranked up and went on the road toward home.

Late that April afternoon Mr. Crisp went over to the Joneses to check on his fishing pal. Uncle Walter was sitting in a chair by a window in the dining room. The afternoon sun brought out the blistered glow of the two fishermen's faces. Their noses were a startling red.

"Just wanted to check on you, Uncle Walter," Mr. Crisp said.

It was hard to tell which red-faced fisherman looked happier. In fact it was a grateful family circle that gathered around to hear their story.

"There's one thing I want to ask you, Brother Crisp, do you still feel like you did about wanting to die?"

A sun-red smile played games all over the face of Mr. Crisp. "No," he answered, "what about you? You want to stay here awhile?"

"I'm in no big hurry to go," Uncle Walter remarked.

Well, they stayed on awhile. Sure they went fishing again. Many times, and back to their beloved Cooter's Creek. They used their old folding chairs again and again but not in the little aluminum boat.

Some Things Are Best Left Alone . . .

Frances Greene

When young William Edward Nichols walked into our lives, we were, my husband and I, a well organized, hard working, middle-aged couple. Our list of priorities included publishing a weekly newspaper, keeping a house and garden, enjoying our friends and stealing an occasional weekend at a nearby lake to do a spot of fishing. But in less time than it took to transplant Billy Nichols' bargain priced wild azaleas or to make jelly from his "cheap as dirt" muscadines, our tried and true schedule was not only disorganized, disrupted and disconnected, it had completely disintegrated — which is only a nice way of saying that it went straight to pot.

Literally, Billy Nichols never walked into anything. He hopped, bounced or skipped, and the first time I ever saw him in my life he skidded to a stop at the typewriter table, turned slowly and stood there, a mite of a codger, his eyes meeting mine squarely, unflinchingly across the cluttered desk.

Wiggling his snub nose a little, he stuck out his lower lip, blew upward to dislodge the mop of hair on his forehead. "You know something?" he asked finally.

I shook my head.

"If I was in your shoes," he paused, drew a deep breath, "I sure would be looking for somebody to sweep up this mess."

I looked around the office. By some standards it could have been considered dirty; trash was spilling out of the yellow basket; an ash tray was running over.

"I work," he blurted finally, watching me closely, "by the hour or the job."

Opportunity was knocking, and any good newspaper woman worth her salt can recognize a combination of perseverance, stubborn determination, honesty, shrewdness and integrity when she sees it; she also can recognize a tow headed youngster's need for money. And in that instant, the woman and the boy reached a silent agreement to respect and accept each other at face value, no questions asked.

The deal was signed with a smile.

My husband, who, in time, came to be called "The Boss" to his face and "Your True Love" to his back, was not too enthusiastic about the arrangement. Coughing his way through the daily clouds of dust, he was quick to point out that the last thing we needed was a juvenile custodian who actually stood guard over the trash can.

"Almost daring me to put anything in it," he complained. "And while we are about it, I frankly think you are getting in too deep," he warned, evidently referring to the box of chocolate chip cookies I had baked the night before and which were now on the counter. "In the first place, you do not know one thing about him."

Frankly, I knew more than he thought I did. I knew that William Edward Nichols was named for his Pa but that his three sisters, Barbie, Beautye and Betsy, and Ma, along with his closest friends called him Billy. I knew that the five of them had moved from the mountain to the old Bohannon place south of town when Pa was sent away for a spell; I knew that he did not believe in "taking something for nothing" and that his Pa always said it was better to get things done yourself than it was to sit back and hope somebody else'd do it for you. But Pa also believed that what was to happen *next* week was the Lord's business yet what was happening to a fellow *now*, this very minute, was *his* business. All of which was quite a bit to know but nothing compared to the final bombshell.

"His Ma," I hesitantly admitted, "is in the family way."

"And," The Boss said tiredly, "you are involved up to your neck."

Actually, I was not involved at all. Although I had volunteered to drive the little ones to a nursery every morning and to pick them up every afternoon and then keep them at our house every night while Ma was "laid up," my work at the newspaper would not be affected; neither did it mean that his meals would be late. As for our sleeping on the sofa bed, it would be for only three or four nights.

"And surely you do not begrudge that," I accused loftily.

If he begrudged it, he did not have time to admit it. The youngster was coming through the door with a coffee can of violets, and his face was as bright as the sun. Miss Mary, the welfare woman, had made all the arrangements for Ma at the hospital ten miles away and for an ambulance to take her. Not only that, she was going to bring them a case of milk, baby blankets and clothes which meant that he could use his week's work money to make a down payment on a baby bed because Ma had never in all her natural life owned one to put her babies in and that just wasn't right.

The Boss silently went back to work at the ad table but that night I noticed he tested the sofa for softness.

Waiting, regardless of what one is waiting for, is nerve wracking, but waiting for a new arrival whose time of appearance was based purely on guess work played sheer havoc with the nervous system. Billy Nichols suggested that Miss Mary might know since she was the one who took Ma to see the doctor. But Miss Mary informed me over the phone that the doctor had decided to give or take a few weeks from the fifteenth.

"Of which month?" The Boss asked.

I presumed either next month or the next. But, according to the almanac, four calendars, a schedule of the moon's change, tides, fishing hours and the sun's rise coupled with the last week Pa had spent at home, I figured a month from now. And since I was impatient anyway, I dared Ma to double-cross me.

Billy Nichols insisted with a jerk of his head that we did not have a thing to worry about. "Everybody's just going to a lot of trouble." he pooh-poohed. "Gosh a mighty, she might not even go to a hospital; we can do everything they can."

Either he had a lot of faith in what we could do or he was an expert at boiling water.

However, our anxiety was temporarily given a respite in the form of a tall, soft spoken salesman driving a faded green paneled truck. His quiet, understanding, sympathetic manner was just what Ma needed to brighten her days.

Billy Nichols had another word for it. Trying to keep his chin steady and his lower lip stiff, he said simply, "Ma was took."

And Ma was. The traveling man had sold her a blue satin bedspread and a "mess of pots and pans."

I did not believe it.

Billy Nichols nodded once, keeping his eyes lowered to the pencil in his hand. "She's got to pay him something every week for might near the rest of her life," he said sadly.

I suggested that we call the sheriff; there had to be a law against taking advantage of a woman so hard up. It was unfair and dishonest, and the interest rate was probably so high she could have bought a bed to go under the spread.

The Boss replied calmly that I was prejudiced. The salesman was only trying to make a living, and if Ma wanted that spread and those pots and pans, then that was *her* business.

He was, it seemed, on her side. Which led me to suggest that maybe he also had an answer for finding a baby bed, now that the week's work money would have to go for food.

He said that he had not given this a thought but that when he did, he probably would find an answer.

Billy Nichols said that when he was cutting the grass for old lady McElhannon, he had found what looked like an old cradle in her barn and he reckoned she might let him work out whatever it would cost. "But it'd take a lot of fixing," he admitted with a deep sigh .

The man who was not going to get involved suggested matter-of-factly that the youngster should see about it. He had the tools, he said, in his workshop.

Billy Nichols, who did not want to appear too excited, fidgeted silently from his perch on the stool behind the counter and then with a casual "See ya," bounced from the office to the street.

At exactly five minutes before closing time, he was back. The deal had been made and all we had to do now was to go by the old lady's barn, load the cradle in the trunk of the car and haul it to our basement.

The Boss was now not only deeply involved, he was into it up to his neck.

"At least," I offered, looking at the dusty frame, the missing rungs, the broken piece of the front rocker, "it has good lines."

Billy Nichols said you just couldn't buy wood like that no more and he just never had seen anything like it.

The Boss muttered that he could not agree more; I pointed out that it had to be an antique.

Battling against time, we spent every night of the next week holed up in the room behind the furnace. While the man and the boy sawed, glued and sanded, I refinished each piece of the wood we "couldn't buy no more of." Our

friends were positive that we had slipped away on a
vacation; our neighbors kept the television repair man on
call to check out their grinding reception; my house became
a hangout for spiders, and our meals featured toasted
cheese sandwiches. But by the fifteenth, give or take two
weeks, the cradle, in all its resplendent glory, was loaded on
a borrowed truck and duly delivered to the old Bohannon
place.

Ma's surprise was genuine; in fact she wondered aloud
where in the world she would put it?

Billy Nichols suggested the bedroom but she quickly
pointed out that it was already crowded, what with her and
Betsy and Barbie and Beautye in it, and she reckoned the
best place would be in the sitting room.

The Boss reckoned as how it was getting heavy, holding
it like he and the youngster were doing at the moment, and,
until she decided, how about leaving it on the porch?

Ma smiled sweetly at him and said that suited her fine.

"I really believe," I confided on the way home again,
"that she does not know how to express appreciation. So
many folks don't . . ."

But the man at the wheel only shrugged; at the moment
his mind was on a thick steak followed with an uninter-
rupted hour in front of TV. He had accomplished what he
had set out to do; from here on in, Ma and the girls and
Billy Nichols were my problem. "But it really is a beautiful
piece of furniture," he mused aloud, "Even if I did remake
it."

And indeed it was but he was not the only one to think
so. As Billy Nichols said the very next afternoon, "I just
don't hardly know how to tell you this . . ."

From the look on his face, from the hurt in the dark
brown eyes and the nervous wiggle of his snub nose, neither
The Boss nor I hardly knew if we actually wanted to be
told.

"It was the traveling man," he said quietly, simply. "He
came by to collect."

I think we knew what had happened.

"I don't reckon she could turn him down," he said
loyally. "He gave her some money and threw in one of
those fancy kimonos." His eyes were on The Boss. "But he
told her it was about the nicest cradle he ever saw."

For a long minute, we sat there in the office, the man, the youngster and I. All of our work had been in vain, but then maybe we were trying to please ourselves rather than trying to please Ma. And the salesman was, after all, only trying to make a living.

With a sigh and a slight shrug, the man at the desk turned back to his work. "Maybe," he said finally to no one in particular, "the kimono will match the blue satin spread."

Billy Nichols stuck out his lower lip and blew upward to dislodge the strand of blond hair across his forehead. And then, hitching up his jeans, he headed toward the back where he kept his broom. There was no reason to cry over spilled milk, and anyway what was going to happen next week was up to the Lord. Right now, he had an office to sweep, a trash can to empty.

"But I still wish," he mumbled, moving toward the front door where he was sure to raise a cloud of dust, "I'd a filled that road with nails."

We were, the Boss and I, suddenly much too busy with our work to lecture properly on forgiveness, turning the other cheek, compassion or grudges. But, picking up a pencil to proof a page of copy, I silently wished that he had dropped just two or three. The soft spoken traveling man in his faded green truck might have been above the law but he was not above reckoning with a couple of flat tires. And somehow or other, I had the feeling that Pa and the Lord would have considered that today's business.

Ole Shug—The Last Mule in Morgan County

Basil Lucas

There was a time in Georgia when mules were very important animals. They did much of the hardest work around the farms and the farmers were proud of these strong, hard workers. When tractors came along, however, mules began to disappear. The old mules died out and there were no new ones to replace them.

There is still a mule living in Morgan County, however. His name is "ole Shug" and he belongs to Mr. Lonnie Huggins. If you were to pass through the little farming community of Bostwick, you'd probably become wide-eyed and roar with laughter to see Mr. Lonnie creeping his '53 faded denim Chevy pick-up down the edge of the road with "ole Shug" tailing along behind on a fuzzy old rope. Mr. Lonnie's pick-up travels every bit of five miles per hour when Shug is hitched up like a caboose!

Mr. Lonnie has got a good many years on him now and Shug is no kid, either. Shug is 18 years old, which is like a man being over a hundred years old. Not as fast or as strong as he was when he was entered in the county fair contests as a youngster, Shug is still a good, steady worker. He and Mr. Lonnie do the plowing in small vegetable patches around the little North Georgia wide-spot-in-the-road. Doing this, they keep pretty busy during the farming season, but in the cold winter "ole Shug" gets restless and bored just like many of the other citizens of the sleepy little town.

One certain winter night, though, Bostwick was anything but a boring little place. The thermometers were stuck at minus 3° when somebody screamed out into the crystal, cold night, "Fire! Fire!!"

Frightened people leaped out of bed when the alarm whirred through the icy, black air. Light from the fire flickered into houses as if it were coming from a giant hearth. Although everyone was hurrying, it seemed to take a nightmare-like forever for the volunteers to get to the tiny town hall and the old fire truck. It was there that their worst fears came true. The old engine would not make a sound in that icy weather.

A crowd of hearty souls began to huddle together, hopelessly watching the cotton gin burn. The water lines were frozen and even if they could get water, they figured it wouldn't do any good now. They stood still and silent as the snowy clouds low overhead reflected a spooky red back into the seemingly frozen eyes of the citizens.

Some of the shivering men were trying to comfort the owner of the gin who had begun to shake wildly. He was crying and beginning to shout at the fire as if it were some kind of monstrous devil. All of a sudden he burst away from his comforters and dashed into the blazing gin. A couple of friends started after him, but they jerked to a sudden stop when they saw the giant roof begin to sag. Their feeble calls to the owner were silenced by the creaking and cracking of heavy timbers. Everyone scattered wildly as flames, ice, cotton, wood and tin flew everywhere with a thunderous roar. Then in the flickering hush that followed, the crowd inched like a big iceberg back toward the fire where they, almost in perfect unison, sighed relief to hear the owner's voice and know that he was still alive. But he was moaning helplessly and the people watching seemed to be equally helpless.

Suddenly, from the ghostly shadows around the cuckle pile, some children came running, saying that "Mr. B" was trapped under a big rafter around the other side of the gin. The excited townspeople jockeyed around the blaze in hopes of saving the poor man, but when they saw the giant timber lying across "Mr. B's" legs they, this time, groaned in unison. The rough timber was burning and there just was not enough room for the men to get a strong hold on the crushing weight. And the tractors and trucks were all frozen up.

It was when that thought jabbed Lonnie Huggins' dazed mind that he started running for the first time in years! He ran straight through the dark toward "ole Shug's" shed. He grabbed the biggest rope he could find, scrambled up on Shug's wide back and spurred so hard that Shug actually hurried back toward town and the fire! Cheers rang out as the crowd made room for Shug. Lonnie threw the rope around the timber, pulled it snug and yelled a deep-throated "Giddap, haaaaa ..." right into Shug's big, rabbit-like ears. The old beast must have thought he was back at the county fair. He strained, his huge hooves chewing up the mud and ice. Every muscle he had must have stretched to the breaking point. The timber began inching slowly when, "Twanngg ..." went Lonnie's aged rope. Another moan went up from the crowd only to be chased away by another cheer as a quick thinking farmer pulled a chain out of a frozen-up truck and hooked it to Shug's collar. Lonnie tied the other end around the rafter while the crushed man watched every move with terror in his eyes and a prayer on his tongue.

Again Lonnie yelled his command and Shug dug in. With mud and ice spattering the frenzied crowd, the monstrous timber began to slide again. A couple of alert men gave it enough guidance and lift to clear the broken legs and the night's loudest cheer burst into the January air as "Mr. B" was dragged away from the crackling gin.

All the children rushed around patting "ole Shug" with congratulations and tugging on Lonnie's sleeve as if he were a football hero. Lonnie's face broke into a happy grin while he was patting Shug's sweaty, soot-covered snout. He was thinking, "Yep, the last mule in Morgan County ... and probably the best 'un that ever was ..."

Christmas
Is for
Surprises, Too

Frances Greene

Somebody somewhere said that the Christmas season is a
lonely time of year.

Though I am sure that the statement was made in good
faith, I have a sneaking suspicion that the fellow who said it
had neither a country weekly newspaper printed on a
second hand, temperamental eleven ton press held together
with baling wire, rubber bands and tender loving care, nor a
stubborn but enterprising and energetic towheaded, snub
nose youngster by the name of William Edward Nichols to
sweep, sharpen pencils, empty wastebaskets and, in
general, manipulate the lives of his bosses.

Either of the two discounts any theory about a lonely
holiday season. In the first place, any old newspaper editor
and publisher worth his salt will admit as quick as a flash
that the advertising from Thanksgiving through the greeting
edition – the one in which every merchant in town wishes
the customers a Merry Christmas – fills the till. This
year-end revenue pays the taxes and the interest on the
notes and buys another twelve months' supply of baling
wire and rubber bands. But, in turn, it means "go-go-go"
from dawn till dark for everybody in the print shop,
including the sweeper.

As for William Edward Nichols, called Billy, every season
was "go." Being the head of a household that included Ma
and four younger sisters while Pa was away for a spell

paying his debt to society, was enough to keep any youngster on his toes.

"After all," I pointed out to The Boss who also doubled as my husband, "would we have done as well at his age?"

He did not have to answer. His heavy sigh coupled with the "are you kidding?" look in his eyes said more than words. He and I both knew that anybody with two middle age Patsies who could make a full time job out of one pencil sharpener and two waste baskets had it made.

But, in all fairness, Billy Nichols did not work more than an hour or two a day. He was, as he said, "just sort of in and out" and he was more out than in unless the current needs of his brood demanded a special project above and beyond the part-time wages. Some of the projects had merit; all of them involved me as a partner.

"Some day," The Boss warned following the decline and fall of the cricket bait business, "you are going to learn to say no."

It was not, I assured him, a matter of learning; in the case of the crickets it was purely and simply a hole in the screen that covered the box, and until the night of the great escape we had a good thing going. As for the roasted chestnut deal, he could very easily have told us before the explosion that the shells or husks or whatever covers the mealy meat had to be stuck or pierced. And though we did not make a profit on the calf, I pointed out defensively, we did not lose anything either. In fact, we still had half a sack of powdered milk and a bucket with a nipple if ever we . . .

"Please," he said quietly, his voice tinged with a shade of warning, "not until after the new year."

He did not have to worry. Everything, it seemed, was ship shape with Billy Nichols. He had passing marks in reading, spelling and math, and Ma's welfare check was keeping the larder supplied with fat back, dried beans, potatoes and coffee. Not only that, the baking powder can behind the dictionary had a nice rattle, but to cap it all, Pa had written that he was saving a little cash and would send it home to buy presents.

"I reckon," Billy Nichols said with a sniff, his eyes shining as he took his perch on the stool behind the counter, "I'll let the girls hang up their stockings this year."

He could as well have announced that Pa had circled the moon in a space craft of his own making.

I was happy for him, I said. And I thought it was most noble of Pa to turn over his savings.

Sighing a little, he tried to hide the pleased smile tugging at his thin lips. "Sometimes," he said, cocking his head slightly, "you are just like him."

I did not know Pa; in fact, I had never seen him. But I gathered that I had been paid a rare compliment.

"When he gets out," the boy said dreamily, "and we move back to the mountain . . ." He drew in his breath quickly and hopped from the stool. "See ya," he called over his shoulder, closing the door behind him.

But as Thanksgiving came and went and the days dissolved into an endless chain of getting the right picture with the right article and the right ad with the right price interspersed with the groans and grumbles of the big press, there was nothing in the mail for Billy Nichols.

"You don't suppose," I suggested to The Boss early one morning, "that it got lost . . ."

He shook his head.

"Couldn't you maybe just put a twenty dollar bill in an envelope and . . ."

He looked for a long moment at the copy on his desk, and then shook his head again.

He was right as usual. With Billy Nichols, it was measure for measure; nobody, in his book, took something for nothing, and he also was an honest young man who expected honesty in others.

Still and all, I grumbled to nobody in particular, walking to the window to check on the weather, Pa was cutting it mighty close. Already the thermometer was taking a dip; the air was crisp, the sun was having trouble shining through the snow clouds — just right for Christmas shoppers who were even now circling the block to find an empty parking space. Maybe tomorrow I could steal a minute and buy a few presents of my own; maybe even Billy Nichols would pamper an aging editor and let her help with those stockings.

But tomorrow and the tomorrow after that were made up of clicking typewriter keys, flash bulbs and checking the post office box. And then quite suddenly, tucked beneath a Christmas card, there was the envelope; inside there was a note. We did not have to ask to know that it contained an apology instead of money.

Slowly, deliberately, the youngster tore it to shreds. Carefully he picked up each small piece and then, hopping from the stool, walked to the empty wastebasket.

The Boss studied the notes on his desk; I studied the Garden Club photos on mine. Billy Nichols climbed back to his perch, propped his elbows on the counter and silently studied the street beyond the window.

The phone rang; I listened to a complaint about a misspelled name on an address label.

The Boss cleared his throat; picked up a pencil.

I picked up one of the pictures, and then another. "Mmmmmmmmm," I said to no one in particular.

The Boss turned in his chair; Billy Nichols lifted his head slightly.

'Mmmmmmm," I said again, looking more closely.

Billy Nichols got slowly from the stool, ambled to the desk.

I handed him the photo. "If the program chairman can make Christmas decorations out of pine cones and galax leaves . . ."

The Boss cleared his throat again.

"Then fifty-five club members in town are on fire to try their hands at it . . ."

The boy's face brightened. The woods were full of both, there for the picking.

I lifted my shoulders a bit smugly. "A classified ad would help . . ." I had the bull by the tail now and I was not turning loose.

The Boss had a grim look in his eyes. He was, his silence implied, reserving an opinion.

"Of course, you will need dozens of boxes . . ."

The youngster grinned broadly, and without waiting to put on his jacket, headed for the door.

"Who knows?" I asked no one in particular, reaching for a sheet of paper to write cutlines, "The supply may not meet the demand."

It did, but only because we devoted every spare minute to tramping the countryside and filling the boxes. The response was unbelievable, overwhelming, and, in time, a pain in the neck. Every little woman in town had a yen to make her own decorations; several placed two and then three orders. Four paid Billy to do the spraying.

Not only did I keep tabs on the accounts, I also sacked and labeled and then hauled. And the office, in the process, contracted a chronic case of woodsy hiccups. The Boss, in the process, contracted a case of frustrated grumps, making it a point to glance at the calendar whenever he thought I was watching.

"We'll make it," I assured him every morning after coffee. "The papers will get in the mail on time."

He did not believe it but it took energy to argue.

"We passed the crest," I announced one beautiful, cold afternoon.

He looked at the bedraggled worn calendar; unless the housewives intended to decorate for Lincoln's birthday, then the peak had to be past.

I shook the baking powder can; the coins rattled musically. Christmas morning in the Nichols house was going to be one to remember for years to come. There would be gifts of sweaters, socks and dolls and a bottle of 49¢ perfume for Ma. And Billy would pay for the lot of it with money he had earned by the sweat of his brow.

That, too, was a matter of opinion, The Boss said with his scorching glance.

"He is even studying the ads for a good turkey buy," I tossed in matter-of-factly. "The first one ever."

He might have softened at this except the last section of the paper was ready to run, and once we put "A" and "B" and "C" together, labeled and then sacked, we could walk out and lock the door behind us.

But after that, there was little at home to remind us of Christmas. The cooky jar was empty; the refrigerator was bare; the tree was in the living room but the lights were in the attic. Stores would be open until the usual time tomorrow but what would be left on the shelves?

Over a bowl of soup for the fourth night in a row, I looked tiredly at the drab and dirty kitchen. It should, I mumbled, be reeking of spices, and yeasty breads and rolls, the makings of turkey dressing. Instead, the bowl of ivy on the window sill had died for the lack of water and one lone onion stared back at me from the vegetable bin.

"We should," I suggested suddenly, "do like the Hudgens. Go to Florida for a few days."

He tilted his head with interest. We had the time; our

own family get-together was the Sunday after. And a couple of days in the sun . . .

"Mrs. Hudgens said that it is surprising how much rest you can get . . ."

He nodded as if he were not accustomed to surprises.

We sat there, looking for a long time at our empty bowls, both of us tired to our bones. But, we silently assured ourselves, our subscribers would get their annual greeting edition tomorrow, and Billy Nichols would be like a buzz saw buying the candy and gum and oranges and then supervising the popcorn chain on the tree.

The youngster would tell us all about it next week, I thought on the way to the den to listen, for a change, to the six o'clock news.

"Maybe we could fly," I suggested to the man on the sofa who was already removing his shoes. "I could try to make reservations in the morning."

He nodded, wiggling the toes of his aching feet.

Of course, we would have to give our sons and their families a call, too. And, of course, they would fuss because we would not join them for the day but how could parents make a choice of children?

No, I mumbled, staring unseeingly at the newscast, we had worked that out years ago. But it was strange how time had a way of going by so quickly; not too many holidays past we, too, had to stay at home for Santa's arrival.

"It will take a lot of cooking before next Sunday," I said aloud. "We would almost have to fly if we got any rest."

He nodded again, his eyes opening and closing and opening heavily.

"Yep," I said suddenly, "we'll just do nothing for three whole days. Have Christmas dinner in a restaurant . . ."

And even as he dozed, he nodded.

But over an unhurried breakfast of a tad of grits, one strip of bacon divided between us and toast from stale bread, he scanned the morning paper for flight schedules. Outside, the clouds were getting heavy and the windows were fogging over. I tried desperately to remember some of the exciting activities Mrs. Hudgens had mentioned. Maybe it was croquet or two handed canasta in a motel room. But she had raved over the friendliness of the other couples; everybody, she had said, wanted to speak and even talk a while. "We could stroll on the beach," I offered, breaking the silence.

But he was walking to the phone now, the paper in his hand. He dialed the operator.

The back door opened slowly. Billy Nichols stood there, his green corduroy jacket covered with snowflakes. He twitched his red nose, stamped his feet, shook his shoulders.

The Boss replaced the receiver; the boy must surely need more money.

For a long moment, the youngster wiggled, twisted, wiggled again. He wet his lips, drew in his breath. "You don't have to lessen you want to," he blurted finally, "but we sure want you for Christmas dinner."

I swallowed hard.

"We got a turkey that'd knock your eyeballs out . . ."

I looked at The Boss. Neither of us had ever had that kind of turkey.

"And Ma's making three punkin pies." His eyes sparkled.

The Boss looked at me. There was no doubt but that the Florida sun would do us a lot of good but there was a doubt that we would ever again be given the opportunity to share dried beans, pies and a rare bird with Billy Nichols and his brood.

"We accept," I said firmly. "We accept with pleasure."

The youngster grinned broadly, and with a lift of his hand headed toward the door. "See ya," he said with a swagger. But he turned back suddenly, his eyes dancing happily. "Don't worry," he called out, "about bringing your stockings, I already hung two extra."

I looked at The Boss. His mouth had fallen open. But as I poured another cup of coffee, he folded the newspaper neatly and placed it in the trash can.

"I reckon," he said suddenly, giving his head a swaggering tilt, "lessen you just don't want to, we'd best be putting on our shopping britches to buck the last minute rush."

I agreed wholeheartedly. But as I passed the bowl of ivy on the window sill, I stopped. Maybe if it were replaced with pine cones and a bow . . .

From the den came the most un-boss-like yell I had ever heard. The snow, he called out, was really peppering down . . .

I cleared a spot on the window. The fluffy, lazy flakes

were big and soft and thick as they rolled and tumbled in every direction. Already the needles of the pines were edged in white, and the children across the street were racing across the lawn, their arms lifted as if trying to catch a handful.

It was going to be a beautiful Christmas Eve. It was going to be a wonderful Christmas Day. And standing there, watching the world around me take on that special glow of the holiday season, I pitied all of those somebodies somewhere who were lonely; lonely enough, in fact, to try to run away from it all.

Figs from Thistles

Evalyn Newlands

Almost a half century ago in South Georgia, a small, ten-year-old black girl sat on the bottom step of a cabin with her mother's arms around her. Tears drenched the child's cheeks.

"Ain't no use moanin', Minnie Mae," Mandy said to her daughter. "Aunt Duck is sleepin' sweet next to her Rufus out there in the cemetery. Jest be happy, chile." She wiped a tear from her own cheek, kicked off her steaming shoes and wiggled her toes in the sand.

Mandy's sad eyes looked above a blossoming pineapple-pear orchard and a cotton field to the steeple of a white frame-church. Tall pines spread sheltering arms over the church and a cemetery embroidered the grounds. Mr. Oscar, Mandy's boss-man, had given the land for the church and cemetery. The property was a part of one of his farms on the edge of town.

Minnie Mae raised her face from her mother's bosom and rubbed the tears from her eyes. "Ma, wuz it a fine funeral?" she asked.

"It sho wuz, Minnie Mae." Mandy smoothed the wrinkled front of her best dress. "I wish I'd let you go but you get so upset 'bout things. Mistah Oscar 'n Miz Bitsy wuz there. Aunt Duck cooked fur them years ago. Don' worry, honey, yo Pa's sister looked mighty peaceful-like lyin' there, smilin' a little."

But Minnie Mae remembered Aunt Duck's ravaged face and her mind struggled to suppress the wasted image. A twig from a liveoak tree lay within her reach and she began to draw slowly in the sand. Often when troubled, her fingers busily eased tension by creating pictures of birds and flowers and soon a song would rise within her, drowning the confused longings of a child's bleak world.

Mandy's lumpy hips rippled as she moved up to the porch. She took a gourd from the water bucket and began to water her flowers. The begonias, ferns and geraniums splashed a swatch of cheerfulness across the ugly face of poverty.

Mandy looked up to speak to her daughter but the child had disappeared. She called loudly, "Minnie Mae, where you?"

"In the scrubbery, Ma, chasin' a butterfly." She captured it and emerged from the tangled undergrowth cradling it in cupped hands.

Mandy smiled and hesitated to interrupt her daughter's small delight, "Always lovin' pretty things," she chuckled.

Minnie May examined the wing-flowered swallowtail, its long wings, bars and black dots. Then she dropped a kiss on it and released it.

Mandy settled herself on the steps again and sighed, "Lemme straight'n yo hair befo' yo Pa cums home. Get de comb 'n beautifier on de shelf."

As she ran the comb through the child's mass of hair, the touch of her daughter made her love flow like sap in the springtime. Mandy yearned to give her some of the good things of life!

"Ma, did Pa go to town after the funeral?" Minnie Mae inquired as she wiggled free with disturbing memories of her Pa. Sometimes he wuz mean to her Ma 'n her — usually after his trips to town.

She crawled quickly under the front steps to make a doodle-bug wish and stirred the little concave hole in the sand with a twig, chanting, "Doodle-bug, doodle-bug cum outta yo hole 'n make ma wish cum true." Presently, the larva of an ant lion crept from the sand nest and Minnie Mae squatted on her heels and laughed gleefully, banishing momentarily all fear of her father.

After a supper of collard greens, side meat and corn bread Minnie Mae went to bed. She attempted to erase apprehension with dreams but she tossed and turned under a worn patch-work quilt until she heard her father's heavy footsteps. Soon the springs of the other bed groaned and his great weight settled for the night. Then the child slept.

Minnie Mae got up the next morning without waking her parents and ate a hurried breakfast. She grabbed a hat woven of corn shucks and skipped on bare feet out to the dirt road. She hummed gaily, "Today is a happy day 'n I'm gonna spend it wid Miz Bitsy, doin' little odd jobs on the cook's day off. She *always* gimme a nice present, besides the pay!"

She walked by the blossoming pear orchard and was filled with ecstasy over the lacy beauty. Its fragrance aroused her senses, accented the sweetness of nature and gave the promise of new hope. She buried her face in some of the blosssoms and broke a branch for her friend, Miss Bitsy.

As Minnie Mae approached the fringe of the cemetery she remembered Aunt Duck. Vacillating between the bliss of the morning and twinges of grief, she wound her way between bunches of buckfoot, hopping around one grave after another in search of fresh earth enclosing her aunt. After a while, a mound of red dirt, topped with some withered flowers, showed the burial place.

Minnie Mae sat down on a stone and rested her chin in her hands. She watched a red-headed woodpecker drill on a pine tree while she sifted her muddled thoughts. She lingered on. Eventually, her eyes swept upward and she whispered, "Lawd, is Aunt Duck down here or somewheres up there wid you now?" She decided to place the spray of blossoms on the new grave.

Waves of music poured from the front parlor at Mr. Oscar and Miss Bitsy's house. Minnie Mae knocked several times on the kitchen door but there was no answer. She began to think that Miz Bitsy wuz gonna' play them sweet Jesus songs all day 'n forgit 'bout her 'n the odd jobs.

She sat down on the back steps and gazed at a fig tree, spreading its leaves like an umbrella against the sun. Soon she began to sketch it in the sand with her finger.

"Mawnin', Minnie Mae," Miss Bitsy said unexpectedly.

She looked closely at the drawing in the sand. "You have talent, child!"

"Yes'm. I draws everthing pretty. I'd like to draw you, too."

"Oh, Minnie Mae, I'm not young or pretty anymore. You draw the fig tree." But she flushed with pleasure.

"Yes'm you is. Yo eyes is as blue as the sky 'n sometimes the angels make a halo of you yallo hair."

Miss Bitsy was touched and she began to think about a *special* present for the little girl: her sister's art supplies left there after her wedding! "Minnie Mae," she said, "you draw the fig tree this morning. The odd jobs can wait."

She went into the kitchen and soon returned with a tray of food for the child. Then she turned her slim back and left to search for the present.

When Miss Bitsy reappeared, laughing and loaded with the gear of an artist, Minnie Mae jumped off the back steps and did cart wheels around and around the backyard. Her hat flew off and her skinny legs circled like miniature windmills. And then she hugged Miss Bitsy's knees and Miss Bitsy patted Minnie Mae's head until she became conscious of the greasy beautifier.

"Miz Bitsy, I ain't never bin *so* happy! Kin I use'm — now?" Her white teeth flashed in a wide grin.

"Of course, Minnie Mae. They are for you. I'll play the piano while you paint."

Minnie Mae picked up her corn-shuck hat, pulled it down over her ears and began to assemble the easel, canvas, brushes and paints. Time passed. She was oblivious of time as she painted the squat Smyrna fig tree. Only its glossy leaves and sturdy stems had meaning and she had the joy of creating them in color.

Miss Bitsy looked out of a back window again—and again—as the day slipped away; but she *would not* disburb the child's absorbing hours. Finally, the brilliant colors of sunset swirled across the west and she called, "Minnie Mae, bring the canvas into the kitchen and put it on the marble biscuit slab. It's late and Mandy will be worried if you walk home in the dark."

Miss Bitsy drew a long quivering breath when she saw the painting — marveling! A sensation of weakness swept over her with the impact of a discovery. Genius and destiny must be handled sensitively she felt and she groped for guidance.

A phrase from her Bible lighted the way and she said, "Dear Child, you have a great gift and it *must be* nurtured. Shall we call the beautiful painting, 'Figs from Thistles?' " And silently she pledged that she would weed all the thistles along the wayside as the little one's talent blossomed and bore fruit.

"Is That You, Jesus?"

Jane Underwood Sweat

It was my good fortune to grow up in a remote area of rural Georgia where the past was an integral part of our daily lives. The farm where I was born, my grandparents' "homeplace", in Hancock County, was of moderate size and prosperity, but their lives remained very much the same as their pioneer ancestors. There was no electricity, they drew their water from a well, washed their clothes in an iron washpot, cooked on a wood-burning stove, heated their home with wood fires, and illuminated it with kerosene lamps.

In those pre-television days, devices for entertainment were few indeed on this isolated farm. The evening's activities usually consisted of sitting on the front porch after supper, with the sound of the whippoorwills from the woods nearby, exchanging tales of the past. The elders usually held forth while the younger members of the family listened eagerly to stories of Indian days, eccentric family members, wars, the knavery of Sherman's men, and "hants" (or ghosts) in the cemeteries.

Frequently, an elderly black man would join us for these evening sessions. His name was John Thomas, a grizzled giant then in his late eighties, who had been a slave of my great-grandfather. He and my grandfather, both great raconteurs, swapped stories. So many of them are lost to my memory, but the following classic stands out. They would laugh uproariously at every telling.

Shortly before the turn of the century, a balloonist was appearing at a fair in Augusta, some sixty miles away. The airship broke loose from its moorings with the balloonist aboard and drifted over the area of my grandfather's farm. It happened to be a clear, moonlight night, and John Thomas spied this floating white object while on a visit to the privy. John had led a very sheltered life, probably never having left his home county, and knew nothing of airships. On seeing this wondrous white object floating silently in the moonlight, his keen mind could reach only one obvious conclusion: The Second Coming — Our Lord had arrived! He eagerly cried out, "Is that you, Jesus?"

The frustrated balloonist answered with enough profanity sprinkled in to convince John that he was not Jesus but rather a disciple of the devil. Whereupon John rushed into his house, grabbed his shotgun, and let loose both barrels into the evil object. The airship settled to earth in a pasture near my grandfather's house. The balloonist made his way to the house and knocked on the door, a startling enough event in the middle of the night, since such knocks usually meant birth, death, serious illness, or fire. As he explained the plight of his airship, a sleepy Papa said, "What did you say you landed in?" The balloonist, by this time at the end of his tether, shouted, "An airship! An airship! Good God Almighty, man, ain't you never heard of an airship?"

Papa admitted that he had not, but the man was welcomed, fed, and taken by buggy to the nearest train to Augusta. The remains of the airship hung on the back of the smokehouse when I was a child; I believe they hang there still. —*Jane Underwood Sweat*

Christmas Is the Time to Say "I Love You"

Willa Francis

Willa sat a long time just holding the letter in her lap. She was feeling so blue. Seemed like at least one of her sons could come home for Christmas.

The air was crisp and Willa knew there would be heavy frost again tonight. She should get in some firewood before it got too dark but she kept sitting there. She couldn't remember when she had been so lonely. Somewhere a tiny memory stirred and became stronger. The crisp air reminded her of a long time ago when she was only six. Six was the age of Crissy, her granddaughter. How young and unknowing one is at six. Such a long time ago, nearly fifty years ago.

Christmas was only a week away. She could almost smell it in the air. The pretty little pine tree was already cut and in a bucket of water. Willa loved to smell the pine and couldn't wait to have it put up.

Grandma and Aunt Thelma had been baking for a week and the house smelled of fruitcakes in their tins with a cut apple in the middle and just a little spirits poured on for moisture.

Grandma and Aunt Thelma were going to decorate the tree in the living room. Grandma had the children fixing strings of popcorn for the tree all evening and she brought out the little red folding paper bells to hang on the tree.

She also had some little boxes of lead paper cut in strips that looked like silver and made the tree shine. The most important of all the ornaments were the little candle holders which fastened to the branches and held the candles which Grandpa would light on Christmas Eve night before everyone went to bed. It was so pretty and the fresh pine and candles smelled so good.

At last Christmas Eve came and the children were so excited. Everyone in the whole community went to the little red school house to see Santa. Nobody ate supper at home because everyone brought a dish and had supper there. The long table was set up in the auditorium and the big Christmas tree was over at one end. It was the prettiest thing Willa had ever seen and even had shiny balls on it. The kerosene lamps were all lighted in the wall brackets and the old organ was all ready to be played. It had to be pumped with the feet.

After supper, everyone gathered around the organ to sing the carols. Grandpa had a big voice and he loved to sing. Santa came in. He was so fat. He had on a red suit but his voice sounded like Cousin Glennis's father. Glennis said her father had gone out to take care of Aunt Lizzie's horses so Willa guessed she was wrong. Santa gave her brother Johnny a little red car with wheels that turned. It was only six inches high but looked like a real Model T Ford. Willa and her sisters all got rag dolls. They were soft and cuddly. Soon it was late. Johnny was asleep, hugging his car. Grandpa held him on his lap. Everyone loaded up to go home. Grandpa pulled the blankets up over the children and told him to lie down and they would soon be home.

When they arrived home, Grandpa lit the little candles on the tree. Everyone said a good-night prayer for tomorrow would be Christ's birthday. Grandpa held Johnny, who was asleep, as he said his prayer. Everyone said amen.

The dim light of the morning was peeping in the window. Her sister Elouise was whispering to Willa, "Let's go see if Santa left something under the tree". They crept out into the big hall and could smell Grandma's coffee in the kitchen. Grandpa came in. He was in his long white nightshirt and Grandma scolded him because he didn't have on his slippers and robe.

Santa had left some little gifts. There were oranges, nuts, colorbooks and crayons. Grandpa had a new cap and Grandma had some new leather gloves.

After breakfast, the children dressed for church. Willa wished her starched dress wasn't so scratchy. Grandpa had heated some bricks to put in the buggy so that their feet wouldn't get so cold.

The preacher usually talked loud and sometimes shouted, talking about sin a lot. (Grandpa thought he talked about it too much.) But today he told a Christmas story and then everybody sang. After church all the children told each other what they had new.

Christmas dinner was fun. So much food. The fire was burning in the fireplace and Aunt Thelma kept rushing in and out filling plates. Dessert was pumpkin pie and fruit cake. Willa didn't want dessert. She had eaten too much ham and chicken dressing and spiced peaches.

After dinner Grandma and Aunt Thelma had a great bustle to get straightened up because everyone went calling and drank eggnog and ate dessert at each other's homes. Grandpa wasn't going so the children stayed home and played in the great hall.

When it got late and turned dark, Grandma fixed cookies and milk. She said the children had eaten too much heavy food. Willa would be glad when she could take off her scratchy dress.

Grandpa was telling a story. He was telling the story of himself, of how he had been an orphan in an orphan home. He had been born in Philadelphia and his mother and father had died and later his brother. He said, "I want you to remember I love you. I'll love you all your life."

Less than two years later Grandpa died. He had been very sick. One night at three o'clock Aunt Thelma came and shook Willa and her sisters awake. She was crying softly, and saying, "Papa's dying, and he wants to say goodbye." Grandpa was in the big front bedroom and his bed was propped up high at the head. Willa and her two sisters and Johnny stood in the hall. Her feet were very cold and she was shaking. Her sisters were shaking, too, but Aunt Thelma was holding Johnny. The doctor said to go in. Grandpa said something and reached out his hands. Elouise put her hand in one, and Willa put her hand in the other, and LaVerne put her little hand on top of Willa's. Grandpa's hands were cold but he squeezed tight and said, "Remember I love you."

The doctor took the children out. There was a fire in the fireplace in the hall and they stopped to warm their feet. When Willa went past the room again they had pulled the sheet over Grandpa's head for he was gone. Willa could still hear him saying, "Remember, I love you."

Now Willa knew what it was she had forgotten. Grandpa had once told her when they were sitting quietly and talking. "You never need to feel alone if someone has ever loved you. All you have to do is open up your memory and take out a page, thin and folded as a piece of parchment paper, and unfold it. It will have the time and the people as they were then. That way no one ever gets old and leaves you because in your memory you can feel the time you had then. When you get through with the memory, fold it back up and put it away. It is better than a picture because it is real."

Willa could still feel Grandpa's rough wool overcoat as they went to the Christmas party and she could still hear his deep voice singing. She could never be alone. She could take any memory out and then put it away.

Suddenly the phone was ringing and she knew it wasn't fifty years ago. She went to answer it. It was Crissy, her granddaughter, and she was saying, "Grandma, I love you."

The Oracle of Screven County

Richard Dowis

W henever I read something about Jeane Dixon it starts me to thinking about my Uncle Mac. I don't suppose you ever heard of him. Dr. John MacNulty? No, probably not, unless you happen to be from Screven County. He was an oracle, so to speak, though he never got to be famous like Miss Dixon; and he never made any money out of the prediction business. Not that he cared. They say he never collected half of what was owed him, for all those sick animals he treated in fifty years of practice.

I miss the old man; I remember blumping along in his old Chevy, traveling between Sylvania and Dover and Middle Ground and Buck Creek, eating a peck of Georgia dust every mile of the way. By the time I was fifteen I had seen more sick horses than anyone in the county, except Uncle Mac himself. I was with him so much that people took to calling me "Little Doc," or "Docky." He called me "Son." I think that was because he and Aunt May Ree had no kids of their own.

My buddies thought he was something special, because of the thing about the mad mule. He had been bitten by a mule that had hydrophobia — they call it rabies now — and he had three or four brownish marks on the back of his right hand to prove it. I always thought only dogs and foxes got rabies, but a mule is what got ahold of Uncle Mac. He nearly died of it, even after taking all those shots.

But what I want to tell you about is how he began making predictions right after he retired from his veterinary practice. He was seventy, and he told everybody he wanted to catch up on his fishing and hunting, which he hadn't had time to do much of in the last twenty-five years or so. For a long time he kept getting calls from his old friends wanting him to come out and see about their stock. They all said he'd forgotten more about animals than that new vet would ever know. And when they said that Uncle Mac would just smile and say, "Guess that's my trouble, I've forgot *too* much." But Aunt May Ree and I knew the reason Uncle Mac retired was because his eyes had gone bad. He just wouldn't risk making a mistake that might cost some farmer a calf.

Retirement didn't suit Uncle Mac. He just didn't know what to do with himself. We went quail hunting a few times, but he soon gave that up. "I can't see no fun in spending a whole day looking up a dog's rear end," he said. But the times we went he missed most of his shots; and I'd often heard it said that Doc MacNulty could get two on the rise any day.

We fished a lot. It was fun, I guess, but he didn't smile as much or tell as many funny stories. Aunt May Ree said he was bored because he had worked so hard all his life, and if his eyes were still good you couldn't have dragged him away from his practice with a twenty-mule team. About the only thing that really fired him up was baseball. He was a New York Yankee fan and he liked to brag about seeing Ruth and Gehrig.

We were talking baseball the day he made his first prediction. I can just see him sitting on the bank of Brier Creek, leaning against a big tree, fishing pole tucked under his arm, his sweat-marked old hat pulled down over his eyes. A pal of mine, Bobby Ross, was with us. Bobby and I were fishing hard, not paying much attention to Uncle Mac, and all the while arguing about the National League pennant race. I was saying the Dodgers would win; Bobby thought the Phils would take it because they had better pitching.

Just about that time Uncle Mac got a bite. In a minute he was holding up a bream that must have weighed half a pound.

"You're both wrong," he said casually, stringing the fish. "Cards are gonna take it. They'll win their next seven games and move up the middle while the Dodgers and the Phils are knocking each other off. Yanks'll win the Series, though. In six games."

We thought he was joking. But he was as serious as a preacher talking against sin; and when a man who knows baseball like John MacNulty says something, you better listen before you place your bet. Still, Bobby and I couldn't keep from laughing. Uncle Mac set his jaw hard and closed his mouth so tight his brushy-looking mustache came down and covered his lower lip. He didn't say anything, though; he just took a fresh worm, hooked it, spat on it for luck, and tossed it into the creek. The line had hardly hit the water when the quill bobbled and went straight down. Uncle Mac pulled out a bream almost as big as the other one. That ended the baseball talk, which was just as well, because I was afraid Bobby and I had hurt Uncle Mac's feelings.

The funny thing was, it all happened just like Uncle Mac had said. Pennant race, Series, and all. It came to me when I was listening to the last game, which the Yankees won, making the prediction come true. Uncle Mac told me after the game that a vision had come to him one night when he was reading his Bible. I wanted to ask him what chapter but I didn't want to sound like a smart-aleck.

His next prediction was about me. We were raking leaves, a job Aunt May Ree had been after us to do for a month. Without any kind of a warmup, he looked at me and said, "Son, you're going to start Friday night against Millen."

You could have knocked me over with a chinaberry. I was the second-string fullback and had the shiniest pair of pants on the football team. "Uncle Mac," I said, "Charley Mills might have something to say about that." Charley, our star fullback, was a cinch to make All-State.

"Charley won't be able to play," Uncle Mac said as if the matter had already been settled.

"He looked great in practice today," I said, feeling a little tingle of excitement at the thought of starting against Millen.

"He won't play. You'll start." That ended the conversation, although I tried hard to keep it open to see what Uncle Mac had in mind.

Well, I guess I don't have to tell you Uncle Mac was right. Charley Mills twisted his knee chasing his little brother Thursday afternoon. He didn't even dress out for the game. I started, and Millen beat the stew out of us.

After that Uncle Mac started making all kinds of predictions, and the word got around. Soon, people were pestering him to predict things like football scores, probably so they could make little bets here and there. At the barber shop, where baseball and politics were the main topics of conversation, he would get more attention than the Governor got the time he stopped in for a shave before talking to the Rotary Club.

And boy, did Uncle Mac like being the center of attention! He was enjoying life for the first time since he retired. He seemed to hold his back a little straighter and his head a little higher. He even took to hitching his thumbs into his suspenders and wiggling his fingers when he talked.

I remember the night old Armistead Hess came by to ask Uncle Mac's opinion on some property. Mr. Hess didn't mention *predictions* but it was clear what he had in mind. He told Uncle Mac he wanted his opinion because Uncle Mac knew Screven County better than anybody.

When Uncle Mac heard that he broke out laughing. "Mr. Hess," he said, "it seems mighty strange that a sure enough financial wizard like you would be seeking advice from a broken down old horse doctor that ain't never had a pot to cook his peas in. No, sir, I can't give you any advice about land, but I can tell you one thing: *mend your wicked ways before it's too late.*"

You should have seen old man Hess! He turned red in the face and almost choked on his cigar. After he'd gone, Uncle Mac laughed so hard he turned over a cup of coffee. Aunt May Ree chided him for being rude, even if Mr. Hess *was* a scoundrel, because he was a guest in their home.

Not long after that they wrote up Uncle Mac in *The Sylvania Telephone.* A man with baggy pants and pockets full of flash bulbs took his picture with a big camera and asked a bunch of silly questions, like had he ever thought of playing the stock market. Uncle Mac tried his best to be funny. When the man asked about clairvoyance, Uncle Mac said the only *Claire* he ever knew was a waitress down at the cafe that married a feller *Mock* that farmed over near Po' Robin and he couldn't recall her maiden name though he was pretty sure it wasn't anything like Voyance.

It was a good piece. It made my Uncle out to be something special, which he was. A few weeks later I began to notice a change in Uncle Mac. He had begun to go pretty far with his predictions. He still hit most of them, but he missed a few; and when he missed he took it pretty hard. While he was waiting to see if one would come true he was nervous and edgy. Aunt May Ree noticed, too. She tried to get him to stop, but he was obsessed with what he called "my gift from God." Personally, I began to think that some of his predictions came, not from God like he always said, but from John MacNulty. Funny thing, though, most of the really *important* ones came true; it was the little ones that failed.

I finished high school that year, and in the fall I went up to Athens to the University. I had to study hard, and there was little time to think about Uncle Mac and his predictions. Besides, I met Peggy Carson and I was spending my spare time with her and thinking how Peggy MacNulty might sound.

One morning just before the Christmas holidays I was surprised to get a letter from Uncle Mac. Not a letter, really, just a short note. On the single sheet of ruled paper was written, "By midnight Friday someone you love will die in an automobile accident."

That was all. But it was enough to make my scalp tingle and chills run up my backbone. I could think only of Peggy.

She laughed when I told her; but Bobby Ross and I had laughed, too, that afternoon on the back of Brier Creek when Uncle Mac made his first prediction. Finally I got Peggy to agree to stay out of cars until after Friday. You can imagine how I felt. I couldn't sleep and I ate almost nothing, which was right unusual for me at the time. I had trouble paying attention in class, which *wasn't* all that unusual.

On Friday afternoon Peggy was still all right, and I felt a little easier. After all my Uncle Mac *did* miss occasionally. After supper I sat in my room, waiting, looking at my watch every few minutes. At midnight I rushed down the hall to the pay phone and called Peggy. Her voice was the most beautiful sound I had ever heard. I felt a little silly, but she didn't make fun of me like some girls would have. That shows how special she was.

I went straight to bed and fell asleep almost immediately. It seemed like only minutes before I was awakened by a knock. Somehow I knew that Uncle Mac's prediction had come true after all.

After the funeral I talked with the sheriff. The car had crashed into a bridge at a high rate of speed, almost at the stroke of midnight. No witnesses. No skid marks on the road.

"There's just no way to explain it, Docky," the sheriff said.

He was wrong. There was an explanation. Aunt May Ree and I knew. She carried it to her grave a year later. I've carried it in my heart ever since.

The Blue Ridge Pilgrim

Margaret Meaders

This is the story of a gentle adventure, a 60-year-old happening of wonder and transport in the life of an almost-vanished species — a true hill woman of the Georgia Blue Ridge.

I treasure my good fortune in having shared in it, as a little girl; for wonder (like those old-fashioned hill people) is, it seems to me, in increasingly short supply. Becoming ever more widely informed and "sophisticated" via TV and the movies, vicariously experiencing every imaginable situation and sensation, today's Americans come (for the first time in the flesh) to the rim of the Grand Canyon or the rim of the world burdened with such awe-dispelling foreknowledge and familiarity that we risk losing the keen edge of what Joseph Conrad called our "capacity for delight and wonder ... our sense of the mystery surrounding our lives ... our sense of pity, and beauty, and pain."

Not so, 60 years ago; especially, not so for Leodacia ("Dace") Garney on her one and only pilgrimage from the mountains to Atlanta.

When I was a child, radio and television, CCC roads and bookmobiles, consolidated schools and tourists hadn't brought "progress" into the coves and creek bottoms and ridges of the Blue Ridge. Mountaineers were considered a breed apart — hardy, scantily book-taught but impressively (even fiercely) self-reliant, God-fearing, and independent. And well enough — those people living "away back over yonder" beyond my North Georgia village Dahlonega — for theirs was a tough life. Especially that of the women, who in almost every instance served as wife, mother, cook and dairymaid, spinner and weaver, nurse and exemplar, field hand, even not rarely as draft animal alongside men and boys. A 15- or 20- or 30-mile trip to the County Seat was for most of them only a once-or-twice-in-a-lifetime journey.

Occasionally, circumstances forced such a woman, with or without her family, into town to hire out as a cook. Most were willing workers, but sorely unversed even in village ways. Some responded quickly to on-the-job training by their employers; others never learned and so returned to rocky, hardscrabble farms. Dace was among the former. (Leodacia Garney wasn't really her name, but it's close enough.)

I was seven when Dace took command of our kitchen — and a good share of our daily lives. The first sight of her sent my little brother and me backing to the edge of the pantry. Her ice-blue eyes gave us such a severe let's-have-no-lalligaggling look that we shrank from her. Even without that glance, we'd have been intimidated. She looked to me, somehow, like a large and unfriendly duck — an old, unfriendly duck. Actually, she wasn't a big woman — except to little children. But she was thick-bodied and ungainly and unsmiling.

When she arrived that day — the first "white help" we'd had — she was wearing (set board-flat) a stiff, narrow-brimmed, shallow-crowned black straw hat, which age would never wither nor changing custom successfully displace and which soon after became known in our family as The Hat. Her shoes were men's brogans; her quilted "cloak" was pieced of somber woolen swatches from a men's-wear sample book, and underneath were a black skirt and a white shirtwaist. Everything was as clean as a battling stick after wash day — and about as soft and inviting.

Without one word — and with five pairs of eyes watching every movement — she yanked out a lethal-looking hatpin anchoring the hat to a tight coil of gray hair, hung hat on a nail, replaced brogans with heavy felts from a flour-sack carryall, set shoes in a corner, removed coat and hung it under hat, produced a spotless feed-sack apron, tied it on, thrust a leathery fist across her forehead, turned, and said to our assembled family:

"Now, spell out what's to be did around here. Then ever'body git on about their bizness!" It sounded like the Commandant of Cadets at North Georgia College barking commands on the Drill Field. The effect was the same. The troops, including my parents, all but scurried to follow orders.

But Dace's bark, we learned in double time, was far, far worse than her bite. Considering her previous life, that was surprising. Dace had been born on a cramped and scraggy farm in a remote mountain valley at the back of the county. Orphaned early and shunted from one behind-handed farm to another (sometimes kin's; but mostly not), she'd had no chance for schoolin', had at all times been "put to her toilsomest shifts," and had eventually borne and raised, alone, a large family — all members grown when she came to us. I doubt that she'd known an easy day in all her fifty-some years.

Aside from those with her family, Dace's human contacts had been few and then usually unrewarding. But her contact with Mother Earth had been close and compensating. She was on first-name basis with many a tool and technique and "sich stuff-another" that were largely mysteries to town folks — women, anyway — harrows and scythes, wedges and adzes, double-bitted axes and bull-tongued ploughs, springhouses and corncribs, manners of wild things and rules of the calendar.

"You ever see a corn-shucks doll-baby?" she asked me one day. Assured that I had not, she went into our garden, returned with the makings, and soon produced a quite-respectable small girl's companion. Could we have reached the places at the proper time, Dace could have showed me wake-robbins in bloom, and Dutchman's britches, and lemon honeysuckle (wild azalea), and Indian pinks. Such spots were those she'd "knowed in days a-gone," out along Nimblewill Creek or the Etowah near Davis Chapel; but

springtime roads to such places were quagmires scarcely
navigable by even the staunchest RFD mailman. One single,
blessed time my father managed a trip almost to Winding
Stair Gap; and, though that was farther than Dace's known
world, she knew Nature's signs and signals and took us
almost straight as an arrow to a leafy, mossy spot where
pink lady's slippers bloomed.

"Has it ever been that you've seed baby possums?" she
asked my brother and me once. Again assured of our
meager background, she described to us "fresh-dropped
possums so little-bitty as to look no more'n dried field
peas." (Private checking with our father supported the
description, freeing us forever of any doubts at whatever
Dace told us.)

"You'd ought to know critturs and varmints and their
traipsin' places," she declared. "They's much to be learnt
that-a-way. Did you ever hear-tell how doves is partial to
pine stands for nestin' in? Did you know that owlses does
their daytime hootin' only deep in the dark timber? Would
you be a-knowin' that deers hankers as much after acorns as
ever did a gray squirrel or a white-footed mouse?" We knew
none of these things. "Has yore teacher learnt you how Bob
Whites — little 'uns — allus rests in a circle neat as one
drawed in the dust by a settin' .washtub, with all their
downsey heads a-facin' out'ards, watchin' close till their
mammy has come home, agin?"

Dace knew that root vegetables ask for plantin' in the
dark of the moon, but above-ground bearers need a
light night for a proper start. She knew to put a flintstone
in a fireplace corner so as to some way skeer off circlin'
hawks hovering over fresh-hatched chick-biddies busyin'
theirselves in the backyard sunshine. She watched, among
other signs, the thick-or-thin fluffiness of squirrels' tails for
a measure of the winter firewood to be split and the
foodstuffs to be dried or "put up" in pantry and cellar.

Without Dace I'd never have known that the heartwood
of an oak log makes first-rate splints for formin' up a
basket, but that shingles from the same source will curl up
like a carpenter's shavin's and split like a tree laid fair open
by a lightnin' bolt. How would I ever have known, in later
years, to try a mixture of vinegar, sourwood honey, and
North Georgia moonshine for my arthritis? (It didn't cure

the ailment, but it did make it easier to bear — at least for a while!)

My life never has depended for its continuance upon such items of knowledge. But each one taught me that an individual's inward satisfaction and sense of kinship with Nature and the sensation of never being entirely solitary are greatly enhanced by just such wee bits of lasting lore. And, of course, every one of us came to love Dace deeply. What else could we do in return for the loyalty and steadfast service and love that she gave to us for many long years? Singly and as a group we often put our minds to the problem of doing something extra-special for Dace. Just because. My father came up with what was perhaps the very best idea: we'd take Dace — who'd never been farther than 25 miles from Dahlonega — to Atlanta!

As it turned out, strong persuasion was required. Dace wa'n't no city slicker; she'd not took to the summer folks from Atlanta she'd seen when she'd worked, briefly, in the kitchens at popular Porter Springs at the foot of Cedar Mountain. She felt city folks to be most times a-fallin' all over theirselves, a-funnin' and a-skitterin', without manners enough to put in yore apron pocket. Besides, she hadn't — nor had we — time to be hurtled away on jest any fool-trip-or-other.

My parents felt that Dace's reluctance sprang largely from her uncertainty as to what would be expected of her in the Big City. It was the danger of embarrassing us, they believed, that worried her.

"It'll be for only one day," my father reminded her. "We'll start before sun-up." In those years such a trip took all of daylight and considerable darkness on either end.

"And" — my mother added — "we'll take a picnic lunch and eat at Grant Park." That seemed to lessen Dace's apprehension enormously. Clearly, she'd been dreading a hotel dining room or a city restaurant. This way, she'd not be likely to attract any particular attention.

"Well, then," she said finally, "I'll not higgle more. I'm sure it'll be a true double-footed time." *Double-footed* was Dace's strongest endorsement for anything. Not till long after her death did I learn that the adjective is a moonshiner's, denoting whiskey that has been run twice through the still. Had she known its origin, Dace probably never would have used it, for — except medicinally — she did not hold with likkerin'.

A dorned in her best outfit (black bengaline skirt, white basque shirtwaist, "gold" breastpin, high-buttoned shoes, and The Hat) plus a "genuine" caracul throw (a recent Christmas gift from one of my aunts; price in our store a few years back — $4.95), Dace was ready and climbed without comment into the back seat of the new Hupmobile with my mother and me. As long as we were in the foothills — still in her own land — she talked easily with us. But when the peaks dwindled and stood singly along Sidney Lanier's Chattahoochee, itself growing steadily broader and more languid, when the towns became more numerous and getting through them took three minutes instead of one, then she spoke less and less, but was increasingly curious. Her gaze darted from side to side; and she turned frequently, if stiffly, to peer at something we'd just passed. Some while after we'd first encountered out-moving city traffic, Dace said, "They'll not be one saved soul left when we git there; we've done met ever'body a-comin' out. You reckon maybe could be they's some kind o' ruckus or mishap up ahead?" (North Atlanta had burned a year or so before). Assured that the growing numbers of wagons and buggies, automobiles and drays were normal, she subsided again.

At Peachtree Station (or was it Brookwood?), then on the edge of town, a long train was moving slowly through the underpass. My father pulled to the curb to give all of us the whole effect, for to tell the truth my brother and I were only slightly less thrilled than Dace; the city was still a great adventure for us country kids, and trains would excite us for many years to come. This was, of course, Dace's first train, and she was astounded.

"What in the world keeps the varmint in its path?" she asked, craning to look down upon the rattling cars. "And what in tarnation pushes all them wheels around?" My father tried to explain, but Dace shook her head in continuing wonderment. "I've heered about these contraptions," she said, "but seein' one for my ownself is a pow'ful caution. Puts me in mind of a nervous caterpillar, backin' out of a chicken run!"

When we were well into the city and my mother had identified the famous thoroughfare we followed, Dace said, "I'd allus figgered this-here Peachtree Street to be a road amongst somebody's fruit-tree orchard."

The increasing hubbub — cries of newsboys and hawkers, chug of motorcars, rattle of horse-drawn vehicles, percussion beat of hooves, hum of the crowds of pedestrians — was another astoundment. "Whomsoever listens?" Dace demanded. "Seems-like nobody's a-givin' heed to anybody else. Sich a howdy-do and roody-how I never thought to see!"

Then we met a trolley! and then a fire engine! Then two ladies and a gentleman in an electric automobile and then a pair of matched and elegant grays drawing a Stanley Steamer, which obviously had quit steaming. And then a cavalry unit, clop-clopping along (on loan, my father surmised, to Fort McPherson from Fort Oglethorpe). I guess Dace took it that the whole world was on parade.

My parents had decided that Dace must see inside one big department store. We parked, therefore, and went into one — I can't remember which. Instantly, Dace stopped in her tracks, eyes wide and lips clamped. She quickly regained her composure, however, and got into the family line, and plodded along behind my mother.

The crowds — most of them women — the showcases and display racks crammed and burdened with all kinds of wimmen-folk allurements, the buzz and hum of conversation — these were things for which Dace had no background. I'm sure that the largest crowds she had ever known were the camp-meeting crowds when she was a child or those during Court Week in Dahlonega or maybe at a country "singing school," none of which bore any resemblance to the throngs in that big-city department store even so long a time ago.

Dace made only two comments while we were inside. Once my mother asked, "Well, Dace, what do you think of all this?"

Dace paused, looked around again, shook her head, and then declared in no uncertain tones: "I never seed in all my borned days so much truck ever'body could git along without!" Then we rode an elevator, Dace entering reluctantly and murmuring, when we got out, "My innards'll be along terrikly — I *hope.*"

When we were once more in the Hupmobile headed toward Whitehall, with an almost furtive (and, there-

fore, uncharacteristic) motion Dace sort of smoothed the
bengaline skirt and touched The Hat with clumsy fingers.
Young as I was, the gestures made me feel somehow that,
of a sudden, Dace felt awkward and out of place. With all
my heart I wanted that trip to be a splendid thing for her
with never a ragged edge. So I remember clutching a fold of
the skirt and leaning against her and looking up and saying,
"Dace, you look just beautiful!" The old woman neither
turned her head nor said a word; but she caught my small
hand in her rough, worn fingers, and she never let go till we
reached Grant Park.

Once, along a particularly busy stretch, Dace volunteered that she'd "as lief be the bottom nut in a
bushel-basket of chinkypins as to try to scrouge out" a
place for herself "amongst all them scurryin' bodies."

"Just like ants," I agreed, having heard some adult make
the comment somewhere, sometime, and wanting to sound
wise in the ways of this roaring metropolis.

"Antses has got order," Dace corrected me. "Them out
there is like cockroaches one scurry ahead of the broom!"

The State Capitol (then several decades away from
acquiring its golden dome overlay from our county) was
broader in the beam than any other structure Dace had seen
or would ever see. She doubted aloud that, settin' up there
in that monstrous big place, our local representatives could
hold their sights to the needs of folks in Wahoo or
Cavendar's Creek or Hightower District. Better, she opined,
they should traipse from county seat to county seat to do
their gover'mint palaverin'.

Under pressure she admitted a desire to see the home of
the Brer Rabbit feller. So we turned aside to the Wren's
Nest, with Joel Chandler Harris dead less than ten years.

And so, finally, to Grant Park — and everybody out.
Dace, who was by then "stiff as the corpse at a all-day
funeral," was glad. The picnic was a marked success. The
food was delicious, and our small group seemed caught up
in a special glow of comradeship. Then, to the zoo and the
Cyclorama.

I don't know which was the greater amazement to our
old friend — the animals or the huge, circular, canvas Battle
of Atlanta. Standing before the cages of the big cats, Dace
startled us by murmuring, "The leopard will lay down with
the kid." And then somewhat more audibly: "Was I the

kid, I'd close nary a eyelid!" The giraffes necessitated a far-back tilting of The Hat; the sight of the elephants all but dislodged the caracul throw. "I've heered-tell seein' is believin'," she said; "but this time tomorrow I'll not be able to give credit to this day's seein' — not one chit of it nor dottle."

Inside the dark Cyclorama, turning slowly to follow the battle raging before her, Dace spoke in a gentle, wondering way: "Reckon is my grandpappy pictured anywheres here? He was felled at Rough 'n' Ready." And: "My pappy, too — he ketched a bullet somers around Kennesaw. I heered him tell many's the night about layin' all day a-feered of burnin' with the bushes."

The next turn was homeward. All the winding 75 miles Dace sat silent, now and then dozing a bit, now and then shaking her head over something not to be believed, yet seen with her own two eyes and never, then, to be forgot. When she was very, very old, she still recollected in amazing detail and with great pride the day she'd seed Atlanta.

One poet has said: "For want of wonder the world was lost." But not for Leodacia Garney; not for Dace — and because of her not for me.

About the editor

Ann E. Hatton Lewis began her writing career as a country correspondent for *The Greenville News* and other dailies when she, her late husband, William W. Lewis, and their five children, lived in Whitmire, South Carolina. She soon became a feature writer on historical subjects, matters of human interest and adventures travelling with her children. Active in civic affairs, she established a public library and also a weekly newspaper in Whitmire.

Moving to Atlanta in 1952, she was impressed by the lack of readily available information about her adopted state and equally impressed by the number of able writers she came to know. So in 1957, she founded *Georgia Magazine* with the slogan, "In which Georgians Tell the Georgia Story." The magazine was built on the strength of Georgia's folks.

Mrs. Lewis sold *GM* in 1971 and it ceased publication three years later. The next year she returned to publishing with the colorful quarterly, *Georgia Life*. The stories in this volume, full of humor and pathos, have been collected from both magazines.

About the illustrator

John Kollock, well-known artist and illustrator, has been capturing the magic of his beloved North Georgia mountains in drawings and watercolors for many years. Some of his watercolors have appeared on the covers of *Georgia Life* and many of his sketches have enlivened its pages. He has illustrated each of these *Fifty Georgia Stories*. His own book, *These Gentle Hills,* full of his paintings and drawings, reflects his love for the farms and the people of his native Blue Ridge.

10903

10903

AUTHOR
Lewis, Ann
50 Georgia

TITLE
Stories

DATE DUE

BORROWER'S NAME

DEMCO